TREADING AIR

Also by Jaan Kross

THE CZAR'S MADMAN
PROFESSOR MARTENS' DEPARTURE
THE CONSPIRACY AND OTHER STORIES

Jaan Kross

TREADING AIR

*Translated from the Estonian by
Eric Dickens*

THE HARVILL PRESS
LONDON

First published with the title *Paigallend* by Virgela, Talinn, 1998

2 4 6 8 10 9 7 5 3 1

© Jaan Kross 1998

Introduction and English translation © Eric Dickens, 2003

Jaan Kross has asserted his right under the Copyright, Designs and
Patents Act 1988 to be identified as the author of this work

First published in Great Britain in 2003 by
The Harvill Press
Random House
20 Vauxhall Bridge Road
London SW1V 2SA

Random House Australia (Pty) Limited
20 Alfred Street, Milsons Point, Sydney,
New South Wales 2061, Australia

Random House New Zealand Limited
18 Poland Road, Glenfield,
Auckland 10, New Zealand

Random House South Africa (Pty) Limited
Endulini, 5A Jubilee Road, Parktown 2193, South Africa

The Random House Group Limited Reg. No. 954009

www.randomhouse.co.uk/harvill

A CIP catalogue for this book is available from the British Library

ISBN 1 843 43036 3

Papers used by Random House are natural, recyclable products made from wood
grown in sustainable forests; the manufacturing processes conform to the
environmental regulations of the country of origin

Typeset in New Caledonia and Century Old Style
by SX Composing DTP, Rayleigh, Essex
Printed and bound in Great Britain by
Mackays of Chatham plc, Chatham, Kent

INTRODUCTION

TREADING AIR is the fourth work by the Estonian writer Jaan Kross to be published in book form in English. It is preceded by two historical novels, *The Czar's Madman* and *Professor Martens' Departure*, and a book of six semi-autobiographical stories, *The Conspiracy and Other Stories*. A number of Kross's short stories have appeared in English in books and periodicals, including those published in Britain.

Although a fiction, *Treading Air* contains many elements of the author's own successes, failures, lucky escapes, trials and tribulations. Jaan Kross was born on 19 February 1920 in the Estonian capital, Tallinn, where many of his novels are set. His birth almost coincided with the formation of the Estonian Republic, which emerged out of a partial break-up of the Russian Empire following the Russian Revolution and World War I.

The first twenty years of Kross's life were, to all intents and purposes, uneventful – bar events of an amorous nature – and after leaving the Westholm Grammar School (changed to "Wikman's" in this novel) he studied law at Tartu University. Just before the outbreak of World War II, Kross became an assistant lecturer in law, but his luck, like that of his country, did not last long.

In 1940, already having forced military bases on to its tiny neighbour, the Soviet Union took over by sleight of hand, claiming it had been called in by Estonian Communists, who in reality belonged to a movement more dormant than active. For one year the Soviet Union ruled the roost and as this was only three years after Stalin's notorious show trials in Russia itself, it proceeded with its usual recipe: deportations of middle-class people, of *kulaks,* of anyone else who posed a threat to the new conquerors, censorship and the disappearance of members of the former government.

When the Germans invaded Estonia in 1941 and pushed out the Soviets, they were initially hailed as liberators – except of course by Jews who feared for their lives. The honeymoon did not last long. Soon, even for average Estonians, the German occupiers proved as intransigent and imperialist as their predecessors. Young Estonian men were now recruited into the *Wehrmacht* and the *Waffen SS*, instead of into the Red Army. National aspirations on the part of the Estonians were stifled. This is how, as a young man, Jaan Kross spent his first months in prison – suspected by the Germans of nationalist activities.

In 1944 the Soviets pushed the Germans out, who fled in disarray back to a disintegrating Reich. This time the Soviets consolidated their hold on the Baltic states, which now became, as before in Czarist history, the Baltic provinces, geographically near to Western Europe but virtually impossible to enter from the West.

Kross was again arrested, this time by the Soviet authorities. He was sentenced to a 5+5 term in a labour camp, meaning five years of camp plus five years of Siberian exile. In those days, people could be sentenced to up to 25+5, and they were not necessarily entitled to return to their native land. In Chapter 22 of *Treading Air* an episode from the narrator's own camp years is described. During 1949, one of the more "academic" tasks which Jaan Kross himself performed was drying out felt working boots in the labour camp – a "career" somewhat better than that of working outside in sub-zero temperatures or down the mines. Kross alternated his boot-drying activities with translating poetry by Russian writers such as Blok and Simonov.

After serving his sentence in Inta, near Vorkuta in the Komi SSR and working in a brickworks while in exile in the Krasnoyarsk region, Kross was pardoned "early", in 1954, because of the thaw and amnesty under Khrushchev. Some of Kross's experiences in both German and Russian captivity are set out in the tales which make up *The Conspiracy and Other Stories*.

On his return to Estonia, Kross wrote poetry for a while, and published poems he had brought back from his captivity. However, by the 1970s Kross had decided that he would prefer to write prose, and started the series of novels for which he is now famous. Since that time, Kross has built up a reputation as the most important Estonian novelist to deal with the history of the country. From 1992 to 1993, Kross was Member of Parliament for the Mõõdukad party (Social Democrats) in the Estonian parliament, the Riigikogu.

Kross's novels can be divided into two types: historical novels focusing on aspects of Estonian history, and semi-autobiographical novels that reflect scenes from his own life. Estonia and the Estonian people figure prominently in all his works, and he also refers to other European countries. Kross often examines the life and times of real historical figures, those somewhat marginalised, playing a bit part on the periphery of great events.

Aside from the novels already available in English, a number of Kross's other works merit a mention. Most of these have appeared in several languages. Between 1970 and 1980, Kross published *Between Three Plagues*, a tetralogy of novels about the ethnic Estonian Balthasar Russow who, despite his German name, was of humble local origin and a chronicler of life in Tallinn. All four volumes were published in first editions of 32,000 apiece, which is remarkable for a country where there are only approximately one million native speakers of Estonian. Kross soon became genuinely popular, not least because of his veiled criticism of Soviet reality.

Other novels include: *The Third Range of Hills* (1975), dealing with Johan Köler, an artist of peasant origins who ended up as court painter at the Czar's court in St Petersburg in the 1870s; *A Rakvere Romance* (1982), a novel about divided loyalties which deals with the struggle between the burghers of the provincial town of Rakvere and the feudal von Tiesenhausen family in the 1760s; *Ship into the Wind* (1987), which tells the story of the astronomer from the island of Naissaar, Bernhard Schmidt (1879–1935), who moved to Germany in the 1930s and became world famous for his telescope; *Untouchability* (1993), where a Kross-like figure, fleeing from the Germans himself, is writing a work about the member of the Committee for Estonian National Salvation, Jüri Vilms (1889–1918), who was executed by the Germans in Finland on suspicion of spying; and *Tahtamaa Farm* (2001), which deals with a Western speculator trying to trick an Estonian out of the deposits of medicinal mud on his land, recently restituted during the 1990s.

Two further novels should be mentioned: *The Wikman Boys*, a *roman à clef* dealing with many of Kross's schoolfriends (1988), where the protagonist of *Treading Air*, Ullo Paerand, appears very briefly; and its quasi-sequel *Mesmer's Ring* (1995), which deals with some of these same boys when they go to university. Neither of these novels is closely linked to the present one, and *Treading Air* is perhaps the most engaging and representative of Kross's semi-autobiographical works.

Kross has also written a score of short stories and novellas. Three of the most important historical novellas are *Two Mislaid Sheets of Paper*, about the collector of Estonian folk poetry Friedrich Kreutzwald (1803–1882), co-compiler of the *Kalevipoeg*, the Estonian answer to the Finnish *Kalevala*; *Michelson's Matriculation*, which tells of the life of an Estonian serf Johann von Michelsohnen (1735–1807), who rose to become a general in the Czarist army and helped put down the Pugachev Uprising in 1771; and *Four Monologues on the Subject of St George*, which tells of the life of Michel Sittow (1469–1525), who was born in Tallinn and spent seven years as court painter to Queen Isabella of Spain.

In addition, Kross has penned two plays, *A Hard Night for Doctor Karell* and *Brother Enrico and his Bishop*. The former deals with the life of a physician to the Czar, the latter is based on the life of Aleksander Kurtna (1914–1983), an Estonian polyglot who studied and worked at the Vatican archive between 1936 and 1942, survived the labour camps and went on to translate plays by Dürrenmatt, Mrożek and Ionesco. Kross has translated several works of world literature including *Macbeth*, *Othello*, *Pericles*, *The Tempest* and *Alice's Adventures in Wonderland*. He has recently published a book of collected speeches and lectures, and the first volume of his memoirs is about to appear.

Treading Air was first published as *Paigallend* in 1998 and deals with the tragicomic fate of Ullo Paerand, by way of notes jotted down by the narrator Jaak Sirkel (i.e. Kross's alter ego) during a series of short interviews. The narrator is trying to piece together Ullo's life between his schooldays in the late 1920s, and his final years in the mid-1980s. The episodes and anecdotes that make up the novel are largely self-explanatory, but some introduction is necessary. It is also necessary to describe the numerous real-life characters who have walk-on parts in the novel, so that the reader understands some of the jokes and nuances that characterise Kross's novels. These are listed alphabetically at the end of the novel, and the chapter(s) in which they appear is given. Translations of the poems written in German in the novel are also given at the end of the book.

During the 1990s, Estonia had once more "appeared" on the map of Europe, and a glance at an atlas can tell the reader a good deal, not least since place names are nowadays spelt in the Estonian manner, using the Roman alphabet, instead of being transliterations from the Cyrillic as in Soviet times. Many of the events described here occur in the Estonian capital, Tallinn, on the northern coast of the country just across the gulf from the Finnish capital, Helsinki. A number of Tallinn's streets are mentioned in the novel. During Soviet times, the names of streets with religious or bourgeois connotations were changed. After independence in 1991 they were changed back again.

The history of the Old Town of Tallinn stretches back to the Middle Ages. Nowadays, there is an area of shops, restaurants and ministries in the Lower Town. In the Upper Town on Toompea Hill, the pink edifice of the Riigikogu, the parliament, and the grand nineteenth-century Alexander Nevsky Russian Orthodox cathedral stand facing one another in almost symbolic fashion. The Lutheran cathedral stands further up the hill. Attached to the Riigikogu building is Pikk Hermann (Tall Hermann), the tower at the top of which the national flag is raised at sunrise and lowered at dusk (see Chapter 37). Flying the blue, black and white Estonian flag was illegal during both Soviet and German occupations.

Raekoja plats (Town Hall Square) in the Lower Town is regarded as the absolute centre of Tallinn, and Vabaduse väljak (Freedom Square), where the House of Art which contains an art gallery and flats for artists is situated, is nearby. They are separated by Harju Street. Pikk Street is also right in the middle of the Lower Town, as is Pagari Street where KGB headquarters was based right up until 1991. This building now houses the Ministry of the Interior. Kentmann Street, which changed its name with the regime as mentioned in Chapter 28, is where the US Embassy now stands.

The episode with Monsignor Arata, the papal nuncio, in Chapter 22 reflects the strange relationship between the Roman Catholic Church and Lutheran Estonia. There is, to this day, a small Vatican Embassy in the Kadriorg district (see below). The church complex that is mentioned is grouped around a former Dominican monastery on Vene

Street in the Lower Town. This includes the former mediaeval monks' granary, now a pub-restaurant, Kloostri Ait, where the small group of Catholic convert students tend to sit and drink tea or mulled wine. Above, there is a theatre where Symbolist plays by Maeterlinck and Pessoa have been staged. There is also the ruins of a Brigittine convent out at Pirita, north of Tallinn. Kross has written a play, *Brother Enrico and His Bishop* about the Proffitlich episode alluded to in that same chapter and the inscription *Hic vere est domus Dei et porta coeli* has recently been restored.

Oleviste Church (St Olav's) in the Old Town dates back to the thirteenth century and has a tower plus a newer steeple 124 metres tall. The tightrope walkers mentioned in Chapter 22 would have tied their ropes to the base of this steeple. Between Niguliste Church (St Nicholas's) and the Writers' Union building there is still a tiny patch of rough ground and a plaque, where, on each anniversary, candles are lit for the seven hundred residents of Tallinn who died in the 1944 March bombings. Anthony Powell based the geography of much of his 1932 novel *Venusberg* on the split-level Old Town.

The Estonia Theatre stands just outside the Old Town, as does the bank building with its Red Tower. The Wikman Boys' Grammar School is based on the Westholm Grammar School in Tallinn, which Kross attended in the 1930s. This school became the 22nd School during Soviet times, but has now had its original name restored.

The Estonian President's Palace stands in the park at Kadriorg, Catherine's Vale, named by Peter the Great of Russia in honour of his wife, Catherine I, a woman of Lithuanian peasant stock. From 1712 until the time of the Russian Revolution in 1917, Estonia formed part of the Russian Empire. Seewald is the main mental hospital on the outskirts of Tallinn and, as its German name suggests, it is near the sea and in the woods.

In parts of the novel, the district of Nõmme is mentioned. This is, in effect, the garden suburb of Tallinn. Even during Soviet times, people managed to keep hold of their private villas, although the best of these were inevitably taken over by the Communist Party nomenclature. Kalamaja, the district of Tallinn where Kross grew up, is between the Old Town and the sea, to the north-west of the centre. During Soviet times, no one except the military was allowed near the sea shore.

Rannamõisa, where the narrator's family rent a flat for the summer, is near the coast and a few miles to the west of Tallinn. Estonia's second city Tartu was the country's only university city in the 1930s when Kross studied law. Tartu University was originally founded in 1632 by the Swedish king, Gustavus Adolphus, but was shut down between 1710 and 1802 by the Russian authorities. Nowadays, it has around eight thousand students. The Stone Bridge mentioned towards the end of Chapter 27 was destroyed in the Soviet bombing of the city.

The city of Narva used to be within Estonian territory, and the border with the Russian Federation ran further to the east. In the mid-1940s the border was shifted to the Narva River itself, where it has remained to this day. Narva, once an architectural pearl, was bombed during World War II and is a ghost of its former self. It is now 95 per cent Russian-speaking.

Pärnu, a holiday and health resort on the west coast of the country, is still popular today with Estonians, having earned the epithet of "the Summer Capital of Estonia". The poet and politician Johannes Barbarus (see Chapter 20) had his ramshackle home there and Ullo spends a couple of summers at the resort. Two other provincial towns mentioned in the novel are Rakvere in the north of the country and Viljandi in the south.

In 1944, as the Germans retreated and the Soviets advanced, about 80,000 Estonians took the opportunity to flee to the West, either via Germany where they ended up in displaced persons' camps, or to neutral Sweden, sometimes via Finland. The vast majority of them travelled in small and overloaded boats over to Sweden from such places as Puise, mentioned in Chapter 34. This small village is situated on the west coast of Estonia, south of the coastal town of Haapsalu and to the north of the Matsalu inlet.

The largest islands off western Estonia are Saaremaa and Hiiumaa. The small bird-sanctuary island of Vilsandi forms the westernmost tip of Estonia. In some history books and documents, the old German place names can be found. The most relevant ones for this novel are Reval (Tallinn) and Dorpat (Tartu).

Estonian history is coloured by occupation, war and famine from the thirteenth century onwards, with occasional bouts of peace and harmony. Parts of Estonia have, at various times, been occupied by Sweden, Russia, Poland, Germany and Denmark. A layer of Baltic–German nobility formed a cushion between the occupying power of the day and the Estonian peasantry. German cultural influences on Estonia have, over the ages, been stronger than more local Russian ones, leading Estonians to look westwards, rather than eastwards.

The first key date in *Treading Air* is 24 February, Estonian Independence Day. This commemorates the day in 1918 when, as Estonia was being invaded by the Germans, the Provisional Committee proclaimed the independence of the Estonian Republic. Estonians would collect – illegally according to Soviet law – around the statue of writer Anton Hansen Tammsaare to commemorate their republic.

In November 1918, during the War of Estonian Independence which followed the Declaration, Estonia had to stave off the Soviets and the Germans. She was backed up by a British fleet who sent fifteen warships, including destroyers and light cruisers, under the command of Rear Admiral Sir Edwin Sinclair. Estonia finally signed the Treaty of Tartu with Soviet Russia in 1920 in which it was stated that Russia *"definitively recognises the independence of Estonia and will renounce for ever every sovereign right that Russia has had on Estonian land and the Estonian people"*. "For ever" lasted until 1940.

A Communist coup in 1924 which involved some three hundred armed fighters – but only lasted a couple of hours – the emergence of the fascistic Vapsid (League of War of Independence Veterans) and especially the ruinous Wall Street Crash, all resulted in the autocratic rule of the Riigvanem, State Elder, Konstantin Päts, now termed the Period of Silence.

The Riigivolikogu (Chamber of Deputies) was the first parliamentary body to be created when, in 1938, Päts's autocratic rule began to slacken. It survived until the Soviet annexation of Estonia in 1940. (Since 1992, an independent Estonia has had a new 101-seat parliament, the Riigikogu).

On 23 August 1939, Soviet Russia and Nazi Germany signed a non-aggression treaty, the Molotov–Ribbentrop Pact, which marked the beginning of the end for an independent Estonia. In a secret protocol to this document, the Baltic states were left in the Soviet sphere of interest. One month later the Russian Foreign Minister, Vyacheslav Molotov, put pressure on Estonia to accept a pact of mutual assistance which, in effect, meant the stationing of huge numbers of Soviet troops on Estonian soil.

While still a province of Russia, for centuries Estonia had been run by Baltic Germans. Famous Estonian Germans include the aristocratic philosopher and oriental expert Hermann von Keyserling, the short-story writer Werner Bergengruen and Hitler's ideologist Alfred Rosenberg, who was born in Tallinn and executed at Nuremberg. When Hitler summoned them "back" to a fatherland they had never known, about 14,000 Baltic Germans – termed *Umsiedler* in German – disappeared from the Estonian scene.

Bitter battles took place between the Nazis and the Soviets around Narva and in the Blue Hills towards the end of World War II, with Estonians conscripted on both sides. The Omakaitse was a home guard that originated in the War of Independence and was revived with the German occupation of 1941–4, during which its 32,000 members acted as security police for the occupiers.

During World War II, Tallinn was a frequent target for bombs, the most notorious being on 9 March 1944 when Soviet women bomber pilots – led by a Canadian Communist, it is said – missed the key harbour installations, instead destroying many houses in the city itself, and the Estonia Theatre. In September of the same year, the Soviets managed to hit the port. Evidence of the former raid can be seen to this day on Harju Street in the centre of the Old Town.

On 18 September 1944, Otto Tief proclaimed a new independent Estonia, exploiting the vacuum created between the retreating Germans and the advancing Soviets. But this was more of a gesture than a deed and a few days later the new government was forced to flee to Sweden. Soviet rule was consolidated and Estonia unwillingly became the Estonian Soviet Socialist Republic.

The secret police made its presence felt during the two Soviet occupations, 1940–1 and 1944–91. It was originally called the People's Commissariat for Internal Affairs (NKVD), later changing its name to the KGB. Its methods were the same, despite the name change. In early 1941, during the first Soviet occupation, one thousand or so people disappeared and a further ten thousand were sent without sentence to Soviet labour camps. During the 1949 March deportations, a further 20,700 Estonians, mostly women and children, were deported to the Krasnoyarsk and Novosibirsk provinces of Russia.

The Forest Brethren were Estonian guerrillas who went underground as the Soviets arrived and whose activities did not cease fully until the mid-1950s. During the rest of the Soviet period, up to 1991, many of the top posts in the Estonian Communist Party were held by what are termed "Yestonians" – i.e. Estonians brought up in Russia, as Russians, with Russian as their mother tongue and with a lamentable inability to speak Estonian. This expression has nothing to do with yes-men, but is based on the tendency for Russians to add a "y" sound to the vowel "e" at the beginning of words.

The Estonian language is closely related to Finnish, as closely as German is to Dutch, or Spanish to Portuguese. Loan words have come from the Low German, and from the Russian. Neologisms were introduced with some success in the mid-twentieth century by Johannes Aavik. The language is agglutinative: many suffixes are affixed to the ends of words, especially nouns.

Until about 1900, very little secular prose literature was written in the Estonian language, although folk poetry has a long history. The twentieth century saw an enormous increase in the number of novels and poetry published. During the last two decades of the Soviet Union, and the first decade of renewed Estonian independence, many new writers joined the fold (and the Writers' Union).

Throughout *Treading Air* there are veiled allusions to the Estonian literary movement Noor-Eesti, Young Estonia. The movement began around 1900 and lasted into the 1920s. Several of the poets and cultural figures mentioned in the novel were associated with the movement. Young Estonia looked for cultural inspiration towards Europe, especially France and Scandinavia, and modelled itself on the Nuori Suomi (Young Finland) movement. The Young Estonians' slogan, coined by poet and critic Gustav Suits, became: *"More European culture! Let us remain Estonians, but let us also become Europeans!"*

Despite all the drollery and slapstick, there is something indisputably sad about the fate of Ullo Paerand. His family circumstances and those occurring nationally and internationally all seem to conspire to bring him down. And yet he remains eternally in opposition, fighting from a position of quasi-hopelessness against forces much greater than him. While he somehow remains buoyant after every setback, one cannot help feeling that each of these brings him a little nearer the brink.

Eric Dickens

TREADING AIR

1

AND SO SOME TALES about my old friend, the object of my sympathies, suspicions and admiration, Ullo Paerand.

I have already described him briefly elsewhere. But he deserves to be treated as the bones of the story. For his own sake, but also because of the early part he played as his own chronicler. And lastly, because his role, if not exactly seminal, was at least decorative against the backdrop of history.

I first got to know Ullo at our famous school, the Wikman Boys' Grammar. He remained outside the circle of Wikman boys dealt with in my novel about that school because it focuses on a group of my own form mates, while he was four or even five years our senior. Another reason for Ullo's absence there was my feeling that the treatment of Ullo as part of that group would not be sufficient, that a more extensive, yet more individual, approach was necessary.

Anyway, I first clapped eyes on Ullo on the steps of Wikman's, and also in the yellow assembly hall, as early as, let's say, 1933 or '34, when I was twelve or thirteen years of age and he, seventeen or eighteen. When I was maybe in the top form of the junior school and he a tenth-former at the grammar, ready for his leaving exams. He was tall and thin, with a narrow face, a longish and sensitive nose and a large Adam's apple, a beanpole whose face often looked as if it were freezing.

I do not recall whether at this stage I had heard of the comparison between the size of Turgenev's brain and that of Anatole France (if I am not mistaken, that of the former weighed 2,018 grams, and of the latter 1,343). But I presume I knew this fact, because I do not remember ever questioning that Ullo, with his small birdlike cranium, had room up there to house a brilliant intellect. I had noticed, early on, that he was very intelligent. But even before that I had managed to notice that his clothes were of rather poor quality, something rarely encountered at Wikman's. Sleeves short, elbows frayed, his blazer tight, his trousers bagging at the knee. Though there was nothing raggy about his clothing: cuffs and buttonholes were neatly sewn, the patch on the seat of his trousers was in place, and of more or less the right material. What struck me most about his dress was the fact that he wore the small proud maroon school cap with black edging even during periods of severe frost. He wore it when other boys were coming to school in fur hats with earflaps which mothers had rammed on to the heads of the smaller boys back home, and ordered the older ones to put on, on account of the biting cold, and which many did, of course, wear quite voluntarily; though they would have liked to brave the cold in their school caps. At other times, except when the frost was severe, they did not want to wear their caps at all, and wearing a cap was the badge of being a mother's boy. On frosty days, however, wearing one was an act of hardiness and bravado. My mother, of course, pushed my fur hat on to my head without the least resistance on my part. I tried to blame this acquiescence on a recent bout of ear inflammation, but it was a nuisance nonetheless. And so, in my eyes, Ullo was all the more enviable in his actions. Till it emerged that Ullo simply didn't possess any winter headgear. Once I had heard this, wearing his school cap seemed a trifle desperate, no longer a quirk to envy.

Tenth- and eleventh-formers did not generally associate with younger boys. Unless, that is, they had a whippersnapper of a younger brother in, say, the sixth form. And then only if their mother had ordered the older lad to make sure that the younger one didn't run off to the gym in only his blazer in twenty degrees of frost. The gym stood a kilometre away and boisterous teenage lads were quite capable of showing off how big they were. So when an elder brother had received orders from home to make sure that his younger brother had his overcoat and scarf on, he could often be seen at the door of the cloakroom yelling at his younger brother: "Oi, you! You tuberous lump! Do you really expect me to come over and put your coat on for you?! Put it on right now!"

Otherwise, it was not normal for older boys to have contact with younger ones. And Ullo was responsible for neither my overcoat nor my scarf. But we did nevertheless establish contact. This happened once during long break:

Our strange German form master Schwarz wanted to hear us tell him something that day – material which would first be dealt with in the ninth form – he wanted to hear, next lesson, what sort of man a certain Adalbert von Chamisso, a man with a French name, was and what he wrote. And I happened to have swotted up a bit about him, and as soon as we arrived in class, Herr Schwarz dragged me up to the blackboard and started asking questions. He wanted to know the name of that accursed island in the Pacific, about which Chamisso had written a narrative poem. Its name had slipped my mind and I was not allowed to leave the vicinity of the blackboard to go and look it up in my exercise book. Troubled by this, I went up to Ullo during the next break.

While three hundred boys – from the seventh to the eleventh forms – were walking slowly and in a tight huddle around the hall, not of course all together and mechanically, but still in decent order, i.e. with some bustling around in a large circle and others in dribs and drabs beyond it – at the same time as all this was happening Ullo was standing, his back to the room, hands on his rump, under the plaster-of-Paris bust of Tõnisson that stood between the yellow curtains, and looking out of the window. I went up to him – he must have realised that he could be of assistance – and asked (I now think it was on that occasion I noticed that his left eye squinted slightly towards his nose): "Ullo, tell me, what's the name of the island Chamisso wrote a narrative poem about?"

Rather surprised, he looked me in the eye with good-natured condescension: "Does Herr Schwarz want to know that from you lot? What a weird chap he is! The next thing you know, he'll be putting questions like that to the pap-chinned nippers in the seconds. Anyway, the island was called Sala y Gomez, named after the man who discovered it. Some Spaniard or other, no doubt. But as to the size of the island, how many kilometres square it is, don't ask me. I've seen three different figures in three different encyclopaedias: 0.12, 4 and 38.5. Which only goes to show how little you can trust reference books. Anyway, Chamisso went there in 1816. He had gone along with Kotzebue on his round-the-world voyage, as a botanist. Kotzebue, by the way, was born in Tallinn."

I said: "There's a street with his name. I walk past the end of it every day."

"Really," said Ullo, "where do you actually live?"

I told him my address and even now, sixty years on, I seem to remember he came round to our house for the first time that very same evening.

We sat in my room and felt a bit awkward, at least I did, he too no doubt. He eyed my test tubes and spirit lamp and pieces of pyrites picked up from the beach at Merivälja, and everything else that made up my "laboratory", and muttered: "Want to make the philosophers' stone?!"

I shrugged one shoulder and changed the subject.

"Tell me something more about Kotzebue's voyage around the world."

Ullo was, however, not a fluent teller of stories. He would speak in small staccato bursts, and then leave the sentence hanging in the air, his mouth half open (a fact I noticed much later) and then say: "But perhaps it was, in fact, like this . . ." Or, in keeping with the content of some story: "Maybe we could do the opposite now . . .?" and would add something almost absurd.

"Kotzebue, you say? Surprising litter he came from. Five brothers. All of them are in the larger encyclopaedias. The first: the sailor we've already mentioned. Discovered 399 islands. The second: a writer, officer and explorer. The third: a general, and not just any old general, but a full-blown infantry general, and the Governor-General of Poland and who was made a count. The fourth: a diplomat and a writer. Russian ambassador to Switzerland. The fifth: a battle painter. And again, not just any old painter but one who painted half of the Winter Palace collection, by imperial appointment. But there is still one even more surprising individual: the father of all five. A dramatist. Sent to Siberia by the Czar and was stabbed to death by a German student. Lived for a good number of years in Estonia, and wrote 216 plays. According to many accounts he was a schemer, a boor and an informer. But there again, maybe he wasn't – if he managed to sire such sons?"

Then we played chess. He, of course, won. Even when he had given me one rook's start as a handicap. His strategy was to perform quite unexpected moves right from the outset which would quickly lead to a welter of confusion. Only when I had grown a little more familiar with his style of play (and when he offered me a queen instead of a rook) did I sometimes win. But that occurred much later.

On that first occasion, as on all subsequent ones, my mother invited Ullo to eat dinner with us. At table he had to answer my father's questions:

"What does your father do for a living?"

"He's a businessman. As far as I know."

Father raised an eyebrow. "What are we to make of that – as far as you know?"

"Well, in Estonia he was a building contractor. But he's been abroad for some years now and I don't really know what he's doing there, business or otherwise."

"Otherwise?"

"Well, some say he's gone into hiding, in Luxembourg or wherever, to escape his creditors –"

"Then we can assume he will have his reasons –" said Father, slowly.

"Or maybe not," said Ullo. "Maybe it's because he's got a French wife out there, but doesn't want to upset Mum –"

"Oh, I see –" said Father – "then the story's more straightforward. Or maybe, in fact, more complex."

After dinner, Ullo and I went back to my room. At half past ten my mother came in to tell me it was time for my wash. Ullo rose, thanked my mother for the meal and went home. Mother summed up his first visit:

"He's a well-brought-up boy all right. But his clothes do have – didn't you notice – the smell of the cellar about them. It's that mezzanine flat halfway down to the cellar at some market gardener's out Nõmme way where they're now forced to live. And he certainly doesn't know when to call it a day and go home –"

And when Father (who never suspected anyone of anything, but would smile wryly about many) didn't say anything, Mother (who would never smile wryly about anyone, but was suspicious about almost everyone) said: "Jaak is still a child. But that Ullo is almost a young man. I wonder what he sees in Jaak?"

What Father said pleased me greatly. "Well, in his eyes, Jaak can no longer be a child."

WHERE AND HOW I got to know about Ullo's childhood, and how I came to write about it, is something I am no longer in any position to explain. I must have heard fragments early on, both from him and from my mother. For, with a little exaggeration, it can safely be said that in a city as small as Tallinn, everyone knows everyone else, or at least everyone knows something about everyone else. It turned out that our mothers, that is to say the ladies who later became Mrs Paerand and Mrs Sirkel, had once been classmates at junior school, years of course before the births of either Ullo or myself. Every girl and future wife is always more interested in what occurs to classmates than in the fates of other childhood friends. When I once happened to mention to my father that the name "Paerand" was in fact an Estified name, and that the surname of Ullo and his parents had once been "Berends", my father had said: "Ahaa . . ." And then added that he had in fact heard odds and ends about them. So I presumably heard something from my father, too.

Finally, five or six years ago, I had the bright idea to start asking Ullo about his life. But Ullo had still not developed into a fluent story teller. So I said to him: "Listen, now that I've understood that you're not going to do anything literary with your life story, what if I should do so?" And to my great surprise – he did not demur. Well, we didn't get very far in our conversations. But we did manage four or five sessions.

His father, whom I never met, and whom Ullo had probably seen on only one occasion after 1930, was the son of a village tailor from the province of Harjumaa. Imagination and restlessness seemed to have been in the genes of those who plied that trade as the genes were passed on to their own children, and theirs. Let us not forget that tailor's son from Gudbrandsdalen, Pedersen, who managed to succeed in attracting the most fulsome praise of his people – and a quarter of a century later, now known as the novelist Knut Hamsun, brought on himself their strongest condemnation. Not, of course, that Ullo's father or Ullo himself ever deserved either. The father never thought to praise his own nation. His son perhaps did, but half ironically and, when it came down to it, he simply couldn't be bothered. As regards wholesale condemnation, they both managed to let that pass them by. The tricks they would have deserved it for were either of all too personal a nature, or were rendered sufficiently irrelevant against the turbulent backdrop of the world at the time.

With the education you received by attending five or six classes at the local school – and that was all that Ullo's father had had – you would not exactly be counted as an intellectual in Tallinn, but you would at least be regarded as more or less educated. Especially when, as in Ullo's father's case, you had a pretty decent command of Estonian, Russian, German and French, not only of the spoken language, but also an ability to write them, a fact borne witness to by some of Mr Berends's letters which Ullo had kept. Where Ullo's father had obtained this knowledge is not clear. If you cannot, that is to say, derive some explanation from one of the tales I heard from Ullo: when Ullo was in the ninth form, he had been accused during a German exam set by the headmaster, Wikman himself, of learning the appropriate pages of *Dichtung und Wahrheit* by heart, in the manner of a child, rather than retelling their content in his own words. And Wikman had only very reluctantly believed Ullo on hearing his explanation: that Ullo had managed to get the passage into his head, in Goethe's own words, after reading it only once.

When I asked Ullo whether his father ever wrote poetry in his youth, Ullo shook his head vigorously: not one single line!

But the tailor's son had come to the city and learnt his languages well. He had become an errand boy with some banking house, and had soon risen to the rank of bookkeeper. Then as a bank clerk, with a stiff collar round his neck, young Berends had gone and got married. To Trimbek's daughter, who had been christened Aleksandra, but was known to everyone as Sandra. Her hair was almost black, and she possessed a foreign brand of beauty. This was the very same girl who had been in my mother's class at junior school. Ullo's mother had told him much later during sorrow-filled days what Eduard, his father, had been, at the start of their marriage – "Well, I thought he was

7

marvellous. Only later did his hollowness and frivolity emerge . . ." In the adjoining building there lived one of Eduard's boyhood friends from Mõik, who ran a draper's shop. From here Eduard would bring home the finest of materials on Saturday evenings – "Well, there wasn't any silk in that shitty little shop. But there was glossy satin." Eduard was especially enamoured of shades of red and pink. Half of Saturday and all of Sunday he would busy himself with it, draping it around his naked young bride with the help of dressmaker's pins.

But then the last years before the First World War were at hand, and the young Mr Berends had made the acquaintance of a surprising number of people, principally from among the Russians and Germans who were local civil servants. And mainly those who were a little, or a lot, more important than he was. From them he obtained the necessary information – whether over a tot of vodka or not (as he didn't really drink himself). So that he suddenly left the bank and managed to get a loan of several thousand, not of course from the Baltic German bank where he had been working, but from a certain Russian one, and went and bought a couple of hundred *desyatina* of the most stony and flat land in the poor soil region, out towards Vääna, some fifteen kilometres west of Tallinn.

A year later, he sold the land to the state at ten times the price. For a year later – on the grand imperial scale of the time – they had begun building a line of defences, named after Peter the Great, to protect the capital, that is to say St Petersburg . . .

Mr Berends paid back his loan and the interest on it – in those days they were reasonable percentages, not the thirty which bankers of today regard as their patriotic norm, but your good old twelve – paid his dues, and suddenly acquired standing and respect in business circles, plus an amount of free capital. And the main thing was – and one which proved fatal – that he had acquired a taste, or rather fingers, for it.

Work on the defences continued, and opportunities grew. Those who popped up like mushrooms after rain were, generally speaking, failures, albeit temporarily successful business geniuses, pocket Vautrins of local proportions. They felt themselves initially to be innocent and in no way representative of a morality to which the real Vautrin had subscribed in his native land one hundred years before: gobbling each other up – like spiders in a jar. Oh no! Young Berends dived into this maelstrom with innocence and enthusiasm, enthusiasm and innocence, behind which still lurked the Lutheran work ethic of his village forefathers. Which, of course, began to clothe itself in the latest sports suits.

Mr Berends speculated – and with increasing success – in land, forest, limestone, pig iron and cement (it is said that in 1913 he had bought up half the production of the cement works in Kunda). Then came five years of various brands of war and occupation. So that Mr Berends's riches multiplied unceasingly. I do not know – because Ullo didn't either – how his father had managed to do so, but he had saved half his stock, or at least a good proportion, on the collapse of the Russian Empire, through the Kerensky year, through the Bolshevik episode and the German occupation. When the Russians carried off the Czarist gold from the Estonian banks and you could wallpaper the privy with the portraits of the Empress Catherine, and when that great husbandman, History, had swept the Kerenskys and Oberosts of this world into its dustbin, it emerged that Mr Berends's money had been deposited at a London bank in pounds sterling a good while before. So by the time of the Estonian War of Independence he had become, if not one of the most pivotal, then at least a significant financier of the young republic. Not, shall we say, like the Puhk brothers, but certainly like Jakob Pärtsel and other men of his calibre. This selfsame Jakob Pärtsel is supposed to have said of Mr Berends, maybe, admittedly, still during the mid-twenties: Berends wants to do business in too proper a manner, and earn too much by doing so.

At first, Berends clearly did succeed in his undertakings, although his business activities were limited, in the main, to those of the "potato republic" itself. Incidentally, among those the Berendses received at their home in the early 1920s were Russian emigrés who were in an important, even dominant, position in this emerging society; these emigrés viewed Estonia as a potato republic indeed, this attitude being, in the eyes of Mr Berends, and even more so his wife Sandra, a poor show and an affront. Even the five-year-old Ullo was aware of these tensions. Especially after the business with Rolly.

Rolly was a beautiful black Dobermann, which Mr Berends had bought recently, in the spring of 1921, from an emigré university student, young Master Burov, a small man with a black moustache who was forever in need of cash. He had paid three thousand marks for the

9

three-year-old dog. Such a high sum was the result of Mr Berends's weakness for small gestures of largesse – and also of the outstanding quality of the dog itself. Master Burov had done a good job promoting the dog, and Mr Berends knew why Burov, his frequent guest, needed the money, the principal cost being that of courting one of the seven daughters of one General Tretyakov (who by then, of course, transliterated his name as *Tretjakoff*), a sometime regular guest at the Berendses'. As regards the dog, Burov had said: "Well, you know, *gospodin* Berends, Rolly is such a creature that his master's name isn't Burov, but Durov – Russian fool that I am! I have taken great pains with him – but the result has been worth the trouble! *Gospodin* Berends, stand up, I beg you, say '*zdravstvuite*' to him, and see how he reacts!"

Mr Berends had stood up with a smile and said "*zdravstvuite*" to the dog. Whereupon it stretched, got to its feet, walked up to him, stood on its hind legs, placed its left front paw on his right shoulder, extending its right paw towards him – "woof!" – to be taken and shaken. An enraptured Mr Berends slipped the three thousand on to the table for Master Burov and got a kennel ready for Rolly in the front garden of their block of flats on Raua Street. And Burov had himself put Rolly on the green pillow in the kennel, showing the dog his new place and home. Ullo did not leave Rolly's side for two or three weeks and Miss von Rosen, who lived in the building and taught the boy French, had to drag him out of the kennel in the evenings and to the bathroom, and so to bed. Until Nadja, one of General Tretjakoff's seven daughters and, for some strange reason, the one whom young Burov was courting (seemingly without success) had turned with a tinkling laugh to Mr Berends and his wife and said: "Well, that's what the sloppy great hound does when he hears '*zdravstvuite*'. But have you tried to see what happens when you say '*tere*' to him in Estonian instead?"

No one had tried this yet, so Mr Berends immediately obliged. Rolly turned his rump towards the master of the household, raised his left hind paw and peed with a gurgle against the trouser leg of his light grey summer suit.

Despite her almost urban proletarian origins, this was something that Ullo's mother simply could not abide. I have the feeling that during their marriage she played a relatively low-key role, but precisely for this reason certain of her decisions were all the more absolute regarding her Eduard. At least while he still had some respect for her. And in those days he still had a good deal. So Ullo's mother said: "Eduard! Get rid of that creature at once! Can you imagine my mother having to say '*zdravstvuite*' to it, when she comes to see Ullo on Sunday? Because she won't be able to greet us with '*tere*' like any normal Estonian, unless she wants to get –"

And so no doubt that very day Mr Berends sold Rolly to some Russian immigrants. They were, at all events, not likely to start saying "*tere*" to their dog. And he got at least half of his three thousand marks back. Regarding the grandmother, she could now come to visit Ullo on Sunday as she pleased. The arrival of Grandmother, that is to say, was always an important occasion for Ullo.

Ullo's grandmother, Old Mother Trimbek, was a woman more gruff than over-kindly, at least to many others, maybe all others, in the house. However, along with her dark, stout presence, and a pair of lively bright blue eyes, she brought Ullo a sense of security. At least protecting him from the loneliness, something which Ullo told me he was half aware of in this home constantly filled with strangers. But it wasn't only a feeling of security which the stern woman with her cackling laugh instilled in the boy (for she always chose others as the butt of her laughter – never Ullo). No, it wasn't merely a question of feeling secure. But also because she told the eight-year-old Ullo such wonderful stories. He would see everything she said with frightful vividness in his mind's eye. Such as what had occurred when she was seventeen and had sung Estonian songs in some provincial Harjumaa choir in Tartu at the first All-Estonian Song Festival. She had even gone, accompanying the conductor of her choir, to the home of the Jannsen family, the widower Johann Voldemar and his daughter Lydia, whose pen name was Koidula, on Tiigi Street. She had seen for herself old Jannsen himself – "a very kind and good-natured old gent". And what is more – and it is amusing, in looking back, to think that the grandmother had understood that this was more than merely seeing Jannsen – she had also seen Koidula with her very own eyes. Ullo's grandmother remembered exactly how Koidula had cried "Come in!" as they had stood there knocking at the door of her father's study, and how they had entered whereupon Koidula had cried: "*Ach, ihr lieben Leute* – wipe your feet carefully! There's so many as comes in here, and wi' t' streets so full o' mud . . .*"

11

So they had wiped their feet for such a long time on the jute doormat that the young poetess had cried out, amused, perhaps even with a measure of irritation: "All right, that's enough, enough, enough! Step inside, if you're ever going to!" and handed them their scores herself.

And Ullo's grandmother explained: "I don't know how the others responded, but the next day I sang more diligently from the score. Because Koidula, the Nightingale of the River Emajõgi, had handed us our scores personally. Even allowing for her lesson in foot-wiping –"

His grandmother also told him about things which, as he gradually realised, she could not have seen with her own eyes, since they had occurred earlier even than his grandmother's youth, namely about Ivan the Awful, almost a pet name, as he was called in Estonia before being termed Ivan the Terrible, the Estonian term being almost masochistically mild compared to the Russian "Grozny".

And the grandmother also told about the Dog Snouts, the principal assistants to Ivan the Terrible. She described them in such detail that it was as if, incomprehensibly, she had actually seen them, although they had, along with Ivan himself, vanished long ago from this country into the mists of time, so that no one had clapped eyes on them since the good old Swedish days. Ullo's grandmother explained: they were all under four foot tall. No, there were no women among the Dog Snouts. Only men. And dog-snouted, the lot of them. Or maybe more fox-snouted. Or wolf-snouted. With long fangs. And they panted through the villages and forests, sniffing the ground as they went along – hnff-hnff-hnff – and if they were after somebody, then they began to whine and howl and drool at the chops. But what they did with those who fell into their hands, that Grandmother glossed over – "Oh yes, what they did with them – well, they did what they could to maul them." Although Ullo demanded to know what they did in more detail, he didn't insist too much. For he was afraid that at night he wouldn't be able to escape from wrestling with the Dog Snouts and having to breathe in their fiery, foul breath and wouldn't be able to fall asleep for fear that they would sneak up on him. So his dreams remained more or less free of Dog Snouts, and were exorcised by the security of Grandmother's presence. But he nonetheless had his own nightmares. And one which he had more and more frequently, worsening progressively for several months at a time:

12

There he is, the eight- or nine-year-old Ullo Berends, sleeping in his room in the luxurious flat on Raua Street. He wakes up all at once, in the night, not out of a dream, but *in* one, and sees how he is not for some reason sleeping in his own bed, but is on the floor. The first time this occurs, he doesn't at first know what is happening, but on every subsequent occasion he knows, knows, knows, and is duly afraid. For next to him on the floor lie large grey sacks, smelling of earth and filled with some terrible living substance. They begin to stir, rise up, drag around and move in on him, threatening to bury him. He tries to push them away. He struggles, cries out, wakes up for real, and is afraid of going back to sleep. For then the attack by the horrible sacks would begin all over again. And the ghastly dream repeats itself. At first, every second or third night. Then twice or three times the same night and every second or third night. At first, the red-haired, somewhat menacing Miss von Rosen takes the whimpering little boy who has yelled himself awake to her own bed, delivering him from his night-mares. When this only improves matters for a short while, his mother puts him on the sofa in his parents' room, to fall asleep there. But the nightmare recurs and even progresses. Progresses in a satanic way, so that with each repetition the boy becomes smaller but the sacks, which approach him with their unknown but fearful contents, become ever larger, heavier and more oppressive. In the end, the boy has shrunk to the size of a tailor's dress pin, he has in fact become a dress pin. His pinhead glows with the fear of the suffocating proximity of the approaching, wriggling, tossing grey sacks. Fear, so that now, now and now he burns the sacks with his glowing head or pokes his sharp length into the holes – and the Fearful Thing pushes its way out to kill its liberator.

This nightmare subsided over several months. His mother and father, Miss von Rosen and whoever else, even including the family GP, Dr Dunkel, came in between his bouts of nocturnal weeping, during times when he was awake and through days that followed so that he might at least tell what it was about the dream that was so frightening. He never did tell. I can now, however, read from the notes I made during conversations in 1986 (when he was seventy years old):

"They tried to coax it out of me with all sorts of tricks. They

13

promised me that they'd stop the dreams recurring. My father promised me that the next summer I would go with him on a trip abroad: so long as I told them the dreams. I didn't tell. I can't explain why. And it is only now for the first time that I am telling you."

To tell you the truth, this admission still makes me wince now, eight years later, and six after Ullo's death. For it shows how seriously he took his own revelations. But how seriously did he take what I have been doing with them? Unless, of course, the whole business was simply one huge game on his part. Where the boundary between game and truth lay for him is something that I have never quite been able to work out.

3

ALTHOUGH ULLO HAD NOT given his father any grounds on which to keep his promise, he was nonetheless taken on a trip abroad. This was in the spring of 1923 and the travellers comprised his father, mother, Ullo himself plus the seamstress Charlotte, a St Petersburg German of around forty years of age who lived with the Berendses, dividing her skills between the family wardrobe, nursery and kitchen when the need arose, sometimes as overseer of the forever changing female cooks, sometimes as skivvy.

Their destination was the Germany of the day. Although trips to France and Holland had also been mooted, Germany's towering inflation, which rendered the currency fantastically cheap in comparison with that of Estonia, made a trip there especially attractive.

They boarded the grand, white, two-funnelled *Rügen*, in Tallinn, settling themselves in a first-class cabin (with Charlotte travelling second) and arrived the following day in Stettin. On that first day of the voyage they went to the dining room. But Ullo only mentioned this with reluctance some sixty years later:

"*Nojaa*. It was actually due to the rocking of the ship. But I had convinced myself that the very slow rocking of such a large ship could not make such a brave boy as myself sick. So it had to be the lunch, to be more specific, the celery soup. I have always told all my friends and women that the damned Germans fed us such disgusting celery soup on the *Rügen* that I puked my guts out!"

But the next day, as the ship was approaching the German coast, and especially during the afternoon as it steamed across the Stettiner Haff and up the River Oder, the boy stood proudly at the rail, giving the impression, and he could certainly give such an impression, that he had never had anything to do with seasickness. Which had been made easier by the fact that Charlotte had rinsed out his

15

blue sailor suit in her cabin and dried and ironed it to perfection. Out of a sense of prudence, no one had come to fetch him to come to the table.

As far as Ullo could manage to discover, Stettin was in every respect a top-notch city. But all he saw, in fact, was on the cab trip from the harbour to the railway station, although his mother suggested staying the whole day. A certain Dr Schleich was meant to be living there, a doctor and a writer whose book *Besonnte Vergangenheit* Ullo had seen on his mother's bedside table back in Raua Street. But he had not felt the urge to start reading it. Because he was at the time halfway through Sir Arthur Conan Doyle's *The Exploits of Brigadier Gerard* in German translation – at the time he couldn't yet read English. As they emerged on to the street from the customs house, with porters carrying their luggage, his mother was saying: "But Eduard, you yourself have had a look at Dr Schleich's book. The reviewers even write: 'the most idyllic work to have come out in the madness of post-war Germany'. I'd really like to meet the author and have a chat with him."

Whether Ullo was surprised by his father's reply I cannot tell, but usually Ullo's father was a good deal more keen on meeting people than his wife. But now (while the porters were lugging their yellow-strapped suitcases to one cabman, and his father was helping the ladies take their seats with the second cabman, then taking his own with Ullo by the suitcases) he replied: "My dear, if we did that we would lose a whole day of our stay in Berlin. And that just isn't possible judging by how many people you want to talk with there. Granted, Goethe's dead, but as you told me yourself there are so many different types of people there, everything from actors to clairvoyants – and I have my own negotiations to conduct. So we don't have any time for Dr Schleich."

Ullo, of course, wanted to get to Berlin as quickly as possible, for he had heard of its allure, and nothing about that of Stettin. So the boy could afford to interpose at this point. "But Mum, I read a year ago in some paper or other that Dr Schleich is now just as dead as Goethe."

They did not spend any more time in Stettin, but hurried on to the railway station and sought out the first-class carriages to Berlin.

Ullo did not recall his impressions of the railway journey. But he did remember the taxi journey to Unter den Linden in the dark evening, through the bustle and the city lights. And his disdain when the hotel, the "Adlon" as he remembered, was not at all situated under lime trees

16

(whose crowns the lights in front of the hotel lit up as a greenish-gold roof from underneath – he had imagined this all with tangible clarity) but stood instead under the open sky. The Hotel Adlon was grand enough, nonetheless, certainly the most noble in Berlin at the time, standing as it did on the corner of Unter den Linden and the Französischer Platz. From the outside it was not particularly imposing, rather reminiscent of the headquarters of the Bank of Lending that was being built in Tallinn at the time. But from the inside it was extra grand. The porters and lift boys wore red uniforms and their bows and smiles were multiply reflected in the mirrors lining the walls. But at the time it seemed to him that this was how it should be in hotels where he stayed.

Father, Mother and Ullo went to their hotel apartment which consisted of a lounge and a double bedroom leading off, and to which a dressing room and a bathroom belonged. What would nowadays be termed a suite. Charlotte went to her smaller room nearby, which proved not to be so small after all. As well as a single bed, there was also the couch on which Ullo was put to bed of an evening when Father and Mother had gone visiting, or to the theatre or the cabaret. Looking back, it seemed that the weeks spent by them in Berlin consisted only of such evenings.

Ullo always slept badly on the couch. On the fourth or fifth morning in Berlin he woke very early and found that Charlotte was not in the room, and that the clock on the chest of drawers said a quarter to six. Even seventy years later, Ullo was loath to admit that he had been afraid, or that he had called out for Charlotte and when there was no response, he had gone looking for her. Or was really, in fact, looking for his parents. Their door was only a few dozen paces away.

Ullo arrived at their door, turned the handle and found the door to be locked, as it indeed should have been at that hour, so he cried out and knocked, cried out and knocked, until it was opened by his father. Ullo bounded inside and saw that both his parents were fully dressed and sensed that they had just come from the company of others. He could smell tobacco and perfumes and God knows what else, but little trace of alcohol. Because of these strange smells he did not want to be hugged by either of them, but he did want to get on to their still made-up bed which had not been disturbed that night. Since they were standing in his way, he ran round the bed and saw, between the bed

17

and the wall, his parents' yellow-strapped suitcase, the lid open. It was in his way, and so he stepped with one bare foot into it in order not to lose his balance. He then jumped under the silky orange eiderdown, pushed his knees in between the smooth sheets and cried – looking all the while at the suitcase – "Oh, how rich we are!"

The suitcase was brim-full of violet banknotes, each with the figure of a blacksmith striking an anvil. Written on each and every one of them: *Eine Milliarde Mark*.

His father began to laugh and said: "There's only a modest sum in that suitcase. Come here." He sat down on the edge of the bed and pulled Ullo towards him. He pulled his wallet out of his jacket pocket and took from it two 5,000-mark notes – of Estonian currency. (Estonians will remember the one designed by Nikolai Triik, yellow, green and brownish in colour. In the middle a Madonna with child, men with swords and shields kneeling around.) His father asked: "Well, how much have I got here in Estonian money?"

Ullo was as quick as lightning at mental arithmetic: "Ten thousand."

His father glanced at his mother, implying she should agree with her son, and continued: "And is that a great fortune, in your opinion?"

"It's no fortune," said Ullo briskly, "but there behind the bed are billions. That," pointing at the money in his father's hand, "is only enough to buy two model train sets as you yourself said at Wertheim's only yesterday when I was trying to get you to buy me one –"

"And thank goodness he didn't," his mother said, smiling.

"Of course I didn't!" cried his father. "Not because it would have been too expensive, but only because it was too big. I did explain. The tracks form an oval some five or six metres in length. Too long to fit in the middle of our living room on Raua Street. Anyway, as I was saying, over here, ten thousand of our currency is enough to buy two such children's train sets. And that pile of billions over there under the bed is worth exactly the same amount. So now you see how ridiculously low in value German money has become. It doesn't tell you anything at all about how rich or poor we are. Wait a minute –" his father looked at the clock – "this is perfect timing."

His father went to the window and rolled up the white blind with a swish. "Ullo, come over here!"

Ullo went pum-pum-pum over to his father's side and his father lifted him up on to the warm edge of the radiator under the window.

They could see the Französischer Platz lit up by street lamps, and when they pressed their noses against the pane they could see the lower row of young lime trees of Unter den Linden. The empty pavements were yellow in the lamplight. At the brightly lit main entrance of the Adlon, several taxis were arriving with tra-la-laa-ing foreigners, and trainee waiters in red uniforms were thronging to open the car doors. And round the corner vehicles from bakers' shops and dairies were going through the tradesmen's entrance of the hotel to the kitchen yard. Ullo's father squeezed Ullo's elbow.

"Look there! Sandra, you too come over here and watch!"

Four goods vans pulled up in front of the main entrance of the hotel. Men wearing greenish uniforms like the *Schutzpolizei* jumped down and divided into pairs – each pair unloading from the vehicles grey washbaskets which were carried impetuously, and at a running pace, into the hotel. There were eight baskets in all, each around two cubic metres in volume.

"What are they delivering? Clean bed linen?" asked Ullo's mother.

"Money. Filthy lucre," said his father, laughing. "Forty printing houses across Germany are busy printing paper money round the clock. It's distributed each morning, in lorries for longer distances, carts for shorter ones. So that before the start of the working day all institutions and businesses will have their money by the start of the working day. In the morning, each basketful contains the equivalent of some fifty thousand Estonian marks, but by the evening this has diminished to ten or twenty thousand. That is how rapidly the value of the German mark is falling."

His mother said: "So, the more of that money there is, the cheaper it becomes!"

Since he was fond of sentences which sounded as if they contained philosophical profundities and paradoxes, Ullo's father said: "That means that the more it appears to be, the less it in fact is."

Ullo cried: "Explain to me, how can it work like that! I just don't understand it at all!"

His mother said: "Maybe no one really understands."

His father said soothingly: "One day I'll explain."

(Here I wrote in my 1986 notes: Ullo thinks that this early-morning scene could have primed the time fuse which set off the crisis in their family fortunes, seven or eight years later.)

4

ULLO REMEMBERED FOUR MAIN things about their late-spring visit to Berlin, before they travelled on to Baden-Baden.

Firstly, he remembered the bronze memorial to Bismarck in front of the Reichstag. The four of them had passed it to go and look at the interior of the Reichstag building and the press gallery in the main hall where his mother remembered that Eduard Vilde, thirty years previously, had listened to Bebel's speeches and, enthused by them, had become a socialist himself. As they passed the monument and were walking towards the main entrance of the Reichstag, Ullo read Bismarck's name on the bronze plaque, a name he had already heard of, and he stopped to ask: "But why is Bismarck trailing his coat along the ground?"

They all laughed. But no one did know why. His mother said: "A whim of the artist. Or what do you think?"

Ullo replied in a clear voice: "'Cos that Bismarck didn't have an Auntie Charlotte to tweak his left ear if he dragged his coat along the ground."

His father laughed. Aunt Charlotte remained stony-faced, Ullo too. But his mother had to smile. "Poor Bismarck not having an Aunt Charlotte, and all those passers-by smiling at him."

His father asked: "Ullo, Vilde's just been mentioned. Do you know who he was?"

Ullo said: "The commander of the Estonian forces during the Mahtra War."

They all burst out laughing. Even Charlotte. And Ullo cried: "What are you laughing for?! Laidoner wasn't around yet during the Mahtra War!"

His second memory was of Noah's ark.

This was on Alexanderplatz in the central hall on the first floor of Wertheim's department store. The model ship was some five or six metres in length and according to my notes, Ullo had said: "Clearly, I was still at an age where the size of something played an important role in how impressed you were. But many people in this world never grow out of this." The ship was as black as pitch (and must have been made of gopher wood and coated with tar). It was broad in proportion to its length ("Like one of those wherries on Lake Peipsi which, at the time, I hadn't yet seen") and covered with a black awning whose ridge stood, from stem to stern, much higher than its eaves which rested on the boards at deck level. In a word, a ship like that in the famous picture by Doré. With the difference that three rows of ninety-nine square portholes had been cut, each ten or fifteen centimetres high. And wide. At the stern there was a door some two or three times wider, like on car ferries nowadays. But this door was not for cars, but animals.

The ship stood in a large tank with water sloshing around its base. There was nothing extraordinary about the spectacle so far. However, at the edge of the tank stood a man in a yellow uniform who performed the tasks of cashier with his left hand, and mechanic with his right. When Ullo's father stuffed the appropriate number of millions into his left hand, he cranked a handle with his right, whereupon the mechanism started and things got exciting. Along a green strip of grass which emerged from bushes behind the tank, the animals began to appear. Two by two, smaller ones, larger ones. Smooth ones, shaggy ones, bison, hippopotami, lynxes, dogs, cats, lions, tigers, elephants, wolves, hyenas, rhinoceroses, bears, snakes, eagles, crocodiles, horses, cows, sheep, pigs and donkeys. The audience of nippers and adults consisted of some two hundred people for each session. Ullo understood what was going on, as most children his age understood. The smaller ones did not need to understand. The animals made walking motions with their legs, but did not actually move forwards by themselves, being transported by the green strip of grass itself. This strip rose up to the rim of the tank on trestles supported by stones moving the whole of zoology into the innards of the ship. Inside, the animals were clearly lined up along the portholes, for they poked out their respective muzzles, paws, horns, heads, trunks, and shook them about. The cobra raised itself to half its length and stretched, now shaking out of the higher, now the lower row of portholes. All the animals made noises: they roared, squeaked, howled, whined, barked, screeched, whimpered and bellowed. And then from the heaps of clouds above, it began to rain. And in the clouds a lit-up calendar page could be seen:

Am 15. September des Jahres 2205 v. Chr. Geburt.

The rain lashed down so fast that in the first rows behind the barrier children got their faces quite wet, Ullo included. Then out of the rain appeared a one-foot-tall Noah on the roof of the ark wearing a black sou'wester and sporting a red beard. He pulled a tube which looked like the funnel of a samovar out of the roof of the ark, and pressed a bar on its end. At every press, a cloud of steam appeared from the pipe and spread thickly over the ark, with a hoot higher than that of the *Rügen*, but still convincing. The ark worked itself free of the bottom of the tank and floated in the foam that had been whipped up by the rain. Finally, the anteaters quickened their pace and leapt on board. A song emerged from loudspeakers, mixing with the sounds of the animals, and Ullo heard a hoarse cabaret voice intone:

O, du Faultier – schnarche, schnarche!
Dich braucht Gott kaum, sieh die Arche
fährt schon los! Doch nein, doch nein –
O, du Faultier, hast noch Schwein . . .

This was the only fragment of the long song which Ullo managed to remember in 1986. Next, Noah steered the ship back to the edge of the grass strip and the sloths climbed yawning on board, their eyes half closed. With the plashing of rain on the decks, the ark moved to the far end of the tank and there turned round majestically. In the sky, the calendar pages flashed forwards and the rain thinned out, until five months had passed and the ship came to a standstill in the middle of the tank. The waters began to immediately recede and the ark was revealed to be standing on a summit consisting of purplish crystal blocks, i.e. the summit of Mount Ararat, rising out of the waters. Noah released a raven from the ark which flew croaking under the ceiling of Wertheim's before returning to the ark, then a dove, which vanished into the shrouds of the ceiling draperies, which the clouds had now

22

become, then a second dove which returned with an olive branch. Then the year 2205 BC became 2204 BC and the day became 27 April. The waters had receded into the base of the tank, the doors at the stern opened, and the green line of animals started in motion again, now in the opposite direction: the whole of the family of animals marched bellowing, whimpering, screeching, barking, whining, howling, squeaking, roaring, back on to the purged terra firma. Then Noah himself emerged with his family and built an altar in gratitude at the edge of the tank (by employing a good puppet-theatre technique this did not take a minute), lit a fire and sacrificed a white hare, whereupon Jehovah's rainbow appeared as a sign of reconciliation. At that point, to the sound of music, the children dispersed noisily, but Ullo stood there, his legs straddled, wiping his face dry, saying: "I want to see it again!" thus forcing his father, mother and Charlotte to watch the whole show, which lasted some three-quarters of an hour, once more.

His third memory of Berlin was of the guinea pigs' castle which had been built at the zoo. But in this case he hardly elaborated on his experience, other than to say that it was constructed largely of glass so that the actions of all the inhabitants, i.e. the *Caviae porcelli* or whatever, could be observed with the naked eye. I didn't ask him whether he could find in this – neither as an eight-year-old nor in subsequent years – any analogy with God's omniscience and the fate of mankind. But I see from my notes that there was no shortage of philosophical musings out there at the Berlin Zoo. Throughout what was left of the week, Ullo pondered on the story of Noah's ark. And about what ensued. Even including the question of whether God still existed or not. Over a cup of cocoa in the children's café at the zoo, he decided to do an experiment to put this to the test.

His mother and father had gone to town and Ullo had come to the zoo accompanied by Charlotte whom he couldn't, for the main part, stand. So he sipped up his cocoa and said to her that he would take a little walk around. Charlotte, a woman with the mentality of a deaconess, looked him straight in the face with her harsh, bright fish eyes and asked sternly: "Where are you going?"

Ullo replied, in a manner inappropriate for a well-brought-up boy in 1923: "For a pee." He turned his back on Charlotte so that she would hopefully not see him sticking out his tongue at her and strolled along the path between the tables, his hands balled into fists in the pockets of his sailor suit.

The plan was remarkably simple and Ullo executed it immediately, all due caution notwithstanding. He walked up to the counter of the café and casually eyed the wares on display, chocolate, marzipan, sweets, cakes and the like. Then he made sure that Charlotte could not see him from her table and that the few people sitting at adjacent tables, a few children, a couple of grown-ups, were not watching him attentively. He smiled briefly at the black-moustached old codger across the counter, sizing up how dangerous he could be. Maybe he realised, though not at that age from experience, but subconsciously, that the gent was harmless. Since he regarded him, Ullo, as harmless. If Ullo were hanging around the café, the old man knew that he would have paid his five million to enter the zoo and would not therefore be that type of urchin who would start stealing things from the counter. He saw the old man go up to the adjoining cash desk, open the drawer in it and begin counting money into it. Ullo waited, instinctively it seemed, until the man was completely engrossed in his work – and then, like lightning, he sprang into action. He raised his hand, snatched a packet of carob pods, or St John's Bread, in their cellophane and silver-paper wrapper from the counter and stuffed them into his right-hand trouser pocket. If, in this zoo café, zoological experts had been observing his movements, they would have concluded that the boy's actions had the rapidity of a chameleon's tongue.

Ullo stood there a moment longer, in order to subconsciously emit an expression of complete indifference, then walked over to the toilets, where he had originally not intended to go. A minute later he emerged, re-entered the café, and came and sat down at Charlotte's table. He would now sit and see whether he was punished or not. If no punishment ensued: God did not exist. If it did: He did.

Back at the hotel, he wanted at first to rip open the packet and put them, pod by pod, down the lavatory, i.e. do what he had failed to do in the café toilets – but then reconsidered. Over sixty years later he explained: "You must understand, I thought if I did so, then my whole action would have been too superficial, too formal, to deserve real punishment. For the test to work, I would have had to be at one with the damned pods, so to speak. Only then could I be sure that God would punish me – and in so doing reveal His own existence. So I had

24

to eat up my St John's Bread. But just as I had ripped open the packet and begun to nibble at its contents, my mother happened to say: 'And where did you get those from? Did Charlotte buy you that Turkish rubbish? How many times have I told her . . .' So I was obliged to lie, and said I'd bought them myself. This gave me the comfort of adding a lie to the theft and making punishment all the more inevitable. If the punisher Himself did in fact exist. And I added a further lie to the first: I told my mother that I would throw the uneaten pods in the waste-paper basket in the lounge, but I munched them all up on my way over and only in fact threw away the packet."

After that, Ullo simply had to wait. But for how long? How quickly would punishment have to follow on a deed so that it could be clearly interpreted as its result? He waited the whole evening, the whole of the next day, and the next. By the evening of the day after that he had reached the conclusion that God did not exist.

The relief derived from this knowledge gave his fourth Berlin recollection that extra something. Despite the unease involved, Ullo also recalled even more vividly the knowledge born of the experiment. This last major memory was of the one-and-a-half-hour flight above Berlin and its environs.

The representative of the flight organisers, a young gentleman with a thick briefcase, accompanied Ullo and his family from the hotel. The five of them took a taxi to Tempelhof airfield, which was situated pretty well in the centre of the city. There, by the old hangars, they waited for their plane. But first they had a walk around. The young gentleman with the briefcase handed it over to the cashier in the hangar office. In it was the flight fee. Ullo's father, with his somewhat reckless humour, said: "A good thing that bundle of money is being handed over before our flight. I got the impression that if we were to have taken it with us, the plane would never get off the ground in the first place, or even if it had done, it would come back down prematurely."

Well, all his life Ullo was interested in the technical details of things, as well as in models of vehicles and cannon. It was a platonic enough interest, because at the time of his flight he had not as yet built any models of ships or planes himself. But his knowledge of them was surprising. He described the plane used for the trip as follows, but of course with the knowledge of hindsight:

"It was what is termed a 'frame tail'. Constructed presumably by the French rather than the Germans, and dating from the end of the First World War. It was originally a light bomber built, no doubt, by the Farman brothers and shot down by the Germans and redeployed. The fuselage was made of three-ply and fabric stretched over slats, for its new civilian purpose. There was a four-metre-long 'saloon', in front of which was the engine with its yellow propellor. Behind this was a convex cockpit with two seats for the pilots and behind their backs a space for the passengers, a box made of wood and fabric with side windows and hatches in the floor which had once been intended for dropping bombs and were now sealed, with two tiny seats on each side. The wire tailplane was so called because the tail, a vertical rudder with horizontal ailerons, was fixed to the cabin, well, not solely with wire, but still only by the thinnest of struts some four or five metres in length."

The flight company representative handed back Mr Berends's empty briefcase and the four passengers took up their seats. Ullo's mother sat behind him and his father next to his mother. Charlotte sat next to Ullo on the opposite side of the foot-wide aisle. The pilots were wearing leather overcoats, leather caps and goggles that looked like those worn by welders. They shut the passenger door from the outside, took away the steps and climbed into their own seats. After giving a snort or two, the engine started and the propeller began to whirr so that it became invisible. Then the plane set off and began to tremble and judder, taxiing along the rather potholed asphalt. The juddering decreased, but the jolts increased apace – until, all of a sudden, but not until half a kilometre is likely to have been traversed, they took off. The plane was in the air. And they were already high up, with the roofs of the city, now on the one, now on the other side of the plane, far below.

Ullo had been afraid of being afraid. During the three or four days, while waiting for his punishment for his theft and his lies, he had known that they were going to take a flight above the city, and was afraid that he would start being afraid. For where and when could be more suitable for God to mete out his punishment than there and thus: by making the plane crash! Nothing happens to his mother. She says, after they have crashed: "Well, if you fly you have to experience that too." Nothing happens to his father either. Nothing now. Only his gold-framed spectacles fall off his nose and maybe break . . . Charlotte sprains her wrist. Nothing serious. But she does it in her knickers out of sheer fright and shock. But no – then Ullo would have to put up with her dreadful smell for a while, so a sprained wrist would be quite sufficient . . . For Ullo takes his punishment with a meek heart – he would not deserve death for the mere theft of six carob pods. These were, roughly speaking, his thoughts on what punishment to expect. But then, presumably growing weary of anticipation (and, of course, on account of the feeling of relief which a release from punishment affords), he drew the conclusion that God did not exist. And felt relief at this. And now, having risen high above the city, and despite all the unease which arose from the void below and the unusual swing of horizons, plus the mixture of blue sky and grey rain clouds into which they seemed to be about to plunge any moment – despite all of this unease Ullo had a feeling of relief. If the engine of the plane should stop or the fabric be ripped from the sides of the cabin – look, there it is flapping round the window, so the fabric will soon rip away – nothing is going to happen to Ullo or the others. For the others have nothing to do with the matter. So if anything were going to happen to anyone it would be to him alone. But what could happen to him? If the plane breaks up and he falls out, he is so feather-light, so weightless, so insubstantial that the wind will bear him down on to the shores of the great Müggelsee, over which they now are flying, bear him to earth so gently and in one piece, like the dove bore the olive branch back to Noah's ark.

And that was that. The exaltation of escaping into that godless world lasted until the end of the flight, but was soon over after that. Sixty years later Ullo thought that the change occurred that same evening. He was dozing off on Charlotte's couch, when the thought had suddenly struck him: God could simply be playing a trick on me! He could exist after all – but will refrain from punishing me for my theft and lies until I am no longer able to associate the punishment with my deeds!

I asked: "And how did you get out of that one?"

He said: "On that occasion – simply by forgetting!"

5

THE THIRD AND LAST week of their sojourn in Berlin was filled with memories for Ullo. In general he only mentioned them in passing, and my notes only record a couple of specific instances. That week, he went on three separate occasions to the circus: with his father, with his mother and with Charlotte. On his own insistence, of course. Elephants splashed around in water that had been poured into the ring, and afterwards, when the water had been let out, on came cavalry in Cossack uniforms, clowns, fire-eaters and beauties sawn in half. Along with the strongman Siegfried Breitbart with his tours de force.

With cords attached to his hands, Breitbart restrained horses whipped to pull in opposite directions. He also broke horseshoes in two, clink, clink. Then a bed of nails was brought into the ring. He lay on his back on the nails and an anvil was placed on his hairy chest. An open forge was placed next to him and two blacksmiths beat new horseshoes on that very anvil.

One evening his mother and father had taken Ullo to the opera, to see Wagner's *Ring of the Nibelung*. Ullo had soon – I remember his roguish smile as he told me this – fallen asleep. "So all the cracks about Hitler and his entourage turning up at performances of Wagner are quite true –" But before the scene where the dragon is slain, the fortississimo music had awakened him. So he had seen every detail of Siegfried's victory over the dragon. They had seats in the third row, as befitted their station. Incidentally, for a long time afterwards Ullo had thought that the singing dragon-slayer on stage was that very same Siegfried Breitbart, whom he had so admired at the circus, but made up a little differently here, of course. What he particularly recalled was the pure white trace of a linden leaf on the otherwise red back of Siegfried, covered as he was in dragon's blood. The same place where

Hagen's spear kills him. Ullo explained: "That night, I dreamt that I was fighting the dragon. And dreamt this so vividly that the next morning, in front of Charlotte's mirror, I removed my pyjama jacket and tried to see whether there was a trace of a linden leaf on my back."

They were leaving Ullo's father behind in Berlin to attend to business. The day before departure, they went on a trip to the zoo. There, his father had begun to poke a crocodile with his walking cane, to encourage it to open its jaws to give Ullo a view of its teeth. The crocodile had indeed opened its jaws wide. Quite wide, and for quite a while. But as they finally snapped shut, they darted a metre or so forward, took the end off his father's cane and ate it crunch-crunch-crunch as if it had been a chocolate bar.

Sixty years later, I asked: "Did you see this as an omen of the imminent failure of your dad's business enterprise?"

Ullo said: "Good question – that never entered my head. But my mother did say: 'Eduard – that's a bad sign.' Father, of course, only laughed."

After that, Ullo had travelled with his mother and Charlotte to Baden-Baden. They had gone straight to the Kurhaus, which was not really particularly new any longer and a little worse for wear, but was still an incomparably large and noble construction, made principally of glass. They had taken an apartment there consisting of three adjoining rooms with bathroom, and the waiters and lift boys had smiled just as they had done at the Adlon.

What did Ullo remember of Baden-Baden? That in the park there stood a stork with a red bill which spurted mineral water. And, in the evenings, darker than those we are used to in Estonia in the summer, the Kurhaus was enveloped in the pop and twinkle of fireworks. That a brook flowed from the hills into the park, under a bridge, and in the purling waterfall with its marble tiers trout played and were caught, braised forthwith by the chef and served to the guests with white wine.

One evening the three of them had driven out to the Black Forest. Ullo did not start botanising along the way, but Charlotte tried to teach him the names of the wayside flowers. As his mother and Charlotte sat drinking their *Sauermilch* and fighting the midges on the hotel balcony, Ullo was scribbling down verses containing the names of the plants he had just learnt to the light of the setting sun and the rising moon. This is the earliest verse of his which he allowed me to copy out:

Schwarz dräut der Wald.
Bergab tropft Born,
blüht Rittersporn,
blaut Eisenhut.
Sei auf der Hut!
Wes Hifthorn schallt?
Aus feigem Hinterhalt
Raubritter bricht
Ins Mondeslicht.

It had clearly been admired by his mother and Charlotte to such an extent that he himself thought it rather good, and he had committed it to memory.

He also told me, with a wry smile on his lips:

In Baden-Baden, he had made the acquaintance of a clever little boy, two years younger than himself who came from Holland and was called Cornelis. He had also been staying, along with his mother, at that same Kurhaus and had come to play chess with Ullo on a couple of occasions. Once, during their pre-lunch game of chess, both mothers and Charlotte had gone into town and were to be back by lunchtime, i.e. two o'clock. When they were some three-quarters of an hour late, eight-year-old Ullo said to six-year-old Cornelis: "Let's go to the restaurant and have lunch."

He explained this to me, sixty-two years later. "You must understand, it wasn't so much because our stomachs were empty, well, to a certain extent for that reason too, but mainly for the pleasure of feeling older and in charge."

And so they had gone to the Kurhaus restaurant. The waiters had recognised them since they were guests and had come here before to eat lunch, even if not every day. They were served with complete seriousness. Ullo ordered crab soup and veal kidneys in madeira sauce for each, followed by two portions of strawberries with whipped cream. And, of course, wine and beer; only that instead of wine they were brought orange juice and *Malzbier* instead of the real thing.

At the end of their stay in Baden-Baden, Ullo, his mother and Charlotte had travelled one hundred or so kilometres to the south-west, through the wonderfully scenic Württemberg Hills, to arrive, in the evening, at the small town of Überlingen. Staying at a tiny hotel, they embarked the next morning on a ship which made, as far as I could gather, an afternoon excursion on Lake Constance. Presumably, the ship also dropped in at the ports on the Swiss side. But I am not sure.

Ullo explained about this trip. "Well, this was long before the birth of the authors Peter Handke and Mati Unt, and I didn't intend riding across the Bodensee. The lake didn't interest me particularly. It was as smooth as a mirror and slightly misty. If anything did interest me on that trip it was the paddle steamer, the first and the last on which I have ever sailed. And the Alps, in their pink haze, snowy, untouchable. Retikon and all the rest, whatever they were called. So I was thinking: if I could reach them, then . . . oh, I don't know what then . . ."

I asked: "Listen, aren't you really still living by the same rules even now, as then on the lake? What's immediate, vibrating around you, right under your feet, is interesting, as is what is intangibly distant, ditto. But everything in between is so tedious, so dreary."

He looked at me sharply for a moment and then replied absent-mindedly: "Maybe you're right. I'll give it some thought."

Any answer he might have given has slipped my memory and is not to be found in my notes.

6

WHEN THEY ARRIVED BACK from Germany, the Berends family continued to live in their seven- or eight-room apartment on Raua Street and life resumed its normal course. Perhaps not quite as wildly as three or four years previously, but nonetheless "dynamically". In the 1920s so many dramatic events involving guests had taken place, and the events of this era were unlikely to reoccur. In those days, some White Guard Georgian army captain had danced the *lesginka* on the Berends family's fully laid table, wearing his ammunition belt across his chest, without knocking over one bottle or breaking one dish. Some Americans had arrived at the Berendses' house, three years before, during Rolly's time. Diplomats, businessmen, God knows who they were. Journalists, maybe. Mr Brown brought a briefcase full of bottles of whisky, Mr Clarke brought one filled with tiny paper Stars and Stripes, attached to wooden flagpoles, which ended up on all the Berendses' tables and in the niches by the open hearth. But one morning, when running out to Rolly's kennel in the front garden, Ullo had found one of the gents, his gym shoes placed neatly in front of the kennel on the grass, his striped socks and chequered trousers protruding from the doorway of the kennel with Rolly lying at its door, obliquely across the man.

Ullo went back inside and thought feverishly about what he should do. He finally decided that only his mother could solve the problem with the discretion necessary. Which she did by coaxing the dog into the house with a bone and waking the hungover man, by saying gently but firmly: "Mr Brown, *razbudityesh*!" Ullo's mother spoke Russian to Mr Brown, since she did not know English. "*Razbudityesh*! Come inside. What if people see you over the hedge from the street! Or people from inside the house spot you through the window!"

Mr Brown woke up, quickened, understood and sprang after Ullo's mother into the house through the back door, then into the bathroom. He gave his trousers to the maid to iron and became awfully polite. That same day, he brought Mother a litre bottle of "Crabtree", a New York perfume named, presumably, after crab apples, as a token of gratitude. The pungent yet sweet fragrance was characteristic of Ullo's mother for years afterwards. She was still using it when the bottle was half full, one-third, one-quarter full, when it had become their only relic of halcyon days.

Temperamental captains from Tiflis, stylish generals from Petrograd, and drunken gentlemen from New York were no longer to be seen at the Berends residence by the mid-1920s. However, more mundane visitors still turned up. Composer Raimund Kull, sporting officer's uniform complete with glittering flashes, by then conductor of the Navy orchestra, would still, to Ullo's delight, push lighted matches up his nose and rotate them with his nostrils, in opposite directions. Dr Dunkel would smoke one of his black Katlama cigars and put drops in Ullo's ears when he had earache. And Eduard Hubel, alias Mait Metsanurk, with his tiny pince-nez, once discussed with Ullo's mother how to proceed with one of the novels he was working on (Ullo thought it could have been *Jäljetu haud – The Unmarked Grave*) and once played Tchaikovsky's *Souvenir de Hapsal* on the violin to the assembled guests.

In the early autumn of 1924, the Berendses stayed for a while in a genuine stately home.

An old acquaintance, friend and business partner of his father's, the Dutchman van den Bosch, who was consul and whatever else in Estonia, had rented Maarjamäe Castle. He only used a few rooms of the building, and suggested to Papa Berends that he might bring his family to stay towards the end of the summer. Ullo could remember some stuffed bears from those otherwise bleak rooms, and travelling back and forth between town and Maarjamäe, driving in a two-horse calèche with high wheels along the long, crunching gravel roads. And, beyond the grand silhouette of the city, the sea, now grey, now green. And the stench of rotting seaweed, brought in from the bay by the south-west wind in through the windows of the manor.

And then – they had been back in town for two weeks, and it was now the middle of September – crunch, crunch, crunch into their Raua Street apartment, which stood full of furniture and packing cases, came men with broad-brimmed red caps on their heads and brass badges on their cap rims – Express-Express-Express. Things were shoved anyhow into crates, and in the space of two days they had moved out of their eight-room apartment!

Ullo said that he had never received a full explanation why. The owner of the building had suddenly demanded a significant rise in the rent, and Ullo's father, in a fit of rage, had let it be known irrevocably that he was not paying. God knows. Ullo said: "Father was the type of man who could smile tolerantly for ages, thinking *laissez-faire, laissez-passer*. But then he would suddenly explode, disregarding what was in his own best interests."

At any rate, the removal from Raua Street occurred with flags still flying. The furniture and other objects were stored in a warehouse on the Narva Road at some incredibly expensive rate, and the Berends family moved into three rooms, with bathroom of course, at the Kuld Lõvi – the Golden Lion – hotel. Ullo said: "I have read that, during the last century in the Mediterranean region, it was the habit of rich, though not very cultivated, families, e.g. those of Athens, to have an apartment in the city, while they found it more chic to live in a hotel. Well, the only difference in our situation was that we didn't possess such an apartment as a back-up, but were looking for one, and found one just before Christmas."

So for three months or so, the Berends family lived in a three-room suite at the Kuld Lõvi and ate at the Kuld Lõvi restaurant and allowed waiters and chambermaids to bow and scrape in their presence. Then they moved on to Pikk Street, in the middle of the Old Town, into a grand apartment block with lift. They still had six rooms, two of which had a fine view of the sea, so that this could not be considered coming down in the world. And Miss von Rosen came as usual every day and lorded it over Ullo, and Charlotte continued at the Berendses'. Only she now had to live out. The actual removal occurred at the new year for an amusing reason: the Berendses' furniture and bedclothes which had been stored at the warehouse on the Narva Road at such great expense, were now full of bugs . . .

Ullo told me in 1986: "Mother had been a stickler for hygiene all her life, and her efforts at cleanliness increased by the year. I first noticed this obsession during the bug attack. But it entered my consciousness only later, perhaps. I remember my mother walking around diligently

34

with her anti-bug liquid, paraffin or whatever they used in those days, and preparations of sulphur smoke, and having the wallpaper changed in the rooms we were going to move into. But in the spring, when we had more or less grown accustomed to our new, clean apartment, we moved again although still on Pikk Street, this time to Suur Rannavärav – the Great Coastal Gate. Still a pleasant block, but now we were on the second floor, with no view whatsoever of the sea, though it was, of course, even closer than before. Now we had only five rooms, one of which was quite dark, since the window opened out almost directly on to the wall of the neighbouring building. And the physical darkness, which cast shadows on that one room, somehow extended mentally throughout the whole flat."

I do not remember whether Ullo said this to me *expressis verbis*, or whether I wrote the description on the basis of fragments: across from the door of this dark room, a door with a glass panel, in some room like an entrance hall, there was a cylindrical pier glass which reflected darkness across all the rooms, whether their doors were open or shut.

The source of this darkness which dulled colours and voices was, of course, the depressed presence of his mother.

I never quite understood when and how it was that Ullo became aware of this, and when and how he found out about the source of his mother's sadness. This can, however, be reduced to the trivial formula of *cherchez la femme*. It must have been during their stay at their second Pikk Street flat that he began to notice his father's frequent absence from home – including night-time absences, which Ullo's mother explained were due to business trips to Tartu or Narva or Helsinki – as well as the worry on his mother's face and her tenderness towards Ullo himself.

I do not know when Ullo first heard of his father's new sweetheart, but it was, no doubt, early on. Ullo's own awakening to the ways of the world was also early. My information about the lady in question comes of course from Ullo. Maybe his father even told him these details himself, because I don't think the final parting between father and son took place in complete enmity.

The lady had originally come from Luxembourg. Her maiden name was Monod, Marie Monod. After attending some convent school or dropping out of school halfway, the sixteen-year-old girl had moved in with relatives in Paris – no doubt to seek her fortune. And fortune she managed to find. In that she became acquainted with a Russian nobleman by the name of Koshelev, from the Serpukhov *gubernia* near Moscow, and went off with him to Russia as *bonne* for his five-year-old child. And in the summer, she went with them to the Black Sea coast, to Sukhumi no doubt. There she met a young engineer by the name of Fredriksen. He had been working in Baku, drilling for oil for the Nobel company and had come from the oily Caspian Sea to a clean Sukhumi, for his holiday. They got married in the spring of 1915, and in autumn 1920, fled revolutionary Russia intending to settle in Norway. They had travelled through Estonia on the way, and after passing through quarantine for ticks and typhus in Narva, a young person entered their compartment at one of the following stations who, introduced, proved to be the Director of the Estonian Oil Shale Works. As Ullo remarked, this was the engineer Märt Raud, no doubt. And before the train had reached Tapa, he had made a proposal to the Fredriksens which changed, not only the lives of the Fredriksens, but those of the Berendses. Raud recruited Fredriksen for the Estonian Oil Shale Works. The Fredriksens remained in Estonia and settled in Tallinn. And sometime in the 1920s, Marie met Eduard Berends.

"She was amazingly similar to Mother," Ullo said. "In appearance, at least. I didn't get to know her well, myself. But she looked like Salome. So in that respect, Father had remained true to type, only Mrs Fredriksen was, well, a little slimmer, a little more easygoing. And some ten years younger than my mother, of course."

I asked: "Had your father and this Mrs Fredriksen found the love of their lives?"

Ullo replied: "I don't really know. But they did stay together until Father's death in 1969."

In other words, they stayed together for some forty years. Through what was, no doubt, an insecure and hardly very rosy period for them. I note that I asked: "Ullo, did you ever come to understand your father in the end?"

He had said: "That I can't answer, as I don't know all the circumstances. In 1929, I deeply regretted what he had done. Then, understanding was far off. At that point, the break-up of our family and the decline of our financial and social fortunes were, in my opinion, the fault of Mrs Fredriksen."

T HE DECLINE — THOUGH NO one actually mentioned it in
these terms — manifested itself in everything, but most clearly
in the move to ever more modest flats. In the summers, this
decline was less noticeable. Maybe because, while they were still
taking summer holidays at all, their holiday homes were harder to
compare than their city flats. They still went abroad, even as late as
1925, spending several weeks in Munich and surroundings, where they
went on a visit to Mad King Ludwig's castle. Incidentally, the interior
of the castle was so overdone, it made Ullo feel sick. The parks with
their various trick fountains were, however, of great interest to him.

They also visited Munich's crematorium. Ullo remembered how
they were on their way to the room where it was possible to actually
watch the cremation of bodies through a window, when his father, of
all people, had asked his mother: "Sandra, do you really think that Ullo
— hm — should see all this?" And his mother had replied: "Let him
look." Ullo said: "I was very pleased that my mother regarded me as
mature enough for something, when my father wasn't sure. For it was
usually the other way around. And only later, maybe years later, did it
strike me: my mother's 'let him look' was a sign of deep despair . . . The
spectacle itself was of course horrific to an extent. But not only
horrific. Something more, something uplifting. The body burning in
the pale red flames, its contours bathed in a bright yellow light. This
triggered off no nightmares. But the memory remains with me to this
day."

They had gone round various museums in Munich. Ullo remembered especially the knights' weapons, suits of armour and the
bombards and mortars of solid wood with their rivet-studded bases.

For some strange reason, Ullo could not remember precisely where
they had gone after Munich, but it was some port on the Rhine where

they boarded a white river steamer, the *Lorelei*, and sailed down-stream, first past steep hills of vineyards and chateaux, then past factory chimneys and finally between river banks, as straight and flat as if drawn with a ruler, past windmills, and right up to the Dutch border.

Mr Berends's principal link with Holland was his Tallinn acquaintance van den Bosch, who was still the Dutch consul to Estonia. Ullo had even called him a good friend of his father's. This was one of the advantages of our minuscule Estonian society: even I had managed to catch a glimpse of this Consul van den Bosch during my childhood. His wife was pale in a white outfit and a little like someone out of an Eduard Wiiralt portrait (as I would now say). The Consul himself smelt of cigars, had bluish-grey hair, a rubicund complexion and a portly bearing. He and his wife had drunk coffee with my parents on the veranda on Purde Street. I am not sure why the Consul was there. I have the vague recollection that he talked with my father about constructing radio receivers and told my mother about the wonderful and unexpected works of art to be found in Tallinn – and asked her whether she had seen, from close to, the altarpiece depicting the martyrdom of St Victor which stood in the Niguliste Church? It is supposed to have almost reminded Mijnheer van den Bosch of his namesake who could even have been related. What the Christian name of our unexpected guest was I never found out, either then in 1925 or subsequently. And that gap in my knowledge has become confused with all manner of Bosches – Carl, Jan, Juan and of course Hieronymus.

Ullo and his parents took the train from Amsterdam to The Hague, where they stayed for a few days with the Bosch family in their noble and very darkly panelled home.

In the mornings, while his father was spending time negotiating with van den Bosch, Ullo, his mother and Mevrouw van den Bosch went off to the beach at Scheveningen. There he flew a balloon – a gift from the Bosches – on the sands and along the pier, several hundred metres in length, which led to the summer casino (a swimming baths like an elegantly winged T far out in the sea, accessed by means of a tum-tum-tum-tum-thudding plank bridge). An extraordinary red, white and blue balloon, filled with an unfamiliar gas. It was one metre in diameter and had a silk net around it which supported a gondola underneath with two celluloid gondoliers. On the second morning, he lost his grasp of the string. So that the balloon, borne on the westerly wind, soared into the sky above the beach, flat as a die with its multicoloured collection of bathers, and vanished into the glow of the sun.

Mevrouw van den Bosch said approvingly: "Brave boy, you didn't start crying."

And Ullo, his cheekbones jutting more than was usual, said: "I'm just thinking about how much they'll get to see –"

"Who?" asked Mevrouw van den Bosch.

"My balloonists. With that wind, they'll be in England in three hours!"

The next morning, under a phantasmagorically leaden sky, *mijnheer* van den Bosch took his guests to the railway station, still to a *comme il faut* first-class carriage, and showed them how to find the canal port and the sloop which would take them to the holiday house which Mijnheer van den Bosch had rented for the week. "There you will experience Holland, *par excellence*!"

The stubby skipper with white eyelashes and his ten-year-old son – a true chip off the old block – heartily welcomed the passengers on board. The Berendses would be staying in the skipper's house on the island of Marken, a two-hour trip from Amsterdam. Ullo remembered: "In Amsterdam, and on its canals, I did not notice the gloom of the sky. But I did when the sloop was chugging towards the Zuyder Zee. *Nojaa*, there was absolutely no wind, and the petrol-engined boat chugged between the still, grey mirror of the sea and the low grey sackcloth of the heavens. When we had turned out to the Zuyder Zee, the skipper said that a storm was brewing, but that we would be in Marken before it broke."

Under the press of the gathering storm, Ullo and the skipper's son had begun to wrestle in the low murky stern cabin of the sloop and Ullo at least had put his fear of storms quite out of his mind. They had reached the island by the time of the first gusts. When Ullo mentioned a number of dates connected with the island, I asked him if he had also remembered them back in 1925. He explained that of course he hadn't: "You must understand: the less accessible such information became in later years, the more . . ."

So on account of the fact that Marken soon became inaccessible to him, on account of their own family earthquake, their penurious state, the war and the Iron Curtain – his information about this island was a good deal more detailed than I reproduce here:

The island had been a peninsula up to the year 1164. Then, on St Julianus's Day, a large tidal wave had turned this into an island proper. Which it still was when Ullo visited it, an absolutely flat and verdant piece of land amid flat grey waters, several kilometres long and broad, located some ten kilometres from the western shore of the Zuyder Zee, near the town of Monnickendam. So flat indeed that people had begun to raise it for reasons of safety, building the foundations of the villages on small earth hillocks and constructing their houses right on top of these molehills. Some on piles. And now, in 1986, the island had once again been joined to the mainland for the last thirty years by a dyke. And the whole of what was now called Markwaard had become – after being separated from the Zuyder Zee in 1932 by a huge dyke, the Afsluitdijk, from the North Sea – five hundred or so square kilometres of polder land. When Ullo was on the island, it was surrounded by sea and on the evening he had arrived there with his parents, the rage of the first white horses had begun to trouble its smooth grey surface. And when they were eating their evening meal at the house of the skipper, with its thick reed-thatched roof, the hurricane hit. The wind had veered to the south, so the water did not rise significantly. Ullo felt more than safe in the thick-walled farm-house, happily rescued from the storm. The whitewashed walls were covered in rows of white delftware with blue patterns and pictures, the largest at the bottom, the smallest at the top. And the stove, standing almost in the centre of the room, was decorated with tiles with blue cabbage-leaf patterning.

What more did Ullo remember from this trip? That they had sailed in their host's sloop, that week of wind and sun, to the town of Monnickendam and seen all there was to see there, and on the second or third day of their holiday they had gone to Edam. There, they had tried the famous local cheese and entered the Great Church where they had seen the graves of the Fat Man and the Tall Girl. The former was supposed to have weighed 440 pounds and the latter was eight foot two inches tall.

Ullo also remembered that before their departure he had put on the Dutch folk costume and clogs belonging to the skipper's son. The garments were a wee bit too short, and a good deal too wide. His father

40

had unpacked his Leica camera, bought in Germany shortly before, and had taken pictures of him in the room with the delftware plates. And had then taken others of his mother and Ullo, and his mother had taken Ullo with his father on the latter's insistence. But when Ullo, a moment later, had himself picked up the camera and had asked his father to show him which button to press to take a picture of his father with his mother, she had vanished from the room that instant. So that no picture was ever taken of Ullo's parents on the island of Marken. And when, on deck, Ullo had begun to pester his father to give him the camera so that he could take a snapshot of his parents, with the puffed-out sail of the sloop as backdrop, on the return trip to Amsterdam, his father had said: "Don't you understand that Mother doesn't want to be in the same photo as me?"

Whereupon Ullo had cried, shriller than he would have liked, as I imagine: "But I want her to be in it!"

His father responded: "Ullo, if your mother doesn't want to, then nor do I – and you don't get a say in the matter."

They took the train back from Amsterdam to Berlin, where his father alighted – for business reasons, Ullo was told – and Ullo and his mother travelled home the day after. Ullo said: "But as we still had two-thirds of the summer before us, my mother and I left Tallinn to go on holiday again . . ."

8

A T THIS POINT I asked: "Ullo, could you tell me about all the summer holidays you spent in Estonia?"

"You mean, before our family split up? Well, OK. But Mrs Fredriksen was with my father from 1923 onwards. As I later found out. But anyway, let's take the summer of '23 at Karila Manor which we spent in the Kymmel *pension*. Mum and Dad were happily together – at least that's how it appeared. After returning from Germany.

"We were driven there the forty kilometres by a paid cabbie. The manor house was enormous. More interesting from the outside than within. Burnt down during the 1905 Troubles and rebuilt before the Great War. Pretty bleak inside. And the Kymmels, a married couple of around fifty years of age, somehow gave the impression of being poor. From our perspective, or mine. We had two huge but sparsely furnished rooms. We ate rather ceremoniously in the old manor house dining room, three times a day, about twenty-five to thirty people at table, children included. At the head of the table sat the ninety-year-old Baroness von Rellstein. She was a very tiny, very thin, very quiet and spry old dear, whom I immediately christened Baroness von Rollstuhl – i.e. wheelchair. About one-third of those staying at the *pension* were Estonians, and there were a few Russians too, but most were Baltic Germans. Of the children, the one I noticed right from the start was the Kymmels' daughter, the twelve- or thirteen-year-old Dora. She was that type of elf who would behave in the dining room as if she were a lady, but in the park turned out to be the wildest climber of trees and exceedingly quarrelsome with the boys. One day, a real prince came to Karila, as a guest of Baroness Rollstuhl, I believe. His name was Maximilian von und zur Lippe, and he was a middle-aged gent with a beer belly, who had come straight from Germany in a black Mercedes.

It was whispered that he was a close relative of Kaiser Wilhelm, but this meant nothing, at least to the boys. What the boys did gawp at – what *we* gawped at – was the Prince's car. And when this jovial uncle in Bavarian lederhosen invited the Baroness and a number of others for a ride, he also asked two children along: Dora and myself.

"Well now, maybe I really did become a little drunk. Next to me on the back seat the usually twittering Dora gave off a faint whiff of eau de Cologne, and sat silent as a mouse, with all around us the paint- and leatherwork of the fairy-tale car and the slight smell of oil and petrol. And what a speed – this prince was almost crazy – bowling along from Karila to the main road at seventy kilometres per hour! And on the main road he went up to, God, one hundred, one hundred and ten! And all the while the whiff of eau de Cologne. And the bird-boned shoulder almost against my chin.

"From then on, the boys at the *pension* were green with envy. I don't know whether they said anything to Dora, but they began ribbing me almost immediately. How did your car courtship proceed? Have you decided when you're going on your real honeymoon? Et cetera. It was all quite unpleasant and embarrassing for me, but titillating too, as such comments tend to be. I suppose I tried to avoid Dora, but actually glanced in her direction all the more.

"And then one day, I noticed in the park: Dora had clambered up to the top of a large linden tree and four or five German boys were standing under the tree yelling obscenities at her. She saw me and shouted that I should fetch someone to drive them away so she could climb down. The boys neither attacked me nor prevented me from doing so. I went into the house, found Herr Kymmel and asked him to come to the park. Kymmel sent the boys packing, and Dora came down from the tree and disappeared off somewhere. That day, during the children's customary nap at the *pension*, from three to four, I was lying on the iron-framed bed and had just been telling something to young Tomson, who occupied the adjoining bed and had now dozed off, when the door opened a fraction and Dora slipped into the room. She sat on the edge of my bed and seized my wrists. I was afraid she was going to hurt me. She had done so before, but this time she didn't. She came close and looked me straight in the face. She had hazel eyes with black flecks. I could feel her breath on my skin. She whispered: '*Du, kleine Fliege, kleine Fliege –*'

43

"Suddenly, she threw herself on top of me, still holding my wrists – so that I felt through my blue-striped melton shirt and her pink chintz frock the hard beginnings of wild apples underneath. She lay there motionless on top of me and, after a while, whispered: '*Du kleine Fliege, erzähl mir was –*'

"And I told her in a half whisper how El Cid besieged Granada and the Moors forced their way out of the city. And how the beard of their leader was so long that the whole army rode on it. And how, when they spurred on their horses to rush at El Cid and his troops, all the horses slipped on the beard, pomaded with musk and nard oil, and could make no headway. And how El Cid slashed off the turbaned heads of every man jack of them.

"'*Erzähl noch was –*' whispered Dora.

"As I had already started on the subject of decapitations, I told of how Dietrich von Bern met the dragon and began cutting off dragon heads till he was trapped in the heap of heads with only his sword-arm free. And how the last dragon's head seized the sword in its jaws and tried to chew it to pieces and how the sword pierced its throat.

"'*Du kleine Schwertfliege –*' whispered Dora, releasing my wrists and running from the room.

"There was no time for anything else to happen, as my mother and I returned to town a few days afterwards. Only much later did the thought strike me: Dora had never called me by my name – Ulrich as I was in those days, suitably German-wise, though everybody called me Ullo. But only *Du kleine Fliege*. Though she no doubt knew my name. And twelve years later, when I was an editor at the *Sports Encyclopaedia* and met her again, now a tired bank clerk in the transactions hall of Scheel & Co., she did not, of course, recognise me, nor could my signature – i.e. Ullo Paerand – have meant anything to her."

Ullo continued: "Let us descend three more steps down those stairs of decline – to our summer at Lootsaar in 1926. Father had been given an assignment, obtained by underbidding competitors: the Ministry of Agriculture was planning to deepen the River Lootsaar. So we moved, the family *still* together to all outward appearances, to Lootsaar Manor, into two rooms that were markedly larger and markedly more hideous than those we had rented at Karila. And Charlotte was no longer our maid, instead some Estonian girl or other, who moved into the attic room so coveted by me. And the fifty or so labourers, paid by my father, were housed in the ancient workmen's cottages on the other side of the completely mossed over and rank orchard and park.

"The only residents of the manor house itself were ourselves and the Poolmanns, a tenant couple, both somewhat pitiful figures, who had three daughters, the eldest of which I scarcely remember. But the youngest, the eleven- or twelve-year-old Valja, whom I remember particularly well. She was a curly-haired redhead with an incredibly freckled face, surprisingly green eyes and a snub nose. With her I felt a happy complicity for the first time in my life. There was also an instant rivalry with Jaan, a boy one year older than me, who lived somewhere nearby, and was no doubt a townie but tended the Poolmann cattle herd. The rivalry grew to such a pitch that a week later we arranged a running race which was to decide who was to get the girl. The distance was a kilometre paced out somehow along a stretch of village road between brushwood. I led for nine-tenths of the way. Then thickset Jaan began to gain on me. Valja, who was waiting at the finish, clapped her hands and screeched shrilly, filled with enthusiasm – but I didn't know who she was cheering for and still don't to this day. At any rate, about fifty metres from the finish Jaan overtook me. And won. Yet didn't win the girl. For it was I who went around with Valja right until the heart of summer. And Jaan disappeared from view with his cattle.

"That summer, the labourers built temporary dams on the river and a dredger puffed and wheezed along its banks. There were enormous numbers of crabs in the river which we boiled and ate every other day. Once Father even entrusted me with his FN revolver. And there on the river bank he showed me how to use it, then left me alone there to practise. For three-quarters of an hour, I sat and watched a river pool. And then it happened: in the river I saw the sharp, stickled crest of a pike appear. And I fired three shots – and brought the bloody, thrashing fish on to dry land. That pike was the biggest I ever caught. It was one metre eleven centimetres long and it weighed twelve kilos. Its flesh was like wood, as is always the case with large pike, but the fish soup was delicious.

"We were sitting at the table eating the soup, when Father asked: 'Ullo, could you give me my revolver back now?'

"I said: 'Right away.'

45

"Then Father looked at the clock and cried: 'Dear me, everybody –
I've got to be in Lihula in an hour to pick up some building material!'
and with that he rose from the table, rushed outside, got into his car –
he had, or we had, a blue Ford convertible, our first car. Anyway, he
drove off, leaving the revolver in my hands. But the pleasure was short-
lived, as Mother took it off me right away ('Your father must have gone
quite barmy, letting a child play with a weapon like that').

"Father returned two days later ('Oh, I had to have dinner with my
suppliers in Haapsalu that evening . . .' That was his excuse that time.
But, when I was in the next to last class at school, someone finally told
me: Father had gone to Haapsalu to meet Mrs Fredriksen at a hotel.)
He did remember the revolver. He immediately asked where it was.

"'Mother's got it,' I said.

"'Where did she put it?'

"'I don't know.'

"'And where is she, anyway?'

"'She went out for a walk down by the shore.'

"And I quite failed to understand why Father rushed frantically to
the bedroom and began rummaging about in the drawers of the tallboy
and the bedside table, growing ever more agitated – till he found his
revolver among the clean sheets in the linen cupboard. Sometime later
the thought struck me that he had believed that my mother's state of
mind was such that it would be better not to leave a loaded pistol
within her reach.

"By the time we spent our summer holidays in Paldiski, Father was
no longer coming with us. It was summer 1929 and we had rented two
rooms on the main street in Paldiski, in one of those two-storey
buildings, of which there were about a dozen in those days. The rooms
weren't that bad and there was a cake shop across the road which sold
the tastiest gooseberry tart you could imagine. Along the siding by the
sea, interesting armoured trains equipped with exciting cannon were
being shunted to and fro. When I say that Father no longer came on
holiday with us, that is not entirely true. It was even worse: he wasn't
there, and yet he was. He was supervising the construction of a new
railway line and some kind of granaries for the Ministry of Defence. I
saw him several times that summer. He would come up to me, pat me
on the cheek and ask how I was getting on. I couldn't answer him, went
all stiff, hated him, but didn't want him to go away. But he did, every

46

time. For he was living a kilometre or two away. At Leetse Manor. With Mrs Fredriksen."

The last year that Ullo went on holiday was in 1929. A year previously, they had moved, still with his father, into a new city flat in Toomkooli – Cathedral School – Street, on Toompea Hill. This was a three-roomed flat, a strangely contradictory dwelling: in one room there was a genuine Venetian mirror, in the other a chandelier; on the other hand, not even one lamp in the long, dark corridor. "Instead, there were rats, which we tried to kill by pelting them with logs," Ullo said.

"We only lived there for a couple of months before moving to the next, on Toom-Rüütli – Cathedral Knight – Street and now only in two rooms. Father never turned up there at all." All he had done was pay the removals men. The same ones, with the red caps and brass badges on their brims, who had, in Ullo's opinion, been witness to the whole five-year process of decline, right from their real home on Raua Street.

"Well," Ullo said, "in my boyish pride, I tried to remain indifferent to what was happening around me and stay as undramatic as I could. But the situation was beginning to haunt my dreams with its drama. I had oppressive nightmares. In our penury, with our belongings still piled up in the bedroom on Toom-Rüütli Street, behind what was then the Rahu Courthouse, i.e. the Moorish Assembly House, was where I first had them. And though the frequency admittedly slackened, that they have continued. Most recently – was it last year? Maybe the night after I had gone to the Tammsaare statue on 24 February to hear TV commentator Talvik, or whoever it was, vainly trying to get his point across?

"In that dream I am still a fourteen-year-old boy and my mother is still correspondingly youngish. Although with the white streaks in among her darker locks, as she had in the end. And we walk along in a procession along Vaeste patuste – Poor Sinners' – Street up to Jerusalem Hill. Some passers-by shake their heads or even spit or cross themselves, and around us walk our bearers, executioners with red caps and brass badges on the brims, at any rate they have bundles of firewood tied together with string on their shoulders. I do not know whether they intend pelting us to death with logs on Jerusalem Hill or constructing a stake for us to be burnt at . . . In my dream, I always come to understand that the former is much more likely than the latter – for what is happening to us, happens throughout, well, the eighteenth, nineteenth or even twentieth centuries, and behind my thinking, which seems torn to quivering strips, I think another, namely that there is not such a vast difference between being pelted to death and being burnt at the stake . . . But I say to my mother: 'Look, how nice. They've decided to build a bonfire over there to keep us warm. My limbs are like ice. Yours too?' Mother replies: 'Everything'll be all right. We'll manage . . .' And then I notice that the number of people following in the wake of the executioners has increased. And, arm in arm in their midst, hiding behind the backs of other people – Father and Mrs Fredriksen are walking.

"At that point in the dream, I pull a small brass flute from the pocket of my cloak – I have never actually had one like that, but it doesn't particularly surprise me that I find it there. It is a little dented and dull and scratched and covered with patches of verdigris. When I raise it to my lips, I taste the verdigris. It is poisonous, heavy, disgusting and sweet. I begin to blow. And I find I'm very good at it. I blow a jolly tune, something light. I am playing to comfort my mother and defy my father. Or maybe vice versa. Oh damn, maybe indeed vice versa – to defy my mother and comfort my father. The executioners begin to listen, but continue onwards, carrying their logs. The hangers-on, behind whose backs Father and Mrs Fredriksen are cowering, raise their fingers to their lips when I look round over my shoulder, at least some of them do, and signal to me to stop playing. Others applaud, presumably to urge me to play louder. In other words, people are listening to me play, to what I'm playing, and to how I'm playing it! But in some fateful way I can hear nothing of my own playing. I play as diligently, as clearly, as fluently, as seriously as I possibly can – I can even hear the air rushing through the flute, but not one note of music. And my disappointment on account of this (pure vanity by the logic of those awake, wouldn't you say?) – my disappointment because of this strange brand of deafness is even more frightening than the awareness of where my mother and I are headed: either to be pelted to death with logs, or burnt at the stake. Well, you see, it is such a foolish dream, but one which has repeated itself for sixty years . . ."

IN NOVEMBER 1929, THERE, between Rahukohtu and Toom-Rüütli Streets, in a higgledy-piggledy three-century-old house facing the courtyard, in the two poky rooms that remained to them, the bailiff noted down all their belongings. Then his assistants loaded the belongings on to a waiting cart and took them away, God knows where to. Probably to some warehouse for second-hand goods where they would be put up for auction, to pay off Ullo's father's debts. But only a very small part of them, only symbolically.

When their belongings had been taken away – two vague cart tracks in the delicate ground glass of snow, across the cobbled courtyard, out and away – they remained there, Ullo and his mother, sitting on the two chairs at the oilcloth-covered kitchen table which they still possessed. Which made me think of when my own father was arrested in 1945, for political reasons, not debts. On that occasion, my mother was at least left with a decent oak dining table with brass feet. And two chairs too. Even though I was not actually living with my mother by then. She was living alone and had asked the officer in charge of removing the furniture, a Russian NCO with blue epaulettes, why the state had left her two chairs when she could only sit on one at a time.

And there they sat, Ullo and his mother – when suddenly he said, in a hoarse, commanding voice, as I can well imagine Ullo could muster: "Mother – let's promise ourselves that we're not going to cry!"

They had shaken hands on it, the tears welling up in their eyes. And maybe they would not have been able to stop the flow of tears at being tricked and betrayed, had not the handshake, which in itself threatened to start the tears flowing, been meant to prevent them. But some time later Ullo fell ill. When talking about this, he felt that as his adolescent pride had not permitted the shedding of tears, he was bound to rot away in sickness. At any rate, he was attacked by his third or fourth bout of earache of his childhood, this time the most virulent and serious of all. He suffered acutely and ran a high temperature. Dr Dunkel, whom his mother summoned and who, being an old family friend, turned up quickly on Toompea, shook his head. A Red Cross ambulance was sent for Ullo from the Juhkental Military Hospital, and Dr Dunkel made a point of attending to him there for the next two or three weeks. Ullo only began to recover when an incision was made behind his right ear and the pus was drained off. Incidentally, I wrote down verbatim what he himself told me: "This was a depression which had manifested itself physically."

When I asked him what the draining operation had been like, he said, sixty years later: "Revolting. It wasn't even that painful. It was done under powerful anaesthesia. Dr Dunkel held a chisel in his left hand, a hammer in his right. And my brain simply juddered. As far as my eyeballs. I don't think I cried out. A couple of days before, I had celebrated my fourteenth birthday. And this was a military hospital. Not a place to start crying. But later, and for the rest of my life, when people have started talking about physical pain, a pain shoots through me from the base of my skull. I remember reading Lepik's poem 'The Painter', which appeared in 1951 in Sweden, that's right, isn't it? I think I managed to get hold of a copy in 1954, i.e. twenty-five years after the operation. But when I read, you remember the words –

> In my paintbox only black,
> Of white not a single nuance.
> A neurologist
> my brain will crack
> In his hand bright, a chisel, white.
> I cry out in horror, loathing, fright:
> "The chisel too should be black!"

When I read those words, even now, a pain shoots through my head and my eyeballs. An imaginary pain, but still. And when I came home from hospital, I was so unhinged that for some time my mother took me out of school. In those days, I was in the seventh form at Wikman's."

At that point, I asked: "Ullo, couldn't you tell a little about the schools you attended before you ended up at Wikman's? And about your home tutors before you went to school?"

Ullo told me the following:

His first tutors had been his mother, and Miss von Rosen who we already know. They started teaching him to read when he was five years old and it transpired that the boy could already read both German and Estonian pretty fluently. Miss Rosen also happened to speak very decent Estonian, though Mr Berends thought it better that she didn't teach his son Estonian and left it to a native speaker. But French was still left to Miss Rosen. That young woman with smooth, auburn Titian-style hair, rather severe in Ullo's recollection, but with a wish to please and always smelling of "4711", no doubt played a significant role in the boy's development. And here I had noted down an anecdote, admittedly from a little later, which involved this same Miss Rosen:

"I must have been fourteen by then. Miss Rosen had not, at any rate, been teaching me for some while. I was living with my mother in Weseler's house on Toom-Rüütli and attending the Wikman Grammar School. And, as far as I know, Miss Rosen taught history and French at the Hansa School. Mother sent me off to Mr Weseler, our landlord (who also doubled up as my German master at Wikman's), to pay off the rent arrears – Mother and I had managed to survive until the money sent from abroad by my father arrived. Mr Weseler's flat was on Aida Street. And to my surprise, Miss Rosen was there visiting Mr Weseler who was bald, with a goatee, rather like the writer Hindrey. Miss Rosen seemed to be aware that my father had abandoned us. She asked in passing, quite tactfully, how we were getting on. But I imagine she already knew. And I wanted to get back at her for that knowledge. Miss Rosen had, after all, been very close to me – alongside my mother who had been much preoccupied with the family's society aspect – had almost been an ersatz mother. This increased my desire for revenge and made me put my feelings into practice. In some way, the presence of old Mr Weseler awoke a cheekiness in me, maybe clothed in a measure of jealousy, which I was unaware of at the time. I answered Miss Rosen: 'Oh, we're more or less surviving . . .' and then asked, in my newly awoken interest in contemporary Estonian history and wishing to cause her embarrassment: 'By the way, Miss Rosen, I've always wanted to ask you, are

51

you in any way related to Otto von Rosen, author of the Rosen Declaration?'

"She replied: 'Yes. If you go back two hundred years.'

"So I asked: 'How do you then respond to your great-great-great-uncle's idea that Estonians have, throughout history, been objects – in principle *servi res sunt*?' I had picked up the expression recently in some article or other by some Sepp or Vasar.

"Miss Rosen looked at me for a long time, then said, gently: 'My dear boy, you've always had a very lively, even rather wild, imagination. So you can easily imagine yourself away from this room and sinking down through the stone floor and through two hundred years of history. And imagine that you are in the same room as my great-great-great-uncle, at the same time he was there. Very dark. Very cold. Like a cellar. And that you are one of them. That you belong there. You don't have an inkling of the brighter storeys somewhere above. Because they do not yet exist. Don't you think that, in his shoes, you'd think a little less radically, a little differently, than the way you do here and now? Or what if Otto von Rosen suddenly rose up through the floor in front of this fireplace, removed the wig from his head and screwed up his eyes? What would he have to say to us? That Estonians are objects? Or, rather, would he say what the German member Hasselblatt said only last week in the *Riigikogu*: that it was now time for the Germans in Estonia to live loyally alongside the Estonians . . .?'

"I'm afraid I had no answer to give Miss Rosen. Otherwise, the question would not have remained so long, and so disturbingly, in my memory."

So much for the *glossa* on the part of Ullo. But I have interrupted my story about his pre-school education.

Anyhow, on his father's insistence, an Estonian tutor was found for the boy, someone who taught at a private junior school somewhere on Vladimir Street, a young Estonian who wore pince-nez and went by the name of Peterson. He wasn't quite as astute as his famous namesake Kristjan Jaak Peterson had been (this one was in fact called Nikolai) but he could speak Estonian at the level demanded by that university linguist Jaan Jõgever, and taught in an irreproachable manner. With hindsight Ullo realised that the fact that he came to employ some of the neologisms introduced by Aavik was thanks to Mr Peterson.

In 1923, on the insistence of his father, they had tried to send Ullo to the primary school situated on that same Raua Street, entering the second or third form there. But his classmates were those who had the year before, and the year before that, taken part in inter-yard battles and skirmishes across garden fences, and had been in the opposing camp to Ullo. So Ullo had begun to protest and announced that he was simply not going to mix with these savages. Consequently, he stayed at home. That year and the next he was thus under the tutelage of Miss Rosen and Mr Peterson. Both came to tutor him, came to the first and second Berends flats on Pikk Street, and both managed to convince his parents that their offspring had made remarkable progress under their guiding hands.

Eventually, in 1925, he attended the German-language Knüppfer Primary School on Süda Street, entering the fourth form. The headmistress and presumably owner of the school was one Mrs Knüppfer, who was around fifty years old. Ullo said that she was a respectable, well-meaning woman. A lady. Taught singing and German. The other teachers, as far as he remembered, were a certain Madame von Buxhoevden ("a swarthy broomstick of a woman, who taught mathematics and natural history") and some redheaded witch or other, a Baltic German, or would-be Baltic German, who taught Estonian. There were eight pupils in the fourth form, four boys and four girls. Sixty years on, Ullo remembered the Jewish boy Lurje, whose mother was a city-centre dentist. Incidentally, in 1940 when, fifteen years later, Lurje had returned from Russia, he had become the head of the militia for the Pärnu Road area of Tallinn and had done Ullo a few favours. And at that school, as Ullo told me on my insistence, there was not the slightest hint of anti-Semitism against the jolly and witty young Lurje.

Of the girls, Ullo could remember three, a Stieren and a Mohrenschildt, two girls of noble extraction, plus the Estonian Martinson girl, who exhibited tangible intolerance towards the first two. But to return to the boys: Ullo's best mate in class had been Jochen von Brehm. A boy from Pikk Street, a cheerful, fat and freckled lazybones, whose father was some kind of clerk and philately buff (especially Austrian stamps), that is to say a philately buff to the extent that the family were sometimes down on their uppers. Nevertheless, Jochen had various rather unusual things at home, with which Ullo never grew tired of playing. He had, for instance, a thousand tin soldiers, half French Napoleonic, the other half in German uniform. Each army had a gun which worked on air pressure and shot wooden balls a centimetre across at the enemy. Battles were fought of an evening on the large and quite worn kitchen table, Jochen mostly playing Blücher or some other German, Ullo unfailingly Napoleon, even at Leipzig, at Waterloo, at the Fall of Paris – always Napoleon.

Actually, what drew Ullo to the Brehms' was partly, of course, the presence of Jochen's sister Benita. The girl was ten years older than her brother, i.e. already over twenty. Her presence always gave Ullo a feeling in his innards, part painful, part sweet. And later, when dabbling in art history, Ullo understood who Benita von Brehm really was: the woman whom Dürer had immortalised in his *Melancholy* . . .

Naturally, nothing happened between Ullo and Benita. Apart from that feeling of throbbing hollowness in Ullo's stomach when they played musical chairs at the Brehms' and Ullo always tried to end up last with Benita – which he nearly always succeeded in doing, and which meant that one would end up sitting on the other's lap. And to be sure, the best days at school were those when Benita appeared at the school on Süda Street, having been sent out by their mother to check whether Jochen, oaf that he was, had managed to stay there, or play truant as he so often did.

As far as learning went, Ullo at least was convinced that there at the Knüppfer school he had learnt – nothing. Apart, that is, from conventional behaviour, to some extent at least. But he thought the same, and this in his mature years, of his schooldays at the Wikman Grammar School, having there too learnt practically nothing at all.

10

A S I HAVE NO DOUBT mentioned, Ullo was sent to the Wikman Boys' Grammar by his mother, in that very same autumn of 1929, about a month before his father finally travelled abroad for good. Or fled.

That spring, in late May, his mother had put on her very respectable grey-and-black chequered costume, in front of the Venetian mirror, still in their Toomkooli Street flat, and had gone to sign Ullo up for the seventh form at the school.

Mr Wikman twirled his meagre moustaches: "Ah, I see, Mr Berends is a – businessman? Mm yes . . . That we already know. But there isn't actually any entrance examination set for the seventh form. You see, the places in the seventh are all filled by pupils coming up from the sixth. So I'm afraid I can't really promise you anything, my dear lady. But do send your boy along next Tuesday at nine o'clock, and I'll have a word with him then."

So Ullo shined his boots – the maid who used to do such chores was no longer with them – and went off to the old schoolhouse on Hommiku Street and approached the school secretary to request an interview with the headmaster.

Wikman's office sported paintings by Raud, Laikmaa and Weizenberg. The headmaster received him with a good measure of what Ullo felt to be condescension.

"Ah, Ullo Berends, hm? Your mother came along last week and asked me to let you join the seventh form. She claimed you were a real young polyglot. *Elle m'a dit que tu parles librement français. Est-ce-que c'est vrai, ça?*"

Ullo had shrugged one shoulder: *"Si ma mère l'a dit, évidemment c'est vrai."*

Mr Wikman had conversed with him for a quarter of an hour, first

55

in French, then in German, then in Russian. Ullo had never actually learnt the last of these languages formally. But while they were still living on Raua Street, and the Tallinn of the time being what it was, later too, he had heard Russian pretty frequently, so that several hundred elementary expressions had stuck. He had managed to keep up a five-minute conversation with the headmaster in that language with a reasonable measure of success. And was taken on for the seventh form. Wikman had kept fairly mum at the time, but it later reached his mother's ears what he had said after the conversation with Ullo. While telling me, Ullo suggested: "Well, I don't know, but maybe kind people said this to my mother to comfort her after her recent abandonment. Mr Wikman was supposed to have said: 'Take note, in the autumn a particularly remarkable *Köpfchen* will be joining our sevenths.'"

Sometime in the spring of 1986, he was sitting in his study in that low, uncomfortable armchair with too low a base, his sharply outlined knees together, his hands on his stomach or at least there where people of his age sport some kind of belly, which, as if belonging to a younger generation, he didn't yet have. He placed his fingertips together, then separated them, now pressed together his thumbs, together, apart, together, apart, and said with a wry smile: "It is quite likely that decent people wanted to comfort not only Mother, but also myself. Not only the jilted wife, but also the abandoned son. And clearly I was very much in need of such comfort. Otherwise, it wouldn't have stuck in my memory so clearly."

A week later, our next conversation at Ullo's went like this:

"Ah, the Wikman Grammar School? Well, I'm not going to start telling you about that. You know the place just as well as I do, even a bit better. You were there all the time – and years more than me. I only stayed a few months. Then my mother had me stay at home, on account of that ear infection. The scar behind my ear was very slow to heal, and that second and less tangible wound took even longer. So I'll just tell you about that first year without Father. Agreed?"

"Agreed."

"Well, in the early winter we moved yet again to a new, that is to say cheaper, flat. For being without money was so new to my mother that she couldn't bring herself to ask Mr Weseler to lower the rent, although I think he would have agreed to a reduction. We moved out to Nõmme, where the rents were lower, to Põllu Street and a house belonging to a former haberdasher, a Mr Tõnisberg. It was a furnished room with a tiny kitchen attached, furnished because by now we no longer possessed any furniture. Half of the first money Father had sent from Holland or Luxembourg was used by my mother to pay my school fees – for she thought that it wouldn't look good to start asking Wikman for the fees to be waived right from the word go. So in the late winter – no money, no furniture, no fuel. However, Mother had managed to save something. Along with the furniture, all the paintings had been taken away. We had had plenty of them. Not particularly valuable ones, but pictures at any rate from before the War of Estonian Independence: a few Neffs, a few Repins, a few Clevers, Maxolls, Vihvelins. Now all these were gone. But by some miracle there were still two paintings in Chinese lacquer, framed bird murals, one of yellow-beaked ducks, the other of red-billed cranes. Interestingly stylised, yet true to life. Quite fantastic works. At home we'd been told that they'd been stolen from the Palace of the Emperor in the Forbidden City in Peking, and been sold by some immigrant, newly arrived from the Far East, to my father. Mother now sold them. Through some acquaintance or other, because she could not bring herself to do such things herself. Not yet, at any rate. I seem to remember that they were sold for some ridiculous price, but I couldn't tell Mother that. Nor did I start protesting when she sent me to a third-rate antique dealer's on the Tartu Road, where I was to receive the third and final instalment of the money paid for the pictures.

"An old man with drooping lips and a foreign-sounding voice received me in the shop. I put the IOU for the three thousand marks or thirty kroons on the counter, and said who I was. The old man immediately started making difficulties: yes, of course, but Thursday – Thursday eez wery bad day. Wery leetle money earnt. No, no, he weell pay nonetheless. He weell pay vonn sowzant right avay.

"'And dzen – you know vot, yong man: vee vill closse ze shop. I from morningk hevv vonted to gou to sauna. Let's go toogezzer. I know wery good sauna.' He looked at me with his red-eyed satyr's face – 'Let's take leetle beer. You already big man. Leetle beer. There is wery good sausages. Dzen, in sauna we towk about we arrainzh last sowzant in next month.'

"Well, the old codger must have thought I was still wet behind the

57

ears. Which of course I was. But I did happen to have read through August Forel's book which we had on Mother and Father's book-shelves, hidden behind the other books, and had also peeped in the Magnus Hirschfeld tome. So, after a second's incomprehension, it became clear to me what the old antiquarian bookseller was after. So I shoved the IOU back in my pocket and darted out of the shop. And talked the matter over with Mother when I got home. She blanched with shock. But listened to what I suggested we do right to the end. And that consisted of going along to Mr Mahoni at the Ministry of Justice or to his legal practice and asking him for advice.

"Mr Mahoni, a jovial and humorous elder gent, once a notary, once assistant to the Minister of Justice, once the Minister himself, had been one of our most frequent visitors when we were still living on Raua Street and, unlike many others, still visited us afterwards. He still came along when we were living in our flat with the Venetian mirror and the rats in the corridor, i.e. came to drink tea with Mother and Father up to a couple of years ago, more rarely than before, but still. And my mother did indeed go and consult him now. And got her money from Droop-Lips on the Tartu Road after arriving there accompanied by Assistant Commissioner Schönrock in full police uniform. Whom Mr Mahoni had rung.

"We lived on the proceeds of the sale of those two imperial murals in Mr Tõnisberg's rented flat for a month or two. I recovered gradually and my mother, ever more nervous and pale, looked for work. But it was the worst possible time for doing so. The tsunami caused by the Wall Street Crash reached Estonia by the 1930s. Not only private businesses, but also government departments began laying off staff, rather than taking them on. Well, I have all my life thought that such social waves need not play any role in individual cases. And experience has proved me right, at least in my own situation. But my mother did not find suitable work – for there was initially no question of her doing anything manual. Despite the fact that she spoke faultless Russian and German and some French too, she didn't have any experience of secretarial or translation work. She could have got references from former acquaintances, but couldn't bring herself to ask them.

"We lived from hand to mouth and learnt to count the pennies, to know whether an open tub of milk cost nine or eleven cents – and ignore bottles marked with labels with cows on them standing there on the shelves of the milk shop, and where the exact percentage of fat was marked. We got to know the price relation between birch and aspen, and the relative heat each could produce. And we got to know a new route from Mr Tõnisberg's house to the railway station which did not take us along Põllu Street, past the windows of Truup's grocer's shop. We took this new route when we had chalked up a debt for bread and milk in excess of ten kroons."

At that point I asked: "But Ullo – wasn't your father sending you anything at the time?"

And Ullo explained: "Something, yes. But very little. And more and more rarely. About fifty kroons a time. Every two or three months. And what's more, these consignments caused tension between Mother and me. I would demand noisily that she didn't accept the money. And such demands got on my own nerves, since I couldn't really be consistent. Because an empty stomach is also a factor to be taken into consideration . . . It was all the more difficult, since Mother asked me to accept the money Father had sent. Try to understand me. Our mess wasn't only my father's fault. In some way, though she didn't seem to understand how, it was her own fault too. And the responsibility for the fact that their boy now had to do without things fell on her shoulders too. My refusal to accept Father's support seemed to make her burden all the heavier, for it appeared to show that as well as not having been able to keep the family together, she was not able to use my father's financial support for the benefit of their son.

"And besides, the strain between us awoke because of my, how shall I put it, vacillation between pity and censure. We had agreed that we wouldn't cry. I did not shed tears, neither in Mother's presence nor behind her back. It became more and more impossible to do so. For by now I had reached the age of fifteen. As for Mother, I never saw her with moist eyes either, although on occasions they were red. That would always make me nervous and insecure. By the way, how Mother handled money was always dreadfully inconsistent. At times, to save a few cents, she would not buy something essential, then she would squander hard-earned kroons on some trifle or other."

I then asked a question which, despite having a certain predictability to it, now embarrasses me. "Ullo – in all that unaccustomed misery, did you never get the idea, either you or your mother, and since you can't really know about your mother, did you personally never have suicidal thoughts?"

Ullo replied instantly. "In Mother's case – no. We did actually discuss the matter, later on, in slightly better days. She had never thought seriously about it. Sometimes, out of sheer inertia, just for something to say, she would sigh to herself: Oh, I ought to jump in the ocean. Or: I ought to string myself up. But she had never seriously thought of doing so. Since my presence would not allow her room for such thoughts. And as for myself – such thoughts are even more alien to me. But in a quite different way and surprisingly early on in life – well, how shall I put it – they *were* familiar to me.

"I was five years old, Father and Mother had gone abroad and I was staying for the summer with Charlotte at Kose, opposite the Kochs' residence, I don't remember whose summer house it was. We had four rooms, I think, on the ground floor, above which was a small tower with four upper storeys. This tower contained the ship models made by the owner of the house, fascinating objects they were, and at the top was a platform with an observation balcony. I was only allowed up in the tower and on the balcony in Charlotte's presence. We had my dog with us at the summer house. A sandy-haired dachshund. A wonderful creature. I had named him Traks on account of the rhyme with 'taks', i.e. a dachshund. As I said, he was a wonderful creature with a completely smooth, yet tough, coat. It was as if the skin were electrified. Made to stroke. One morning the dog was ill. He ran around whining, then lay down on his cushion. He did lap up water cautiously, so Charlotte concluded that he couldn't have had rabies. As I said, I was five years old at the time, and I couldn't be with him and worry about him all day long. I probably wouldn't have been able to even now. I dragged Charlotte up into the tower. I was holding a pair of binoculars in one hand and wanted to go and look out from the balcony as I usually did. At the tops of the trees, the roads, people, rivers, rowers. Then we heard Traks coming howling, or rather bellowing, on account of the pain. He rushed up the tower staircase – we could do nothing to stop him – and out on to the balcony, between our feet and between the slats of the balustrade – straight into the air. By the time we got downstairs, he was lying on the sand below. Dead.

"When the first shock had passed, it suddenly occurred to me: so if you really want to, you can *step out of it all* – voluntarily.

"This discovery struck me forcibly, as if you've been standing behind a door and the wind blows it into your face, not painfully, but with enough force to make you think. It was an unforgettable experience."

Ullo continued: in the autumn of 1930, his mother had once again approached Mr Wikman and asked him to re-register her boy for the eighth form, now that his ear infection had more or less cleared up. Mr Wikman had clearly not forgotten his positive impression of the boy from the year before. Into the bargain, Mrs Berends added that the boy had been keeping up with the school syllabus all year long. Well, that wasn't entirely true, but it wasn't a complete fabrication either. Somehow, his mother had found the necessary kroons and (although Ullo had found this unnecessary) had had some matriculation pupil come along to check Ullo's work at home a few times a week, before the school year began. Ullo said: "He was a quite intelligent, but peculiarly embittered young fellow. The son of a drunken farmer from near Tallinn, but also the nephew of a well-known Tallinn lawyer, with whose family he was living. And when we had nothing better to do, we'd play chess together. And argue. What about? He made up a horoscope for my mother. He knew that work – if you could call it work – pretty well. And for her he predicted, oh I don't remember exactly, something like kidney disease, long trips and possibly suspended animation. And I, of course, tried to dash his predictions to pieces. With what arguments? With quite elementary ones, really. I claimed that the destinies of people born on the same day weren't at all like one another. He said that even a few seconds' difference could mean large differences in their fates. I said that hardly anyone knew their time of birth to the nearest second, and that his horoscopes were floating in a morass of good faith. Or charlatanism. No, we didn't become friends. And as revenge, he kept my copy of Lasker's book on the philosophy of chess, sent to me from Holland by my father. It was in Dutch, and at the time it was quite likely the only copy in Estonia."

At that juncture, a small but embarrassing argument about languages arose between us. I pointed out that it couldn't have been much of a loss. It was, after all, in Dutch.

He cried: "What d'you mean? I could read it with no difficulty at all. I also read Frederik van Eeden's *Van de koele meren des doods* – there were hundreds of things in there that I couldn't understand exactly, but I understood the chess book perfectly. It presented no problems at all."

11

ULLO CONTINUED: "IN THE autumn of '31, when we were on our uppers, Mr Tõnisberg helped us in an unexpected way. What sort of man was he? Well, perhaps about sixty, maybe younger. Short, pale, his hands trembled slightly. A scrubby little ginger moustache. A bit like Piłsudski's. But very quietly spoken. And even quieter in the presence of the exuberant Mrs Tõnisberg. In their home, the adjoining flat to ours, there were an unexpectedly large number of books. At least for a haberdasher. There was nothing very special about them, but there were thousands of books, in Estonian, German and Russian. Our first more personal contact came when I began borrowing books from him. Because we didn't have anything left of our former library, and I had flitted about for the last few years borrowing books from here, there and everywhere. They had God knows how many – we never had that many books anyway. There must have been two or three thousand. Then one day, Mr Tõnisberg suddenly said to Mother: 'My dear lady, I've heard that your boy has an excellent command of the French language. Please forgive me for saying so, but you don't really have that much money to hand, if I understand rightly. So, look, I happen to have tried to learn that same language at one time in my life. And I thought that the twenty kroons you pay every month in rent for your room could come in pretty handy for yourself and the lad. And so I thought: you can have the room for nothing. If, that is, your son undertakes to give me French lessons. I had thought, let's say, ten a month, and two hours at a time. That would be a pretty decent fee – one whole kroon per hour. Only experienced teachers are paid at that rate – but your young man hasn't got any teaching experience – and would be paid a kroon an hour, even when having to travel to the pupil's house. But in this case it would be me who came to you. No, no, why should he come to our place? No need to do so at all. My wife has her own activities going on there, friends with their coffee mornings and so forth. And I only have to cross the corridor. If we would be a bother in the living room, then there's always the kitchen – but I would imagine . . .'

"We agreed that I would start the lessons the day after next. We would be using my own textbooks, and he would bring along some texts himself. When he had gone, my mother clapped her hands quietly and said: 'Ullo, this truly is the finger of God! We would have had to pay him the day after tomorrow, and I didn't have the slightest idea where we were going to conjure up twenty kroons from.'

"Two evenings later, at seven o'clock, a sprightly Mr Tõnisberg turned up. He had a copy of *Le Figaro* from the previous week under his arm. And I had my *France*, volumes I and II, ready on the corner of the table.

"Mother withdrew to the kitchen with an assiduous smile. 'No please, Mr Tõnisberg, please make yourself at home.' And he did. Actually, even more so.

"He put his newspaper on the table. And began with how great a disappointment it would be for Mrs Berends should nothing come out of these lessons on account of my wilfulness. But then again, he wasn't imagining any such problem would arise. For I was too sensible and inquisitive a boy, or rather, young man. And so forth. Then he opened his copy of *Le Figaro* and there, between its pages, lay a pornographic magazine.

"At the time, I hadn't seen such things before. But I did know they existed. What lay between the pages of the newspaper was hardly what we nowadays consider pornographic, what with the existence of such things as *Kalle* and the like, which find their way across the Gulf of Finland. The photography here was much more primitive. And there were so-called 'artistic' illustrations – by Félicien Rops and others."

I asked: "But what did he need you to go through them for?"

Ullo explained: "There was a text section, too. That was what I was to translate."

"And you did?"

"Well, you know, to a certain extent. At first I felt kind of hollow inside and my throat pinched. But I was in a most awkward situation. Jump up and refuse – that was quite out of the question, for Mother's sake. At the same time, I felt that if Mother were to know, the whole business would come to an abrupt end, there and then. But the curiosity of a fifteen-year-old also played its role. I wanted to look at the magazines. Despite the reluctance and embarrassment I felt."

"And was it some straightforward porn mag? Or one for some special kink?"

"I couldn't really tell, at the time. Looking back on it – but then how analytical are we of these matters in this country? – even now I suppose it was, as you put it, a straightforward one. I seem to remember that Mr Tõnisberg took the greatest interest in lesbian themes and, well, the *manusturbatio puellarum*." (I, of course, desisted from smiling – but it did amuse me that his seventy-year-old prudery forbade him from expressing such things in anything other than Latin.)

I asked, then, in '86: "And did he comment on your translations?"

"No, he didn't. From time to time he would ask something. But in the main he just listened. Or muttered from behind the shelter of his moustache. But did his wife know of his hobby? Yes, she did. I'm convinced that they looked at the pictures together in bed. With Daddy doing the explaining. I nicknamed the wife the Volumnia. And Volumnia knew, for sure. How do I arrive at that conclusion? Well, when Mother came into our lessons a couple of times from the kitchen – she had managed to get some temporary job in a Nõmme market garden firm doing the bookkeeping – to get a ruler or a rubber, Mr Tõnisberg covered his magazine with the newspaper, at lightning speed. But when Volumnia came to our lesson in search of her husband – 'Listen, I think you've put the keys to the pantry in your pocket' – then he would conceal his magazine in quite another manner: he would hide it on those occasions too, but without any fuss, carelessly, for the sake of form. And Volumnia would look at us ironically through the blonde locks of her perm and smile: 'Is the young man trying to make a Frenchman out of my hubby . . .?'

"When did this saga come to an end and how? Pretty soon. When Mother found herself a job. At that same market garden firm on Jaama Street where she had done the bookkeeping on occasion. Now the owner, Zopf or Topf or whatever his name happened to be, wanted to offer Mother a permanent position. At first he offered forty kroons a month, then he pared it down to thirty and suggested: for ten kroons a month you can move in to the spare room in the watchman's and stoker's house in the same horticultural centre. And so we did. And then I told Mother of Mr Tõnisberg's special interest."

"And your mother?"

"Mother went completely berserk and tweaked my hair for the one and only time in her life – because I hadn't told her until now. Then she hugged me – but that wasn't the first or the last time – because I had nonetheless told her."

In the end, Ullo got round to telling me about what things were like at the Wikman Grammar School and about his relations with the school: In the seventh form, the autumn before falling ill, he was all of a sudden asked by a stubby individual from the eighths whether he, Ullo, remembered Valja? Nudge, nudge, wink, wink.

Ullo had blushed to his roots. He recognised the cowherd Jaan. Who had grazed the tenant farmers' cattle on Lootsaar the previous summer. And with whom he had run a race to try to win Valja's favours. And lost, but in fact won.

"I turned my back on Jaan in silence. In silence, and I felt, that I was blushing profusely. And I ignored him, right up to when I fell ill. And I ignored him after my return to Wikman's. Ignored him for three long years, till Jaan himself left school and vanished from my horizons. I didn't exchange one word with him. I really don't know why not."

Ullo continued: "I wasn't really accepted by the class as a whole. I would have had to have been more of a chatterbox than I in fact was, and sporty, which I wasn't. It would have been hopeless for me to try. Dr Dunkel had forbidden me from taking part in any kind of sports for at least two years. And I would clearly have had to be much more like the others. Not that I lacked quirks of vanity. Concerning, for instance, Racine in Mrs Lüllii's class, or Ohm's Law in Hellmann's. Well, I couldn't keep my mouth shut all the time, tending to mutter the answers half audibly – and that didn't exactly endear this 'clever dick' to the class in general. So it took me some while to gain their confidence.

"Of course, I made friends over time, long-term ones. Like you. But now they are, yes, where are they? As you once wrote: anywhere from Norilsk to Nordhausen, from Katanga to Karaganda. Some made it, some snuffed it. D'you know, I even managed to get one or two pupils thrown out of Wikman's. Yes, that's right. What are you staring at?

"Have you heard of that trick of pulling someone through the bench? Called 'piping'? No? Well, ask your older brothers. In my day,

65

this practice was still in full swing at Wikman's. It was forbidden, of course, but practised with great fervour. Do you remember the plywood sofas from the Luther factory which they had in the yellow assembly hall? Each had an armrest at either end, horizontal and squared-off. This created a rectangular hole between the ends of the sofas, the dimensions of which were (I actually measured them): height, 18 centimetres; length, 43 centimetres. Through such a gap the older boys pulled the younger ones. Usually during long break, and not every day. As rarely as befits a ritual. The crowd of inquisitive folk and watchmen surrounding the bench in question. The guinea pig was made to lie down on the sofa and was pushed and pulled, head first, under the armrest – bonce, shoulders, ribcage, backside, legs. Those whose bellies or shoulders didn't fit were pulled back halfway and given a thwack on the backside, then let go. Some stronger types struggled so vigorously that they didn't succeed in piping them. Such as my classmate Viktor Viisileht. And he wouldn't have passed through anyway. But then again, he did become Estonian and Soviet heavy-weight boxing champion. I, at least, had no difficulties passing through, neither my head, my shoulders nor my backside. My first reaction when pushed down on to the bench was to go limp and help my 'pipers' along with their task. To get from under the armrest all the more easily. For what else could I do – when I was being handled by two sturdy lads from the tenth form? But they didn't like the fact that I wasn't putting up a fight. One sat on my knees and started twisting my arms. The other pressed my right cheek against the bottom of the bench so that a shooting pain went through my sick ear. But it was more the indignity of it all rather than the physical pain which caused my anger to suddenly well up in me: the fat-arsed idiots trying to be clever! Who did they think they were? How dare they! I wriggled my right knee free from under the boy sitting on my legs and kicked him straight in the face with the heel of my shoe. Well, for that I was dragged a second and then a third time through the 'pipe'. And when I said that I was going straight to the headmaster, they grinned and said: 'You, pathetic weed, you're not going anywhere. 'Cos if you do, we'll belt you one, just round the corner! Just you remember!'"

"And did you go . . .?"

Ullo said: "I did. And straightaway, too. If I had hesitated, I wouldn't have gone. And I told him everything. My appearance confirmed what

I said. Nor did I omit to mention their threats. Wikman said that I shouldn't worry and should go quietly off to class. He wasn't intending to expose me. And for ten days nothing happened. Then all of a sudden both boys were summoned to the headmaster and expelled. The previous evening, Mr Ambel, the Second Master, had seen them in Kadriorg Park sitting on a bench, smoking. That was sufficient to have them expelled. I do not know to this day whether it was coincidence, or whether something had been cooked up. No one mentioned my name in connection with the business."

I thought, as Ullo was speaking, and I think it again now: this is interesting, but is my gut instinct failing me when I imagine that he actually regretted going to see the headmaster? Then, when he told me in 1986, I left the question unasked. And now it's no longer possible to ask.

We carried on talking, changed the subject, it would appear. I asked: "Ullo, you once used the expression *expand on my admission*. Would you like to say a little about how, and thanks to what, the admission arose and how it developed?"

Ullo had to smile. "You mean that the mongrel now has to raise his tail all by himself? Which is all he can do if no one else does it for him. Well, the whole thing began, I think, when someone, I can't remember who, maybe Plaks's lad or whoever, came to me: could I do his German composition for him – his homework for Mr Krafft, that is. I don't remember what it was about on that particular occasion. But it certainly all began in the eighth form. I wrote his composition for him. And he got 4 out of 5 for it. I didn't want to write anything better for Plaks – even getting a 4 could be a bit dodgy in his case. But Mr Krafft fell for it and was telling everyone right, left and centre that Plaks had actually begun to think for himself and had only made four silly grammatical mistakes! Plaks (if it was him) paid me the agreed two kroons quite honourably – and by the next month there were four or five pupils commissioning compositions from me. And these were in Estonian language, that is to say, for Mr Kõiv. Some people were prepared to pay up to five kroons each for them. And so when I was in the top forms I managed to earn forty or fifty kroons a month. Because my list of clients just kept on growing. And I had fun, as well. I remember, it was in the tenth form I think, but the subject matter makes me think it must have been earlier: Mr Krafft gave the topic of

67

the Nibelung for homework. And I wrote twenty-three compositions on that topic. There were forty of us in our class. Sixteen wrote their own compositions. So I did twenty-three, leaving aside my own. Well, I tried to write each of them so it would reflect the mentality of the person who was supposed to have written it, weaker for those who were weaker, better for those who were better. I varied the points of view and the emphasis, but in the end, I was so fed up and felt so wrung out that as for my own composition – which I had left till last and only had a couple of hours in the night to complete – I could just no longer bring myself to write it. Mr Krafft always expected at least four or five sides. And at least ten from me. But nothing was coming to mind any more. Then I had an idea: I would write my essay in verse. That would excuse a certain amount of impudence in me, for after twenty-three regurgitations, any other approach would seem hopelessly insipid. And written in verse, it could be got over with in a page, a page and a half. So there, in the stoker's room where my mother and I had been lodged for getting on for two years, I wrote:

> *"Die Nibelungen*
> *sind in den 'Nibelungen'*
> *künstlerisch nicht besonders gelungen.*
> *Obschon rein arisch,*
> *sind sie literarisch*
> *und sowohl philosophisch*
> *als auch strophisch*
> *fatal*
> *und katastrophal*
> *unbeholfen, hölzern und trocken.*
>
> *Man könnte sagen: neben dem glanz*
> *der Helme*
> *und Locken*
> *gehen die Schelme*
> *unterhalb des Gürtels in ganz*
> *ungewaschenen Socken.*
>
> *Und sucht man*
> *unter den geharnischten Onkeln und Tanten*

nach einem höheren Repräsentanten
von Werten,
sieht man mit Unbehagen:
es gibt da eigentlich nur den verehrten
Herrn Hagen.

Der wird von uns anderswo gründlich erörtert.
Ich merk' nur dazu, dass
Herr Hagen den germanischen Judas
par excellence verkörpert –

"When Herr Krafft gave us back our work the following week, he had placed my poetic opus on top of the pile, and spluttered on about it for an extra quarter of an hour. How could I bring myself to be so trivial and vain?! While the class on average, even many of the weakest among them, had done particularly well on this occasion! It turned out that Herr Krafft had given at least half the class very good marks. And – what didn't come out at the time but made many of us smile – those who got top marks included fifteen I had written essays for."

"I have to say," explained Ullo, "that it never came out in the open, but more or less all the boys knew. And when you asked what it was that gave me status in class, well, it was largely due to such affairs. And I have to admit, thanks to the fact that I didn't go around boohooing about what happened, simply scoffed at the fact that I got a miserable three for my own efforts. How could I help it if I had grievously overestimated Herr Krafft's pliability and sense of humour to an unrealistic degree?

"So, Herr Krafft's splutterings and my three strokes of the cane – and this was not the only occasion – did not prevent me from continuing as scribe in the same vein. But I've already mentioned that people were now ordering homework for old Kõiv, in Estonian language. For the compositions could be much more natural if written in Estonian than in German – which had to take into account each boy's level of language knowledge. The Estonian efforts were much freer of their obligatory kindergarten-level qualities. I didn't become particularly philosophical in them, but they didn't expect that from me either, given the fact that the boys were paying two kroons a shot, five kroons in the case of the better-off."

12

ULLO WENT ON:
"I remember Christmas 1932 particularly well. Father was no longer sending us anything, hadn't even sent us anything that Christmas or the one before, as far as I recall. We didn't even know his address. We didn't know what country he was living in, Germany or Holland or Luxembourg, or God knows where else. The economic crisis was deepening. At least that's what everybody was claiming. The boss of our market garden was no exception. Out of thrift, he began to do the bookkeeping himself. He paid out the agreed thirty kroons a month – under pressure of circumstances, as he put it – only if Mother would take over the chore of stoking the greenhouses, and clearing the street of snow, piling it up along the edge of the pavement. Well, between us we got that done, and that's what Herr Topf, or Zopf, had reckoned on. Thirty kroons a month plus the odd kroons I earned for the homework essays I wrote for the boys was, to feed a family of two, how shall I put it. Well, it kept the wolf from the door and was almost enough to live on, but it was a pittance, nonetheless. Although it did teach us, my mother too, but principally myself, to regard Mammon with superciliousness. At least theoretically speaking.

"In the spirit of this feeling of superiority, we did try to maintain the traditions of Christmas. We had gone out to the edge of the marsh near Pääsküla and brought back – using a small saw from the nursery garden – a small Christmas tree of one or one and a half metres in height. I had whittled the bottom of the trunk to a point. We pushed it through the fingerhole of our kitchen stool and placed the tree in the corner of the room, with six white candles and a sprinkling of silver foil which my mother had obtained from somewhere. That kind of nostalgia. Ha, ha, haa! And then, on Boxing Day morning, suddenly – knock-knock-knock-knock. And in walks Mr Kõiv. Kõtsberg, as he was called in your class, I believe, a pun on the writer Kitzberg. Or Kõtsu, as we called him.

"Anyway, you've known him longer and better than me. For you, he is much more the *magister*. But in 1932, he didn't yet have his MA. And it was in connection with that, that he turned up at our place. He rattled off what he had to say, just like, well, oh I don't know, some animal, some boss-eyed, bespectacled squirrel, but one wearing a smart black astrakhan-collared coat.

"'Gd mrning, Mrs B'rends. I'm yr yng ld's 'Stonian lnguage tchr.' And so forth. Skipping half his vowels, as always, and being extremely concise. He had started writing his Master's, and needed help. Someone who could type. Who could read and summarise books competently, ones he himself couldn't get round to reading, or simply couldn't read. Because, for instance, he didn't know enough French. He had followed the exploits of Ullo Berends at grammar school, as Berends was his pupil. So he thought he'd give him a try. If he agreed. For fifty kroons a month. You and your boy, Mrs Berends, must please decide."

No, no, don't get me wrong. Mr Kõiv did, in the end, take a seat. And placed his astrakhan cap on his knee. But didn't take off his overcoat. Why bother? The proposition had been uttered. Let them now weigh up the pros and cons. If Ullo should agree, then he was to turn up at eight at number such-and-such Kaupmehe Street in Tallinn. There were still ten days of the school holidays left. A perfect time for doing uninterrupted work. Thank you. And goodbye.

Well, Ullo and his mother danced around the room several times – which more or less amounted to gyrating on the spot, given the size of the stoker's cottage. And the next morning Ullo took the electric train from Nõmme into town at a quarter past seven.

Mr Kõiv received a very decent salary at Wikman's. Between 120 and 150 kroons a month. So the pleasant two-roomed bachelor flat where he lived came as no surprise. Nor did its furnishings. Chairs, tables, a writing desk, two armchairs – all solid stuff from the Luther Wood Products Manufactory. A couple of paintings by Krims and Ole. Nor could he have hung any more, as the walls were lined with so many bookshelves that there would have been no room. Ullo got the impression that Mr Kõiv must have collected his books with great care during his university days. For how many could he possibly have

71

inherited from his draper father? There were bound sets of *Eesti Kirjandus – Estonian Literature* – starting from the year 1908, and *Eesti Keel – Estonian Language* – from 1922, in leather bindings with gold lettering, and *Looming – Creative Endeavour* – from 1923, plus copies of *Olion,* starting from 1930. And all sorts of other periodicals too. And all the linguistics books by Saaberk-Saareste, Aavik, Mägiste, Kettunen, Veski, Muuk. And metres of shelves with foreign authors. Names which Ullo may have come across before (Jespersen, Setälä, Mommsen, Wilamowitz-Moellendorf) but others which he encountered for the first time (with the blithe hope of one day gobbling down the contents of the lot).

The room where Mr Kõiv received Ullo, his living room and study rolled into one, was of linear neatness: books on the shelves, papers in stacks, card indexes in boxes. The card index took up the whole surface of a low table next to the writing desk, and was stacked up in two layers.

Ullo would have concluded that his patron would not prove to be a particularly jolly fellow, since he wasn't a lively teacher at school. But there was no denying his expertise, and no reason to doubt the dry correctness of his behaviour. It soon emerged that Mr Kõiv was a good deal more familiar here at home than in the classroom. This was not in itself surprising, for at home the master of the house could feel master of the situation, while in class he had to always be on his guard on account of his youth, friability and increasingly jumpy falsetto voice, when intercepting paper aeroplanes, or what were often blunter objects in flight, whisking them out of the air as they threatened his teacherly authority. At home he compensated, still acting with some authority, but now domesticated, his shirt collar open, his feet pushed into tasselled mules. He directed Ullo to a seat at a corner table and pushed a dozen or so handwritten sheets under his nose.

"I thnk y'll sn be able to rd my hndwrting." But he gave Ullo no more than three minutes to familiarise himself with it, distracting Ullo's attention from the sheets, with the explanation that the topic of his master's dissertation was: research into language innovation in Estonian within the current system of linguistic science. It went under the title of "The Structural Linguistic Factor in Johannes Aavik's Language Renewal". To write this he needed to penetrate the arcanities of structural linguistics, then fashionable, to their very roots. What these consisted of, Ullo was soon to glean from his sources.

When, at this juncture, he raised the question (oh, accursed vanity and superficiality!) as to whether the main source wasn't surely Jakobson – i.e. Roman Jakobson's *Prinzipien der historischen Phonologie* – Mr Kõiv raised his eyebrows, looked Ullo full in the face, smiled and explained: yes, yes, of course, but that would be something he could cope with himself, because his own knowledge of German was quite good enough for reading purposes. Which made Ullo blush and he explained, for his part, that he himself hadn't a clue what Jakobson's book was actually about – just that he'd heard the title mentioned somewhere. Mr Kõiv continued: he could certainly cope with Jakobson and Co., and the English linguists. But their knowledge was based on that of a French-speaking Swiss, one Ferdinand de Saussure with his *Cours de linguistique générale*, which had appeared in Geneva back in 1916. And he, Mr Kõiv, just didn't have enough French to wade through that book. So this became Ullo's first assignment: to read through the volume and make a note of the contents, concentrating on those passages which referred more exactly to Mr Kõiv's field of study.

"D'you thnk y'll mnage?"

Here Ullo was plunging into completely unknown waters, but to refuse, or give up before trying, would have been just plain foolish, so he said, jauntily enough: "I imagine I can make a start . . ."

Mr Kõiv took down the Saussure tome from the shelf. "Rd it thrgh. Trnslate it. Mke a smmary of it. If thre'r'ny frthr questns, jst'sk."

He sat at his writing desk and became engrossed in his papers. Ullo told me that that first uninterrupted work session lasted some four hours. Four hours of complete silence. During which Ullo realised – to an increasingly depressing degree every quarter of an hour – that he had taken on a hellishly demanding task.

Word-for-word intelligibility with regard to what were pages of quite modest format, nonetheless proved quite elusive. And not only because the central tenet of the text was that all its meanings were relative. When Ullo did at last manage to make something of it, it came out like this:

Other sciences operate with given objects, which can then be viewed from various different angles. In our field of learning, i.e. that of linguistics, there is no such thing. Someone utters the

73

French word nu: *the cursory reader tries to imagine in this a concrete linguistic object. But on closer inspection three or four entirely different objects are revealed, depending on the point of view of the viewer: firstly, a sound or noise; secondly, an idea or expression; thirdly, the equivalent of the Latin* nudum. *And so on. In contrast to the claim that an object presupposes a point of view, it can be said that a point of view creates an object, and we cannot thus predict whether any of the ways of viewing the object in hand are higher or lower in comparison to others . . .*

Well, any textual transparency and clarity were immediately compromised because the text itself spent so much time stressing its own multifarious meanings. Furthermore, Ullo realised that while experienced in everyday French, and even with the literary language, he had no experience whatsoever of the language and exigencies of a scientific text. So what seemed clear at first glance, even in draft translation, over time grew ever more intangible and dubious. For instance, the scope of, and difference between, *langage* and *langue* . . . And yet – or for that very reason – the text (and the circumstances of its background) became an addictive challenge for Ullo.

He leafed through the pages, read, and asked for a copy of the small *Villecourt*, the only French–Estonian dictionary at that time, and the large French–German dictionary. Mr Kõiv lugged them over to his desk. Ullo read, took notes, collated facts, marked translation variants. He became engrossed in his task, enthusiasm and pleasure welling up out of a sense of duty.

Around half past twelve, Mr Kõiv jumped to his feet.

"Brnds! Hre's a kroon fr you. Go t'the bkry rnd the crnr – four sltd brd rlls. Buy sme sgar fr what y've gt lft. I'll mke the cffee."

Ullo went to the baker's. The coffee pot was already steaming when he got back. Mr Kõiv took out two smallish blue plates and put two rolls on each. He poured the coffee into attractive Meissenware cups which almost matched those which the Berendses had used right up to the end of their residence on Toompea Hill. He tipped the bluish-white sugar lumps into the sugar bowl with a clatter.

"Wll, cme on. Lt's rvive the spirit."

Ullo's stomach was painfully empty. But his training in etiquette as a child did not allow him to more than a nibble at the fresh, salty and

74

crisply crusted rolls, soft inside. While Mr Kõiv, who had no doubt had the same training but was not obliged to apply it in his own home, bit into his roll with such gusto that the flaky pastry surface of the roll remained around his mouth, crumbs sticking to his four o'clock shadow. Ullo looked away forgivingly, finding it hard to conceal a smile.

But even more than this foible, another event made Ullo tolerate his gauche, if strict, teacher: the way Mr Kõiv reacted to his answer to the question as to whether he had managed to make out Saussure's train of thought on the subject of language renewal.

Ullo replied through the last mouthful of his last roll: "*Nojaa*. He approaches the matter rather indirectly. But does approach it nonetheless. On page 31 it says, and I quote: *Let us once more read over the characteristics of language: Firstly: language is a well-defined object in a motley collection of well-specified speech facts. It can be placed into this restricted area of the subject matter, where the auditive image begins to be associated with definition. This is the social sphere of speech, beyond the relations of the individual, who cannot create it, nor vary it; because that is to say, language exists only thanks to the conventions of participants.*"

"And what comes next?" asked Mr Kõiv, very attentively.

Ullo interjected: "No individual can create language? I would like to ask: why not? When there is clear proof to the contrary. What kind of proof? That of Dr Zamenhof and his Esperanto!"

"Quite true! Quite true, Berends!" Mr Kõiv cried out excitedly in a semi-falsetto. "Then we will take a stance which is diametrically opposite to that of Saussure!"

Ullo continued: "Or that the individual cannot change language – Saussure uses the verb *modifier*. But again I ask: why not? If we take in any way seriously, say, what our Madame Lüllii – sorry, I mean our Madame Zelkovsky – says about the importance of Boileau. This is more on the stylistic side of things, but still, it can surely be allowed that the individual can modify any given language to a very significant extent as we can see in Johannes Aavik's work on Estonian. Most clearly seen in the case of his morphological and syntactic neologisms . . . ?" For simplicity's sake, let's write out all of what he now said in normal orthography:

Mr Kõiv cried, now not in a half, but full falsetto: "Berends! You're a clever boy! And Saussure is clearly a clever boy too. But in all practical terms his argument doesn't hold water. So that is something we must bring out in our work. I'm grateful to you. Please continue!"

And Ullo continued. Initially, at least, up to the end of the Christmas break. And once school had started again. Not from morn till night as before, naturally. But in such a way that he went straight over to Mr Kõiv's place after school, with double the usual ration of school sandwiches made by his mother, as Mr Kõiv didn't provide any meals. Ullo would stay at Mr Kõiv's until seven or eight in the evening. Or he would take home Mr Kõiv's copy of Saussure (and soon books by several other authors as well), bringing back the noted or translated pages the next day, or the day after, either to Mr Kõiv at home, or to school. The choice of what to translate or make notes on was left more and more to Ullo's discretion.

One evening in mid-January, when Ullo was just about to leave Mr Kõiv's house to take the train home, divide up the evening hours between the work for him and his schoolwork, and have that ready for him the next morning, Mr Kõiv said: "B'rnds. Jst a mmnt."

"Just a moment. You've now been working for me for sixteen days. I think it is time to pay you the first instalment of your first monthly salary. New year, new expenses. Otherwise, your mother might start worrying that Mr Kõiv is trying to shortchange her son . . ." He smiled awkwardly behind the thick lenses of his spectacles and pressed two blue ten-kroon notes and one pink five-kroon one into Ullo's hand. As Ullo had, if the truth be told, been waiting for him to do. When was he finally . . .

Yes, indeed. But then (half a century or more later it still feels as if this was the very next day) Plaks's son or some other lad said to him at school: "Listen, my friend, Kõtsu gave us homework the day before yesterday – what was the subject again?"

Ullo said: "'*The Hunchback of Notre Dame* or Romanticism as exaggeration' . . ."

"That's right, it was," the other boy continued, Plaks or whoever it was. "You've still got a whole month in which to finish it. But remember that I'm your first customer. Otherwise you might say in the end that you haven't got enough ideas to go round for two dozen essays. For your first customer – and a full five kroons – you have to have!"

"OK, agreed –" said Ullo. And grunted more or less the same

message to a second, a third customer, thinking all the while: tomorrow I'll order two fathoms of nice ready-sawn half-metre lengths of birch from the Raudtee Street wood dealer's, so we can keep the fire going until the spring, and Mother won't have to keep on worrying.

But then, on Sunday morning, his mother had cleared the required stretch of street from overnight snow, and received from Ullo, who had woken late, the due reproaches and hugs (and noticing with a start how much of her dark hair had lately turned grey). His mother had gone off somewhere and Ullo had got up and eaten his fill of porridge oats and sat at the table looking out of the window. The pages for Kõiv the next day had been finished the previous evening. His homework for Monday was done, or was manageable in ten minutes under the desk in the scripture lesson. There were still three weeks to go for the essays the boys had ordered. No feeling of being hounded by deadlines, no panic of any kind. And the weather outside – so calm, so clear, so white that on such a blank screen ideas and images must begin to project themselves . . . And project themselves they certainly did: Victor Hugo himself, as Mr Kõiv in his rather cackling way described him – a picture of the author gleaned from God knows where – a small, loud-voiced, theatrical romantic, which in his case meant hyperbole, as Mr Kõiv himself had said. And the mark of Hugo's hyperbole or romanticism: Good and Evil distributed in unequal parts between all the characters from Quasimodo to Esmeralda and Frollo – of course Ullo couldn't waste his best ideas on the Plaks boy. It was not that he felt sorry for him, just that it would have been very dangerous to do so. Mr Kõiv would instantly have seen through what we nowadays would call their alien quality and exposed the fraud in an instant. So Ullo would have to put forward his selected ideas in a much simplified, very primitive manner – but even in such a guise, the ideas resisted their own liberation.

Ullo related: "Yes, you know, *kurat*." *Kurat* was, incidentally, number one in his vocabulary of swear words. And he always pronounced this word very slightly more quietly than the rest of the story, so slightly that it was something I only began to notice years later. Because there were so few occasions on which to observe the phenomenon.

"You know – *kurat* – I had ended up in a particularly awkward situation. Mr Kõiv had bought me – I'm not saying with his bread rolls, but rather with the crumbs thereof, which stuck around his mouth even on days when his face was cleanly shaven – he had bought me with a matter-of-factness that lay within him. I couldn't let him down any more, or pull the wool over his eyes. On average, that was going to cost me as much as he paid me for my help with his Master's, not counting all the fuss I brought down on myself from the boys, when I refused to do their essays for them. First of all, complete incomprehension. Then, bit by bit a kind of understanding which showed itself through their scoffing. Which I tried to get over by way of a, so to speak, soft landing. Instead of whole essays, I would sketch out for them the content, development of themes and arguments. This seemed to me less of a betrayal of Mr Kõiv, compared to full-blown essays, and writing them seemed to be something I could still practise. Especially when I refused to accept money for writing them and also, of course, for any advice . . ."

13

"WITH REGARD TO GIRLS –" Ullo said, in answer to my question – "they entered my life in a problematical way quite late in life.I remember that the sevenths and eighths girls had already begun to interest me with some urgency, but I would still shun them. It seemed to me, well, at least on the Nõmme–Tallinn suburban train, they would giggle about me. I tried to avoid sitting next to them. To sit on a nearby bench with a girl – still at some distance – was something I wanted and even sought to do. While chance touches would almost burn me.

"Well, anyway, it was the same in your day: the field of interest of Wikman boys, with regard to girls, tended to reach out in one direction, or rather, in two – that of the Commercial College and Bürger's Grammar School. I belonged to the first category. Because I had cast eyes on Lia, the pretty sister of my classmate Armin Borm. And she was a Commercial College girl. Hair like in a Titian painting and green eyes, a stunning vision, in my eyes. So when our form had to vote for ballroom dancing-class partners from either the Commercial College, or from Bürger's (such trappings of democracy had been extended to us by Mr Wikman, no longer the case when you, Jaak, were at Wikman's, by which time only partners from Bürger's were considered), I of course voted to dance with the Commercial College classes. But the majority plumped for Bürger girls, and the dancing classes were organised with them. So I dropped out.

"I had to ask Armin's advice – he was, after all, one of my friends in class – whether Lia could go to the school dance with me. Armin scratched his pate and thought that I had better pay a visit to their mother first. Those were the rules of society at the time. If I were to make a good impression on the mother, she would allow Lia to go with

79

me. I remember very much wanting Armin himself to put in a good word for me with her, but said nothing to him.

"So, a visit to Mrs Borm. Ha-ha-ha-haa! Now [i.e. in 1986] my tenacity at the time astonishes me. But for a sixteen-year-old there was simply no other way.

"The story of the Borm family was simply this: the father was at the time an almost odious figure in the eyes of the general public. He had been taken to court while a minister and although he had been exonerated, he had not been reinstated. And had, by the way, left his family. And I have thought that this whiff of scandal associated with his name, and parallel with that of the Berends family (a very relative parallelism, but still), made Lia all the more attractive to me. I say a relative parallelism, since Mr Borm, the father of Lia and Armin, was nevertheless a well-known lawyer and did still pay visits to his family. And of course, something we didn't yet know at the time, there was no comparison in their respective fates – that of my father and Mr Borm, that is. My father remained abroad, Mr Borm, here. My father survived all the subsequent upheavals, though I have no idea of the details. Mr Borm, on the other hand, was invited to visit the NKVD in the autumn of 1940. And, realist that he was, he put a bullet through his head that very same evening.

"So that's how it was. I had taken notice of Mrs Borm before, as she was Lia's mother, and managed to neutralise her idiosyncrasies for myself. Mrs Borm, Lidia Ivanovna, was an exceedingly dynamic woman, weighing some 120 kilos. She was Russian by birth. Educated at the Smolny. A lady by any standards. Who was eminently capable of dealing with a kid like me.

"As you can imagine, I spruced myself up for the occasion. I went to the barber's and gave my shoes a polish. I had arranged my visit in such a way that Mr Kõiv had paid me my dues the previous day. I went along, ears red and with a bunch of red roses in my hand.

"The Borms also lived in Nõmme, in the centre at Old Nõmme, and not far from where we were living. It was an oldish wooden house with a veranda amid a snow-covered garden. Which had once been quite a noble dwelling, but was rather ramshackle by then – as was the social standing of the Borms themselves. There were expensively furnished but poorly heated rooms, those same sunsets by Clever on the wall as we used to have, all much more than was required for three people.

80

"Lidia Ivanovna billowed in, smiling, accompanied by a russet-coated, snot-snouted bulldog.

"'Ahaa. *Ja, jaa*. Of course. But Lia will have to make up her own mind . . .'

"I handed half the roses to the lady of the house, keeping back the rest for the daughter. The mother went out to call her, and I remained standing in the middle of the room looking at myself in the large glass doors of the bookcases. I eyed, with much intolerance, the stripling I saw there with his large Adam's apple, his brow moist with nerves, and would have liked to have hopped from one foot to the other, but my upbringing kept me standing still. The bulldog shambled towards me and guarded me, growling, full of misgivings. Then it began – I don't know what bout of playfulness, or whim, had come over him – to chew at the heel of my left shoe. I tried, not too suddenly, to move my foot from left to right, in order to free my heel from the dog's jaws. But in so doing, I only occasioned a more threatening – or goodness knows, maybe more playful – snarling, and I began to feel the increased pressure of its teeth through my insole . . . Then Lia appeared, quite as flushed as I was, and perhaps even more tongue-tied: Yes – she muttered over the roses which I now handed her – but she would have to think things over. She couldn't agree, just like that, without considering the matter, I would of course understand . . .

"Then her mother came back, shepherded her out, and offered me a seat, so that we could have a little chat, as she put it. Thank God she didn't expect me to proclaim my affection for her daughter, or anything of that sort. She took the reins of the conversation with some firmness and did at least suggest my becoming acquainted with her daughter. Go for strolls with Lia. Take her out to the theatre. Give her the opportunity of deciding for herself whether she wanted to go with me to the dance, or not.

"Good Lord, I had nothing against this proposal. But when I turned up, the following Sunday at ten o'clock in the morning (looking at my watch while still round the corner and waiting seven minutes to avoid arriving too early), two people had come to go with me for our walk: Lia, plus her lanky girlfriend. This irritated me no end. The three of us trudged around what was then Nõmme Park through the snow covered with the pattern of frozen dog prints, and I tried to be as spirited and polite to Lia as ever I could, and to Vanda, or whatever her name was – well, not as impolite as I could, but giving her a clear feeling of superfluity. But she didn't take the hint and, what was worse – nor did Lia. Simply announced, as we parted, that we would be going to see Anton Rubinstein's opera *The Demon* at the theatre on Friday evening as a threesome. I was given no room for protest, and the girls just slipped in through the house door, leaving me standing on the snowy steps.

"By the way [this question was addressed to me by Ullo]: have you over the years managed to gather why girls behave in this manner? I have to admit that I have not, I still don't know to this day. I can only speculate, but thinking on it, any explanation would seem foolish. If it is a game on the part of the girls, which would have to mean that they were not interested in prospective advances from the boy – why waste their own and their girlfriend's time?! Let alone my own! But if it were in fear of any advances by the boy, these actions being an attempt to procrastinate, an attempt to save themselves from them – why do girls allow themselves to get into situations which cause them fear in the first place?"

At this point I remarked: "Ullo, it's always a bit of both, both game and fear, in ever changing proportions . . ."

Upon which, he replied: "You know, I understand both games and fear. But one element ought at least to be the dominant factor. Let us say the game takes the upper hand, but with a fleeting, enriching, tinge of fear. So that you can suddenly feel: maybe fear is in fact the principal spur? Or then, fear is dominant – with a nuance of play – so that you don't quite know if the game actually dominates? But the way Lia played it – flatly, greyly, fifty-fifty – that is tiresome.

"But Lia was not irredeemable, as she managed to prove. When, after lunch on the Friday, I saw her on her own and explained that I only had two tickets (in order to get rid of Vanda I was even prepared to use the excuse that I simply didn't have the money; nor would this have been far from the truth), she said with her Mona Lisa smile that she agreed for just the two of us to go. And when I arrived at their house, she said quite calmly that Vanda had turned up in the meantime, and that she had sent her away. Lia had made great efforts to do herself up, looking blindingly beautiful to my eyes.

"If you were to ask how they sang in *The Demon* that evening, I have to admit: I can't remember. Nor, for that matter, who played in

Raudsepp's *Salon and Cell* which we went to see that same week before the school dance. Not even who sang in *Tristan and Isolde*, which we saw on the eve of the dance. Each time, without her lanky girlfriend. Each time, just the two of us. Each time, in her striking *Aufmachung*, and as sweet as sweet could be. Sweet, especially after the interval of *The Demon* when we took a walk from our places on the fifth row, out into the aisle, past the first orchestra pit, and shook hands with Raimund Kull over the balustrade, flourishing his sweaty paw – as he himself put it – 'Hello, Ullo! Well, what's new? How's Mrs Berends getting on?' And me pressing his hand and introducing Lia. 'This is Lead Conductor Raimund Kull – and this is Miss Lia Borm.' Whereupon the lead conductor cried: 'You mean the daughter of Ferdinand Borm? Really? Just look at what a beauty she is!' And he kissed the schoolgirl's hand with its gold filigree ring.

"And so to the school dance. But I'm not going to say much about that. The whole Lia business grew to be too long a part of my life as it is. But the school dance was entirely *comme il faut*. Lia seemed of a slenderness and brilliance that far outshone the other girls: her dazzling auburn hair and her olive-green dress, an evening dress, of course. And her figure – mmm. So not only Ambel, but even old Wikman, danced with her.

"Afterwards – I'll be brief – I started going regularly to the Borms' house. Perhaps too regularly. And began being too clever with it. For one day a rival appeared: a red-cheeked, thickset type, a research student with a face like a farmer. Then it began to happen that when I turned up at their house, Lia would sometimes be out skiing with this research student. Ah well, maybe I wasn't resolute enough on those occasions to get up and leave. I don't know whether it was when she began to notice what was happening, or through her own choice, that Mrs Borm would keep me company. For instance, she had me expand on Russian literature – of which I had a pretty superficial knowledge. Mrs Borm talked of my intellectual kinship with Pechorin – and while the lady was conversing with me, with me trying of course to be as spirited as I could, at a remove of some seven metres, Lia and her research student might be conducting their own conversation. Lia's behaviour was irritating, but I did not manage to give her an ulti-matum: either August the research student – or me. And to an extent, Lia's mother was a crucial support to me in this matter. For I felt that in her own gentle and sociable way, she was keeping me in the family orbit. Or perhaps it was so that she could, time after time – when Lia had gone out with August yet again – play cards with me in front of the stove, usually *viissada*, which I nearly always won.

"Of course I did, now and again, manage to see Lia alone. Especially after she had forced me to accede to a number of agreements, for example, that I only kiss her arm, and then not higher than the hollow of her elbow.

"I tried not to think what she may have been allowing August to do at the same time. Until the spring of 1934, I used to go along to the Borms' in a kind of somnambulist daze, and even felt a measure of relief as the burden of Mr Kõiv's assignments became ever more pressing, and my final examinations at Wikman's began to draw near.

"It was the custom to dress up a little more than usual for the exams and I remember examining the patches worn shiny on my only suit, too dark for that sunny day in late May, and especially the area around my trouser seat, but trying to conceal this from my mother who couldn't have remedied the matter anyway. And when I tried on my only white shirt of a more formal cut, it emerged that it had become awfully tight round the shoulders, too short at the cuffs, and the collar was too small. So I hung it back on the hanger and put on a looser polo-neck shirt instead. The top came over the top of the jacket collar. And so off I went, orange polo-neck above the jacket lapels, to the maths exam, my heart touched slightly by my proletarian appearance – despite my feelings of superiority with regard to Mammon. At the exam I received a formula for combination maths and I do not remember for what I effortlessly gained my five, then I walked out towards the station along Hommiku Street, and took the train out to the Borms' place. Knowing, of course, that my exam result would neither impress nor overwhelm anyone there. It was I myself who was overwhelmed. Because instead of Armin, or Mrs Borm, or Lia, a completely unknown young lady opened the door. Or, not entirely unknown. I had seen her flash by somewhere before. But I had not known her name or spoken one word to her . . .

"Ruta Borm. A close relation of the family: Lia's cousin, a student at some theatre studio or other, she had started to become rather visible in small roles recently at the Workers' Theatre. A girl from the same genetic stock as Lia, so to speak, and yet completely different from her.

Firstly, not by any means as impressive as Lia. And not, of course, as pretty. At least that's how it struck me then. But quite a nice girl, nonetheless. As I started to notice fairly soon. With lithe movements. Small, almost tiny in stature. But in no way skinny, simply of nice womanly proportions. There was a certain dignity in her languid movements. Unfortunately, she was rather lacking in bold colours: her hair was an ashen blonde, with a slight auburn tinge. Her eyes, a light amber, but beautiful, large, oval. Her eyelashes were a little too lacking in prominence. But her mouth was small, well proportioned, almond-shaped. And the way she used it, chopping up words into particularly small units, was sur-pri-sing. Very unassertive. Not at all snappy. Quiet. Friendly. Precise.

"That afternoon of our first acquaintance, at the tea table, Lia mentioned a play which was running at the Estonia – 'evidently some Polish play or other called *Pan Joll*'. Upon which I corrected her almost in a whisper, out of sheer sympathy: 'Lia – the play you're referring to is *Les marchands de gloire*. And its author is the Frenchman, Pagnol. Marcel Pagnol . . .' To which Lia had replied: 'Ah, maybe you're right . . .' and changed the subject. But Ruta had said quietly but audibly, and it has always stuck in my memory: 'Ullo – you shouldn't lay on the general knowledge too thickly in front of Lia. Lia herself does so, but in different matters. Perfumes, for instance . . .'

"And I thought, for an instant: What's this now? Pure chance? Or is this damned girl deliberately allowing herself such an almost frivolous joke? If so, then I am in danger of falling in love with her. And as regards perfumes: her own fleeting honeysuckle was, of course, more moderate than Lia's eternal Soir de Paris.

"And I noticed that Ruta began to drop in on the Borms more often. At our next encounter, one rainy June evening, she rose from the table – Lia, August and Armin remaining seated – wanting to go home that very instant.

"'Armin,' she said, 'find a man's umbrella – Lia, if you will allow, Ullo is going to walk me home . . .'

"Lia, sitting next to Armin on the basket sofa said, well, not in the most tactful of tones: 'Goodness gracious – he's free to do what he likes, isn't he? Whether he takes you home, or round the back of the house . . .'

"They bustled about and fussed a bit looking for the umbrella,

85

because Armin certainly did not possess such an old man's appurtenance. In the end, they found their father's, ex-minister Borm's, old brolly and I walked Ruta home in its shelter, through the showers of the summer night. Mother Borm had draped Ruta's shoulders with some kind of jacket against the cold and I made sure it did not slip off. I got to know where she lived: at her parents' house, a kilometre away from the Borms', out Männiku way. But I made no attempt to kiss her in the porch, nor did I ask if I could come in. Because I had already realised: this is going to work, work, work. Everything's working extremely well.

"Six months later, in the late winter of '34, when everything had indeed worked, Ruta reminded me:

"'Do you remember that evening when you took me home under Mr Borm's umbrella?'

"'But of course! What of it?'

"'That evening, when Lia and I were looking for that umbrella at the Borms', I said to her: "If you carry on treating that boy the way you're doing now, I'll pinch him from you."'"

14

I DIDN'T HAVE TO RELY solely on Ullo's stories with regard to Ruta, since she is, or was, one of his girls I remember meeting.

In the spring of 1935, Ullo was still living with his mother in Nõmme, at the market garden on Jaama Street. I, Jaak Sirkel, was living with my parents in Kalamaja, in various houses belonging to the Vöölmann factory where the white-collar workers lived. By now, Ullo had been working for about a year as an editor for the *Sports Encyclopaedia*, and I had just done my school-leaving exams in the eighth form at Wikman's, a couple of weeks earlier. And I was living with my mother and father, mostly my mother, with my father in so far as he could get away from work during holiday periods, when we were staying in our summer flat out of town. No longer in the house on Purde Street in Nõmme where I had spent the first ten or twelve impressionable summers of my life, for that house had been sold.

I remember how my mother accused my father, on occasion, of groundless optimism. And maybe there was a grain of truth in this accusation. Because I also remember how my father would argue: Imagine me at the front (he had never been there himself, and had he been things would have ended up differently from how he described them). I'm at the front, and they're shooting at me. Why should the bullet hit just me when there is *so* much room for it to miss . . . ?

So Father was an optimist in matters of destiny. But with regard to the financial security for himself, or for his wife and son, it has to be said that he was a sober realist. I do not believe that his suspicions in this area were exaggerated; I don't think he ever exaggerated in a downward direction. But he said: The Vöölmann factory is a private company, and I never have had, or will have, any guarantee that they, or their descendants, will trouble themselves about me for the sake of my wife and child. So I have to fend for myself. As long as I possibly can.

In the early 1930s, my father began to build a largish block of flats in Tallinn, the rental income from which was intended to instil in him the confidence that he was coping. But the money saved from his salary made this an enterprise of rather pinched proportions. To free money for his project, Father sold our house on Purde Street, and we became summer nomads, who lived one summer here, another there, but always somewhere in the vicinity of Tallinn, if at all possible. So that Father could come out after work during the holidays.

In 1935, we had rented a summer flat in Rannamõisa. For my parents, the area was associated with some summer during the early years of the First World War, but the building in which we were now staying was new to them.

It was a four-roomed affair, a wooden house painted green, with a veranda and kitchen, and surrounded by a low limestone wall, amid scrubland and forest. The house was a few dozen steps to the left of the road out to Tabasalu, a few hundred paces from the steps, cut into the limestone, down the cliffs on to the beach.

It would not be worth the reader's while trying to locate the house from this description. It was pulled down several decades ago in Soviet times, when they wanted to extend Ranna Sovkhoz, to grow more flax.

We lived there, the four of us: Father, who at least came out on the bus, or in our old green Ford, at weekends; Mother, who had puffed at cigarettes for a whole week previously against the midges (although she didn't normally smoke), would leaf through novels such as Semper's *On Jealousy*, or Colette's *Duo* which was much heavier stuff, or Goethe's *Wilhelm Meister* – of course more famous than either of the previous two; then there was me. What I spent my time doing during that first Rannamõisa summer I really can't recall. We stayed at that same house again in 1937, when I remember writing my very first and no doubt last, political satire in my life. It was never published, then or later, and was aimed at the prime minister of the time, Eenpalu, whose public servant at large Ullo had maybe managed to become by that time. In the same house lived a, well, in my eyes at the time, almost a middle-aged woman, a damsel who had reached the ripe age of her mid-twenties, and who went by the name of Ella. She was our maid at the time, whose walks along the beach at weekends with the man she was courting, a sausage-maker, were condemned by my mother, while she nonetheless tried to conceal her maid's goings-on from Father. This was out of fear that my father might too categorically forbid such jaunts, or (and this would seem more plausible) would not, on hearing of them, condemn them nearly strongly enough.

Anyway, in 1935, on the second Sunday morning of our sojourn out there at Rannamõisa, I woke very early. Through the green of the lime trees and the black of the firs, I saw the blue sky with its patches of white cloud, saw from the clock next to my bed that it was a quarter to seven, and marvelled at the fact that I had woken up so early. There were no sounds coming from the direction of the kitchen, not yet the hiss of the Primus as Ella boiled water for the morning coffee.

Then I noticed through the net curtains what I had first taken to be the familiar shape of a vase, if positioned rather oddly, but turned out to be something quite different. It was Ullo's grinning face. He had pushed his sharp-chinned head through the open window and, with a lightly cross-eyed gaze, was resting it on the window sill. I asked, in a whisper: "Ullo! What are you doing hanging around here in the middle of the night?"

He smiled ironically and answered in a normal voice, which resounded exceptionally loudly in the room (Ullo was usually rather quietly spoken): "I was trying to see whether it would be possible to wake you just by watching you. It was. And easy, too."

I said, now in a half-whisper: "Speak quieter. They're all still sleeping. And climb in through the window, will you?"

He said: "No. Not now. Besides, there are two of us out here. Stick your nose out and take a look for yourself."

My bed was right under the window. I had raised myself on my elbows. When I looked out over the low window sill, someone's head rose to meet me, a metre to the left of Ullo's face. The head of a complete stranger. A girl. Ullo put one of his paws round my neck, the other round the girl's and brought our foreheads together over the window sill:

"Bump. Well, the introductions have been made. This is Jaak. Who I've spoken about. And this is Ruta. Who I probably haven't."

The girl's reddish-blonde hair, her large yellowish-brown eyes, her bared white laughing teeth and her faint scent of lilac withdrew, and Ullo then said: "Here you are, Jaak, take our rucksack inside for safekeeping. We're bourgeois enough to have even brought one. So we

89

can pop down to the sea. By the way – Ruta and I have got three kroons between us. But we would be most grateful if the household here would be so kind as to offer us a cup of morning coffee after we've had our dip. At what time is coffee usually served?"

I said: "On Sundays – at nine."

"*OK!*" said Ullo, as I looked at the gorgeously bronzed Ruta, sitting there under the window among the lilac bushes. I looked – and couldn't tear my eyes away from her attire or, rather, her state of undress. For she was wearing little more than the briefest of brief lilac-coloured bathing costumes.

Ullo said, in my direction: "Just one more thing," and then to Ruta: "Wait a minute, I'll give him the poem." And she said, laughing: "Give it to him, by all means. I'll wait. I'm *lilacking* around in the lilacs for a bit." And I thought: Well, I'll be damned. What a girl – *lilacking* around . . .

At that moment, Ullo stretched out his bare and hairy leg – he was in shorts – and I got a closer look at the contraption he had attached to his shin. It was a leather tube, about fifty centimetres long and four or five centimetres thick, which had a base to it, and which was closed by a flap with a press stud. It was clearly a piece of his own handiwork. It was attached to his leg by two straps, the lower one made of leather, the upper one made of garter elastic. Ullo opened the flap and pulled out of the tube a neatly rolled sheet of paper.

"Read it – while we go for a swim. Comments afterwards."

I cast a glance at the paper. It had been neatly typed out ("Well, of course. You too have got a typewriter in the office . . .") and looked like an inverted pagoda. I slipped it under the green paper table cover and gave him a slight, conspiratorial nod. And felt how such expressions of confidence affected me. He was, after all, someone who had finished school, someone about to enter university, and a real poet, though he had, admittedly, never published a line of verse – and he expected me to comment on his verse. I thought to myself – only a friend would show me such appreciation.

I informed my parents that Ullo would be joining us for breakfast. Father yawned: "Oh, you mean your friend Berends . . ." and I said: "That's right. And there'll be a girl coming too – Ruta Borm, Ferdinand's niece, a friend of Ullo's."

"That Ferdinand Borm's just a speculator," said my mother quite categorically, so I could not resist replying: "But his brother need not be. Even less so his brother's daughter . . ."

And so they came to breakfast. And my worst misgivings were proved right to 100, even 150, per cent. Ullo was quite *comme il faut* in his brief shorts and sandals and a sober enough shirt. But as I had feared all along, Ruta was not wearing one stitch more than when I had seen her sitting outside the window. And her hair was tousled and wet. She may still have had drops of water on her face and skin. But her lilac bathing costume – well, as was the case in those days, it covered a little more than what now passes for fashion, which exposes the wearer's hips more or less up to her armpits, but for those days it was as skimpy as skimpy can be – was only a little wet here and there, most of it being still quite dry. Ruta was also barefoot and had bright pink lacquered toenails.

Father pursed his lips and raised his eyebrows – with an element of moderation nonetheless – over his spectacles and waited for an introduction on Ullo's part. And the latter said no more than "Miss Ruta Borm . . ."

Father said: "I see. Well, please take a seat."

Mother stiffened visibly and uttered as the two of them sat down at the table: "Isn't the young lady feeling cold – in that attire? Maybe I could give her something to cover her shoulders with?"

"Oh, don't bother!" said Ruta brightly. "When you come straight from the sea you feel so warm . . ."

Mother asked: "Ah, straight from the sea? How did your bathing costume manage to dry so quickly?"

"Oh, Mrs Sirkel, it never really got wet," replied Ruta airily. "Because we bathed in the nude – after all, there's not a soul about on the whole beach."

"And what field of activities does the young lady engage in?" asked Father a little hastily, perhaps to forestall any response from my mother.

Ruta said: "The theatre . . ."

"Aha. The theatre. Well, that explains it . . ." posited my father, breaking off his sentence, hopefully before anyone had interpreted what he was getting at. But I had. He was simply suggesting something like "if it's the theatre, then, my child, you can of course allow yourself to bathe in the nude – in the theatre, anything goes".

"And you," said Father, now turning to Ullo, "you work as an editor at the *Sports Encyclopaedia* . . .? As Jaak has told me."

And Ullo said: "Yes, I do. Six months I've been there now."

Father eyed Ullo's sinewy, if rather lanky frame with scepticism. Not with any great scepticism, but still. Because like the rest of his generation my father had had much more direct contact with sport, i.e. the generation of wrestlers such as Lurich and Aberg and all the others of their age. And he had retained the trimness of someone who used to practise sports regularly. And he now asked (and I rather regretted he didn't ask, for instance: "And what have you written poems about lately?"): "And what type of sport are you best at?"

Ullo replied with a smile that was almost a laugh: "I'm in no way active in sport myself. I'm only interested in sport – a bit, anyway."

Whereupon Ruta explained, sipping her coffee, which Mother had poured out for her with a forgiving nod: "He works at the editorial office as their card index . . ."

"Well, they've actually got a card index . . ." corrected Ullo.

"Yes, they have," explained Ruta, "but it's far from well organised. So it's much simpler – for Messrs Laudsepp and Karu and whoever else there is – not to go rummaging around in the card index but ask you instead." She turned to Father. "And he tells them – where and when Kolmpere or Uuk or Erikson were born and in what year they heaved, or lifted or pushed or flung."

"And he can keep all those facts in his head?"

"Yes!" confirmed Ruta with ardour – "And lots more stuff like it, by the kilo!"

But now Ruta had pushed Ullo into a dubious region of conversation or, hopefully, what was in fact for him the most thankful of regions. For this same stuff, well, not by the kilo perhaps, but quite a few grams of it, had managed to nestle between my father's ears too. He wasn't exactly the card index of some sports encyclopaedia. But he was capable of remembering what kind of javelin result it was, and the date, when Gustav Sule began to draw people's attention, and the result (though this, I think, came some time after that breakfast) with which Villberg broke the world record in rifle shooting in Lucerne. And he possessed a certain schoolmasterly tendency to check people's surprising knowledge before believing it, a trait I had noticed in him from an early age. So now it was Ullo's turn to be hammered on the last.

"Listen, young Master Berends – where better to freshen up my memory about some small forgotten facts than when the *Sports Encyclopaedia* card index happens to be sitting at our breakfast table? Tell me, how many points did that Kolmpere get when he broke the record in the decathlon for the second time? I seem to remember 8,100, but by how many points did he win? By how many?"

"By forty-seven," said Ullo.

"Very good!" praised my father. "But do you happen to remember the details – in what sports and what were the specific results?"

"Well," said Ullo, "that I should know – it was the only Estonian world record ever in track events, up to now at least . . . But do you want the results using the 1912 or 1934 system?"

"Let's say the 1912 one. And if you will allow, I'll write them down . . ."

Father took a sheet of paper and a pencil – to tell you the truth his seriousness in this matter rather surprised me – and started writing down what Ullo said.

"Let's start with running. The hundred metres – 12.3 in 1922 when the world record had been 10.4. That gave him 787 points. The four hundred metres. Kolmpere's time was 55.0 seconds. The world record at the time was, by the way, 47.4. Kolmpere gained 751 points with his 55.0."

I shan't bother to list all Kolmpere's records, as Ullo did that morning. Besides, I'd have to look up all the numbers in old newspapers, because I don't exactly remember them that well, neither the earlier nor ones from recent times, and certainly not all the numbers from that strange morning.

I do remember Father then asking: "You're supposed to be interested in chess. Jaak told me. What position do you reckon Estonia will come in Warsaw?" (The following week, the chess Olympics were beginning in that city.)

Ullo said, without even pausing to think: "In tenth or eleventh place, regarding the team as a whole. But Keres could be among the first five."

"Do you really think so?" asked Father. "He's so terribly young . . ."

"Almost one whole year older than I am," said Ullo, in a tone of voice which implied that one extra year was a perfectly adequate guarantee for coming fifth in the world championships.

We rose from the table. Ullo and Ruta excused themselves politely for crashing in on us and thanked my parents for the coffee. Mother suggested coolly that they might stay for lunch if they wished, but they politely declined. Ullo picked up their rucksack and said to me: "If you haven't got anything better to do, come along with us. We're going for a short walk, and you could show us the sights. If there are any, that is."

We strolled through the pine woods for an hour or two, in the vicinity of the old villas, up along the cliffs and down along the shore. We shouted into some dark grottos near the water which in those days were still intact. Then they said they were going for another swim and disappeared from view. I lay on the grass among the limestone slabs and waited for them, my head resting on their rucksack. They were gone for what seemed an age. When they returned, their faces and hair were wet and so too was Ruta's bathing costume this time. But something in them had changed. Their movements were more measured, yet freer than before – so I immediately knew, well, guessed, but that still counted as knowing: somewhere in the bushes they had been doing *it*. It – for which there didn't in those days exist a commonplace, but neutral, word, there were only vulgar ones, euphemisms and scientific terms. When I walked with them down the Vääna Road, so they could walk the other four kilometres to the station, where they would catch the narrow-gauge train at three o'clock, they were in no hurry, Ullo's long strides in step with Ruta's short paces, holding hands, arms round one another's shoulders. And I walked alongside them and thought, almost holding my breath, that they had been doing *it*.

We stopped at the bend in the road, and I suddenly remembered: I still hadn't managed to read Ullo's poem. Nor had he brought up the matter again, whether out of tact or pride.

"Listen –" I said – "I haven't had a chance to read Ullo's poem. If we sit down here on the stone wall, he'd have time to recite it. But I still wouldn't have time to make any comment on it. Because I won't be able to concentrate. What with those blasted curlews with their cries, and the rustling of the leaves and the shadows and the sun. You understand – I'll read it at home. And I'll write to you about it."

Ullo nodded. Ruta held out her hand. She was still only wearing her lilac-coloured bathing costume. Admittedly she was no longer barefoot and was now wearing a pair of thonged sandals. But the pink-lacquered toenails still peeped out from between the thongs.

94

Even now I can remember a few of the comments made about their visit. My mother said:

"That Ullo has at least learnt something. How not to overstay his welcome. But his girlfriend is simply scandalous!"

"Well, perhaps not as scandalous as you make her out to be," Father suggested. "Now that naturists are officially recognised over here."

"They're quite welcome to go around among themselves in the nude," my mother asserted, "there, I would have no objections. But that young miss came to my coffee table almost in her birthday suit, where she knew, or should have at least, that I am from another generation and very likely have a completely different way of thinking too. And that young miss merely spat on all that. Her behaviour was simply scandalous!"

I said: "Mother, Maurois says in one of his books that Shelley and his wife and, I believe, Byron, often went around together completely naked."

Mother said: "Well, I'm neither Shelley nor Byron. And as you said: went around together. That young lady was on completely foreign territory."

I cried: "But Shelley and Byron were doing so 120 years ago! After all that time, in everyday circles they would–"

Mother cut me short: "My dear boy –" when she spoke to me like that, I must really have got on her nerves – "My dear boy – if Shelley and Byron were great poets, then, believe me, this was not *thanks* to the fact that they went around in their bare bottoms down by the seashore, but *despite* the fact. And you young people, if you're going to get anywhere with your poetry or drama, like that young lady is trying to do, then you'd better take that into account."

When Father came out to Rannamõisa the following weekend, he said: "By the way, that Ullo, whose girlfriend behaved so scandalously in the eyes of your mother – such things are, of course, quite relative – that Ullo, it's quite believable that he could be acting as the card index for the *Sports Encyclopaedia*. He threw out various statistics. I wrote down forty-three of them and had them checked. I've got a friend who works in the office at the Kalev sports club. All forty-three of them were – my God – perfectly correct."

Mother asked: "Does that mean that you're trying to excuse that young chit's behaviour because her boyfriend happens to be clever?"

Father grinned from behind his little gingery stump of a moustache: "Well, think it over. Maybe you can . . ."

Mother said, in an almost conciliatory tone, but ironically nevertheless: "OK. If you wish, I'll think it over."

15

I DO NOT REMEMBER EVER writing to Ullo about the poem he gave me at Rannamõisa, even though I had promised I would. And even though the time when I could, and might have done so (and maybe should have done so), was five whole years before that epoch which made us lose familiarity with writing letters for some generations to come. And this went for the majority of the members of those generations, I would imagine. For me, at least. For one self-evident reason: when writing letters in those days, one had to always know of, or at least reckon with, the possibility that the addressee of the letter would not necessarily be the first person to actually read it.

In the same way, although I hailed from the most coastal suburb of Tallinn and the harbour area there, I, like the rest of the local populace, was ultimately cut off from the sea by barbed-wire entanglements and monolingually alien guards. And just as I had turned my back on the sea, with feelings of suffocation, and maybe a few tearful glances over my shoulder – so too, as censorship was introduced, I desisted from sending private letters. Not absolutely 100 per cent of the time. But anything up to 90.

However, Ullo's poem and my promise to send him a letter about it stems from the five years prior to what I have just described, and was a time of joyful letter-writing. Even I, who didn't care much for the fine art of correspondence, went and joined the World Correspondence Club run by New York schoolboys. Five years later, I destroyed the membership card. I had kept it up to then, but all desire to preserve it had vanished under the changed circumstances. Keeping the card could, given the paranoia of the powers that be at that time, become dangerous in itself. So I ripped the pale green shiny cardboard WCC membership card into tiny pieces and flushed them down the WC, on one of those evenings when rumours of house-to-house searches and arrests were circulating.

Before telling about Ullo's "Minaret Poem", as I think I christened it at the time, I ought to speak about his poem writing as a whole. For some longish while, this activity was one of the channels he had for achievement and which remained unachieved.

I can form no systematic picture of his attitudes towards world poetry, nor do I have a clue about the development of such interests. For when I call to mind specific authors and their works that came up during our conversations, I cannot remember their order of mention. But the period involved is, at any rate, from about 1935 to 1940.

I do remember that among the German poets he talked of Rilke and brought me the *Stundenbuch* to read; and several passages have stuck in my mind. For instance:

> *Sein Blick ist vom Vorübergehn der Stäbe*
> *so müd geworden, dass er nichts mehr hält.*
> *Ihm ist, als ob es tausend Stäbe gäbe*
> *und hinter tausend Stäben keine Welt.*

Be that as it may: apart from appreciating Rilke, he admitted to greatly enjoying Morgenstern. Among the French, it was the trio Baudelaire, Rimbaud and Verlaine, the second of whom afforded Ullo special interest, perhaps on account of his strikingly young age. I remember Ullo commenting one day: "It's depressing to think that if I were to live according to his lifespan, I would by now have written all my poetry. All that there would be left to do would be to become an ivory dealer or a tramp or basket weaver or whatever . . ."

With regard to poetry written in the English language, Edgar Allan Poe deserves special mention. Around 1935–6, one of my WCC pen pals sent me the first volume of Poe's selected works. I seem to remember trying to send him some Estonian work in exchange, but it turned out that no such work existed in English. In the end, I found the next best thing, which was the Finnish woman writer Aino Kallas's small collection of stories, *The White Ship: Estonian Tales*, with a foreword by Galsworthy. So I sent that. But to return to Poe and Ullo: in that first Poe volume, I found poems including, of course, "The

Raven", and the essay "The Philosophy of Composition". I read both and then gave the book to Ullo to read.

With regard to "The Raven", we both posited that Aavik's and Oras's separate translations, when compared to the fluent elegance of the original, were hopelessly bad. Aavik's being even more clumsy than that of Oras. Ullo, being just that bit older than me, was also just that bit less of a maximalist. But in this matter – and others touching on poetry – it was him who was the maximalist of us two. I remember talking about the original of "The Raven" (in my room while still a schoolboy, in my parents' place, in the Vöölmann workers' block) and how he became strangely excited, jumped to his feet and expounded, while pacing back and forth, gesticulating: it was a tower built up of fifteen (there were that many six-lined verses) carved ebony pavilions, stacked one upon the other. And "The Philosophy of Composition" was no essay on the psychology of creative endeavour, but a pure thriller in logic.

"Ever read Poe's story 'The Murders at the Rue Morgue'?" he asked. At that time, I hadn't.

Ullo explained: "Well, this murder takes place on the fourth floor. The door is locked, but there is an open window. There are no marks on the wall underneath, or on the ground below. But a clever French detective concludes, and proves this through additional discoveries, that the only possible way the murder could have been committed was by the murderer scaling the flagpole some three or four metres from the window. Therefore, any murderer who could leap that distance on to the window sill of the room could not be human. It had to be an ape."

Ullo explained that Poe's poem and his short story were two structural versions on one and the same theme, the difference being that what is revealed only at the end of the detective story is present right from the start in the poem. What proves impossible from a human point of view is executed by an orang-utan in the story, a raven in the poem. One of these has some communication with human beings. In as much as it possesses evil curiosity with regard to humans. The other has learnt a fateful word in human language. So that it repeats, without getting to the point of idiocy, the word *nevermore*. The vertical axis is fateful in both works: in the story when the orang-utan whizzes down from the flagpole, in the poem as the refrain in building the tower – to the heights of despair.

99

And in general, as Ullo went on to explain in his excitement, a state I very rarely saw him in: reality is said to be that clay from which a poem is born, but at the same time it is the violator of the poem, par excellence. Also that portion of reality which coalesces in the notion of gravitation of reason. Under its influence has come the habitual direction: writing the poem downwards. But by its very nature, it should be written from the bottom upwards! The resolution, the catharsis, the summit can only be placed in the opposite direction of gravitation, i.e. weight. Like Poe's "The Raven", when you can at first think the opposite, but in the end it turns out that way. Which, Ullo added, is accentuated by the magic numbers, fifteen and six – fifteen verses of six lines apiece. When I asked what the relation was here, he directed his gaze, which had been fixed on the roofs of the houses opposite, back into the room, looked absent-mindedly at me and said: "Ah, I can't be bothered to explain that just now . . ."

But I must bother to say a little about Ullo's own poetic endeavours, in as much as I know anything about them. And although I am broadly unacquainted with his production. In fact, I have only seen a very limited number of his works.

I have seen four or five sonnets, not in the English style, of course, but in the boundlessly polished rhyme the Italians have. And a dozen or so poems, very strict in form as regards rhyme and rhythm, where the author has voluntarily placed strictures so as to produce complex strophes. I have seen three or four longer poems of varying lengths, written as an attempt at epic, on exotic historical subjects. One of these reminds me, maybe quite by chance, of the beginning of Wieland's "Oberon". But these were fragmentary and would, if I had known Uku Masing's poetry at the time, with its trips in time and space, have reminded me in a dreamlike way of some of those, despite the fact that Ullo, in those days and later on too, tended to adopt an entirely a-religious point of departure.

Of Ullo's completed poems, I only have two. One, on flags, which I will describe later, and the aforementioned "Minaret Poem". This being the very same text as was housed in Ullo's strange leather holder out at Rannamõisa. Which was pushed under the green paper table cover and read that same evening. The same sheet of paper, then white, now a faded yellow. Under the pressure of chance and con-tradiction, nostalgia and piety, ridicule and pity, but no doubt out of admiration, I have kept that yellowed sheet of paper, never even having folded it. It is a sheet, as I said above, with a poem set out rather like an inverted pagoda in what is now faded typewriting. Here it is:

To the top of a minaret striving
at the sky's edge hovering
with dawn's golden
flag flaming
a young mullah beholden
came in days olden
in faith to pray

The scales had just fallen from his soul
when a tinkling voice bade him behold
down there espy
a roof garden low
a gentle cry
uttered by
a voice melting away

The boy forgot his Kaaba and Mecca
and cried his prayer confused in ardour:
My love's strain knows
no bounds, Rebecca!
An angel tongue
his soul
has given a lick!

A storm then raged down from the mountains
The gate of wrath flung open
in his ship of cloud
Allah heard this
and the heavens
the winds of holy anger
did cause to rage!

"Death, punish, punish, punish that traitor!"
Death ripped at him with golden chains,

the boy was dragged by the storm
down from the minaret
as head
over heels
from the tree a whirling date!

His saviour was the merciful Astarte
She knew the coryphee in artem
all the ways of magic things
with her arms
a huge silk sling
a swing
rushed from the moon him to save!

The lad recovered in Rebecca's rose garden
due to Astarte's loud laughter: "You glutton!
Now you see what you get! You'd better
learn: in the wide world open
it's only from
mortal women
that you can expect faithful love!"

I have, incidentally, had the feeling right up to the present (and I am perhaps more convinced now than ever before) that in the poem there glimmers some of Ullo's general attitude to poetry and also to attitudes noticed in works by authors he mentioned. Or, let us say, ones he listed as vertically important: a movement vertically upwards towards prayer and the downward thrust of the tempest meted out by a vengeful Allah. And instead of the magical combination of six with fifteen, Ullo's poem sports seven times seven. Instead of the tower carved out of black wood, with which Ullo compared the six-lined verses of Poe's "The Raven", Ullo built a minaret – or rather a pagoda – a reverse tower of white elements. At any rate, not out of elements turned on a lathe, as Ullo in his somewhat youthful arrogance characterised Poe's verses. By the way, with regard to the lines with equivalent lengths, the verb "turned" is more useful in the case of poems whose lines are of unequal length. Such verses – and in Ullo's poem the line lengths varied between eleven syllables and two – could better be described as carvings. Let us admit – the poem hardly possesses any profundity of content. But as a carved sculpture it is in a class of its own – a sculpture in ivory made by a boy, hidden in among imaginary landscapes of Alver's *Tolm ja tuli* and similar. A promising work, at any rate.

16

M Y NOTES ATTEST THE fact that Ullo told me the
following: in the summer of 1935, he left the *Sports
Encyclopaedia* and went to do his military service. He went
without enthusiasm, but it was unavoidable. He had to get that
troublesome year out of the way. He was lucky enough to be assigned
to the engineers' battalion whose barracks happened to be in Nõmme,
only a kilometre or so from his home, which meant that as late autumn
was approaching with its snow-clearing duties, he could pop home
from time to time and assist his mother.

I can imagine that Ullo rallied to the call – surprising not least
himself – and resigned himself to the state of affairs, that is to say, he
avoided most conflicts: he simply did not take heed of the dull-witted
irony of the country lads on account of the extraordinary length of his
neck, but when others were the butt of jokes, he would laugh along
with the rest. He was flexible, adaptable, accommodating. He would
jump to attention, shouting: "Yessir, Mr Corporal, sir! My duty, sir!"
and go off to clean the latrines. But he found a predestined form of
intellectual relaxation in conversations with fellow soldier Naum
Mandel.

Naum was some ten years older than Ullo and was doing his military
service so late in life because, being the son of a rich lawyer, he had
spent several years studying at various universities throughout Europe,
most recently Vienna, where he had read philosophy, history and some
other subjects. Now, having returned to Estonia, he was forced to
carry out his constitutional duty, which he did, except that in being a
Jewish citizen of the world at large, he did so with even more
scepticism than Ullo. At any rate, this thick-necked, round-faced
Private Naum Mandel discovered a pleasant surprise in the barracks,
in the canteen and when square-bashing, in this beanpole of a lad who

spoke French and German better than he did, and was no worse than him at English, and knew about those German Expressionists, and the Jews of Prague and Vienna, all those Meyrinks and Wassermanns – hardly yet Kafka – almost as well as he himself did. But their acquaintance never developed beyond a kind of mutual sympathy. Ullo explained:

"I've noticed it on several occasions since: close personal contact between Jews and Gentiles is hardly ever established, except in the broad contact network of childhood, or at an erotic level with the opposite sex. Otherwise, contacts between Jews and goyim are limited at best to feelings of sympathy. Why is this? Being a Jew, and discovering yourself to be one, in all its bifurcated nature, tends to be strongly centripetal, self-centred phenomena, so that all efforts at outside contact are turned in on themselves, back on themselves."

And when contacts between Private Paerand and Private Mandel simply did not develop any further, there were not only ethnic and psychological, but also medical reasons for this. During the third week of their military service, when the head of their unit bawled hoarsely: "Unit, form two lines! Divide, now!" and pushed them out of the shade of the bushes into the blazing sun to run along the edge of the labyrinth of sand and pine roots with thirty-kilo sacks of sand on their backs, Ullo, so to speak, dropped out of the picture. He lost consciousness and came to some hours later in the Tallinn Military Hospital. He was left there for a week for the doctors to examine him with stethoscopes and take X-rays, and was then signed out of hospital and out of military service. *Insufficientia valvulae mitralis*. With a question mark against the diagnosis to be sure, but only now fit for third-grade home guard service, to use Czarist terminology, then still in use.

After Ullo's happy homecoming, he discussed the situation with his mother. Would he simply rejoin the editorial staff at the *Sports Encyclopaedia*? His mother had heard from Messrs Karu and Laudsepp that her boy could return to work there immediately. Or would Ullo take the plunge, and study something at Tartu University for a while, in the hope that he would be taken on again by the *Sports Encyclopaedia* if he subsequently returned to Tallinn and studied extra-murally? And what would he be allowed to study at Tartu in that fashion?

In this matter, so essential for Ullo's future, his mother had her son consult his uncle. Despite everything. Ullo described his own and his mother's relationship with Dr Joonas Berends, his father's younger brother, like this:

"Right from the start, Uncle Joonas looked down somewhat on my father. For him, my father was a half-educated upstart while he, with his doctor's diploma, was an academic and of higher social standing, although it must be said that compared with his somewhat yokelish younger brother, Father seemed to almost be an aristocrat. As Father grew more successful, Uncle Joonas gradually adjusted his position. Criticism grew more veiled, but maybe all the sharper internally, God knows. After Father's financial downfall, Joonas immediately and loudly announced, maybe to make good his softening attitude hitherto, that the only thing his brother could end up as was a mess and that he, Dr Berends, had seen it coming ages before. But Father, his bankruptcy and escape abroad – even the fact that he had run away abroad with a foreign mistress – quickly lost the interest of local society and soon Uncle Joonas was quite happy to keep silent about the whole affair."

The wife of his speculator brother and her son, now some thirteen or fourteen years of age, had stayed behind in the same city and the same country as Uncle Joonas himself, badly affected by the family earthquake. Instead of offering them moral and financial support, which he undoubtedly could have afforded, Uncle Joonas announced (and there are always ears to hear, and mouths to discuss such information) that his sister-in-law and her son were themselves to blame for their misfortune, well, not chiefly to blame, but certainly in part. But he, Dr Berends, was said to treat them on the same premise as he did his patients. He would not treat alcoholics since they were largely to blame for their own misfortune. But nor would he treat such alcoholics for whom society was principally to blame. He, Dr Berends, would not treat such alcoholics, and that was that. Nor, analogously, cocaine addicts. Nor even those suffering from tuberculosis, if they couldn't be bothered to change their lifestyle to suit the exigencies of the cure. To be free of partial blame! Uncle Joonas had said that he would behave towards his sister-in-law and her son in precisely the same manner.

Ullo went on: "When Uncle Joonas's *no help* philosophy was revealed to us by some good-natured go-between, I croaked out: 'But in what way are we responsible for our misfortune?' and then shut my mouth, shocked at my own words, for I knew what my mother's reaction would be. And just as I had expected: when I slammed my thirteen-year-old fist down on the table, my mother put her hand over it and said quietly: 'Joonas has done Ullo an injustice. The child isn't guilty of anything. But I am of course guilty! Well, partially guilty, at any event. Though, in my own slow-wittedness, I don't really know how . . .'

"But in what way my mother or I were guilty of the misfortune that had befallen us, that was, I think, never explained to anyone by Uncle Joonas. For this would have been impossible to do. As regards Aunt Linda, i.e. Uncle Joonas's wife – a quite insipid former beauty with her dyed blonde hair – she had tried, by all accounts, to influence her husband to move in the direction of helping us, or at least get in touch with us. But if such rumours are true, then Aunt Linda was saying this not so much to improve our lot as to improve her husband's reputation as a philanthropist."

But, explained Ullo, I shouldn't interpret this as him trying to convince me that Uncle Joonas was some kind of boor or pathological niggard, and that his spouse was the embodiment of the same kind of egotism and inconsiderate behaviour towards relatives, at least in the outer reaches of the family (since the doctor and his wife had no children of their own). "Our reservations with regard to 'rich relations' understandably went quite deep. But not all the way. We didn't visit them. They ignored our existence. They were, in my opinion, and with hindsight, not particularly insensitive, but quite ordinary, a little boorish perhaps, a little helpless, a little awkward and of course strait-laced like many Estonians, who see everything from their own point of view. I repeat: they were quite ordinary, even pleasant at times, especially when they knew that nothing was expected of them. People who, and this is especially true of Uncle Joonas, had got as far as they had, having been forced to work hard, and then having created their own private stash, continue to scrape together to build that stash, while at the same time trying to hide all they have deeper in the ground (the method adopted by Uncle Joonas) – and there are those who live beyond their means and swagger, flinging the stash to the four winds while bragging about its existence (which is what Joonas accused my father of being particularly skilled at doing).

107

"One way or another, the doctor and his wife's ignoring attitude towards us clearly became a burden for themselves in the long-term. One Sunday morning in June 1933 – I had just left the tenth form at Wikman's – Uncle Joonas turned up at our watchman's and stoker's cottage in Nõmme:

"'Well, hello there, it's been a long time. You haven't got a bad place here, I see. The room's as clean as a whistle. Health OK?' In his clumsy way, Uncle Joonas was now trying to be nice. 'If you'd been ailing you'd have no doubt looked up your Uncle Joonas, but there's been no need, so it would seem. Anyway, be that as it may. Now, the thing is that Linda and myself are going to Pärnu in July. We've rented a flat in a house owned by friends, in a good district. On Papli Street, near the pavilion. So we're suggesting, Linda and myself, that is, that Ullo come along with us. I believe he's not the type of boy to disgrace himself. But how do I know that, when I hardly know anything about him? By chance, by sheer chance. And having no secrets, I can tell you that the tailor on Jaani Street, Mr Kõiv, is a patient of mine. Kidney stones. And one day he happened to ask me, how that very clever nephew of mine, that Wikman Grammar School boy, was getting on. It turned out that Kõiv Junior teaches Estonian at Wikman's and Ullo goes along to his house and is writing his Master's for him! Or something of the sort. No, no, the son described Ullo to his father in the most glowing terms. And when I told Linda, the idea arose . . . Sandra, being a mother you will surely understand that Ullo is beginning to need, well, a little room to flex his wings. We'll be dropping in on selected people, a number of my colleagues, but not only them. And we are quite prepared to forgive your, how shall I put it, embitterment, and so on. And offer the boy the chance to meet people, make acquaintances (man that he already is!) and relax a bit. So: what d'you say? Can we agree on this?'

"Mother replied that she was grateful for the proposal and would discuss it with me. We agreed that Mother would phone Joonas the following Tuesday from the market garden and tell him what we had decided. And after a short talk we resolved to go along with Joonas and Linda's idea. Of course, if Mother had not been very keen on the idea, I would never have given assent to the plan as it would have been tantamount to betrayal. Instead, she said: 'Ullo, be sensible, and go!' and I was given no other choice, nor had I any good reason to refuse. Perhaps we should have been insulted by what Joonas had said about my father, his own brother, but perhaps he hadn't said it in exactly the way it was conveyed to us. I felt it was pointless to feel insulted on such vague grounds. Moreover, everything, or almost everything, which Uncle is supposed to have said, had actually flashed through my head, quite independently of him. It had not lodged there, but flown through in a moment, and certainly past my conscious mind.

"So in early July '33, I went off to Pärnu," Ullo continued. "There, I also got to know (something you had already written about somewhere in your writer's vanity) Barbarus and I met him two summers after that as well, always in the company of Uncle Joonas and Aunt Linda. I could almost say that I mixed with the Barbarus family. A friendship that could have cost me my head during the German occupation. But when I mentioned your vanity as a writer, I only meant it as a joke and as a friend with no ulterior motives. Because I do, at least, have enough knowledge of that *métier* to understand: where else can poor writers suck nectar for their writings if not from the private lives of friends and acquaintances?

"That's where things stood as regards the development and future prospects of Mother's and my own relations with Uncle Joonas during the late autumn of 1935. And for that reason I decided to look up Uncle Joonas and ask his help in deciding whether or not to go and study in Tartu. The advice he gave me was meant ironically in part, but seemed to me to be eminently sensible, taken as a whole. As it later turned out, it wasn't that sensible after all, although the ultimate lack of sense no longer had anything to do with Joonas.

"I mention the irony in his suggestion. This arose when he quoted a verse which, as he put it, belonged to Heine:

> *Wem es bestimmt, der endet auf dem Mist*
> *trotz seinem ehrlichen Bestreben:*
> *ich bin zum Beispiel immer noch Jurist —*
> *das nennt man Leben!*

"He dismissed studying law before weighing up the pros and cons of other subjects. And he not only did so with that verse, but by the clear, objective statement, well, maybe with the bias as befits a medical man, but with clear conviction, and quite convincing: law would be, at Tartu University, and at this particular time in history, the most immature, most superficial, most futile of subjects to study. Upon which I actually began to wonder how well he in fact knew Tartu University. He had only studied at the medical faculty and for a couple of years at that, graduating at Kiev owing to the ferment of the First World War.

"So, after crossing off law, Uncle Joonas went through all the other possible subjects I could study – and ended up drawing a line through these as well. Some, on account of my unsuitability. Theology, for instance, because in answer to his question, I had declared myself to be a non-believer (how else can you answer such foolishly blunt questions?). Or veterinary surgery ('This would require a different sort of contact with country life and nature than you are capable of having'). So Uncle Joonas shoved aside several subjects, but those that remained were impossible for me to study since I couldn't combine them with part-time paid work. For in my case, the only kind of studies I could pursue were those that allowd me to earn my keep. And so Uncle Joonas finally ended up – this I feel was a planned manoeuvre on his part, right from the start – coming right back round to law.

"'So, really there's nothing left over for you to study. And, by the way, if you are the kind of boy who I must conclude you are, given old Mr Kõiv's tale, then it would not be impossible for you to succeed in life by studying law. You just fill in the holes in that ramshackle boat with the necessary amount of your own enterprise. So it proves to be a vessel capable of coping with water and when you have, so to speak, fixed it you can send it off in any direction you like . . .'"

Ullo expanded: "I went off to the town library and found the syllabus for the law faculty. That same evening I consulted Uno Tamm, a Wikman boy, two or three years my senior, who had been studying law for a couple of years and was sufficiently bright."

Ullo told me that he had got hold of the appropriate prospectus and the relevant books, brought them home and sat poring over them for ten days or so. At the same time he asked his mother to write to a schoolmate of hers now living in Tartu who had a house somewhere out near Raadi Cemetery, to ask whether she and her husband could put Ullo up for a few days. As soon as an affirmative reply was received, Ullo packed his books into a suitcase, an old, dreadfully battered one made out of real crocodile skin, stemming from the heyday of the Berends family, which he chose for some superstitious reason over the couple of Russian three-ply ones lying around, and not out of any need

110

to show off (the suitcase was, in any case, too knocked-about for that), and went off to Tartu.

He handed in his papers at the university and the next day received his matriculation booklet and registration number – at the time there were no actual entrance exams for Tartu University. It was sufficient to show your school-leaving certificate, and, of course, pay the necessary fees for the term. Ullo had set aside sixty kroons saved up from what he had earned from Mr Kõiv. He went straight from the university cashier off to the dean's office and asked to be registered for the general law exam which would be held in three days' time. The stubbly red-bearded and very quiet Mr Tiisik (I found him there four years later myself) refused categorically to put pen to paper.

"No, no, no, I can't register someone for an examination if he's enrolled only the day before!"

"Why not?"

"Ah, erm – there's no precedent for it."

"You could set one."

The head of the Dean's Chancellery, the son of a priest and a censor of Czarist days as I later found out, shook his head in vexation:

"Impossible . . ."

Ullo said: "Then let me have a word with the Dean."

Ullo then related, as I remember: "Maim was Dean in those days. Public law, and all that, which you know better than me. That sonorous voice of his. Like a chest of drawers on the legs of a music stand. Not a bad fellow really. He was sitting behind his huge bare black desk and I told him my story standing right there in front of it.

"He said through his nose: 'Mr Tiisik did the right thing. He can't allow you to take the examination.'

"I asked in the same annoying manner as before: 'But why not?'

"And the professor explained: 'Don't you understand? The general law course is two semesters long. You can't possibly have attended it if you've only been signed up for three days.'

"I said: 'But as far as I know, Professor Uluots – general law is, after all, Uluots's subject – never checks whether a candidate who turns up to take an exam has attended lectures or picked up the information from other sources.'

"'No, he doesn't. Quite true. But he *assumes* that a candidate has attended his lectures. In your case he can't.'

111

"I said: 'Then one could assume that I've consulted other sources. It surely isn't forbidden to have done so?'

"Maim said one tone higher on the scale, nasally now: 'Professor Uluots will not be assuming anything in your case. He has gone to Geneva and has asked me to stand in for him.'

"I said: 'All the better, Professor.'

"'In what way?' asked Maim, now on his guard.

"'Then I won't have to explain the matter twice over.'

"He looked at me with his little eyes through his pince-nez, for quite a long time.

"'Sit down.' And when I had taken a seat: 'What sort of fellow are you, really?'

"And I told him. About Wikman's and about *Magister* Kõiv's lessons – Mr Kõiv had defended his dissertation, three days previously. I mentioned my work for the editors at the *Sports Encyclopaedia* and the pioneers' battalion and that I had tried to do what I could with regard to the general law exam.

"'Well,' muttered Maim, 'we'll check on that. Tell me . . .' and he asked something, I don't remember what, probably from Jellinek, I would imagine. I gave my answer. He said: 'Good. I'll give you a *sufficit.*' I said that that wasn't enough. He said: 'Ohoo.' Just like that. Nasally. You know. And then asked me questions for a further three minutes.

"'Very well. I'll give you a *bene.*'

"I pointed out that that wasn't sufficient either. So he chatted with me for another half-hour and put down: *maxime sufficit.* When I stepped back out into the corridor, I had my freshly made-out student results book with me, and someone showed me where the senior common room in the main building was situated, and I asked whether Professor Leesment happened to be present. I had never set eyes on him before either. But there he was. A thin man, balding early in life, with a slight stammer, who drank in everything he saw with his brown eyes.

"I told him my tale. I explained that I had just come from Professor Maim's office where I had taken an exam and that I would be obliged if he, Professor Leesment, could examine me in the same fashion on Roman law. And, kind chap that he was (he was still young in those days and had just arrived back from a spell at the Sorbonne) said almost triumphantly: 'W-w-well, d'you know, if-f-f P-P-P-rofessor Maim c-can examine you – then I c-c-can do s-s-o t-t-too. And m-m-maybe s-s-straightaway.'

"He took me to a table at the back of the common room and asked whether I was related to the Berendses from Kolga parish. On my affirmative response, he asked whether it was the country or town branch of the family, and when I said 'town', he asked whether I was related to such-and-such Berends. He then asked me which books written in foreign languages I had read on Roman law, in addition to the notes from his lectures.

"I said, in the first instance, Beauville's *Histoire du droit romain*.

"He asked which language I had read it in, and when I said French, we immediately began speaking in that language. A quarter of an hour later – five minutes on Beauville, and ten on the rest of the world – he shook my hand and congratulated me on my good mark. And that was that."

And that was, indeed, that. First exams passed with flying colours. But these also remained his last, at least for some time. Of course I asked Ullo: "But for goodness' sake, tell me why?" And I received an answer which reminds me:

I had once written a historical and biographical sketch on the life of Kristjan Jaak Peterson. The poet had to answer the question posed by himself and the people around him, one which we in our ignorance still put to him: tell us, you blighter, why did you break off your university studies, when you had only managed to get in by a great stroke of luck and the good offices of kind people?

I don't know, nobody knows, how Kristjan Jaak replied. But in my text the answer was as follows: "But why should I waste my time there, when I could read all the books from which the lecturers cobbled together their lectures? And much newer books than those? And much more quickly than our professors managed to read them?"

And the twenty-year-old Ullo answered that question in identical fashion, as did the seventy-year-old Ullo. I put his thoughts into Kristjan Jaak's brain and his words, Ullo's words, into his mouth. May both forgive me for doing so.

17

A FTER ULLO LEFT WIKMAN'S, our already rare meetings became a good deal rarer, and even more so when I left the grammar school. Looking through my notes from 1986, I can't really find anything for the years '36 and '37. Except for the fact that Ullo had returned from Tartu and rejoined the editors at the *Sports Encyclopaedia* and shown his booklet confirming his status as a student with its two *maximes*. From which time he was paid fifty-five kroons a month instead of the previous fifty.

Two major events did occur in 1936, two periods of upheaval in the lives of both Ullo and his mother. The first of these events was of profoundly negative character, for Ullo's mother especially. The second event had an intrinsically positive effect on Ullo, in fact on the Estonian people as a whole, although its significance was only to emerge much later.

In February, his mother (but I cannot say whether formally or by way of some special letter – and if the latter, certainly not from Ullo's father) found out that Ullo's father had, somewhere out there in Germany, Holland, Belgium or Luxembourg, managed to annul their marriage. Whether he had taken these steps to allow him to legally marry Mrs Fredriksen, or whether that marriage had already taken place, was not clear from the missive – nor was it any longer of any real importance. The knowledge that she was now officially separated from the husband who had fled abroad with another woman was a particularly severe blow to Ullo's mother. For Ullo, it was no more than the last link in the long chain of his father's absences over several years, but for his mother, as has been said, it was a blow which well-nigh knocked her over. His mother froze inside and it took months for her to thaw out once more. But she never did so to the extent of becoming her former self. And Ullo was obliged to come to the realisation that he was unable to console his mother. Any attempt at consolation was too impatient, too rational, too brittle. The fact that consolation remained so ineffective raised in him a feeling bordering on intolerance, which was, God forbid, on a par with betrayal, the betrayal of his mother. When, with reddened eyes and a distracted stare, she patted him on the cheek with a hand worn leathery by shovelling snow and said: "Maybe, maybe, my boy. I understand, I'm stupid, but please forgive me, I can't do anything about it." Ullo felt that he hated his mother's endurance, her helplessness, which held sway over her in her suffering, was driving him apart from her rather than bringing her closer – as he would have wished. At the same time, the wall of suffering standing between him and his mother did not drive him further from his father. The image of his father was distant and painful, but in some way it was inevitable and immovable.

One evening a month later when Ullo had arrived home from work, shovelled the snow from half the road edge of the yard and swept it clean with a broom, and when his mother had put some bread and the iron pot full of herring and potato stew on the table, and after both had washed their hands and sat down at the table, his mother said: "These days, it's all the rage to Estify surnames and this is even promoted by the state. I don't like such campaigns. Especially when they result in so many tasteless names. Like all those tilly-lilly ones. All those *Helilas* and *Ilusalus* and what have you. But I've been thinking, now that your father has finally turned his back on us – I do understand that this affects an abandoned wife differently to an abandoned son – anyway, I have to admit I'd be glad if we could in some way do something in response to his actions. And so I've thought that we could change our surname. Then he would see – it doesn't really matter whether he worries about it or not – that we're not continuing our life as his abandoned suitcases containing a little pile of things that he's deserted, but with his label still attached, always his property, but that we are deciding things for ourselves . . ."

I can imagine Ullo's reply: "You could take back your maiden name."

To which his mother is likely to have answered: "Yes. But you can't go around using my maiden name. And you must understand: if you weren't to adopt the same name as me, I would somehow feel deprived of you. But OK, if you don't agree, and you want to carry on as a Berends, I'll take back my maiden name."

So Ullo agreed to his mother's suggestion to Estify both their names and to use one new, joint, surname. He regarded this as an unnecessary step to a certain extent. But nonetheless, there was now sufficient distance between him and his father and his father's deceit, and the bitterness had gone on for seven years now, crowned by his father's final abandonment of them. Because the news had inevitably come as a blow to Ullo. All the more so since he didn't regard himself as guilty or partially guilty, in the way that his mother, somewhat apocryphally, did. The last straw had been the divorce. His mother said: "So you can find, word polisher that you are in your own and others' estimation, you can find us a new, practical and sensible surname which looks Estonian." Upon which Ullo set his grey matter to work.

He decided that, while he was about it, the change should also affect his first name, or rather the one that had become current usage should be officially sanctioned. Ulrich, as few knew him, would have to be officially changed to Ullo, as he was known in the eyes of the world. In the same way, his mother Alexandra would have to be officially changed to Sandra. Father Trimbek, a loyal railway worker in Czarist times, had given his daughter the name of the Emperor, in female form, presumably without asking himself what kind of Czar the present one was at the time of his daughter's birth.

When choosing the new surname, Ullo took as his point of departure a couple of factors he hadn't made great efforts to express to his mother. In his opinion, the new surname should not differ markedly from the old official one. And it should remain disyllabic. The "b" or a "p" at the beginning – Estonians pronounce these two letters the same anyway – could remain, although the foreign-looking "b" could be replaced by a "p". Putting two "e"s between the "p" and the "r" did, however, present problems. I remember Ullo saying:

"The association with the Estonian for a fart – *peer* – did make me want to avoid that double 'e' and plump for 'ae' instead. And the 'rand' part (i.e. strand) was no problem. By the way, when some eighteen months later I happened to find work at the Riigivolikogu – the Estonian Chamber of Deputies – the civil servants there insisted on an Estified name for their colleagues, so as to set an example to the nation

116

– several bosses there regarded the fact that a young chap had already changed his name in this way as a sign of staunch patriotism. I denied this vehemently. I explained that I had not set out with any patriotic motives in mind, purely personal and family ones. But it seemed to me that no one there took my explanation seriously."

The other important event of 1936 was the Berlin Olympics. Although Ullo had never taken any active part in sports activities, he followed it more keenly than the average non-sporty Estonian boy, thanks to his work at the *Sports Encyclopaedia*.

Incidentally, in that old mediaeval building on Dunkri Street, in the editorial offices in three tiny rooms behind metre-thick walls on the first or second floor nothing much had changed in preparation for the Games. A recently appointed Estonian Olympic Committee dealt with the organisation of the Games – this consisting of Lieutenant General Laidoner, ex-Minister Anderkopp and a whole host of lesser functionaries – in sports clubs, stadia and training gyms, in as much as these existed, since many were little more than sheds. No one talked about national sporting aspirations, neither the sportsmen themselves nor the provincial sports authorities. Only the sports journalists, having little sense of responsibility and being sensationalist, did now and again – as this had to be to the taste of the colonels of sport – write how the Olympics would *offer a huge opportunity to our small country to surprise the world with our achievements*. Journalists did on occasion speculate as to the likelihood of Gustav Sule or Arnold Viiding winning a medal. In general, however, the editors snuffled along during those months in their usual tranquil way and dealt with matters nearer at hand. Like, for instance, organising spying sessions from the windows of the editorial offices.

In the building across from the *Sports Encyclopaedia* offices, and one floor below, as was known by the Messrs Karu and Laudsepp as well as by young Master Sooper, the errand boy, a married couple from Narva had moved in. The husband was something to do with a film agency, and the wife worked in the kitchens of the famous Feischner cake shop and café. But neither of these were of any particular interest to the editors at the *Sports Encyclopaedia*. Their attention was focused on the couple's daughter, who by now had reached her late teens. She was blonde, with slightly lank hair, but with very erect nipples, and she was studying dance at some ballet academy.

Her appearance caused the work at the *Sports Encyclopaedia* to reach new heights. And surprisingly enough, this happened in the area of job discipline.

Ullo said: "I no longer remember what her real name was, but she was known among the editors as *Muusa* – the Muse. And this Muusa would exercise every morning when her mother and father had gone off to work, from nine till ten in the room across from our editorial office. Right in the sights of the second room there. The result was: the working day at the office, which was supposed to start at nine, but which in practice rarely started before ten, suddenly started as Muusa appeared on the scene, at nine, or even five minutes earlier. Editor-in-chief Karu and assistant editor Laudsepp, not to mention the errand boy Sooper and strangely enough me too were all at work some four or five minutes before nine. Our observation posts, behind the stacks of files on the window sill, were somehow automatically fixed in this order: behind the chink between the central stacks of files stood the editor, his assistant to his right, Sooper to his left, and I was further to the right between Laudsepp and the window posts.

"Muusa never showed us anything unwonted. Every day she would perform exercises from Ernst Idla's sports exercises course to the tune of the same gramophone record. During the last fifteen minutes of her hour she would practise ballet steps, including the splits. She would move around with a slight Mona Lisa smile on her lips. She never once raised her eyes to her observers, but I am dead sure she knew of their presence. How do I know? She would always appear in our field of vision wearing a pair of tights and a gym slip, never after having just climbed out of bed in her nightdress, or stark naked. Now and again, she would allow herself a break, freezing in some lyrical pose or other. Raising her hand in the air she would turn her closed eyes and slightly opened lips in the direction of our window, place the palms of her hands on her breasts and knead them, barely perceptibly but voluptuously nonetheless. The editor would cough rather foolishly and expectantly, his assistant would blow – fsssss – through his teeth, and the small lightweight boxer Sooper would whisper hoarsely: 'What a damned girl! What a damned *girl*!'

"After some time, it emerged that Muusa had five slips in different colours, black, white, beige, yellow and red. She would always appear wearing a different colour from that of the day before, but seemed to change them in random order. Her observers would sometimes indulge in a kind of lottery: in the morning, before Muusa appeared, the men would choose a colour. The winner was, of course, the one who guessed the colour Muusa would be wearing that day. As a prize, the winner would get, if I remember rightly, one kroon from each of the losers and off they would go to the bar on Dunkri Street or to the Roheline Konn – the Green Frog – on Nunne Street.

"This game was played for several weeks in a row and was forgotten only when the first week of August and the Olympic Games were nudging so close that they demanded, well, if not the full attention of the general public who were more distant from sport, then at least that of the editors of the *Sports Encyclopaedia*.

"Things finally got going when Karu bounced into the office even more dynamically than usual and, with beads of sweat on his brow and an expression on his face which exuded significance, told us that he would be travelling to Berlin the day after next – he had been included in the Olympic Delegation as Press Attaché. His assistant shook his hand in congratulation for several minutes, and expressed satisfaction as to the objectivity of the information that would now be emerging from Berlin. I too gave my editor-in-chief a quick handshake and thought to myself: now there'll be a series of enthusiastic reportage articles for the papers, sent back in quick succession from the Games. But I wasn't seriously disappointed that they hadn't sent me instead of him, or at least along with him. Not seriously. Even though I did happen to know the sports statistics for Estonia and the world at large better than he did, and spoke German significantly better than him. At the time, I hadn't yet learnt magnanimity with regard to such disappointments, something we all learn over time. Anyway, I wanted to deflate the egocentric careerist – though he wasn't in fact such a bad chap really. When he waved his pigskin briefcase around, announcing: 'I'm not talking about boxing, wrestling, weightlifting – there we'll do great things – but I reckon we'll bring home at least one medal in athletics as well!' I felt the urge to dispute this, and said: 'Athletics? – I doubt it. Viiding and Sule could be hopefuls if you just look at the scores they get back home. But they haven't enough experience of major championships. They'll simply be too nervous . . .'

"The editor-in-chief gave a twitch. 'At least one medal! At least one bronze! I bet you lot six bottles of Martell that they will! Well, Paerand, what have you got to say for yourself?'

"I really wished Estonia could get at least a bronze in shot-put or javelin. But in truth, you couldn't count on it happening. So I said: 'A bottle of Martell costs fifteen kroons. If Estonia gets at least one bronze I'll buy you six bottles. If it doesn't, you can give me ninety kroons.'

"Laudsepp sealed the deal with Sooper looking on as a witness."

Ullo went on with his story. "We all remember our major achievements in boxing, et cetera, don't we? Six medals altogether, wasn't it? At the time, I was only hoping for a bronze – that Luhaäär would carry off the bronze, which he in fact did. But you tend to think more of Palasalu, and of Trossmann winning his two golds, which was the nicest surprise in the whole of Estonian sporting history. And then there were Neo, Stepulov and Väli, that is to say silver-silver-bronze. All in all, Estonia took fifth place in boxing, wrestling and weightlifting, but we didn't get one single medal in athletics. Viiding managed 15.23 and came eighth, Sule got 63.26 and came eleventh. So I won my bet. But I didn't receive my ninety kroons. Karu bought six bottles of Martell and the editors managed to down the lot over three evening sessions. They said, grandly, that it was my Martell and that I was invited to drink with them. But I told them what I thought of that, and didn't join them. Though the Olympic wins did mean that the print edition of the *Encyclopaedia* was to be increased by half, and Laidoner himself had promised to find the money for this.

"But I started looking for another job."

18

I ASKED ULLO HOW HIS relationship with Ruta developed, a demonstration of which he had given during his stay at Rannamõisa, thought-provoking and memorable as it had been. I can see from my jottings that Ullo had here come up with a lot of chit-chat, maybe some serious things, but had avoided answering my question.

In autumn 1936 Ullo and his mother moved from Nõmme back into Tallinn. Ullo's mother had stopped working for Mr Knopff and his market gardening firm. My notes say nothing about why she left. Or perhaps not nothing. Mr Knopff's name can be found in my notes: a small circle with an arrow emerging out of its north-eastern edge. This should tell us that Mr Knopff was of the male gender. Ullo was hinting that Mr Knopff had begun to make advances to his mother.

In those years, I visited Ullo at his market garden on a number of occasions. His mother was around fifty years old at the time, a somewhat saddened woman who looked old for her age, but was slim and younger in her behaviour, resembling the *Portrait of a Roman Woman* by our drawing teacher at Wikman's, Arnold Kalmus. Responding to Ullo, she said: "A new husband? Quite possible in theory. I have not decided to remain untouched only on account of your father. But in practice, I doubt if I'll ever meet the right man. For he would have to be more or less perfect . . ."

Mr Knopff exhibited no tendencies in that direction. This short man with his brisk ways, little buttons of eyes hidden deep beneath his eyebrows, and balding pate was, as a human being, perfectly respectable. But as a knight in shining armour, a hero, prince, as men were supposed to be to an extent vis-à-vis ageing ladies, in inverse proportion to the woman's demands, here Mr Knopff had no visible advantages. Although the imminent move was a big step for Ullo's mother to take, she took the plunge and left the market garden. Why the Paerands moved back to the more expensive Tallinn was something Ullo was at a loss to explain. But that is what they did.

I have written somewhere that if you divide cities into cities of grass, hedges and trees (the sign of the last form being the trunk) then Tallinn belongs to the tree category. The Old Town, including Toompea Hill, forms its expressive stone trunk. Accordingly, city dwellers flit around, like birds of the hedgerow, the tree trunk or crown of the tree. By this definition, the Paerands, mother and son, were trunk birds who would build their nest in the tree trunk.

They moved to Toompea, to the Danish King's Garden, where to specifically I have unfortunately omitted to note and now it must remain unknown for ever. At any rate, it was to some second-floor flat and – *nota bene* – to a building that was haunted. Anyone wishing to find their address would find it listed among haunted houses of Tallinn. Ullo smiled at the thought.

"People certainly talked about our house being haunted, supposedly by a pale young woman in a long scarlet dress. I, at any rate, never actually ran into her. But then again, we only lived there for a short while . . ."

For some obscure reason, they moved house three times before actually settling down. They were probably looking for something cheaper each time, because Ullo's mother had no work to start with, their only income being what Ullo was earning. But after the conflict over the bet, they could no longer rely on his salary rising above fifty-five kroons per month. He continued to be tolerated because Karu and Laudsepp managed to get some use out of him, but Ullo felt instinctively that as soon as they managed to find some semi-eidetic fool like himself with a prodigious memory, he would be out on his ear.

Following their whim seeking holes in tree trunks, they moved from the house in the Danish King's Garden to an even stranger location: to Neitsitorn – The Virgin's Tower. During the previous century, part of the tower had been converted into apartments. These apartments had a limestone floor, a stove, windows set into walls one and a half metres thick and a limestone privy complete with limestone toilet seat, a dry closet, of course.

". . . Using precise microanalysis," Ullo said, "you could perhaps still find the impression of the mediaeval backside of the tower warden

Hinrik Parenbeke from the year 1373 – the restoration expert Zobel mentions him in his last book."

But here, bringing firewood up from the cellar and hauling buckets of water up from the well – the stone stairs were narrow and the steps high – became such a burden that Ullo's mother decided to move as soon as they could find a suitable place. Even though it was Ullo who had lugged the firewood up the stairs and filled the water buckets each morning before rushing off to the editorial office.

Ullo explained: "And then one day my mother bumped into our former landlord: my old German teacher from Wikman's, Mr Weseler. Whether this was a good or a bad thing I cannot tell. He had asked where and in what circumstances we were now living. Mother had said that we were doing all right. I don't think that she complained very much. She didn't even permit herself to do so in front of people much closer to us than old Weseler. We were in fact having a really rough time just then. I was still earning my fifty-five kroons. Plus the ten or fifteen I would get for tutoring some, shall we say, straggler at Wikman's. Weseler had presumably deduced from Mother's tone of voice that we were in dire straits, and that our flat was unsuitable and expensive to boot: we were paying twenty kroons a month. So he had offered Mother a new flat in a block on Aida Street. And we moved in there. It was there in that fourteenth-century building near the mangling room, half a cellar, that Mother tried her hand at running a laundry. But you yourself visited us there on a couple of occasions."

I said: "I did, I did. When I was in the top form at Wikman's. But listen, I was asking you about Ruta. How did your little idyll develop? I never really got to know . . ."

"Quite so . . ." grunted Ullo. I don't in fact think he'd actually forgotten my question, it was more that he was making attempts to evade it. But as he saw that I had returned to the subject, he stopped equivocating.

"I should be grateful to Ruta. I've told you of how I thought that girls giggled about me. On the Nõmme train, for example. Or that I was burnt by the occasional touch of a girl. My relationship with Ruta completely and very swiftly freed me from these problems. But this relationship didn't start up immediately. I had perhaps been going to her house about half a year. During which time things weren't quite clear. I visited her place about twice a week. With or without an excuse for doing so. Her parents and brother weren't always at home to keep an eye on what we were getting up to. Her father was a very pleasant and jovial figure, a stamp collector among other things, and we therefore never lacked a topic of conversation. Her mother, a twittering brunette, was somewhat more nervous, but there was nothing much wrong with her. And her brother, around thirteen years of age, was hardly a source of danger. And yet this uncertainty went on for some six months, during which time Ruta had nonetheless sat stark naked on my lap on several occasions, before things got serious."

I asked: "But what about your affair with Lia?"

Ullo thought for a moment. "Well, Ruta didn't free me from that at all. I have to say that my affair with Ruta didn't affect my relationship with Lia in the slightest. I would now say [this was in 1986, remember]: I was in love with Lia in a foolish sort of way. I convinced myself that it was all an interesting game. Going out with them both. Going to the theatre with Lia and the cinema with Ruta. Kissing Lia's hand and jumping into bed with Ruta. The former all soul, and the latter all body. Though this wasn't 100 per cent the case. Because I wrote poetry to both of them. I did give a number to Ruta, but I only gave one to Lia – I knew that Lia wouldn't care about them, as she wouldn't understand them. Perhaps even Ruta didn't fully get them (because she didn't study them carefully enough) but she sensed what was in them, better than Lia did. I remember how both of them would read them, Ruta sunbathing on the beach at Pirita, between two swims, spraying drops all over the sheet of paper. I would keep a firm grip on them so that the wind wouldn't blow them away over the sand. And Lia, with that one poem I gave her: on her veranda where she sat in her startling green evening dress. She took the poem, smiled, sat down on the settee, started to read, got up, brought up a footstool, placed her feet on the stool – in her bold purple strapped shoes – and got comfortable until Armin called her to help her mother lay the table for tea, and the poem remained unread on the veranda.

"I never really escaped from Lia's orbit. My chances with her seemed to be improving, at least on the surface: August was sent off to officers' school and Lia began to pay a little more attention to me. She even admitted that in my presence she felt a great contentment of the soul. Yes, she would use such grand expressions as contentment of the soul . . . Oh hell, we were both rather screwed up and unhappy. She seemed incapable of letting me near her – I don't know what fears lurked within her or what old Freud would have said about it all – and I was afraid that I would go and spoil everything if I tried any harder. And so we would play at pretending to find the game interesting. I have the feeling that Lia had an inkling of my affair with Ruta right from the start. Though she never asked, and I never confessed.

"Ruta was extremely easygoing, and had a youthful energy. She was certainly brave. In the autumn of 1936, we saw an advert in the papers saying that the sculptor Sanglepp was looking for a model for a sepulchral monument to a young girl. In those days, everybody knew who Sanglepp was, even you. At least you know what he looked like: fortyish, in those days, sourish-faced, a little nervous. But he was a gifted sculptor. So I said to Ruta: 'Go on, offer your services. He's not going to have an affair with you. And with any luck you'll earn a few kroons extra on top of those from the theatre. Besides, the world will receive an eternal monument to your existence, albeit under another name.'

"Ruta went along to see him. There were a couple of dozen applicants, but Sanglepp chose her. The death of the daughter of Sakkeus, an industrialist dealing in metals, had occasioned the commission. Despite being sent to all the Davoses and Lausannes of this world, she had died of consumption and had been, by what you could see in the photos Sakkeus handed to the sculptor, strangely similar to Ruta – as Sanglepp had said: her bearing, her proportions and her face. Only her coiffure was different, old-fashioned, that of ancient Roman women or those of Jacques David statues. Sanglepp was happy for Ruta to pose in a wig which he found among the props kept at the Estonia Theatre. And there was no improper posing in the nude. Ruta posed in, well, a thin wrap, but one which reached her ankles. I went over to meet her after the sessions with Sanglepp. And saw how his wife twittered happily with Ruta. But I must tell you . . ."

He thought for some while and I felt: if I try to rush him now, he'll brush aside what he was going to say. So I decided to wait quietly, till the silence would force him to speak. And so it did, about seven or eight seconds later.

"Clearly, such a turn of events raised in me – well – a feeling of disappointment. What are you looking at me like that for –? In a word it did. I had apparently steered Ruta in the direction of Sanglepp's studio, well, if not in the hope, then at least thinking that she'd end up

125

in bed with him. Following the literary cliché about artists. But if you were to ask me what I needed her to do that for, I really haven't got a good explanation. Not on account of the fifty years that have passed, but despite them. In spite of the time I've had to reflect.

"Anyway, I suppose I'll have to try to find some explanation. It was presumably because I needed Ruta to be unfaithful to me in order to justify similar foibles on my part. With Lia, if you see what I mean."

I don't remember what I said to Ullo. I am likely to have pursed my lips slightly and said a neutral kind of "I suppose so. To a certain extent . . ." which cannot be avoided in such situations. When we don't want to cry out: "But, my dear Ullo, I don't understand you one tiny bit!" Because I couldn't in all conscience have answered him in that way. To a certain extent I did understand what he was driving at.

"And if you want to know," he continued, "what happened to us after that, well, we carried on seeing each other for about two years. Ruta's grandmother had a cabbage patch down near the Mustamäe swimming baths and on that allotment stood a tool shed with a stove. A stove and an old sofa. Ruta went to the plot in order to help her grandmother tend the cabbages, and I went along to help Ruta. Ruta tended to know when her grandmother was likely to be there, sometimes we would arrive at the same time as her but mostly we were there on our own. Ruta had the keys in any case.

"Occasionally, we would walk along the outer edge of the Mustamäe district over to the cemetery at Rahumäe and would sit on a bench by the Sakkeus family grave, to look at Ruta's monument. By the way, if you were to judge the sculpture on the basis of a photographic likeness, then it is a masterful work. The Sakkeuses were supposed to have been boundlessly happy with it. It was said to resemble their late daughter to a T. But it was always strange for me to look at it, because it also reminded me so startlingly of Ruta, in those rare moments when she was slightly introverted and melancholy.

"One time when we were sitting there, in August or September 1938, I remember pulling a copy of the *Päevaleht* out of my pocket and opening it. I glanced at its pages: news, the leader, sketches and announcements. As if looking at the day's paper for the first time. But this was staged, a lie. That morning I had read the advert which I now slid under Ruta's nose. My dirty trick was now set up. Well, what do I mean by 'dirty'? I said, as if reading the small ad for the first time: 'Look, what sort of ad is this?'

"'Which one?'

"And I read out: 'Elderly German lady living in Stockholm requires companion of Baltic German or educated Estonian background. Duties not too burdensome, salary respectable. A good knowledge of German is a prerequisite.'

"'Well, what about it?' asked Ruta.

"And I said in a reasonably neutral voice: 'Could be something for you?'

"'How do you mean?'

"'Well, we all know what a "respectable salary" means over there, up to four or five times what you earn here. The Estonian kroon and the Swedish krona are about equal in value. How much would you get for a similar job over here?'

"Ruta said: 'Well, if you could find such work here in the first place – as the companion to an old lady – then, depending on such things as food and accommodation, I would say about twenty to thirty kroons a month.'

"I said: 'Well then. Over there they pay between eighty and 150 kronor per month.'

"'How do you know?'

"'Because similar work is four to five times as well paid over there,'" said Ullo – and he explained to me: "I used a story I'd heard from you to back me up. You had told me that summer that you'd been on a class trip to Stockholm. And that along with your new deputy head you'd visited the home of some retired grammar school teacher. A physics master, as I remember. His pension amounted to some eight hundred kronor. Our Mr Hellmann, Ouromaschin as we nicknamed him, was being paid two hundred kroons a month for teaching at Wikman's and that was an exceptionally high salary! I explained to Ruta that a pension in any country is never 100 per cent of the salary, and is, at best, some 20 per cent lower. So if his pension was eight hundred, his salary would have been around a thousand kronor. So about five times as much . . ."

"Ruta said: 'But the cost of living is half as much again as over here.'

"I had to smile: 'But of course. So then you only make two and a half times as much. I don't want to persuade you to apply, just simply to

127

bring the offer to your attention, as something which perhaps merits serious thought.'

"Ruta then asked: 'But don't you see something rather insulting in the advert?'

"I knew of course what she was driving at. But since I had already begun feigning: 'No – what could be insulting about it?'

"'Only educated Estonians are regarded as suitable – but Baltic Germans will do, even if they're uneducated.'

"I said gently: 'Listen – it's only a question of language knowledge. Baltic Germans know German anyway, but Estonians only do so in as much as they have an education. What's insulting about that?'

"When we met the next day at her grandmother's cabbage patch, Ruta said unprompted: 'I don't speak German well enough . . .'

"I replied: 'Where there's a will, there's a way.'

"Ruta said: 'But to be taken at all seriously, I'll have to write to her. I can't really . . .'

"To cut a long story short, it was me who ended up writing the letter of application, and Ruta simply copied it, so that were she to get the job, it wasn't entirely fraudulent right from the start. The first letter led to a correspondence. Three or four letters were sent in each direction. At first, one of the old lady's relatives wrote from Sweden, then the old lady wrote herself. With the pedantry of an older generation. I tried to take everything into account. In the end Ruta was chosen from the seven or eight candidates. She left before Christmas 1938. That was our last meeting. At the beginning of February, I put a crease in my trousers, bought seven roses and went to ask for Lia's hand.

"And was turned down."

19

B UT NOW ULLO'S TALE has dragged my plot pretty far ahead. This goes to show that even with something so firm as describing the biography of one person, thematic and narratological considerations can clash with the chronology of events, boundaries can crumble, colours flow together, and nothing is left of methodological purity.

So, back to the autumn of 1936! At any rate, back to the market garden on Aida Street. To those days when the smell of soil which clung to Ullo's clothing had been replaced by the smell of the cellar laundry at Mr Weseler's house. But I will allow Ullo to describe the laundry and I will write of something else.

Before Christmas 1936, the newspapers said that Paul Keres would be holding a "simultaneous" chess match in the hall of the Chamber of Trade and Industry on Pikk Street. The previous summer, Keres had won several international competitions, most notably at Margate against Alyokhin in twenty-three moves. Interest in this simultaneous match was huge. It interested me a lot too. And Keres's personality even more than the late Sunday morning match, a man who had until recently been a schoolboy but had suddenly proven to be on a par with wrestlers like Palusalu and others and was ahead of them in one respect, and that was something we as a country clearly needed more than we could fathom, and that was to help bring Estonia from being a faceless and nameless entity into the front rank internationally – making our name known to the world.

I wasn't, of course, thinking of actually participating myself in the simultaneous match, because that would have been sheer vanity on my part. As it would have been in the case of a certain gent I met twenty years later in a completely different world – and about whom I have written. That gentleman had met world champion Capablanca on a train somewhere near Baden-Baden in around 1930, and had immediately suggested playing a game. Just so that he'd be able to tell his friends that he'd played a game against Capablanca.

As for me, I wasn't even going to go to watch Keres play his simultaneous match. But that Saturday, Ullo sauntered over to our place and said that *Sports Encyclopaedia* had sent him to cover the match. So he had decided he might as well take part. And could I go with him? No, no, not to play chess, just simply to watch how things turned out. And to have a closer look at Keres. I couldn't refuse. The hall at the Chamber of Trade, with its high ceiling, its cabbage-green walls and its Jugendstil windows with white frames, was filled with the buzz of conversation. There was a double row of small tables that stretched the length of the room which could accommodate forty-four players. The simultaneous player would walk up and down the gap between the tables. At first, some dozen fidgeting players had seated themselves at the tables, but soon the places filled up. All kinds of people, but only of the male sex, from bearded veterans of the Chess League right down to schoolboys.

Ullo signed up on some side table near the wall and was shown to his place at one of the players' tables. I found myself a chair and moved it up close behind him. Then a boy who was even leaner than expected, with his hair neatly parted in the middle and wearing a top-quality dark suit with tails and a white collar entered the hall and applause broke out. Professor Nuut gave a welcoming speech, and Keres listened, gazing at the floorboards with a smile, then walked up to the top table and started the first round, moving pawns on squares *d* and *e* two squares forward by turns.

I no longer remember precisely how everything went – in fact, I only have the vaguest memory of the match as a whole. During the first hour, one-third of Keres's opponents gave up, and during the next hour and a half, a further third followed suit. Then, for about an hour, three or four were trounced. At this point there were also seven or eight stalemates. So by the fourth hour there were no more than seven or eight players still at their posts. And who fell away every ten minutes or so. So that the group of players thinned out all the while, and the group of diehards halved during the course of the day, with ever fewer points between them.

I only remember details of what happened during Ullo's match. In

130

the first round he had already whispered to me over his shoulder: "No, no. I won't be able to throw him. He functions better than I do in confused situations. I'll just try to keep things simple. Avoid falling into his traps."

About an hour later they both lost their queens and after another hour both their rooks were gone. Another hour passed and they were both left with a bishop, a knight and two pawns each. Ullo whispered: "He doesn't want to go for stalemate. But I do. For me stalemate would be more than adequate. But achieving that gets harder the fewer opponents he has."

Then the other Last of the Mohicans gave up the ghost and Keres came and stood opposite Ullo and began to deal with him alone. The last thirty or forty spectators grouped on each side of the table.

Keres is said to have been an extremely sensitive man. This is no doubt true. But he was a chess player first and foremost. And chess is a battle game. Sensitive battles do not exist. Having stopped in front of Ullo he awaited his moves, then made his own. The first. The click of the time clock. The next. The next. The next. And the click of the clock after each move. He was standing facing Ullo, with the fingers of his right hand tucked into his left armpit. And he moved his white pieces with the straightened index and the middle finger of his left hand, making his moves, well, if not with lightning speed, then at least immediately, straight after Ullo's move. Let us say with the speed the second hand of the clock took to move after Ullo had made his, leaving – I don't know whether it *should have done* – the impression that *he* needed no time to think. He was working according to some plan worked out down to the last detail, and as soon as a move by his opponent presented new opportunities, whether intending to or not, his swift reaction revealed a kind of weariness at the clumsy slowness of his opponent. But in this clumsy slowness lay, let's put it this way – Ullo's *greatness*. He didn't allow himself to be tempted into lightning moves himself, though the speed of his opponent should have provoked him into doing so. He had enough time to think. Ullo would sit motionless for between half a minute and a minute, or anything up to two once his opponent had made his move. He would place the fingertips of both hands to his mouth with the tip of his long nose resting on his index and middle fingers, and think. He thought with boundless concentration. When both players' pawns had been taken,

131

they still made a dozen or so moves. At the sixty-first, the grandmaster said – and hadn't Keres already become one? – "Stalemate. As you can see." And smiled as he shook Ullo's hand. One of the supporters – or was it a journalist – then asked: "Mr Keres, what observations can you make about simultaneous chess?"

And the boy replied: "Several. One thing that was very interesting was –" and he cast a glance at Ullo's list of moves which was lying on the table – "the game played with such deliberation by Mr Paerand . . ."

Ullo and I stepped outside on to the street. I felt just as if we'd been through an exam. All the more so, given the fact that evening had crept upon us and it was now dark.

"Come round to our place," I said. "Stretch your legs a bit. My mother'll make us some tea."

Ullo said: "Sorry, I'm afraid I can't. I've still got a huge amount of bed linen to run through the mangle. That's how it is when your mother decides to open a laundry."

I had to admit: "You know, when you announced at the start of the match that you had no intention to surprise us with various tricks, I was disappointed. But in reality – as I now understand – such a barbed-wire style of play came as a yet greater surprise. I even wrote a little ditty about it . . ."

"Oh yes?"

And I recited:

> *"Now comes the fun – your supporter cried out –*
> *For both young lads were as dynamite bold*
> *Your game played like barbed wire payed out*
> *As if Master Salo Flohr had managed to grow old."*

And we shook hands at the corner of the street. And he himself can describe the laundry. My notes show he said the following:

"The laundry was my mother's idea. Firstly, there was the fact that she was unemployed, because she couldn't find work in Tallinn. Even though the economic crisis was supposedly past and the country was now enjoying a period of growth. And secondly, the idea arose because there was a wash house at Weseler's place, right next to our flat. A wash house with a mangle. Weseler owned two adjoining buildings which were like the rest of the buildings on that street with narrow façades

132

on to the street itself, walls from the fifteenth century, interiors from the eighteenth, taps from the turn of the twentieth and electricity from the time of the First World War. But the ceiling vaults of the half-cellar which had become rooted in the earth were surely from the time of the St George's Day Uprising back in the 1340s. Under these arches was the wash house and the mangle. Our living-room-cum-kitchen – this was in the basement of one building and the floor was a little higher – led out there, i.e. down under the second building, by way of an unexpected door and a short flight of steps.

"In all, only two or three families lived in the two buildings. On the first floor, I think. The lemonade factory next door used some ground-floor rooms, which lay just above our ceiling, as a storeroom. Higher up, the buildings were empty. The attic was left to the pigeons.

"My mother easily managed to agree with the rest of the building's inhabitants that they wouldn't use the wash house or the mangle, and in return she would do their laundry for nothing, once a month. This meant that the rooms were in our hands, so to speak, and cost us nothing. And the crucial equipment too, the boiling vats, the washtubs, the wash paddles, and so on. Which in fact belonged to the landlord himself. They were worn, of course, but still serviceable.

"At first, I tried to talk my mother out of her business venture, but I then realised that she had stored up an unexpected amount of unused energy over the years. And indeed a small sum amounting to starting capital, some 150 kroons. Too little to do anything satisfactory with but too much to leave untouched. At any rate we did the best we could, to make a start for ourselves.

"To get the rooms clean required a lot of effort. Mother washed the floors and scraped the stove rings and removed the grime and rust from the pans. I obtained three bucketfuls of chalk and two of lime from the father of a classmate who ran a chemical suppliers. Mr Kalmus had tried to teach us how to paint at Wikman's, an enterprise in which he all but failed. But he had managed to instil in us the foundations of the skill and I now employed my knowledge to good effect. With a mixture of chalk and lime I managed to whitewash both the ceiling vaults and walls of both rooms, the wash house and the room where the mangle stood. Plus the entrance with seven cellar steps which led to an arched passageway between the two buildings, some five paces from the street. We washed the cellar windows till they sparkled, and put up muslin curtains. We burnished the two taps with metal polish. At the street end of the passageway we put up a plywood sign with bright blue letters on a white background: *Aura Laundry*. By the way, I used the word 'aura' on account of its occult connotations as well as the basic meaning you found in the dictionary: a breath of wind. And, of course, the resemblance to the Estonian for steam or vapour – *aur*. In those days, I didn't yet know anything about the medical meaning of the word.

"I made a number of small additions to the interior, replaced the broken window panes in the attic with pieces of plywood to keep the pigeons out, and spanned washing lines across the ceiling. We managed to get some old wardrobes which had been used for surgical smocks and had now been cast out from Uncle Joonas. I did a spot of joinery and built some shelves. These were painted freshly white for the customers' newly ironed and starched laundry, which was packed and had name tags attached. What more was there? From the interior of the mangle I removed the chunks of limestone which had been used as weights, dusty, grimy and mouldy as they were. I scraped the frame clean, gave it a coat of paint and put new ballast in instead. And what did I use? Ha, ha, haa! Mother said that it was pointless to prettify the machine unnecessarily. But I did so nonetheless. From the stone-mason's near the gates of Rahumäe cemetery, I cadged some suitable hunks of marble left over from the Vasalemm stratum (these were the cracked pieces they couldn't use) and took them off in a wheelbarrow. This attracted the attention of our potential customers to our spring clean. I designed and ordered a special barrow for the laundry. It was a tricycle made out of two old bicycles, in effect a plywood box on wheels, freshly painted and, of course, with the words *Aura Laundry* painted on it in blue. In order to collect the dirty washing and deliver the clean laundry it therefore had two interchangeable boxes. Old Trimbek was already retired but he still had his contacts with the railway supply plant and had some of their apprentices knock together the contraption in their spare time. For a few kroons and maybe a bottle of Riigivanem vodka. Or perhaps in those days the latter incentive was not yet needed.

"Well, our first customer turned out to be Mr Weseler himself. Mother asked him to come and inspect our firm. This had, to a certain extent, been put together behind our landlord's back, but he smiled grandly at our efforts, instructing his wife to try the quality of our work. And when he got his shirts back ironed and all *blitz und blank*, they brought us other washing. And it was agreed Mr Weseler would let us off the rent for our living quarters if we did their laundry for them and also, well, all right then, he would let us off the rent, as he put it, for our laundry company, at least for the time being.

"It took a while to build up a clientele, but the number of customers rose steadily. With some surprises. I thought that since Uncle Joonas and Aunt Linda had taken me with them to the seaside at Pärnu for two or three summers running, there would be no problems from that quarter: they would certainly bring their laundry to the Aura if asked. But not a hope of it. Uncle Joonas glanced out of the window and suggested I speak with his wife. And Aunt Linda, can you imagine, answered: Oh no. They couldn't. They would feel embarrassed exploiting my mother's physical toil. I was to understand that if, for instance, Uncle Joonas needed a reception clerk, some kind of nurse or hospital secretary, then my mother would be able to work for them. However, Uncle Joonas didn't actually need one. But as a washerwoman – no. Their delicacy of feeling wouldn't allow it. I don't know who initiated such a strange point of view but they were of course agreed in that respect. It is rather interesting to see the role that events, considerations, feelings and wishes if you like, played on the harp strings of their mental life. But I didn't make a fuss about it and did, by the way, go along with them again to Pärnu the following summer, i.e. that of 1937.

"So anyway, the number of laundry customers gradually grew in number. A few shopkeepers' families came from the Old Town, and a number of doctors too, which made me think on one occasion: maybe Uncle Joonas had at least recommended us to a number of his colleagues . . . ? But I doubt it. At any rate, when my mother and I did the accounts a couple of months later, it turned out that our starting capital had been exhausted, but that along with covering the rent we had nevertheless managed to make a little profit. About forty kroons over the two months. This was, of course, a ridiculously small sum of money. But it meant we had a viable business. It was hard to look into the future, but it did seem at a first glance that our prospects were not entirely hopeless. Admittedly, we had put a great deal of effort into it. In the evenings, I had pulled our barrow-bicycle goodness knows how many kilometres over the cobblestones of the Old Town. And pushed goodness knows how much firewood under the boiling vats. And put goodness knows how many loads of bedclothes and table linen through the mangle. And this was a mere joke compared with what Mother had had to do.

"But – whether in the coal smoke of the smoothing iron (we hadn't yet got a modern 'Siemens-Schuckert' electrical one, instead we had a terribly heavy one that was heated by coal), or in the steam of the wash house – Mother would say, pushing back the strands of greying hair from her sweaty brow, the corner of her eyes glistening: 'This is nothing. I'll hold out . . .'"

Ullo continued: "I wasn't so sure about that. Or that the work had been split up between me and my mother according to our respective strengths. Of course, I tried to do what I could in the laundry. I fetched the firewood – the carter dumped it on the cobbles of the yard, and I had to get it down into the wood store in the cellar. Each day, I would bring a sufficient amount for Mother to stoke the stove. I regarded running up and down the stairs to the attic with the washing to hang it out to dry as my part of the bargain. And then there were the trips with the barrow-cum-bicycle. But one-fifth of these had to be done by my mother since I didn't always have the time. And from time to time I felt a joy at the fact that I was working at the *Sports Encyclopaedia*. The salary I got there was initially very much needed alongside what we made with the laundry.

"But then one day, one December's evening as I remember, I was out delivering clean laundry with our bicycle-barrow. The streets were covered in black ice. The street lanterns were glowing coldly in the darkness – and I rang the doorbell at some address on Toompuiestee from the list my mother had given me.

"An unknown housewife opened the door. I said with a practised smile: 'The Aura Laundry is pleased to deliver your clean washing . . .' and heaved my blue-and-white box into the hall of her flat. The lady called out in the direction of the living room: 'Eevald – come and pay the young man for our laundry . . .'

"There, in the hall, unceremoniously and in his braces – stood my boss. The editor-in-chief of our *Sports Encyclopaedia*, the prematurely balding, paunchy Mr Karu. Who, after the Olympic Games and the money for the editor from our commander-in-chief, had become quite military in attitude. I said: 'Oh, look, it's the editor-in-chief in person. I didn't know you were one of our customers . . .'

"I feel that the surprise on my part was quite neutral. I was even almost pleasantly surprised. Despite the fact that I had by then decided to leave the editor's office as you already know. Because of the bet. And because of the atmosphere of a training school for NCOs in which the editorial office bathed. I will say: I was at least neutrally surprised. But his surprise was not entirely neutral and it was not pleasant.

"'Paerand –? What kind of clowning is this?!'

"'What do you mean?'

"'Well, playing at being an errand boy for a laundry, eh?!'

"'I'm not playing. I *am* an errand boy.'

"The editor-in-chief said didactically, while counting out the three red five-kroon notes which he owed me for the laundry: 'You're an editor at the *Sports Encyclopaedia*. Do you really think that this sort of –' and he pointed to the *Aura Laundry* box '– that this sort of job-on-the-side is *compatible* with work as one of our editors?'

"And then I felt what, presumably, everyone feels in a similar situation, however calmly they normally thought. Anger and insult were visibly throwing a fine-meshed red net over my equanimity, quite transparent, but impenetrable. Discretion foundered, turning into helplessness, paralysis, immobility, rigidity. I announced (and under-stood perfectly well how atavistic this was, but I enjoyed my freedom immensely): 'Yes, Mr Karu, sir. Perfectly compatible. But it's not a job-on-the-side, it's my main job. The work I do for the Aura Laundry is my main job, what I do at the *Sports Encyclopaedia* is my job-on-the-side.'"

Ullo went on: "I remember what you'd told me – and you've surely written somewhere about it – how our old headmaster, Wikman, had problems with Laasik who, wearing his school cap, stood on the market place selling things, and the headmaster had tried to ban him from doing so. But Laasik had said that if he wasn't allowed to, he'd have to change schools – because he simply *had* to help his mother. And the headmaster had backed down, saying he should indeed help his mother, but instead of our school cap please wear a hat on the market place (which was, by the way, just as strictly prohibited under other circumstances). That's how it was. I didn't try to talk Karu round regarding the necessity of helping my mother. Instead, I repeated what I've already said a minute ago, with a provocative grin on my face, adding: 'If this doesn't suit you, I can always drop in at the editorial office tomorrow morning and leave my letter of resignation on your desk . . .' I stretched out my hand in the direction of the five-kroon notes he was holding. And when he didn't react to my gesture – he was presumably looking for something momentous to reply with and that always took him a little while – I turned to his wife, to the lady I now understood to be Mrs Pihl, a gymnastics teacher who, for some reason, did not have the same surname as her husband. The woman was standing on the other side of the Aura Laundry box with a pained smile on her face. She was, I have to say, an attractive blonde with soft features and sad eyes and markedly younger than her robust husband – and I have asked myself afterwards: was there not a tinge of jealousy in my behaviour? I said to the lady, smiling wryly: 'So you see – my editor-in-chief is incapable of doing two things at a time: accepting my resignation and paying me the laundry money. Because this would require the presence of two convolutions of the brain.'"

Ullo laughed: "Well, as you can imagine: he of course sacked me there and then. But I have to admit, even if grudgingly, that he had enough aplomb to do it correctly, at least in appearance:

"'Mr Paerand, I think that you yourself understand that after this – erm – scene you can no longer continue working at the *Sports Encyclopaedia*!'

"I said: 'Of course I understand. I neither can, nor wish to. I will drop in tomorrow and empty my desk. And I would appreciate it if you could pay me one and a half months' salary. You yourself know the law on labour protection, I would imagine.'

"But then I felt I had to say something more. So I turned to his wife, who was still standing on the other side of the box and said, out of sheer spite: 'My dear lady – you'll of course have stocked up the dirty laundry for the past two weeks. I'll take it with me now. You see, now I'll have the time to devote myself fully to my job at the laundry. So your laundry will be done *even better* than before.'

"I looked her in the eye, with suggestion and friendliness. And can you imagine, she actually said: 'Yes, it's all packed up ready. I'll go and fetch it now.'

"The editor pushed his fivers into my hand and called out to his wife: 'Helmi! Leave it! Do you really think –'

"I lifted the Aura Laundry box up from the floor and said: 'Yes. You'll have to sort that problem out between yourselves. Your wife knows where we are,' and looked at his wife with an expression of regret on my face. And then left. And that's all. The next day, when I arrived at the editorial office to take my belongings, Karu naturally didn't ask me to stay after all. But thanks to these events, my mother and I did manage to get the laundry going over the space of the next six months. And how? By means of precision. Courtesy . . ." I remember Ullo raising a lecturing finger in the air and saying: "With fragrance. That's how we did it."

He went on: "We ordered lavender powder from the small Hasselblatt chemical works on the Paldiski Road. This was packed in porous paper sachets, each sachet containing a few grams of the powder. I stamped the words 'Aura Laundry' on each sachet. We'd put one or two sachets in with each clean batch of laundry. And it worked. Soon our customers started asking where you could buy it. So we began to sell them the stuff ourselves. We earned, let's see, I don't rightly remember, ten cents per sachet? Which was, of course, peanuts. But our customers began multiplying in number. Incidentally, Mrs Pihl, that is to say Mrs Karu, continued to send us her laundry. In June 1937, when I went off to Pärnu for the summer at the invitation of Uncle Joonas and Aunt Linda for the last time, we paid my classmate Tomp and his sister Viire to assist us, to give my mother a break too. Viire, a girl who'd recently left school, was without work, and where Kaarel worked, some ski factory or other, they were having their summer holidays.

I convinced my mother that she should seize the opportunity to take a couple of weeks off. She could pop into the laundry once a day if need be, but I insisted she relax for a while nonetheless. I took the narrow gauge train to Pärnu. Uncle Joonas and Aunt Linda had travelled over in the brand new 'Mootor' motor coach, but that cost three times as much."

20

ULLO SAID: "DO YOU know, my three trips to Pärnu, a fortnight to three weeks per time, were episodes in themselves. And my visits to the Barbarus household with Uncle Joonas and Aunt Linda were episodes within episodes. That was all fifty years ago now.

"When I arrived at Papli Street with my crocodile-skin suitcase which contained clean underwear and a dozen books, Uncle Joonas and Aunt Linda were already there. The flat consisted of a living room for the doctor and his wife, a bedroom and a small kitchen. There was also a spacious hall and a large veranda. The veranda led out to the garden and to the hall, and you couldn't get to it through the rooms themselves. The living room contained two basket chairs, a half-empty, that is to say half-full bookcase, a standard lamp, a table and a sofa. As on previous occasions, Aunt Linda helped me make myself at home. Our daily routine began with boiling water for the coffee, and making sandwiches with ingredients from the turn-of-the-century fridge (which was filled every ten days with fresh ice). The rota was the result of drawing lots. I would then wave to my uncle and aunt through their open window as I went out of the gate with a pair of sunglasses, a couple of books, my blue *frottée* bath towel and my swimming trunks, down to the beach. There I would lie in the sun, splash around, and read until lunchtime. And by the second or third day, I realised just how much I had been in need of a holiday, after my working year at the editorial office plus the laundry. And I also realised how much my mother needed one. So I wrote her a postcard – with a suitable picture of a newly opened Strand Hotel. On it I wrote: 'Take a break, leave Kaarel Tomp and his sister in charge, and come and relax!'

"We would normally eat lunch at home and this was prepared for us by Aunt Linda. We only went down to the beach café to eat lunch on a couple of occasions. For although Uncle Joonas and Aunt Linda tried to give the impression that they were well-off summer visitors, we were in fact being as economical as possible. But we did go on a couple of occasions to eat dinner at the hotel on the promenade and also a few times to visit Barbarus. Since he was a colleague of my uncle's, let us call him by his real name: Dr Vares. We went to his castle on Vilmsi Street."

Ullo paused for a moment to think, then continued: "'Castle' was a term used mockingly in this context. But at the time, the good doctor did not deserve malicious comment. He was a well-respected doctor and his patients ranged widely, from unemployed workers to factory directors, on occasion to the richest tourists from America, and everyone appreciated him in equal measure. Those more in the know, for instance, knew that he even constructed doctors' equipment. In other words, he was an inventor. He had invented a portable lung-efficiency meter, one you could carry in a suitcase. Uncle Joonas – and he was quite an expert on internal diseases – thought it a brilliant invention. I suppose it was. And as a poet, Barbarus was equally praised – though I have never regarded him as a great poet. His use of language was too coarse, and especially in, well, the field of rhythm he proved to be unbelievably cack-handed and insensitive. But God knows, Tuglas wrote that perhaps this roughness needed the clumsy form, that these were perhaps entirely suited to him. At any rate, he wasn't a great poet, but he was an interesting phenomenon in our world of poetry, someone who pushed back its frontiers, in the guise of a gentleman blowing the trumpet of social reform. And he was a genuine humanist. He could be called out at midnight to visit a sick patient. He was an erudite man, through and through. An expert on French poetry, for example. And a connoisseur of French wines, too.

"But as for his 'castle', this term was always used malevolently. For in Central and Northern Europe, doctors of his rank lived in much nobler residences. His house was relatively roomy, but it was a wooden house, the ground floor plus an attic, on what was more or less a side street. There were a dozen or so rooms on the two floors. I never went in even half of them. But where I did go – the surgery, the library, the dining room, the drawing room – they were furnished in the manner of the *haute bourgeoisie*. The barrels of the microscopes in his surgery were always polished. Half the furniture, oak, redwood, must have

141

been specially designed for him by Adamson-Eric. Adamson was a close relative or distant relation of the doctor's old friend Semper. Adamson spent the summer in Paris, where he won a gold medal at the World Exhibition. For plates and leatherwork, or whatever it was he won it for. And the doctor had paintings by that very same Adamson on his walls, a painter who fought against his own personal surfeit of elegance in his pictures. Then there were works by Jaan Vahtra, woodcuts and paintings. He had also become a friend of Barbarus, I don't know when and how. And then there was Vardi's brilliant portrait – the portrait of the lady of the house. But the people I met in that house were even more interesting than its objects. Perhaps the most interesting was the wife herself.

"This Mrs Siuts was a fragile and softly spoken woman. Was this not a classical case of the doctor and the lung patient? If so, then she had been brought halfway to health by the doctor, but had retained her quiet beauty and translucent attraction. And also her thankful devotion to the doctor. He enthused about his Galatea. At one time, two portraits of her hung in the house, the Adamson one in the drawing room, a Bergman in the doctor's surgery.

"But as I said, the people I caught a glimpse of here were remarkable as well: Semper, in those days, as you will know, was one of the cardinals of Estonian poetry – if we regard Tuglas as the Pope – with his wife Aurora, who was a former classmate of the doctor's and an old heart-throb of his. Talvik came with his Betti. They got married that same summer. Talvik was already established as Talvik, but Betti had attracted attention with her collection of poems *Tolm ja tuli – Dust and Fire*. And there was the very young, very fair-headed, very lanky Sang. Still as good as unknown, but I remember him from those years on account of his '*Müürid*' – '*Walls*'. With his brunette Kersti. She had '*Maantee tuuled*' – '*Winds on the Highway*' – in manuscript form in her handbag.

"No, I don't remember any memorable poetry readings taking place there. But on my very first visit there and also during the last in the summer of '37, in the small hours, the master of the house, holding an unfinished glass of Barsac in front of him, would start reading out his most recent poems to Joonas and Linda, and also to me."

"What sort of poems?" I asked.

Ullo shrugged his shoulders: "I don't really remember. On the last occasion, something from his collection *Kalad kuival – Drying Fish*. It hadn't come out yet."

Ullo paused, looked at the clouds hanging over the silhouette of Toompea Hill, and changed the subject. Now he spoke of what was in the papers that summer of '37 concerning events in Russia and how they were discussed in the Barbarus household. I had to break him off.

"Wait a minute. I'd like to hear details about all that. But before you do, you once told me that you yourself read out poems to Barbarus with a glass of wine in front of you . . . ?"

Ullo smiled and looked again out of the window.

"Well, it's like this. I have been prattling, haven't I. Sorry, you've even managed to write it down, I see. But luckily, not got round to printing it. That would . . ." He now exchanged his wry smile for a friendly grin. "So in some sense, the Soviet censor is almost indispensable . . . The only thing is, I don't actually remember where and what you had the kindness to write about my night-time poetry reading in front of Barbarus."

I said: "But I remember exactly where I wrote about this. Would you like me to jog your memory?"

"Oh, that won't be necessary . . ." grunted Ullo.

But I quoted:

"Ullo had listened to the doctor reading his poetry with interest, but thought it rather heavy despite all the bravura with which it had been read. As did the majority of poetry readers. Ullo was anything but pushy, but would on occasion raise his Sagittarian head, or that of a secretary bird, and achieve things which one would have assumed to be far from modest. Anyhow, he pulled out a number of his own poems from his pocket and read them out to the doctor."

"There you are!" said Ullo. "I really did tell you that. And it's enough . . ."

I cried: "But you haven't even said what sort of poems they were! And what did he think of them? Barbarus, I mean!"

Ullo muttered: "Well, they were quite different from his own, as you can imagine. But I felt that he almost liked them nonetheless. In general, he had a capacity for tolerating or even enjoying things that

143

were alien to him – you understand – also things which, to an extent, humiliated him. I mean to say, he had a masochistic streak in him . . ."

"And what else did you notice about him?"

Ullo needed no time to think. "His paradoxical nature."

"How d'you mean?"

Ullo explained: "The paradox of the rough-barked nature of his texts as opposed to his mildness with the people he mixed with. A paradox which is almost tragicomic, along with the animosity towards the premature paunch he was cultivating. His paunchiness and his bouncy brand of sporting agility. His learning as opposed to his childlike qualities, if you like . . ."

I waited for a moment. But Ullo remained silent. So I said: "OK. You mentioned the events in Russia as they were reported in the newspapers that summer, and how they were discussed in that household. Tell me more. It's more than just exciting . . ."

Ullo said: "It was the events in Russia which kept the papers going that June. Along with the stuff about the opening of the Strand Hotel and the Women's Home Guard Week and other tittle-tattle. It was set against a background of national events in Estonia of course: the Swedish Foreign Minister Sandler's visit to Tallinn and that of Lord Plymouth, plus the parliamentary sessions at the Riigikogu. The Civil War in Spain was also lurking in the background. But what was happening in Moscow and elsewhere in Russia shook the whole world. First, Gamarnik's suicide. And then rumours about the arrest of the Red Army top brass were published. These being officially denied by Moscow. Three days later, eight traitors to the Rodina were exposed. Two days later, they had been charged. And had admitted their guilt down to the last accusation. And were sentenced to death, and the sentence was executed. And who had these traitors and blackguards been? Gamarnik had been the head of the political authority of the Red Army. The others were Field Marshal Tukhachevski and his generals. *Pravda* wrote about them – and this was quoted in *Päevaleht* :

"Holy rage seized millions of workers when they heard of the heinous deeds of the gang of conspirators in the army. Through-out our huge Soviet Union, unanimous votes were taken at meetings and rallies, by workers, Red Guards, members of the intelligentsia and kolkhozniks, all deciding that the conspirators

144

should be shot, and praising the decision of the court. The eagle eye of the dictatorship of the proletariat has rooted out these dens of conspiracy, created as they were by a foreign power. The dictatorship of the proletariat has crushed underfoot this nest and wiped it off the face of the earth. May dogs die a dog's death!

"I remember discussing the events with Uncle Joonas and Aunt Linda around the coffee table on Papli Street. On the basis of this sparse information provided to us by *Päevaleht*. Plus the odd bit extra which Uncle Joonas had gleaned from the Finnish daily *Uusi Suomi* and its Swedish counterpart *Svenska Dagbladet* during his morning visit to the beach café. Uncle Joonas didn't really know either Finnish or Swedish that well, but managed somehow to get the gist of what they were saying. Aunt Linda explained the situation in simple terms, too simplistically, but more than adequately: 'The Russians have been a bit confused for quite some while. Haven't they already been butchering their political parties for several years now? Putting the Trotskyists up against the wall? Now they really have gone off their rockers. They're dashing to pieces their own war machine. All I can say is: may God help them . . .'

"Then we were invited to Vilmsi Street for dinner. I remember that the lady of the house apologised several times as we sat round the well-laden table, that things were not *comme il faut*, since they now had a new and inexperienced cook. And after the hors d'oeuvres, the master of the house asked if we would mind taking a quarter of an hour's break from eating and disappeared off somewhere, returning a little while later. Meanwhile, our hostess explained: 'He bought a big Marconi radio set recently and every morning and evening, and at midnight, he listens to the news . . .' The doctor then returned really pale in the face after listening to the evening news.

"'Well, yes. At nine, I listen to the Luxembourg broadcast, and at midnight, one from Paris. They are the most sober and objective surveys of world news. But these last few days – it's all been so *depressing*! Joonas, Linda – have you heard about the massacres taking place in Moscow, eh? As Europe comes ever more under the influence of the Brownshirts, Moscow was the only remaining hope and strength for many, including myself. But now, I just heard – this self-destructive paranoia is spreading over the whole land! Yesterday in Khabarovsk, ninety-five Trotskyists were shot. In White Russia, the People's Commissar for Agriculture, Benek, or whatever his name is, has been arrested, along with his whole staff. The charge? Listen to this: in their laboratories they had prepared pills to cure horses and cattle which contained bubonic plague bacteria – and these had been distributed throughout the country. All the kolkhozes in White Russia are said to be secret intelligence centres working for the Poles . . . According to the British papers nine hundred soldiers have been arrested and shot in Kiev, and three hundred in Kharkov. Their families have been sent to Siberia.'"

Ullo said: "Over *rosolye* and stuffed eggs, later coffee and a glass of Benedictine, Barbarus deliberated as to which internal and external powers were manipulating Moscow in this way, in all its length and breadth. But then, during my following and last trip to Pärnu . . . Yes, I did go just one more time – during the autumn of 1939. Not for a summer holiday this time but, for once, to Barbarus's house. I was by then at another stage in my life, already working for Uluots in the Prime Minister's Chancery as a civil servant at large. And ended up in Pärnu on account of the fact that my mother had begun getting annoying pains, rheumatic ones or maybe neuralgic. Uncle Joonas had nagged her into going to the medicinal mud baths in Pärnu. This was a pretty expensive affair, but the sick fund paid some of it and we managed to pay some ourselves, so Mother was there for three weeks. On her last weekend, I took Saturday off and went to fetch her. It turned out that Barbarus, i.e. Dr Vares, had managed to find my mother in her room. 'Mrs Paerand, do you happen to be my old friend Dr Berend's – erm, his sister-in-law?' He had even asked whether she was the mother of 'that young poet Paerand'. Barbarus didn't work as a doctor at the sanatorium, but he was invited to do consultations there, now and again. And had seen my mother there a few times and given her advice with regard to her medication. Mother had mentioned to him that she'd asked to be signed out for that Saturday morning and that I had come to fetch her. And then the doctor had invited us over to Vilmsi Street for lunch. So that is where we went. Well, as soon as you asked me for my impressions of him, I used the word *paradox*. Perhaps *vacillation* would have been more apt, because at the lunch table we talked about the very same things as on the previous occasion, i.e. the time I went along with Joonas and Linda. Because now there was news in the papers about the show trials – Bukharin, Yagoda, Rykov and all those criminals, who had been sentenced to death. It suddenly struck me that now our host's attitude to these matters was an entirely new one. It was no longer perplexed depression. There was no trace of paranoia now. What they were doing was 'well, I suppose, tragic, for sure, but inevitable, very necessary, political steps, unavoidable – Draconian steps, yes, but ones which will cleanse the world!'

"Which caused me to think, not immediately of course, not right then at the lunch table, before we took the late-evening train back to Tallinn, that the doctor had been talking about his trip to Greece and Yugoslavia that spring. Much later, years later, the penny dropped. But I never had the time or the opportunity to research the matter.

"Dr Vares had gone that spring to Greece and Yugoslavia. It would have been really interesting to know if two other people went on holiday at roughly the same time. I am thinking here of the medical doctor, Professor Kirchenšteins and the schoolmaster – and, OK, also writer – Paleckis. The former to, say, Sopot, the latter perhaps to Karlovy Vary . . . And, in those resorts, if they had been contacted by Moscow for the first time. Because they must have been contacted somewhere! It was better to do so abroad than at home where every such step would present danger and such contacts would be obvious to everyone, however invisible they would try to make them. Quite secret trips of some importance to what seemed Western resorts from Moscow's point of view but which were handy for doing important state business . . . I remember, during my last trip to Pärnu, when we had dropped the subject of the fates of Bukharin and the others, and Barbarus had spoken about his Yugoslavia trip late that spring. Both Mrs Siuts and the doctor had related in unison how exceptionally beautiful the landscapes were there on the Adriatic. Barbarus spoke especially warmly of the Bay of Kotor. Looking down from the mountains and out over the sea was said to be the most beautiful vista in the whole of Europe. So I can well imagine that it could have happened somewhere near there, somewhere on a sheltered hotel balcony . . . Mrs Siuts gone to bed with a headache and a sleeping tablet, and the doctor, plus a couple of gentlemen from the hotel, people he'd got to know the previous week, were lounging in deckchairs sipping slivovitz or Zlatna Kapliva. One of these eminently pleasant gentlemen was from the Soviet Telegraph Agency, the other from the Foreign Ministry. So Barbarus was able to have a pleasant talk in the Russian language, which he had by no means managed to forget. And the one from the telegraph agency was a graduate of Kiev University! So they had memories and points of departure from the time before and during the Great War. So, so many. And during their conversation, a number of surprises came up: 'A *my zhe konechno nablyudaem vsyo vremya za dostizheniami nashikh dobletsnyikh malenkikh sosedeii – osobenno v oblasti kulturyi – I gospodin Vares –* we have observed your personal – let us say – almost heroic role in the struggle for culture in your homeland. Pärnu is, of course, only the provinces, but . . .' And so forth. No one in Estonia had, at least in polite society, trumpeted abroad Pärnu's provinciality louder than he had . . . But now that the self-confident Muscovite had said this, so far from home, his gaze falling now on the doctor's ruddy face, lit up by the matt bulb of the night lamp and the stars reflected in the black of the bay at the foot of the mountains, his own face swathed in the smoke of a Papastratos cigarette, now, his declaration of Pärnu as a mere province seemed – well, if not exactly insulting, then almost inadmissible. The only thing was that he had not managed to notice such details since the words about Dr Vares's *almost heroic role* knocked his hurt feelings off their feet at one blow.

"And then, after the second glass from the second bottle: 'You see, *gospodin doktor* – we appreciate your profound interest in literature and humanism as a whole. But diplomacy is something of which you have relatively little experience. That is to say, for a small and entirely independent state to ask the government of its larger neighbour whom it would most like to see in the post of prime minister in the small independent state – such things never happen in diplomatic circles. Officially – they never happen. For instance, if your president were to send Varma from the Estonian Embassy on Sobinov Street on a visit to Molotov to ask his approval – this never happens. But unofficially, merely in order to collect information – that is quite a different affair. Let us imagine Mr Varma's Second Secretary and myself in an intimate corner of your comfortable little embassy, at some reception or other, during a conversation, a mere five minutes in length, champagne glass in hand, and this Second Secretary poses the question – to me: I would wish – especially after our entirely coincidental private meeting on this, our present trip – to say this: I would like you to know that we think that Dr Vares would be perfectly suited to the task of developing relations between Moscow and Tallinn, at this time of complexity for international relations. But I am not allowed to say this. Not as long as I do not know whether you would concur. For maybe your personal peace of existence in order to work on your poetry is more important to you than, well, let us term it, taking the responsibility for guarding you native land, between, and why not say it, Scylla and Charybdis – *pour faire usage de la formule classique* (by which Ivan Ivanovich shows that he is of the Czarist school of diplomacy)."

Ullo's brow had become a trifle moist and a lock of greying hair with three streaks of white, had fallen over his right ear. He looked past me, absorbed in his historical imagination, then continued:

"And then a person from a telegraph office, from the further and deeper shadows, was switched on: '*Gospodin doktor, dorogoi moi* – you don't need to answer right away. Take your time – this is all pure improvisation, for the time being. So: think it over. I'll be coming to Estonia, to Tallinn, in the near future. Also to Pärnu. To receive the plan for the Estonian anthology of poetry from you and your colleagues. This will be published in Moscow. You will put together that plan. And do not reply verbally to the question we have put to you today. The moment may not be the right one. Include your answer in the plan. Let us agree on this: there ought to be a list of authors. And after each name, his proposed work. If you put your own name at the top of the list, this would mean that your answer is no. If you put it in its alphabetical place – no. If you put it at the end – no. But if you put it – shall we say with the modesty of the collator at the end of the list, but then add some forgotten figure – so that yours ends up in the penultimate place – this will mean your answer is yes. Let us agree: twenty names. Your answer will be *no* by default – unless your name appears nineteenth on the list . . . '"

Ullo came from his empty Peter Brookian space back into my study with its view over Toompea, brushed back the lock of hair, looked me straight in the face and smiled awkwardly.

"Well, something like that, anyway – !"

I remarked: "Which means that no one on this side of eternity ever got to see the list?"

He replied: "What do you mean 'no one'? Only the ones who mattered . . ."

21

ULLO TREATED HIS CAREER as a civil servant with greater seriousness, or to be more exact, with a greater muteness of his disdainful superiority than expected. With irony, that goes without saying. But nonetheless with what felt to me like nostalgia. I was a little wary of sounding out the superficial aspects or plumbing the depths, so that the relationship between his ironic surface and the serious nostalgia for his bygone career in the civil service never became apparent.

In terms of how he became a civil servant in the first place, Ullo told me more or less the following:

In around April 1937 he had left the editorial offices of the *Sports Encyclopaedia*, and devoted his efforts to building up the Aura Laundry. But in early January 1938, he had read in *Päevaleht* that the Central Elections Committee needed temporary assistants to prepare for and run the forthcoming elections to the Chamber of Deputies – the *Riigivolikogu*. The elections were scheduled to be held on 24 and 25 February of 1938 and the temps had to be working by 1 February.

Ullo thought that he had energy over from running the laundry, and they desperately needed the extra sixty kroons, for income continued to be a problem. He went up on to Toompea and filled in the necessary application form.

"Perhaps I was toying with the thought that it could lead to something more permanent," he explained. "But I can't say that I took the prospects of this temporary job too seriously, because some two hundred people applied, for twenty paid posts. On account of this lack of seriousness, I filled in the space for *Education*: Matriculated from the Wikman Grammar School, Tallinn, in 1934, removed from the register of Tartu University in 1936 for an indefinite period, until the university is reformed. And in the space for *Family Circumstances*

I wrote: *de jure* single, but *de facto* not quite. Because this was still very much during Ruta's time.

"On the strength of their applications, some fifty people were asked for interview and of these, twenty were picked out. And surprisingly, and yet somehow inevitably, I was among the chosen.

"I fixed up the Tomp boy, who was again without work, to come and help my mother at the laundry. I agreed with him: if needs be, he would lie to my mother that I was paying him thirty kroons a month. In fact, he wouldn't work for less than fifty kroons, and that was what I paid him. This meant that I would only have ten left over from the money I got for the elections work. But the change of environment and the adventure involved in such a change of employment were more than welcome.

"On 1 February, things got going. There were twenty young people, all aged between twenty and twenty-five, fifteen girls and five boys, in the large, bright, four-windowed room in the attic of Toompea Castle. Through the windows we could see snow-flecked red-tiled roofs and above them the sun. At least for the first few days, all I remember is the sun.

"Around the walls there were bookshelves, empty at first, where the election material, newly arrived from the State Printing Works, was put on display. In the middle of the room stood three incomparably large office tables from the Luther Plywood Manufactory where we would spread the material out. We were supervised by three bosses who sat either amongst us at the same tables, or in adjoining rooms: the Head of the Election Committee, Jõgi, a jovial and older man with a crew cut, soon began to show some interest in me. He clearly had the rather dubious idea of turning me into a decent civil servant. Then there was the First Secretary of the Committee, Mägi, who we saw much less of, a man with a steely authoritarian gaze and a kind of matt, ash-grey-coloured hair, though of all my future bosses he had the fairest. And the third boss was the Chairman of the Committee, and the man who involved himself the least with our job – old Mr Maddissoo, a sour little crab apple with inch-thick pebble glasses who mainly exuded a sniffling brand of impatience, but who was in the main quite harmless.

"Of all my colleagues, I can only remember two, one boy and one girl. The boy was Anton Raadik – yes, the very same who was soon to

151

become famous as a boxer. He even became the European middleweight champion, but not until Estonia had become more or less cut off by the sea. In our committee he was some kind of forwarding clerk. He had been trained as a saddler and played the Teddy boy when necessary, but when not doing so he was prepared to act the pub gentleman. And then there was the girl . . ."

When I leaf through my notes I notice that in almost every situation, Ullo made a point of mentioning the women who attracted his attention. I began to wonder whether he was doing so in order to fulfil some artistic exigency. Maybe they never actually turned up as vital elements in such situations? They were indeed present, but were much more some kind of ersatz than Ullo made out. This delicate question sometimes drove me to, how shall I say, a state of perplexity. So unfortunately, I never actually asked him. Though I can well imagine what he would have answered.

"Goodness me, haven't you noticed? Sometimes in our tales we use our best paints, sometimes poorer ones. We apply the paint more thickly where something has remained unachieved, thinner where we achieved something. In general we try to turn our life into art, or at least try to nudge our lives a little *in the direction* of art. Or towards what people at the time consider as art . . ."

Anyhow, on to the girl. Ullo said about her: "Her name was Piia Alkman, and I think she had matriculated from the Kaarli Grammar School. Though I never saw any certificate. But she had to know something, because it was Mr Maddissoo who took her on, on the strength of the interview. As fate would have it, she sat right across the table from me. Kitted up for war in minimal battledress. And maximum warpaint. In some kind of white costume with the odd black stripe. Under the top she wore a white close-fitting blouse, open to well below her caesura. Her limbs were quite unusual: delicate wrists and voluptuously shaped forearms, delicate ankles, rounded knees and further up there was an abundance which was more than adequate for a twenty-year-old, but which made one wonder: what would it all look like in ten years' time? Which was something we did not of course ask. For we were thinking how we could, that evening – or the next day – or the following week . . . All the more since despite her tousled red hair and heavy eyelids, plus her lips, dark with the lipstick applied, Piia wasn't in any way vulgar. Just simply pretty. Though I said to myself, after a couple of attempts at conversation that resulted in receiving monosyllabic replies: these grapes are sour. And my only consolation was that she also rejected the advances of the boxer Raadik in the same icy, or, now it strikes me, in an even more icy way than my own."

To my question as to how the novelette of Ullo and Piia proceeded and how it ended, he answered, after gazing out of the window for some good while: "Wait a minute . . ." So I thought: does he need this short pause to make up his story? And I said, in some embarrassment: "Well, all right then. Just tell me what your work actually consisted of."

And Ullo explained. As I understood it, the task they were to perform was basically this: to divide up the material received from the State Printing Works into piles for each provincial electoral committee and to send this off by post. All the electoral districts were to receive the necessary excerpts from the Constitution and the Law on Elections, plus the necessary guidelines and bulletins up to and including the ballot papers themselves, plus a book of protocol for each district.

Roughly at this point, I underlined in my notes, the phrase: *Ullo manip??* Because I remember that he had proposed some way of rationalising the papers, for simplicity's sake. And his proposal had been accepted. It went something like this. When old Jõgi had begun to explain which of the papers they should be dealing with over the next two or three days, Ullo had said – in his youthful exuberance: "Mr Jõgi, sir, I understand that the ballot papers are, of course, of ballot paper format, but the rest, some nine different papers in all, are all octavo. Would it not be more efficient to cut them all so that they have three different widths and three different lengths in all? Then you'd have nine different formats. These would be easier to deal with when collating them . . . ?"

Jõgi had taken Ullo into his office and let Ullo explain his idea in more detail. Then he and Ullo had walked over to the State Printing Works and discussed the matter with the head of the lodge there. And with only one day's delay, all the material was printed with the appropriate two-centimetre differences in length and width. So that old Maddissoo had cleared his throat and said: "Yes. A good idea, I suppose . . ."

They had sorted for some three weeks, and on the evening of 26 February they had all the material back in the attic of Toompea

Castle. Ballot papers were packed by the hundred, plus the appropriate protocols, in eighty reinforced boxes with brass ribs. The entire evening, night and the following morning, the three Election Committee bosses plus Ullo checked ballot papers and the booklets of protocols. The differences proved to be tiny.

The next day, the 28th, of the twenty temporary assistants, eighteen were dismissed – Piia too, to Ullo's disappointment and relief. Two were asked to stay on – and both accepted the job: Raadik became the courier for the Riigivolikogu office, and Ullo became a civil servant. The former was working for fifty kroons a month, the latter for sixty.

Ullo elucidated: "I have to say that nothing exciting happened during those months I worked at the Riigivolikogu office. I did casual paperwork of the usual kind. From time to time, old Jõgi sent me off to deliver documents personally, even to sittings of the Riigivolikogu, to delegates, or bring them back to the office. Or to settle things with the typing pool. Around a dozen ladies worked there. You will ask me whether I had an eye for any of them. Not really. Or only perhaps for the small freckled redhead, the same age as myself, Leida Saarloo, who had one green eye, one brown. She treated me with friendly and jovial condescension. She was an ideal typist. Six hundred strokes a minute, day and night. I bet her that over a month I could get up to her speed. At the time the bet was made, I was only doing around two hundred. I went in the evening, several weeks in a row – you'll remember this – to the Vöölmann offices, with your dad's permission, and practised on an old Continental. I got up to 550 strokes a minute. I would have needed one more week, but then I dropped the whole thing because I thought it simply wouldn't be fair to beat the diminutive redhead with one eye so charmingly green, the other brown. I took her the agreed sum of ten kroons, plus one yellow rose, but she refused to accept them, and we squabbled for so long over the bet that the whole group of twittering typists, eager for gossip, had written us into a whole romantic novel, or at least a novella . . .

"Then Jõgi called me to his office – it was now August '38 – and wondered if I wouldn't like to go and work at the State Chancellery itself. This would be promotion, would it not? A small step forward, but promotion nevertheless. A senior office worker. At a salary of seventy kroons a month. I joked with Jõgi that at the rate of two rises of ten kroons each per year, within twenty years I could be a minister,

154

and, within thirty, prime minister, going by the state salary scale. I accepted, why not, and off I went to the State Chancellery. Which was not admittedly such a good move, taking into account the further expansion of our laundry business.

"You have asked me what the atmosphere was like in my first three posts. That is very easy to describe. My easiest, happiest time was the first month working for the Election Committee with all the lasses and lads. This was like messing around in kindergarten. But it was there that I gained – strangely enough – a little faith in myself. Then, little by little, as I moved from one post to the next, this surge of joy abated while the feelings of being in a kindergarten remained, and of one's own self-importance increased. That's right. I began to notice all this – and quite against my will – even in myself. Because all those bosses who hovered around the Riigivolikogu regarded it as a historical matter of parliamentary dimensions. Me too, despite all the ironies involved. Especially despite the fact that the Constitution, as drawn up by Päts or Klesment, was very presidential and in places even in some ways resembled the statutes of a student society. Nevertheless, I admitted that after the four or five years of constitutional convulsions, the situation did offer a measure of stability. I thought mockingly that after I had made a career – two salary rises a year – and had become prime minister, then I'd turn to the question of real democracy.

"And as if to justify my mockery – or my wry smile: I don't remember whether it had already happened before Christmas '38 or between Christmas and the New Year, but some boss looked me up at the State Chancellery. Someone who looked familiar, but whose name was unknown to me, from the Prime Minister's private staff.

"'Mr Paerand – the Prime Minister would like to have a word with you.'

"Kaarel Eenpalu had been Prime Minister for over six months. He had been *riigivanem*, the Premier, earlier and had been Interior Minister and so forth on several occasions. In his time, the Social Democrats and, naturally, the Communists, in as much as we still had any, and plenty of members of his 'Amicus' student society, criticised him, calling him a Minister of the Interior with the outstanding qualities of a police officer in the police state of Estonia. Or something of the sort."

Ullo stuck out his lower lip and set his lower teeth out over his upper

155

lip. So that the stubble of his four o'clock shadow crunched between his teeth.

"Well, you know yourself that for forty years it has not been possible to say anything in defence of Eenpalu. Nor do I wish to leap into the breach as his defence counsel. He died in January 1942 of cold and hunger somewhere out there in the Vyatka prison camp before they had managed to serve the death sentence upon him. Out there, thousands of people died, people who deserved their fates even less than Eenpalu. By the way . . ." And here Ullo made an interesting detour into the realms of comparative European political history. And where else should I note his remarks down:

"During those short visits to Toompea, I would catch sight of many ministers up there. Only as they flashed by, but still. On a couple of occasions, I even saw the President himself. And on account of my father – he died just two years ago in Holland where he had been living for most of the past few decades – I've even developed a bit of an interest in things Dutch, i.e. from during the last war and afterwards. This interest has had to remain quite platonic, of course: personal contacts – nil, correspondence – minimal, printed sources – very rare, and censored into the bargain. But a little anyway. And I have managed to compare the fates of the members of the Estonian government and the heads of state during the first Soviet occupation with the corresponding situation during the three-year German occupation of the Netherlands. In Estonia, the situation was as follows: of the eighty or so former ministers, the Russians arrested about seventy-six or seventy-seven. Of these, twenty were shot. The rest were mostly sentenced to labour camp for ten years apiece. Thirty-six of these died in the camps of cold, disease and hunger. Those who were still alive after their sojourn in the camps were not allowed to go straight home, but were sent to internal exile all over the Soviet Union. The years passed and only three returned home, as cripples. Now in the case of Holland, I believe that *one* former minister suffered repression at the hands of the Germans – he was sent to a concentration camp in Germany and was released a couple of years later and sent home. And do you know, to this day I still can't understand how it is possible for people living in the so-called free world to keep quiet about such things – instead of shouting about them for all to hear. But with regard to Eenpalu, I am not going to say anything

156

further except this: he was no angel, but he was not a criminal either nor a genius. And no fool. Although he had an excessive love of power, he loved the legitimacy of his power. So I went to his office, to the very same room in which all our so-called prime ministers have sat – i.e. from Barbarus to Lauristin, Klauson to Toome . . .

"Eenpalu was rumoured to have been a boss capable of very sharp and brusque behaviour when dealing with people, though he looked pretty soft on the outside. He was tall and pretty slim for his almost fifty years of age. If we use novelist Oskar Luts's yardstick for such things, then he was a Kiir rather than a Toots, or a Tõnisson, or an Arno Tali. Yep. A Jorh Aadniel, really. But not in the least comical.

"'You've summoned me, sir?'

"'Yes. Please sit down.'

"I got the impression that he didn't actually know who I was, or why he had summoned me. He sat there at his dull, bare desk, with me in a leather armchair right across from him, to which he had led me. He drew his fingers through his thin, smooth and quite inconspicuous hair, trying to remember who I was and why he had called me, but he didn't succeed – with me all the while sitting reverently with my backside on the edge of the armchair, letting him torment himself – until he finally asked: 'You – are – erm . . .?'

"Only then did I say: 'Ullo Paerand at your service, sir!'

"Happy that he had now at last found an explanation, he then said: 'Yes, yes, of course. Well, let me see now. I'll be brief. I'm in need of a courier. For small assignments, some of which can occasionally even be important ones. I've been told that you could be the suitable person for the job. What have you to say for yourself on this matter?'

"Well, what could I say? I could hardly cry out, oh, yes, yes, I'm undoubtedly the most suitable boy of them all! So I said rapidly, but with some caution: 'I think I could be suitable – as a try-out, sir.'

"He picked up a certain humorous undertone in my reply and it seemed to amuse him a little.

"'Well then, let's give it a try. Go to Major Tilgre, over there, in the next room. He's the Prime Minister's secretary and will run through your duties. You'll be kicking off tomorrow at nine." He rose straightaway and took my hand to shake it in a rather nervous manner.

"And so all of a sudden I found myself in a very coveted post. Not on account of the extra ten kroons I would be receiving, but merely on account of the proximity to the Prime Minister and the seat of power. And to, well – to matters of varying import."

22

"A s for matters of varying import – i.e. secrets, intrigues, affairs – then this thought of mine in Eenpalu's anteroom proved to be completely naive. At least with regard to someone such as myself. I was neither deaf nor blind to what was going on around me but my powers of observation were – how shall I put it – boundlessly limited by my youth. I was principally concerned with small assignments which could, on occasion, be important, as Eenpalu had put it. Even with a more experienced eye I would have hardly caught a glimpse of more universal matters.

"My immediate superior in this new job was, as I have said, Major Tilgre, the Prime Minister's private secretary. He came from the fertile province of Mulgimaa, but was, for all that, a particularly dry individual, a thoroughly correct man of around forty-five. Tilgre had less to do with me than Head of Chancery Terras who was, in hierarchical terms, a much higher and more distant boss. This smallish man was the soul of discretion. He came originally from the Virumaa province near the capital and had graduated from St Petersburg University. He had ideal qualities for a civil servant – he was entirely inconspicuous, but always there when he was needed. Inconspicuous, thus indispensable, to such a degree that he stayed in his post for over twenty years, during all the changes of government in Estonia. And, by the way, he even stayed at his post during the first few weeks of 1946, that is to say during Barbarus's time as Prime Minister. Until one of the informers in place by that time noticed – and then what had to happen, happened. Terras was arrested and given the choice of dying a year later of hunger and dysentery, a normal death at the Solikam labour camp, or freezing to death. Which, God rest his soul, was the normal death for someone of his calibre. As we all know."

And as I leaf through my old exercise books filled with "Ulloica",

I, Jaak Sirkel, think to myself: I myself know this full well. Ullo knew this in quite a mythical way, from hearsay. But as for me, I received a full-blown lecture on the subject (and in an environment of much greater relevance) from a bald-headed chap with major's stripes.

This happened to me during the last days of my career as felt-boot dryer, i.e. in the year 1949. I have described this profession elsewhere. But only now does the thought strike me that my dismissal from what was rather a pleasant job by labour camp standards was maybe the result of this didactic conversation.

The whole thing started because, in the drawer of the desk in the drying room, I had an exercise book in which I occasionally wrote things down, carefully chosen items, let it be said. In those days, mainly poetry. A few of my own, a few translations. Of the last sort I remember Blok's "Girl Singing in a Church Choir" and Simonov's "Zhdi menya". I only wrote down texts which fell within the pale of neutrality, somewhere in between Soviet patriotism and criticism of the powers that be, so that they would not put me in danger, should anyone go inspecting them behind my back. And that someone looked undetected through my lines (as happened with everything out there) was something I was of course quite sure of.

So if you now ask me why I kept such an exercise book in the first place, I can't really give you a satisfactory answer. To a certain extent there arose in me normal feelings such as leaving your mark on the world, an aide-mémoire. But to a certain extent also to provoke the world, as a game, a protest. The informer who read my notebook in my absence (or even in my presence) had, of course, to be Estonian and must have conveyed what I had written to his boss in a manner which put me in a more or less positive light. For months my jottings caused no complications. Then, in the autumn of '49, I was summoned late one evening to appear before the "godfather".

"*Imya? Otchestvo? God rozhdeniya? Statya? Srok?*"

I rattled out the answers and thought to myself: in some strange way this major isn't as wooden as the rest of his colleagues, as far as I have come across them. This sinewy man, fortyish, and prematurely bald, only appears to be sleepy and bored. And right away, he proved my thoughts correct. Instead of approaching the subject by God knows what tangent or other, as was usual here, he plunged straight in.

"What have you been writing in that exercise book out there in the drying room?"

I explained. Expanding my countermove into one involving detail. About my attempts at writing poetry, draft translations, etc., so that anyone researching into such matters nowadays would be tempted to ask whether there was not collusion with the KGB in the way the major and I were talking.

The major asked: "Are you a poet in your own right? Your file states you're a lawyer."

I said: "Yes, I am. But when I'm released, I won't be able to get a job as a lawyer."

The major pursed his lips, stretched his legs and looked at me from under his heavy brow: "Well, you might be able to find work, nonetheless. As a legal consultant for the system of village cooperatives."

I said: "That would hardly do."

"And you think you'd be allowed to write?"

"There are precedents."

"For example?"

"Astafyev. *Alitet Goes to the Hills* is one example."

The major jutted out his chin. "Don't you go around believing all the twaddle you hear. By the way, what are you in here for anyway?"

I thought to myself: that's something you should know – but said: "It's written in my file. For maintaining contacts with bourgeois nationalists during the temporary occupation by German Fascists of the territory of the Estonian Soviet Socialist Republic."

"And did you maintain such contacts?"

I had said "no" to this question so often during interrogation that I said automatically: "Course I didn't."

I thought: well, I hope he doesn't hold it against me that I blamed the Special Commission, i.e. the Soviet Court, claiming they had convicted me groundlessly. But the surprise came from quite another quarter. He thought for a moment, jutted out his chin and said with the aplomb of a superior: "Of course you didn't maintain such contacts. If you had, you'd have received ten years. But you've only been given five."

At this point, the joking and retrospective part of our conversation was exhausted. The second half of our conversation followed, the part which I feel necessary to mention with regard to Ullo. Because herein lies concealed the striving, right up to the present day, of one-third of

Europe to join the rest of Europe. The major's unexpected statement was so provocative that I asked: "But Citizen Major, why are such contacts so deplorable in the eyes of the Soviet authorities that even those innocent of them are punished – as you have admitted in my case?"

The major growled: "What sort of lawyer are you if you can't understand that simple point? Bourgeois nationalists tried to restore their so-called Estonian Republic. Did they, or did they not?"

"I don't know. Maybe."

"But right from the start in 1918, that republic was nothing more than an armed revolt against Soviet power. Your so-called War of Independence was a revolt against the Soviet Union. Leaders of such revolts have to be shot. Their class base has to be eradicated. Those elements operating under their influence have to be scattered. To the taiga, the tundra, the steppe, the desert. Wherever."

I asked: "Does this all mean that everyone who exhibited loyalty to Estonia over a period of twenty years is a criminal?"

"But of course. Everyone. Each in his own individual way."

"And this despite the fact that the Soviet government signed an agreement with Estonia, for what was termed time eternal in the Treaty of Tartu?"

"Good Lord [what he actually said was *Bog pomilui*], an ephemeral little agreement like that can be signed any day you like, when it is in the interests of the immutable policy of the Soviet Union! That is to say – of world revolution!"

Nowadays, the likes of the major would of course substitute "Russia" for the expression "world revolution".

But we should let Ullo continue:

"Work began in the Prime Minister's Chancery at nine o'clock in the morning. At nine thirty the courier would bring post addressed to the Prime Minister or his staff to my desk. It was my job to register it and get it to the appropriate recipient. The majority of communiqués ended up with Terras. He would bring most of these back within the hour having added a few lines of instruction as to how to reply. I would draw up the responses so they were ready for signing. Sometimes, I would receive instructions from Tilgre. For instance, after the Prime Minister's fiftieth birthday, Tilgre brought me 267 telegrams of congratulation which the Prime Minister had received. He said to me:

162

'Reply to them all. But in such a way that each reply seems personal and suitable to the addressee.'

"Luckily, I had been working for almost six months in the job and had some idea about what was demanded of me. The replies still cost me two days' hard work. I used a small stamp and an ink-pad to apply Eenpalu's signature. Incidentally, the stamp was not taken from me at the end of the working day. An act of naivety the likes of which I couldn't even imagine happening today.

"My other work concerned those wishing to have an audience with the Prime Minister. These could be divided into two types: those to whom he had granted an audience, and those whose petitions I had to look through and would have to redirect to other politicians instead. The middle-calibre audience seekers were the least frequent. Mostly it was ministers, generals and directors who tended to come upon invitation. On these occasions I had to make the previous petitioner leave and announce: Mr (or, more rarely, Mrs) So-and-So to see you, sir. Apart from those VIPs, all manner of disaster petitioners would try to sneak in. Once a fortnight, a couple of people, their breath reeking of vodka, would manage to force their way in, people who had received a one-off sum of five or ten kroons and were now, at least during their reeking days, convinced of the fact that the Prime Minister had awarded them a weekly benefit – five or ten kroons was a pitifully small sum anyway. The Prime Minister's small and nasty Cerberuses had to prevent them from cashing in on their luck.

"Not all small-time petitioners were alcoholics. For various reasons, which will soon become apparent, one sticks in my mind. This was old Mr Velgre, a very soft-spoken, very polite gentleman with silver hair and a thin red face. He was not subservient, but very disciplined, as if somehow ashamed of his role as petitioner. A little the worse for wear, but clean-shaven and tidy. He had been a schoolmaster out at Loobre, a country town with city aspirations, and had even become the head of a grammar school out there. But by the time we met he had unfortunately become a little senile.

"I once lent him five or six kroons. Every two months I would announce his arrival to the Prime Minister, who would on each occasion hand me a ten-kroon note, fulfilling a promise or maybe a ritual in so doing.

"Old Mr Velgre's Toompea visit in the first week of June was the third during my time there and he had come for his ten-kroon note from the Prime Minister. He turned up, very correct and quietly spoken as always, with a sunny smile on his face. I showed him to the lacquered black wooden settee across from the writing desk and went to Eenpalu to announce his arrival. The Prime Minister was alone in his office. He gave a brief smile, perplexed and complicit, and with his left hand took from a small strongbox in his desk drawer a tenner, but as I was leaving he called me back and kept me busy with a number of matters by his desk for ten minutes or so. When I returned to my office, the black settee was empty. Restless and fugitive as old Velgre was, he had been unable to wait for me, for he had interpreted my long stay with the Prime Minister as a negative answer and wished to avoid the unpleasantness of hearing this.

"The only thing for it was to go through the ledgers of letters of petition (these were in Major Tilgre's possession) and find out where Velgre lived so that I could take him his ten kroons that evening.

"The street no longer exists, Erbe Street or some such name, but he lived in an old one-storey wooden house. There, the old man opened the door himself, and did not recognise me until I rather forcefully reminded him who I was. He led me through his two-room dwelling which was simple, but quite decent.

"'Precisely, precisely. This is where Maret, my daughter, lives. But let's go to my own area.'

"This consisted of a back room some ten metres square which, apart from a put-you-up couch, was full from floor to ceiling with sheets of paper. There were only a dozen or so books, but sheets of paper by the hundred.

"'I see you're working on something, if I may be so bold . . .'"

"'Well . . . A little.' He seemed to fail to pick up my question about what he was working on, and continued: 'So the Prime Minister remembered. He was, after all, in the battery during the War of Independence . . .'

"Then there she stood in the doorway. This was, of course, his daughter Maret. She was a girl about the same age as myself with an abundance of brown curls, a warm heart-shaped face and observant grey eyes which didn't quite fit in with the rest of her face. Only the next day did I understand why. They were filled with a secret sorrow.

164

"Old Velgre said: 'Well, well, the Prime Minister was good enough to remember. You will have wondered . . .'

"'How d'you mean?' said Maret gently. 'I didn't wonder anything. It was you who was wondering if he hadn't forgotten . . .'

"I rose to go. I shook the old man's hand and let Maret show me out. In the doorway, I asked: 'What's your father working on?'

"The girl shook her head: 'He imagines he's writing – essays or whatever they're supposed to be – about the characteristics of the perfect Estonian youth. But after his stroke, three years ago – physically you'd never notice – after that, his work has become one huge charade.'

"'And you, Miss?'

"'Me – I studied literature for a couple of years at Tartu. But when Dad got pensioned off, I had to leave university.'

"'And now?'

"'Now – oh, I'm a sort of temporary lecturer . . .'

"'Where?'

"'At the kindergarten teacher-training college run by the Christian Women's Union.'

"I asked, now standing outside, beyond the threshold, but egged on by a slight desire to provoke, though I can't think why: 'Are you religious?'

"And the merry girl with the sad eyes replied, looking me in the eye without the slightest trace of embarrassment: 'Oh, that's got nothing to do with it. I deal with the topic of education in world literature.'

"'Oh, how interesting,' I said enthusiastically, as one can say in the heat of the moment, but soon forgets. 'So interesting in fact, that I'd like to hear more about it sometime. Where are those courses held?'

"'On Pikk Street.'

"'You mean in the Young Women's Christian Association building? Can I get hold of you there?'

"'You can if you like. Sometimes –'

"'Goodbye.'

"I never did look her up. Firstly, because this all happened during the time I was going out seriously with Ruta. And secondly, another factor was threatening at the time to become influential, disturbing, sowing confusion in my life.

"Manners in the Prime Minister's anteroom were stiff and formal

165

enough. Ministers and foreign diplomats came to see the Prime Minister wearing tails. Generals rarely turned up in civvies. I had been given instructions about some of the people. For instance, before another visit of Mrs Tammsaare, our author's insistent wife, Terras would comment that she shouldn't be let in to see anyone."

Ullo gave a wry smile, which was both rueful and conspiratorial, and I asked: "So, in what way did you make manoeuvres in this instance?"

Ullo said, the smile aside: "The same procedure every time. In other words, the three 'C's."

"Which were?"

"I conversed with her, calmed her down and convinced her. Then courteously cast her out."

"And was she such a dragon?" I asked.

And he replied: "To an unbelievable extent. But I want to talk about another visitor, before Mrs Tammsaare's time, actually, as she only appeared at Toompea Castle after her husband's death. The visitor I really want to talk about turned up in the late summer of 1939. This was Monsignor Antonio Arata. He had been sent as papal nuncio by His Eminence, the recently enthroned Pope Pius XII. He was to turn up one Monday at ten o'clock in the morning. Eenpalu had already said to me the previous Friday: 'Bring the nuncio in to me as soon as he arrives.' Whereupon he looked at me with those slightly roguish and slightly weary eyes of his and I couldn't help thinking: well, well, all sorts of people seem to be turning up at our gates, so why not a papal nuncio too. We'll receive him, and listen to what he's got to say. Without committing ourselves, as is our tradition, but at least we'll take the trouble to receive him. Because in reality he represented a strange brand of power, or no power at all really, and yet, I don't know, perhaps the greatest power of all . . .

"Preceding the visit, the Prime Minister was a little, how shall we say, on his hind legs. But that Monday, the telephone rang at nine o'clock and it was the Prime Minister himself on the line:

"'Paerand . . .' He must have been in a bit of a state, because usually he would never omit to call his civil servants *Mr* This and *Mr* That. Only when in a funk would he resort to a mode of speech befitting a gendarme, as his enemies, Tõnisson supporters, would have it. So:

"'Paerand! I'm phoning from Aruküla.' (Aruküla, the former manor house of the Baranovs, located in a village twenty-six kilometres from

166

Tallinn, had belonged to Eenpalu for some twenty years. He had presumably received it for services rendered to the Estonian Republic during the War of Independence.) 'Major Tilgre and I have got a problem. My chauffeur can't start the Buick. The nuncio will be there at ten. So you must receive him. Give him my apologies, and don't let him leave. That would cause a scandal. Talk to him. Keep him occupied. Entertain him. Until I turn up. It's important, you understand."

"Well, I replied: 'OK, yes, sir, I understand.' Though I couldn't really see why the nuncio couldn't simply come along the next day instead, once I'd conveyed the due apologies. Didn't really understand – nor do I, to this very day – what it was that the Prime Minister needed to talk to him so urgently about. Then I started thinking about what I could possibly talk to the man about for half an hour, or even an hour – Eenpalu wouldn't allow things to drag on any longer than that. But I couldn't come up with anything and decided to improvise. And then, there he was. A smallish, lively man quick in his movements and with a sharp nose, and wearing a soutane which clothed him well, especially thanks to the purple neckpiece. This sartorial element of Catholicism has nowadays spread to the Protestant countries too. Don't you remember how, while we were still at grammar school, our own Bishop Rahamägi would wear such a neckpiece during morning prayers?

"I met him on the threshold, bowed slightly and said in German: 'Monsignor, the Prime Minister would like to convey his heartfelt apologies, but he has unfortunately been delayed. So . . .' and here I smiled as foolishly and winningly as I could, '. . . he has asked me to converse with your good self until such time as he should arrive. If I were not to do this my duty, I would attract the censure of the Prime Minister.'

"The nuncio replied in good German, as I had expected, though in that rather soft, what could be termed pan-Catholic, accent, the provenance of which is unclear. For us Estonians such an accent can sound rather like Russian, though obviously his was Italian. He said: 'I would gladly spare you the censure of the Prime Minister . . .'

"Initially, he had clearly been offended at the lateness of the Prime Minister. But he now added, more accommodatingly: 'How long has the Prime Minister been delayed?'

167

"I explained. 'He rang an hour ago from his manor at Aruküla. It's twenty-six kilometres from Tallinn. His car wouldn't start. But he'll presumably be on his way by now.'

"'Hm, well – *bene*.' The situation made him smile and the hope that the Prime Minister would be at the door within five minutes made him stay.

"'Since the Prime Minister has tied us down to this duel of words, please allow me to choose the topic.' He crossed his legs after sitting down, swinging his purple socks and black shoes. 'Now, I've come to the conclusion that in my post there is one particular subject on which I ought to get a better perspective: Italians in Estonia. I know a little about Guillelmo di Modena's role in Estonian history. And then – a little – about Mr Indro Montanelli's role in the periodical literature of your country. You picked him out to be correspondent for . . . what was your periodical called again . . .?'

"I said: '*Looming* – which means "creative endeavour".'

"'Exactly. That Guillelmo was chosen by the Pope. Indro was chosen by yourselves. The former was, at any rate, a good choice. But there was a period of seven hundred years between the two, and surely there must have been other Italians during that time. Would you be able to name any?'

"I thought: there have not been many of the blighters over here, but if you've got a bit of patience, I might just be able to keep you here until Eenpalu comes bounding in . . . And what I said was:

"'The first to spring to mind, chronologically after Guillelmo that is, was the cannon engineer Rudolfo Feoraventa who came with the Grand Duke of Muscovy and Ivan III's forces to besiege Viljandi and was killed there in 1481. That's according to what the Baltic cultural historian Amelung wrote.'

"'Not what one would call a very happy encounter . . .' the nuncio noted.

"I carried on: 'Then around 1520 there was a Tallinn doctor, some say the head city physician, Giovanni Ballivi . . .' I left unsaid the fact that he was regarded over here as a Frenchman, feeling that otherwise my minuscule stock of Italian names would come to a rapid end. I added: 'The doctor became famous to the extent that his grave monument was designed by none other than the greatest artist of the period, Michel Sittow. Have you seen the grave in question, against

168

the northern wall of Niguliste Church? With its depiction of Death?'

"'No, I haven't,' conceded the nuncio. 'That's also a somewhat gloomy encounter.'

"'Well,' I said, 'the next one is an altogether happier event. In 1549, several Italian tightrope walkers came to Tallinn and performed quite a dazzling stunt. They attached a rope to the tower of the Oleviste Church. Not right at the top, as I understand, but to some part of the metal roof. The actual tower was some twenty metres higher in those days. And they attached the other end to a post some four hundred metres away in a hayfield. The post was driven into the earth to a sufficient depth so that the rope became taut. And so they danced, or as the chronicles have it, flew along the rope.'

"'*Incredibile!*' cried the nuncio. 'Can you actually see those places here from the castle window?'

"I knew that on the top floor of the north wing there were one or two windows suitable for such viewing.

"'If the *Monsignor* so wishes . . . It's a hundred metres' walk plus a couple of flights of stairs . . .'

"'Listen, we can be there and back in five or ten minutes!'

"'OK.'

"I opened the door to the library. The smooth pate of Halliste, the librarian, plus the fluffy heads of his two girl assistants, turned in our direction. I said: 'Be so kind as to keep the door open. And should the Prime Minister appear, please tell him that the papal nuncio, Monsignor Arata, has gone with me to look at the city panorama from the northern windows and that we'll be back in ten minutes at the most.'

"In the nuncio's opinion, the view from up there in the State Library was unparalleled. I went on to explain: 'You see, over there that's where the rope emerged from the tower of Oleviste Church into the blue sky beyond, on a day I imagine to have been like today. The angle at which the rope descended would have been some twenty degrees. And there it would have disappeared behind the tower of the cathedral. And over there – as we're looking at it – it would have emerged again and stretched all the way to the Baltic station there on the left, which was, in those days, an open hayfield – where Kopli Street runs now. And you can imagine the crowds grouped round the anchor points of the rope, trying to touch the acrobats. And they – in their gilded costumes – would be moving back and forth along the rope, as high as one hundred metres in the air, above the roofs of the city and the walls and towers.'

"The nuncio clapped his hands in delight and cried: '*Fantastico!* But now we'd better return. The Prime Minister has probably arrived by now. But you carry on speaking . . .'

"I carried on telling my story. And why not, I was already in the mood for doing so. On the way back, I told him: 'Monsignor, I don't know whether your position allows you to visit cafés, but you no doubt enjoy coffee, both its taste and its aroma. Coffee arrived in Tallinn thanks to Italians. In Berlin, for example, the first coffee house was opened in 1723. But the first one had arrived in Tallinn by 1702. And the gentleman who opened what was perhaps the first coffee house in northern Europe was Signor Alphonso Carvallido.'

"'Which is of course a Spanish name –' the nuncio pointed out.

"I was quick to add: 'Quite so. But our sources suggest that he came to us from Naples and has been regarded for more than two hundred years over here as an Italian.'

"We had arrived back in my office. The Prime Minister had still not arrived and I said to the nuncio before he had time to utter a word of complaint: 'You, *monsignore*, live in Italy right now –'

"He interrupted: 'No, no, I live in Kadriorg.'

"And I continued: 'Kadriorg is our local Italy. From the window of your office on Poska Street you will be able to see the pond which was scooped out following the design of Niccolò Michetti, with the trees reflected in the water and beyond these the palace, also designed by him. So when you visit the President, you are moving amongst Italian scenery . . .' (Eenpalu had, God damn it, still not arrived.)

"'But if you open Baroness Rosen's –' (I couldn't damned well remember her first name –) '*The History of the Theatre in Tallinn*, you will find there, I believe, information on several Italian theatre troupes that came to cultivate the Thalian arts in us during the eighteenth century. If I remember rightly, they also played things by Alfieri over here.' (God damn, Kaarel had *still* not arrived!) 'If I, again, remember rightly, they played, for instance, *Timoleon* or it may even have been *Saul*, thought it is doubtful whether Czar Paul, in the Russian Empire of the day, would have tolerated plays aimed at satirising tyranny. If you see what I mean . . .' (But hell and damnation, I've practically run out of names . . .) 'Of course, with regard to Count Alfieri – as I've

170

heard people tell, since I personally have never read it in either his diary or his autobiography – he is supposed to have made some travel jottings about his visit to Estonia. During his restless years, he is supposed to have been here. But his remarks are said to be rather spiteful. Well, he was, after all, especially later in life, an extreme misanthropist, if I am not mistaken. Other great men are also supposed to have had sarcastic things to say about our country – or to have uttered things noted down in the diaries of travelling companions – take, for instance, Balzac. He is supposed to have said about an inn at a staging post that, along with a decent enough meal, he was given the most ghastly wine to drink.

"But then, may God be praised, Eenpalu came in to the room, accompanied by Tilgre. Eenpalu of course apologised to the nuncio (he spoke quite tolerable German), but the nuncio broke him off at the door to his office and said, gesturing vaguely in my direction: 'Prime Minister, this young man, whom you had assigned to entertain me, has done so to a most praiseworthy extent. In a most learned and interesting manner . . .'

"I closed the door of the bookkeeper's office and wiped my face with my handkerchief. Because I had just got through a particularly taxing hour. Forty-five minutes later, the nuncio emerged from the Prime Minister's office, walked past my desk, nodded and smiled and then stopped and came up to where I was sitting. I rose to my feet. He said: 'Could you give me your visiting card?'

"I replied: 'Monsignor, unfortunately I don't actually have a visiting card. But if you wish I can write my details down on a notepad . . .'

"I took a notepad and, still standing, noted down my details – all the while battling between vanity and objectivity, letting ambition get the better of me (which I probably don't often allow) and, scraping together my rudimentary knowledge of Italian, wrote down:

Ullo Paerand
l'Ordonanzo del Primo Ministro d'Estonia
Palazzo di Toompea, Tallinn

The nuncio took the sheet of paper, threw a glance at what I had written and burst out in a machine-gun volley of Italian.

"'No, no, Monsignor!' I said. 'I don't actually speak Italian. I'm only *guessing* at what I should write, like any more or less educated European . . .'

"He pointed the index finger of his right hand in my direction and cried *'Furfante! Furfante!'* – and shook my hand by way of goodbye. Which he certainly hadn't done on arrival.

"But the tale is not yet told. A week later I received, still at this very same *Palazzo di Toompea*, a letter written in German. Not from the nuncio, but from the apostolic administrator in Estonia who was, in effect, the Catholic Archbishop of Estonia. This was the German, Eduard Profittlich. The letter signed by him was an invitation to go and talk with him. So I went. Why shouldn't I have done? I imagined the invitation had been made on the strength of the nuncio's impression of me and did think that there could well be a crab lurking under that particular rock.

"I have to say that Profittlich was a much more rigid figure than Arata had been. He was friendly in his way, at least initially, but still retained his German inflexibility. What I remember of him bears ample testimony as to how attitude affects memory. I only met Arata once, but remember him down to the last detail. I went to see the apostolic administrator on two occasions, but I only vaguely remember him. His greyish face and prematurely ageing presence, and the fact that he was wearing a jacket more reminiscent of a *redingote*. He was sitting in an armchair, quite as uncomfortable as my own on Munga Street, in his narrow, thick-walled reception room, with its bluish wallpaper. Beyond the small, narrow window was the back wall of the church, on whose façade was written: *Hic vere est domus Dei et porta coeli.* Some choirboy dunce brought us tea and biscuits and set them down next to our chairs. And the administrator spoke to me for a full hour. Which appears to have been mostly to keep up appearances. Since his mind seemed made up, having based his decision on the information obtained from Arata.

"He offered me the opportunity to go and study, all expenses paid, at the Vatican. He explained that I would obtain the best education in the world there – and of my own choice, whether that was general philology, textology, history, philosophy or even theology. At first I would stay at the Vatican, then elsewhere in Italy, and later, up to doctorate level, at one of the world's Catholic universities of their, and my, choice. 'Please take your time and think our offer over.'

172

"I asked: 'And what kind of duties would I, in turn, have to fulfil?'

"He answered very straightforwardly: 'None whatever. Except for one. And this would be a sine qua non. You would have to convert to the Catholic faith.'

"Major Tilgre – a somewhat suspicious type – asked me several times over the next few days whether I had slept well the night before. I didn't exactly nod off at work, but was clearly more absent-minded than usual. Because Profittlich's question had suddenly caused me to ask myself a whole series of questions. In order to be able to reply to his offer, I would have to know *what* it was I wanted out of life. It turned out I'd never given the matter a thought."

Ullo jumped up from his chair there in my study, pointed a finger at me and said: "You yourself told me once – don't you remember? – how at the same time that I was examining my future in this way – i.e. late summer 1939 – out there somewhere in Tartu, in the garden or cellar of your Amicus student society, you were debating, five or six of you, heads perhaps lightly stimulated by the beer, what and who you wanted to be . . . You remember? Half for fun, let it be said, but that also meant half seriously. And how you said at the time that you were sure in your own case, you'd already made up your mind: you'd like to become Estonian Ambassador in Paris, because this wouldn't entail a great deal of serious work, but you would be living in an environment where there were interesting people and interesting books, and where you'd have a little time to write your own, what you termed your 'poems of dubious value'. So you, at least, had some idea about your future. But I didn't. The Aura Laundry wasn't a serious choice. And what I once said to tease old Jõgi – two rises a year and prime minister in thirty – was also nothing, for God's sake. I had perhaps fancied myself as an arts journalist – someone living in Tallinn, why not, but someone who travelled a lot and from whom papers like *Le Figaro*, *The Times* and the *Neue Zürcher Zeitung* would commission surveys, reviews and commentaries on books appearing round the world. Someone who would whizz articles out for good old pounds and francs . . . But how I would get into this world was something I hadn't yet thought out. And now Mr Profittlich suddenly offers me the best philological and philosophical education the world can offer – of my choice and at their expense. Was this not obviously the road to such success? Plus,

173

think of all the incomparable adventures to be encountered along the way.

"I didn't have anyone I could consult in the matter. My mother would have had heartache for a week and would then have left me to make up my own mind." Ullo looked me straight in the face, smiled and continued: "You weren't – forgive me for saying so – enough of an authority. Perhaps I could have talked with you about the issue, but you were in Tartu, and I didn't think your opinion merited a trip there. Old Weseler crossed my mind, but I abandoned the idea, 30 per cent Lutheran and 70 per cent atheist as he was. And it was just on questions of faith where the biggest problems lay. I realised that in such questions I simply didn't have any fixed point of view. I wrestled with all of this for a week, then went and said: 'I can't.'

"'Why not?' asked the administrator.

"'Because I'm too agnostic.'

"'If your deficient faith is good enough for you as a Lutheran – why should it be too little for you to become a Catholic? Besides, with our help you can consciously cultivate it.'

"I then said: 'I'm only a Lutheran by chance. I would be becoming a Catholic by choice. But regarding the growth of my faith in the future – I can't take on such a responsibility.' What I was really thinking was: I would be for ever tethered to you, and I feel that things would go wrong . . .

"He looked at me sadly and smiled almost imperceptibly: 'A shame. The eloquence of your refusal should have been used for an acceptance. Besides, it would presumably have saved you from so much . . .'

"I am not sure to this day what it was he thought they would be saving me from. But it is not inconceivable that he, during the second half of August 1939, was thinking of what he already knew through his profession: the imminent fate of this country. Things would have turned out quite different for me if I had, some two or three months later, brushed the dust of Estonia off my shoes and had been sitting in some palaeography course or some archive containing documents pertaining to *Maarjamaa* – ancient Estonia – reading William of Modena's account and Henry of Livonia's *Chronicle* in the original with all the hopes which the discovery of these sources entailed and which neither of the Arbusovs, father or son, managed to find at the Vatican.

174

"Concerning Profittlich himself, his knowledge didn't help him either, if he indeed had it. I cannot of course say whether the fact that he stayed behind in Estonia under Zhdanov was ordered by the Church, or resulted from some misunderstanding with regard to leaving or joining the German *Umsiedler*. Or whether it was the choice of a shepherd remaining with his flock. At any rate he stayed behind, was arrested at the end of June and died, he too, as tended to be the case, in the Kirov Prison during the winter of 1942, sentenced to death, but before execution of sentence."

23

H ERE I WROTE DOWN in my 1986 notebooks at Ullo's express request the names of several of his colleagues from the State Chancery. And Ullo's wish *expressis verbis*: "If you ever do anything with my story – then write about them too."

To which I had asked: "How can I? I know nothing about them, except for a couple of sentences you uttered sometime or other."

Ullo replied: "At least mention them. Because no one else will ever do so . . ."

At this point, and I remember it quite clearly, I laid into him: "Why the hell don't you do so *yourself*?! I know, I know. You smile your smile and say: 'Division of labour.' You will say: *"You're* the writer. I'm the maker of suitcases." This would make sense if you couldn't write, but you can. At any rate, no worse than me. So why don't you do it yourself? It must be for one of two reasons: sheer laziness coupled with a lackadaisical attitude worthy of a hippie, or it could be something much worse: *political hygiene*. Letting someone else do it, and letting them carry the can if things go wrong. I'd be a fool to write with no intention of publication, or only in censored or coded form for fear of house searches, but with reasonably good prospects of publication in, say, 150 years' time. For given our experience of the crumbling of empires (according to Professor Taagepera's prognoses on Radio Free Europe) the Soviet Union won't disintegrate before such time has passed. That would make me a fool. And I would come under suspicion were I to write the texts (also using themes from your life), polishing them to such a degree that they would manage to slip under the nose of the state censors. While at the same time you in your angelic innocence were putting together your damned suitcases and in your spare time were studying, I don't know what, Nietzsche, Wittgenstein or Braudel, as much as you could get close to them and as much as your meagre salary would allow (sly fox as you always have been, as my mother at least said), and indulging in collecting things, philately, philocartia, foxomania or whatever they call those pastimes. Plus collecting models of cannon, made out of wood, and cardboard, and lead, and iron and brass. The largest being some seventy centimetres in length and almost pushing you out of your tiny three-room flat. Because two rooms are full of them . . ."

Then I began to feel embarrassed. Because, I don't know, in the end – maybe – presumably – seemingly – surely – undoubtedly – it was simply a dirty trick to interpret his wish for mental hygiene as blind egotism . . .

"So now," I bawled out, "you want to extend a hand *through me* to your poor little former colleagues and save them from oblivion?!"

"Would you be sorry to do so?"

"Oh God, no!"

I should only really feel sorry for him if his refusal to fix the story of his life on paper stemmed from a fear of failure, a lack of confidence behind that birdlike brow of his. That was hard to believe, but maybe now more probable than I had originally thought. The most likely reason at first glance being that he hadn't got the slightest confirmation from any quarter that he *could* write – except perhaps for Barbarus's cries of admiration, maybe also of diffidence . . . Yet were such souls as he in need of such encouragement?

"OK then, let's get down to the names, and what you want to say about them."

And so the names:

Auli Ubin. A twenty-year-old woman with sleek hair cut into the shape of a pail and a jolly pinkish face. She was a cleaner. Whose task it was to keep the Prime Minister's office and the four adjoining rooms spruce. Auli had two more or less open secrets. Firstly, that her left leg was two centimetres shorter than the right, so that she had a slight limp. And the heel pad that she used didn't quite compensate. But those who didn't notice right from the start never did so. Auli's second secret was a little better kept. But all of Ullo's colleagues at the Prime Minister's office knew about it – except for Major Tilgre.

Auli arrived at work every morning at six. She cleaned the Prime Minister's suite. What was there for her to do? Empty the ashtrays. Sweep the carpet. On the odd occasion put some furniture polish on rings left by wine bottles. At five minutes to nine she would disappear, presumably to do the cleaning in some suite on another floor. At around one she would return, flit from one room to the next quietly emptying the waste-paper baskets, wiping the window sills with a damp duster, go into the offices, where there would be officials or guests, and then of course intrude no more. And she would be gone until the next morning. But every Monday and Friday morning at a quarter to nine, she played her little trick, and had never been caught. Though the Prime Minister's doorman, a Mr Tohver, and both of his colleagues, the ancient Petersburger Vilbiks and the Hungarian Jakó, plus the chauffeur and various couriers back in the staffroom would grow nervous and occasionally go out into the corridor to take a look: would she get caught or not?

Every Monday and Friday at a quarter to nine Auli would slip into the private bathroom in the back vestibule of the Prime Minister's suite, so as to clean it, though she had little to do there. Because it was used by no one. Ullo mentioned that it had only been necessary on one occasion while he was there. This was after the Prime Minister's fiftieth birthday, at the end of May 1938, when he had thrown a party for the members of his personal office staff and close associates. Then, Privy Counsellor Klesment and Castle Commandant, Colonel Kanep, had gone in there to sober up (more or less fruitlessly), by pouring cold water down their necks. So anyway, Auli would normally have next to nothing to clean. She would line up the bars of soap in the wall cabinet in a row and give the glass shelves the once-over with a rag. But every Monday and Friday morning she would lock the bathroom from the inside, turn on the hot shower, take off her clothes, put on a rubber cap she had brought with her, rub some liquid soap that smelt of lilacs, also brought, into her palms, apply the pink foam to her whole body and step under the shower. She was always back in her clothes one minute before the Prime Minister arrived, the floor and the bathtub wiped dry and the window opened to disperse the smell.

This prankster would then sit in the staffroom swathed in the smell of lilacs, soothing the concerns of her interlocutors. "Well, what if he did find me out – what sin have I actually committed? I'm not even using up his government soap. He's not likely to give me my cards the first time he does discover me . . ."

The question as to whether the Prime Minister would indeed sack

Auli – living it up in an undisciplined manner in the bathroom, which was intended for the sole and personal use of the Prime Minister – remained unanswered. Because he never caught her once using the bathroom. Neither Eenpalu nor – after 18 October – Uluots. Only when, on 22 or 23 June 1940, just after the coup, unknown checkers came to search the apartment for Barbarus and to decide on who was allowed a pass for what, did things undergo change.

"The first Friday morning when Barbarus was in power," explained Ullo, "I no longer know what date in June it was, one of these outsiders – they were always wandering about with the signature of the Prime Minister proving their legitimacy in their pockets – heard, i.e. at about five to nine, that someone was splashing about in Barbarus's suite. At the time it never struck me – but now we know that such noises could well have suggested an attempt to drown the Prime Minister. After a number of angry knocks at the bathroom door they bawled something of the order of '*Otkroi!*' '*Otkroi!*' Open up! Open up! – until Auli opened up with a rosy smile on her lips.

"The girl was dragged out into the corridor. She was taken away somewhere. She was interrogated. No, she was not sacked on the spot. But she was no longer allowed to work there. And the dismissal didn't take place till three weeks later. So I had to bring her her pink soap and her bathcap out to the guards at the gate.

"When she saw me, she cried joyfully: 'Aha, you've still got a job there? I was silly enough to get caught . . .' And when I accompanied her to the castle square, shook her hand and expressed my regrets, she said, in that same cheery manner: 'But fancy just this particular government giving me the sack. The government of the proletariat should surely have wanted to make me feel at home. What a joke. Don't you think so?'"

I don't remember what Ullo said he replied to the girl, but the following name on my list was the old retainer Mr Vilbiks. About him, Ullo related the following:

"One of Vilbiks's jobs was to arrange dinners and receptions. He was a tall, distinguished-looking, hale and hearty eighty-year-old crust who wore a bow tie. Who expected everyone to enjoy what he did, in the way he himself did. He considered himself an indisputable authority in all matters concerning the Prime Minister's court, was *doktor sekretnikh dvoretskikh nauk*, as he himself termed it – and had, according to rumour, been a chamberlain to Grand Duke Constantine. He had had experience of courts ranging from St Petersburg to Livadia, and in spite of the terseness of his political commentary one thing was clear: all the woes of the world were to be blamed on the Communists. So on the arrival of Barbarus, he left his job in a flash – which doesn't actually mean that he was immediately arrested."

I simply don't know, since Ullo didn't, what became of him. But a number of those who disappeared in the same way reappeared again some while later in suitable posts. Like Major Tilgre, who had gone underground when Barbarus took over but returned in the early autumn of '41 with the Hirvelaan Battalion to Tallinn.

Mr Vilbiks had a younger colleague, the second butler of the State Chancery, the Hungarian, Jakó.

"He too was getting on in years," Ullo said, "over sixty by then. He was of miniature stature, but with the pretensions of a specialist, something he was quite touchy about. For example, which glasses and which knives and forks there should be, and where these should be placed in relation to the crockery. And so forth. In his twenty or so years in Estonia, he had learnt to speak the language almost perfectly and would sit in the staffroom and tell in a gossipy whisper (of course, only when Auli Ubin was absent) of his adventures in whorehouses in Budapest, Warsaw, Berlin and Riga up to the end of the First World War. These adventures never came any nearer, either in space or time."

Then Ullo mentioned the bookkeeper Haljaste. Then there was the junior bookkeeper (also a man). Ullo said: "I don't remember whether he was called Kask or Teder, presumably some name halfway in between – and then the orderlies, for instance Jakó . . . Yes." Something happened to the younger senior butler too, a rather misty tale. During Ullo's first months on the job, Jakó was also responsible for a small stock of goods intended for use at private receptions in the suite, in what was in effect a cupboard set into the back wall of the staffroom. This included a couple of bottles of White Horse, a couple of cartons of Camel and Memphis, and soda-water siphons which were replaced with fresh ones now and again. And the key to this cupboard was kept in Jakó's waistcoat pocket. During stocktaking one time, and I never did ask who did the bookkeeping, something that was supposed to be in that cupboard, wasn't. So Tilgre had called Jakó in to see him and had kept insulting him – presumably just the two of them had been present – to his face, God knows whether he had good reason or not. And then Tilgre had called Ullo, to the latter's great embarrassment, into his office to stand next to Jakó at the desk and had Jakó hand his pride and joy and token of trust, the key, over to Ullo. Tilgre's freckled cheeks were dark with ire – and he said: "Well, sir, if this is the level to which you would stoop . . ."

Ullo commented – almost fifty years later, smiling wryly as he did so: "And I didn't know what level the major was on about. But the results were not as harsh as one would have expected. Jakó was not dismissed. He was simply demoted – from butler to courier. And this only temporarily. There were three or four people in such posts at the time. And I don't really remember them. Except for the boxer Seepere. He was a candidate for European middleweight champion, or similar. Who ended up, a couple of decades later, as a professional in Argentina, I think it was. So you could ask yourself: what with Raadik – from the Riigivolikogu – and Seepere with us, were they not proof that the powers that be at the time, i.e. that of the Eenpalu and Uluots factions, were founded on the power of fisticuffs?" Ullo went on: "I can, of course, confirm that this was the case. And why not? The thought was perfectly logical: assembling a number of young heavies who, in times of trouble, could furnish the necessary physical assistance. It would even have been strange had the idea not crossed the minds of the leaders of the country at the time. Though I think it did. Such jobs would at least furnish promising young sportsmen with better prospects and opportunities for practice. Not so much for their own glory as for the development of national sport as a whole. Yes, that's how it will have been . . ." Ullo jumped to his feet enthusiastically: "In other words, certainly not modelled on heavies of a fascist mould . . ."

There only remains to mention one more name from Ullo's list and that is Tohver, doorman at the State Chancery. And off the top of my head I have nothing to say about him. Or perhaps I do. Wait a minute. I see now that I wrote "Bismarck!" in the margin of my notebook, complete with exclamation mark. Which reminds me of what Ullo said ten years ago: this doorman was the most imposing figure at the State Chancery. Even including three or four prime ministers. That's what the "Bismarck!" denoted. This man had been former porter at Tartu University and his nickname described him well. People used to mistake him for the Vice-Chancellor, until Johan Kõpp took that post. Only then did Bismarck retreat to his post as porter.

So, a decent democratic tradition of attitude in every sense. And Ullo added: "That same tradition, if you like, as with all my experiences during my time at the State Chancery. Because as in stories with a fairy-tale structure (and the more hero-centred, i.e. self-centred, the story, the more obvious this becomes) the conflict between the dangerous and unjust powers that be and tough and shrewd little me, is always resolved to the latter's advantage."

And Ullo now related: "During the first two prime ministers' tenures, I had three such conflicts. The first two at the birthday party held by Eenpalu and both – and believe it or not, being of the sort that did the tradition proud – both put my adversaries in risible situations. But ended in victory for the minor hero, me.

"Eenpalu's birthday was 28 May. The party was held in the rooms of the State Chancery on the last day of May for what were termed 'his own staff'. The Head of Chancery also came with his own staff, and a dozen or so members of the *Riigivolikogu*. Plus the gents I will name presently.

"There was no shortage of drink, as soon became evident from the behaviour of one or two of the gentlemen. But not by that of the Prime Minister himself – tales of the Prime Minister's weakness for drink have been greatly exaggerated. As was said – in his own words – by Mark Twain about his own death. The Prime Minister held out until the end, and was in irreproachable form until around two o'clock in the morning. The first one to start swaying shortly after midnight was the Castle Commandant, Colonel Kanep. Terras took me aside and ordered me to take the colonel across the courtyard. Kanep's apartment was situated in the west wing of the castle. The colonel had had difficulty enunciating earlier on, but pulled himself together and said to me: 'No – yyyou know, if yyyou were at least a mmmajor – or dddamn it ppperhapps a cccaptain – but I wwill not obey ssuch a ccivilian lad like you. Though I know yyyou're tttaking orders from TTTerras. Who's he think he is? He's only a lieutenant . . .'

"What was I to do? I grew angry at my own helplessness, and decided to continue with a desperate bluff.

"'My dear Colonel, sir – perhaps – (this interjection I mumbled as best I could and it perhaps never reached his ears) – perhaps I've

182

reached the rank of lieutenant colonel at the Tallinn Freemasons' Lodge . . .' (There they would have used other ranks than military ones, masters, clerks and apprentices, but such wouldn't have made any impression on the colonel. But a lieutenant colonel – can you imagine!)

"He looked at me with his reddened eyes and blurted out: 'Oh – to hell with you. Let's go. Here, give me a bit of support . . .'

"We walked under the bright sky of the spring night, reeling slightly as we crossed the castle courtyard, and I handed him over to his family at the door to his apartment.

"When I returned to the State Chancery, Terras came to meet me at the door. 'Take Privy Counsellor Klesment back to his house in Kadriorg. The car's standing ready.'

"Privy Counsellor Klesment, one of the main architects of Päts's Constitution, was by general consent the cleverest man among the government legal advisers. His penchant for schnapps was well known, but he wasn't what I would call an alcoholic. But now he was three sheets to the wind, so it took quite some effort to persuade him to descend the stairs so I could drag him in the direction of the car. I had great trouble getting him into the vehicle, but finally managed. We drove along Komandandi Road down from Toompea Hill, and left down Kaarli Avenue. The Privy Counsellor had dozed off and everything seemed to be going smoothly. Then – at the right moment – he opened his eyes and cried out: 'Stop-stop-stop-stop . . .!' and the driver slowed down. 'I'm going in here – if you want, you can come along . . .' he said in my direction. 'But I at any rate am going to the Gloria – st-o-o-p!'

"I said to the driver: 'Drive on!' And since the Privy Counsellor was clearly inebriated, the driver obeyed me. When the car began to pick up speed, the Privy Counsellor did at least stop making attempts to throw himself out of the car and I no longer had to hold him back. And then we arrived, and were it not for the fact that he had now grown limp, I would have had quite some problem pulling this smallish, but plumpish, man out. It was bad enough as it was. At length he was standing outside his own front door and continued to express his dissatisfaction in a loud voice until the door opened and I could hand him over to his wife.

"And this problematical story continued as follows. The next morning, the colonel said nothing whatsoever about the incident the night before. A wall of silence. However, the Privy Counsellor – he was back on Toompea the next morning at nine, having had a good night's sleep – invited me in to his office. And apologised. That he couldn't quite remember how things had gone the night before, but imagined that perhaps not too well. And asked me not to take the matter to heart. So I assured him that he had not allowed himself to do anything untoward and that nothing more would be said about the matter. Upon which he allowed me to leave, but stopped me at the door, came up to me and said: 'Ullo – please allow me, from now on we're on first-name terms. That applies to you too. And he kept his word. And I was forced to do the same, though I tried to avoid doing so in the presence of others."

Ullo continued: "But my third conflict while I was at the State Chancery (folk tales require things to happen in threes) was this.

"One day, during Eenpalu's last month in office I think, a young gentleman appeared at my desk wearing neatly creased trousers and said he wished to visit the Head of the Chancery: please tell Mr Terras of his arrival. And right away, if I would be so kind. The young man told me his name and I will not mention the name for the simple reason that it has not stuck in my mind, not because I want to save him from anything. The young man was at the time the Estonian press attaché in Berlin.

"I do not know what aroused my pettiness. The neatly creased trousers, perhaps. The provocative self-confidence that verged on the obtuse. A kind of self-importance, a hint of loud superiority cultivated in Berlin. At any rate I sat there stiffly on my narrow bureaucrat's chair and felt how the bones of my backside were digging into it.

"'The Head of Chancery is not receiving anyone today.'

"'I know, I know. But go and tell him I'm here.'

"'He's working. He has requested not to be disturbed. I can enter your name in the register of audiences for the day after tomorrow at ten.'

"'Phone him from here. You have a telephone on your desk.'

"'The Head of Chancery has asked not to be disturbed even by phone.' (This was a bloody great lie. He had never requested such a thing. But I had decided not to let the young gentleman in to see Terras.)

184

"'Listen here – if you're going to be bloody-minded, I will make sure, via the Foreign Ministry, that you will not be sitting on that chair tomorrow!'

"'Your threat, my dear sir, is such a serious matter that you leave me no option but to go against the rules. I will convey the message to him immediately . . .'"

Ullo marched forthwith into the Head of Chancery's office, thinking all the while that it would be best if the argumentative young man would follow close on his heels. But he did not do so.

The Head of Chancery had listened to Ullo, gave a snort and remained, as Ullo had imagined he would, true to his principle. He said: "Tell him to phone the Foreign Minister tomorrow. He will hear from him what I think of his behaviour and if and when I will allow him to come and see me."

Ullo grinned: "So, as you can see, this was the triumph of an unimportant individual over an important somebody. A storm of teacup proportions, where the cup was, imperceptibly, slipping from our grasp."

24

ULLO EXPLAINED: "WE WERE so naive – at least I was – that I didn't regard the resignation of the Eenpalu government and its replacement with the Uluots one as anything to do with pressure from Moscow, but simply a result of our own political pliancy. Nothing at all to do with the fact that our room for manoeuvre had been whittled down to almost nothing, but as proof of the superiority of our manoeuvring skills: just you try demanding something from us! Or accusing us of anything!

"In a word – I simply wasn't a political genius!" said Ullo with a smile, and I felt like crying out: "Who is?"

"Eenpalu left on the Tuesday morning with a desultory wave, his portfolio under his arm: 'I'm off to see the President . . .!' This made me question whether something wasn't up after all, as he never used to announce his visits to the President. And at two in the afternoon Uluots arrived and shook us all by the hand.

"I was unable to really decide what that brief and dry, if firm, handshake could mean. Whether it was to show he was now taking responsibility for us – or a plea for recognition of the fact that he really was in solidarity with us (something upon which Eenpalu had never laid any emphasis). Or could Uluots's handshake express an attempt at treating us equally, blending in with us at one and the same level, standing behind us, so to speak . . ."

Ullo went on: "He recognised me by sight . . ." And here I said to Ullo that Uluots will have remembered him too. But not from his spell at university when Ullo had sat the viva voce in law, since Uluots was in Geneva. But Uluots will have remembered Ullo from the State Chancery, as someone sent on occasion from the other wing of the castle, to the office, some score of rooms away, to bring some papers to the Riigivolikogu. Since a rather memorable figure, a thin beanpole of a young man, will have popped into the Speaker's, i.e. Uluots's, office and placed a sheaf of papers on the desk. Or put them in the Riigivolikogu chamber itself on the black baize of the Speaker's yellow table. With a respectful and short phrase which nonetheless covered the contents of the papers. Or stating what it was the sender required of the Speaker when dealing with them.

And allow me to add one thing to Ullo's tale. Professors' abilities to memorise faces varied with regard to the persons in question. Uluots was by no means like, for instance, the legal historian Leo Leesment, whom Ullo had encountered while still a callow student.

Leesment remembered everyone he'd ever seen. One law student of the 1930s, over thirty years of age as was typical, who lived and worked in Tallinn, told me the following story. He had gone, having studied from his lecture notes, to request a viva voce with Leesment in the spring of 1939. He had never seen the professor before in his life. He stepped into the examination room, greeted the professor and said his name. "Student Kallak." Leesment had looked at him with his slightly glassy stare and asked: "D-d-do you c-c-c-ome fff-f-from P-P-Pärnu?"

"Yes, sir. From the parish of Pärnu-Jaagupi."

"Is that b-b-etween Sõõrikese and Parasmaa?"

"Exactly so."

"And you w-w-ork in agriculture n-now and again?"

"Well, when I go and help my father on the farm – well, why not. But how do you know, sir?"

"In n-n-nineteen twenty-n-n-nine – I was in b-between two f-f-foreign bursaries, I travelled around Estonia and collected information for research into domestic households in Pärnumaa county. One May m-m-morning I was riding my bicycle from Sõõrikese to Parasmaa – and you were ploughing the field on the left-hand side. Wearing a b-b-blue sh-sh-sh-shirt and driving a gg-ggrey horse."

Uluots's memory was nowhere near as prodigious. But from at least those meetings of the Riigivolikogu, Ullo existed in his mind.

"On the first or second working day of the new Prime Minister's period of office, Nikitin, the Soviet envoy, came on a visit. Only the rank of envoy, since appointing ambassadors was a fad from more recent years. He was a stoutish man with black hair, straight black eyebrows and grey eyes, pale-skinned but with a somewhat swarthy face: one of those Tartar types who we later got to see by the thousand.

"Of course I hadn't a clue what they talked about for the hour they were together. But at the end of their conversation, Uluots summoned me in to him by means of the electric signal lamp and said in his dry voice: 'Mr Paerand, don't send in any more visitors today.' Half an hour later, he left the building. As was later rumoured: off to see the President. And from that time forth there were far more Cabinet meetings than had been usual. From then on, Terras would step into my office and say in a half-whisper: 'Mr Paerand – tell the Prime Minister that the Cabinet is waiting in the White Hall.'

"And I went in to tell the Prime Minister. And he rose from behind his bureau, nervously stubbed out his papiross among the "Orient" fag ends lying in a pile in his ashtray and slid a pile of papers over the bureau, for me to carry to the White Hall. I do not know why he didn't carry them himself. Looking back on it: some years later he fell ill with cancer, and this was triggered off by ulcers. Maybe he was already suffering pains even then. That would account for the irritable greyish look on his face and his avoidance of carrying a few hundred grams' worth of papers. I walked at his heels, my eyes on the narrow shoulders of his lounge jacket, his white collar, his sinewy neck with two weeks' dark untrimmed hair hanging over his collar, and his tonsure like a yellowish plate."

At that point, I cried out: "Ullo, you seem to be looking at your watch. These descriptions are so interesting that we'll spend some time on them next session, won't we?"

He said: "Oh, there's nothing interesting about them. I wasn't ever there during Cabinet meetings. I left the White Hall before the start of every meeting. And besides – well, an inkling of the approaching catastrophe soon began to seep in through the windows of Toompea Castle. A week later, the *Umsiedlung* of the Baltic Germans began. The representative of the model *Kleinbürger*, Frohwein, went up to see the Prime Minister twice. A few of those being repatriated and who had claims of one sort or another turned up. As far as I remember these weren't Baltic Germans, but Estonians who wanted to leave. Those who were trying to throw in their lot with the ethnic Germans. I don't remember anything Uluots said to them in reply to, or about, them, only his closed and fractious look as if such folk were the cause of his stomach pains. At any rate he ordered me to send them all elsewhere, over to Jürima at the Minister of the Interior, to the Angelus . . ."

"Ullo!" I interjected. "Let's leave Uluots till the next time!"

"Nothing of interest took place!" countered Ullo capriciously. "Or at least *I* didn't take part in any of the events at such close quarters to remember anything out of the ordinary. Barring *one* event . . ."

"Ullo . . ." I said, "you make me damned curious about it – but tell me the next time, and then without hurrying over anything."

"No, what for?" he argued against me, the way he sometimes did: countered my request simply without any rational argument or using what was more or less an absurd one: "Why not now? Why should next time be better? All next times are questionable. Anyway, the only remarkable event in which I took part in an unexpected manner was the trip the Estonian delegation made to Narva and beyond, to the border. On 17 June 1940. A week later, Terras told me under what circumstances I had ended up going. Laidoner had gone to Uluots and announced that he would be travelling, on the President's orders, to the border on the morning of the 17th – to observe the entry of the new contingents of the Red Army. But he had insisted, to Laidoner that is, that the delegation would not be a purely military presence, but that civilians would also be present. He realised that the arrival of the Prime Minister at the border would be out of proportion, as was his own presence, but this had been the President's wish. So would Uluots agree that the Head of Chancery join the delegation?" They had called Terras in to Uluots's office and Terras had refused to go.

Ullo explained: "Terras said to me a week later: 'You have to understand, Mr Paerand – on paper, Laidoner was not able to give me orders. On paper only the Prime Minister could do so. But I understood that he wasn't going to put me under pressure. So I said that I considered that even my own presence there would be out of all proportion. And we discussed the issue as to who could represent the Prime Minister in a civil capacity – Tilgre couldn't, being an officer, you see.' Terras had tried to phone Klesment at home and suggest he go, but hadn't managed to get hold of him. Laidoner had left, saying: 'Let them decide among themselves who they are going to send to join the delegation and make sure that that person is at Tallinn railway station by one o'clock in the morning.' Terras said: 'Prime Minister, I can't see that it makes any sense for the civil authorities to be represented at such a high level in the delegation. What you presumably need is someone to observe the exact process of the entry into our country. I would like to say: there's no better individual for that task than your young assistant Paerand.' Uluots had replied that maybe, but he could hardly send an assistant to represent the Prime Minister. Whereupon Terras had said that we certainly could, if you think it necessary, promote him to Counsellor to the Government – adding, at least muttering: 'Since everything's going to the dogs anyway.'"

Ullo explained: "When they invited me into the Prime Minister's office, the paper was lying on the table with both signatures. 'Counsellor to the Government, Ullo Paerand, is ordered during the official journey of the delegation of the Chief of Staff, from Tallinn to Narva and back again, to observe the signature and implementation of the treaty allowing the entry into our country of the reinforcement contingents of the Soviet Army.'

"When I had put the document in my pocket, Uluots said: 'Only one thing – be careful. You should be aware that tomorrow the Russian prohibition on outdoor photography comes into force. So better not take your camera along at all. And don't write anything down – at least not in such a way that it attracts attention.'

"Once home, I told my mother a little after midnight what I was going to be doing and as usual, she got into a state: did I really have to go? And I should behave, for God's sake, in such a way that the Russians didn't arrest me immediately and shove me in the nick.

"At one o'clock in the morning I looked for the Chief of Staff in the carriage of his private train at the Baltic station and showed my sheet of paper to Captain Jaakson who was standing on the carriage steps.

"'Well, in that case, congratulations on your promotion and please come into the carriage.' This Captain Jaakson, the brother of the colonel who had recently been promoted to the rank of major general and interim Education Minister, was adjutant to the Chief of Staff and vaguely known to me already. He led me to an empty compartment, left me, and returned a quarter of an hour later, when the train was already in motion. He had told Laidoner of my arrival . . .

"'And how did the General react?'

"'With a nod. Which shows that he doesn't know you. And, by the way, that your presence doesn't annoy him – nor interest him, for that matter. In general, he was rather, well, rather distant.'

"Captain Jaakson stayed another half-hour or even longer, and was himself, how should I say, a little distant. But he didn't touch upon the event for which we were in the carriage of this train, fateful for our country. Instead, he told about what he had seen on his trip to Moscow the previous December, when he had gone there as adjutant to Laidoner. Before he got down to telling the story, he jumped up nervously and opened the door of the compartment, but the whole length of the corridor was empty. He shut the door again and came to sit down next to me. And told the following story. He and Laidoner had stayed at the International in a three-room suite. Their reception had been a hearty one. On the third day of the visit, a car was sent to take Laidoner to the Kremlin – but the invitation had been worded in such a way that his adjutant was not expected to accompany him. Well, the general couldn't just fail to go. So he went alone. The captain had remained at the hotel, read a book for half an hour – one he'd found in the cupboard of the night table next to the bed – *Moskva, Stolitsa Mira – Moscow, Capital of the World* – or some such title and so he decided to go and see a little of the city on foot. He had walked around for an hour or more, along Gorki Street, down the Arbat, I don't know where exactly. And had stepped into three bookshops. And stopped at a couple of newspaper kiosks. To ask for a map of the city. But couldn't obtain one."

Ullo explained: "In December of '39, not even the so-called city plan, produced in simple strokes of the pen for use by kindergartens, was on sale, just as now. But when the captain had returned to the hotel he spotted, lying right in the middle of the bare top of his room table, a neatly folded plan of Moscow. You can conclude from that what you like.

"Captain Jaakson left the compartment and I slept a curiously leaden sleep for a couple of hours. Till I awoke and found I had been sleeping on my left side, with my knees under my chin – like the three-thousand-year-old man found buried in a grave in Ardu or Hallstadt. Or a foetus in the womb. At around a quarter past five, the kitchen sergeant major came with a cup of coffee and a sandwich. A quarter of an hour later – my chin was by now neatly shaven – Captain Jaakson appeared and said: 'The Chief of Staff requests your company in his saloon.'

191

"This was some ten paces further up the train. Three compartments had been opened up and in the middle stood a narrow table covered with green baize. The General was sitting at one end. At the table were a couple of officers. The Chief of the Narva Border Guards, Major Kõrgma if I am not mistaken, Captain Hint and another man. Captain Jaakson introduced me to the General.

"'Government Counsellor Paerand, on behalf of the Prime Minister . . .'

"The General looked at me for a moment with his intense brown eyes, but shook hands in what was a most indifferent manner. The others almost in the same way.

"'Sit down, gentlemen,' the General said. 'So, in half an hour's time, in the smaller hall of the Military District casino, we will be signing the treaty. Meretskov for the Russians, me for our part. There will be some 80,000 men entering the country. As reinforcements to those already at the bases. So this is a *treaty* merely in the formal sense of the word. In actual fact it is a *diktat*. And that's all I have to say to you for the present – and perhaps for all time.'

"He remained seated at the table, but made a small gesture with his right hand to dismiss us, and so we rose and went off. I, at least, stepped into the corridor of the carriage and saw: we had just passed Soldina, without of course stopping, just as we had only stopped for five minutes in Tapa.

"Another quarter of an hour, and we had arrived. We got into two large Buick cabriolets which stood in front of the Narva station building and drove through the city glittering in the early-morning sun, like a painting by Jansen or Nyman, miraculously clean, almost empty, bright, the façades of the buildings white. This was, by the way, the only time I set eyes on what is termed the Karling Baroque style of Narva. Because I have never otherwise been to Narva, before or since. And after the time I was there, the city only had five years left anyway. Anyhow, we drove up to the casino – I don't remember where it stood – and got out on to the pavement, Laidoner with a couple of officers out of the first car, myself, Captain Hint and someone else out of the second. And we saw: ten metres from the main entrance to the casino stood the pride and joy of the Russians, a black Zim limousine resembling an overfed greyhound. When Laidoner stepped out on to the pavement, a door opened in the Zim and Meretskov, a fat man in a dark grey shirt and dark blue trousers, stepped out along with a couple of officers. The parties met on the casino steps and Laidoner motioned his guests – he was, after all, still the host – to enter the building. Already, there was a duty officer clicking his heels.

"Once inside, Laidoner led the group into a room which must therefore have been the smaller hall of the casino. I don't really remember what it looked like. Yellow-stained plywood panelling, long green curtains, a long table, a few chairs on either side of it.

"It was said later that Laidoner was so beside himself that he wanted to put his signature in the top left-hand corner of the treaty where he usually wrote his resolutions, and Captain Hint had had to show him where to sign, i.e. at the bottom right of the document."

Ullo wrinkled his nose: "It was all idle talk. I was standing four paces away from him. Nothing special. Perhaps he was a little paler than usual. But he had himself completely under control. As you know: at Wikman's he wasn't particularly popular among us boys. You wouldn't find him there among our busts of honour. His son's suicide didn't increase his popularity one bit. That had happened a couple of years before I started attending Wikman's, but people would talk about it now and again. But no one knew (and still don't to this day) what caused him to kill himself. Maybe the debts the fifteen-year-old had clocked up gambling, or getting the housemaid pregnant or some conflict with his domineering father. Or something else entirely. At any rate, no Laidoner cult sprang up at our school. Nor at our home. Rather, I remember –" and Ullo suddenly glanced at me with a vehement and victorious expression – "how you yourself have told me – your father was supposed to have told, no doubt in the early thirties, how the papers were full of the presidential candidates – Päts, Laidoner, Larka and whoever – that if any of them was a real man it was Laidoner. But this too was no expression of cult admiration. And I would like to say here: Laidoner's behaviour during the signing ceremony was quite dignified. And I would like to add a correction: that characteristic sentence of his, which became famous later by way of rumour, and as a lead-up to which I'm telling you this whole story, was not uttered by him after signing the treaty or diktat, as was said later, but on the border, when the gates were being opened. But not as a throwaway line, but with conviction and pithiness.

193

"So, the treaty was signed. Laidoner and Meretskov exchanged a brief pressing of palms. Someone later said that if Laidoner had refused to shake hands, the Russians would have claimed we were breaking the terms of the treaty right from the moment of signature. But in practice, once the treaty had been signed, we no longer existed in such a way as to give anyone cause for talk about breaking it . . .

"When we climbed back into our cars, Meretskov's had already gone. When we reached the border half an hour later, he had already crossed it.

"We stopped at the border post with its little hut painted in the Estonian colours – blue, black and white. Ten metres on this side of it was a wire gate with metal posts. The road ran through the gated crossing and a ten-metre-long zone between wire fences and then, beyond the wire gates on the other side, there was grey open country stretching out towards Yamburg. On the road itself, and to either side, stood columns of lorries and armoured trucks under the bright sunny summer sky. The bayonets of the twenty men per lorry glinted. In the armoured vehicles were an unknown number of men. Between the columns, soldiers with red flags stood and strutted about, presumably the traffic controllers for the impending deluge. And so it began. My wristwatch was showing 6.43 when an order was shouted from over there. At the same time as the border guards emerged from their respective huts on each side of the border to open the gates, the engines of the vehicles were switched on. Though not every engine fired. Some of the carburettors started coughing and making a hideous noise and the vehicle in question would not budge an inch. But the vast majority of the vehicles did move, so that the principle became clear: groups of ten armoured vehicles alternated with lorries filled with infantry. Some time – maybe only half a minute – before the first vehicles left the other side and reached this side of the border, a slight easterly wind began to blow the strong and alien Russian petrol fumes in our direction. The drone of the vehicles approached us and could be felt in every cell of your body, the dust raised by the vehicles had not yet reached us, the boys of the border guard stood to attention – then Laidoner turned to his entourage. I was standing three paces behind, between us were Captains Jaakson and Hint with a gap between them, so I saw his mouth move and heard him clearly when he said: 'Gentlemen, I hope that what we have built up over the last twenty years will, if needs be, hold out for another two hundred.'"

Ullo rose to his feet. "A claim which you and I have been, however you see it, checking, affirming, refuting since 1945." He sat down again.

"Well, we stood there for another five minutes. Counting the vehicles more accurately was a pointless exercise, since it had already been confirmed that the Red Army was crossing at the same time at Irbosk into Latvia, and Laura into Lithuania.

"Nevertheless, I wrote up my notes for Uluots in the compartment during the return journey. These included the exact procedure followed by the delegation and the exact times, a summary of the speeches made on both sides and only of course an estimate as to the strength of the forces crossing the border.

"On the morning of the 18th, I put this information on Uluots's desk. When, incidentally, I had been about to sign the document, a problem arose in my mind – one of vanity – to wit: how to sign. Should I simply write 'Ullo Paerand'? Or 'Ullo Paerand, Counsellor to the Government of the Republic'? In order to test how real or illusory the title I had been given two days before really was. I understood that a really worthy individual would not put it to the test. *If* Uluots took my title seriously (and such a serious person as he was would surely not be joking in such matters!), then it would come out sooner or later. But if the question of titles was merely an example of Terras's original brand of humour that would also come out in the end. This was, however, one instance where I let my childishness get the better of me. So at the end of the three-page report which I had put together that morning on the train, which had become two pages of typing, I wrote:

Ullo Paerand
Counsellor to the Government of the Republic

in this rather old-fashioned way with, at the back of my mind, the consideration that such an old-fashioned mode of expression would upset the conservatism of the Prime Minister less than were I to have written 'Government Counsellor' and left out the word 'Republic'. This would thus upset him less and would therefore not make him

195

cross it out and declare it impermissible, something which had been done in an ad hoc way and was almost a joke . . .

"He didn't bat an eyelid when I put the report on the table. I don't know whether he read it straightaway or sometime later. Because for the next three days he was occupied sufficiently with other matters: on the 19th Zhdanov arrived in Tallinn and the finale of the drama of the murder of our republic commenced. And against this background, I myself felt it perverse to take an interest in the fate of my report. Even though if that sheet of paper sprang to mind, during the next few days, weeks, months – even years – it was always a source of worry, at least in Soviet times. *If* this paper were still in existence and someone happened to see it, this could cause me no end of problems . . .

"With regard to my promotion, it did at any rate not appear in the *Riigi Teataja* where all state announcements were published. But I never did destroy those papers, where, for the first and only time, this promotion had been set down in writing. And yet I forgot about it completely. When my mother died in 1952, and I had to sort out papers in the flat into those to throw away and those to keep, I found this paper folded up to an eighth of its full size between two sections of the torn lining of my mother's handbag. She too had clearly not had the heart to destroy it, despite the constant danger of keeping it."

25

U LLO CONTINUED HIS STORY. "Three days later, on 21 June, Uluots resigned at lunchtime, but his officials, excepting Colonel Tilgre (who had been promoted to the rank of colonel during the last day of the republic) were all present that evening. They had been ordered by Terras to assemble but would have been there in any case, waiting for news – when the new Prime Minister arrived.

"The officials met in the anteroom of the Prime Minister's suite, around my desk actually, and Dr Vares rolled in, if not quite dripping with sweat, then his skin at least a little moist from the sheer excitement, wading his way forward. He gestured to us in greeting and would perhaps have left it at that and walked straight through to his office, or slipped out into the White Hall where a session of the new Cabinet was about to begin, but Terras stopped him in the anteroom and began introducing us one by one. He shook hands with us all in a row with a tired smile on his face.

"Terras: 'And this is the courier to the former Prime Minister, whom Professor Uluots appointed only the day before yesterday as—'

"The new Prime Minister cried: 'Well, well, well – aren't you Comrade Paerand?! Oh, what a pleasant surprise . . .' He suddenly fell silent and looked with a somewhat perplexed smile straight at the assembled group of officials. He clearly understood that he had exposed me to an unwarranted extent. Clearly what flashed through his round head was that my colleagues would suspect some closer and, of course, political connection between him and myself, and this was unenviable. So he decided to do a little damage limitation and cried: "Comrade Paerand is a poet! My colleague in ministering to the Muse. And a very interesting poet! Which you, naturally, already know . . .'

'This was in fact totally unknown to every single one of those working with me. His additional explanation actually increased, rather than decreased, their suspicions. For instance, Colonel Tilgre, who wasn't actually there at the time, but to whom I had to explain my acquaintance with Barbarus and who will have discussed the matter with Uncle Joonas before he, during Nazi times in autumn 1941, took a decisive step, which was to save me . . ."

At this point I said: "Listen, Ullo – you've been going to tell me about your life under Barbarus at two of our meetings at least . . ."

Ullo enlightened me. "Wait a minute. What was most characteristic was that the State Chancery was purged over the space of a week or so. Those who kept their jobs were the bookkeepers, the couriers and me. In August, when the new Constitution became valid and the whole structure was altered, it was Lauristin who became what was now termed the Chairman of the Council of People's Commissars. Barbarus was packed off to Kadriorg, to the Administrative Building, as Chairman of Praesidium of the Supreme Soviet. And he took me with him. As a subordinate official, not a counsellor, of course. He knew nothing of my spell as counsellor. So that's how I got there. Actually, I was performing tasks pretty similar to what I had been doing before. Only that there were now far fewer visitors. Perhaps one-quarter of the people who had visited previous prime ministers. And the majority of quite a different sort. A group of more or less proletarian petitioners. Pleading for clemency for themselves while bringing dread to their neighbours. Incidentally, I never encountered any people of importance then, such as ministers, people's commissars and the like. On the other hand, the players of *yesterday* turned up – well, only a handful, but still rather more than were to be expected. People asking for posts, favours, support. And *who,* you will ask. Oh, let's forget about the names! But nothing much interesting happened there. Except for – as I have already told you – when the party began manipulating the results of the Riigivolikogu elections, and Barbarus cried to me: 'My dear Paerand, don't you understand anything? But why should you? A month ago even I didn't understand. I felt we could do *something.* Now I know that we won't be able to. I will not be able to do a thing!' Sometimes when he was across from me, at the other side of the President's desk, he would ask me to sit down and, lost in thought, would sigh at me over the incrustations of that table: 'Ah – if I only had an inkling where those speeches on my desk came from, the ones I have to deliver to the people . . .'

198

"To this day, I still do not know for sure where his sincerity began and where it ended. Because he surely *had* to sense the presence of the Central Committee and the KGB behind his back.

"I stayed at Kadriorg for almost a year, a subordinate official to the Chairman of the Praesidium of the Supreme Soviet. Barbarus had a few fleeting and rare moments of semi-sincerity. Usually he was florid, disciplined, worried, and the more time went on, the more worried the smile . . . up to when I helped him and his little suitcase into his car on 15 July 1941, if I am not mistaken. I even don't know when his wife followed later. We drove to the Baltic railway station here in Tallinn. In the back were two security bodyguards, and around us the city was in the confusion of war. The Germans had already taken Pärnu and had almost crossed the River Emajõgi in the south. And Barbarus had to travel to Leningrad to prepare for the evacuation of Tallinn. But he never came back.

"So let me speak of my private life. There are other people who could describe life under Barbarus, in Estonia in general and Kadriorg in particular. But not a soul will be writing about the life of Ullo Paerand."

Ullo reminisced: "I was already telling you about the end of '38, at Christmas, about when I sent Ruta off to Stockholm. And how in February '39 I went with five roses to Lia and was rejected . . ." (I do feel that Ullo was telling me this with his lip held stiff and – yes, even now in 1986 – a little louder than necessary.) "And do you know, even that rejection did not tear me quite free from Lia's skirts. Or from her hands-off approach, as I hadn't as yet got beyond the skirt stage with her.

"Anyway, two years previously, I had gone with Ruta to Kivimäe to visit Lilli, a school chum of hers. I don't know if Ruta would have taken me along had she known that Lilli awakened in me a desire, reprehensible, but all the more powerful for that. This Lilli was a girl with a striking face, rather like Joan Crawford, only coarser, and it soon became apparent that she was an amateur whore. Oh yes, and Lilli's father, a small, fattish and badly shaven individual, was the owner of two nicely renovated little houses in Kivimäe. His family lived in one of them. He always wore his railway official's uniform, black with crimson edging, and seemed to be a typical petit bourgeois type, although he was in fact the first Red I had ever met in my whole life.

When I went with him to the pantry – where there was permanently a metal keg full of beer – he handed me four brown earthenware pots and invited me to have a beer with him. All of a sudden, while still in the pantry, he began to curse Päts and Laidoner. Apropos of nothing. In a half-whisper, true, but using the most offensive language imaginable. Not particularly original words now, since we started to see the same ones used in the papers three years later. But this was the first time, and they struck me as quite offensive. Oppressors. Bloodsuckers. Drinking the sweat of the working classes. He said this as he poured beer into the pots with a gush, raised one to his lips, and wiped the froth off his moustache with his sleeve. For years afterwards, on hearing proletarian oaths, in place of the consumptive cheeks, the tortured faces, of idealists, reduced to despair at iniquity and injustice, instead, the cynical snouts of froth-moustachioed fat men in uniform flashed through my mind.

"Ruta and I went to their place on a number of occasions, and each time I was alone with Lilli's father, he would insult Päts and Laidoner in a half-whisper (I can't remember him ever mentioning anyone else) and I could not understand why he was doing so.

"Maybe he had noticed that Lilli was trying to ensnare me and was jealous, and so this was his way of taking revenge: here, you mongrel anteroom lackey to the Prime Minister, here's to the fact that you come here with your girl and start ogling my child. And as I can't stop her sniffing around you, for that's the kind of girl she is, let it at least be known what serious people think of your boss! You can't be such a bastard that you'd go and rat on me . . .

"The way her father behaved could have been the result of some such thought process. I haven't been able to think of any better explanation. But Lilli's behaviour towards me required no such analysis: it was that of an amateur whore, as I have said. Over a glass of Dad's home-made wine, she had said quite openly to Ruta: 'I'm going to take him over . . .' And she did. At a party she dragged me out with four or five guests to dance to the gramophone, then pulled me off into the sofa corner behind the potted palm – and in no time at all her blouse buttons were undone, her breasts bare, and she pressed my face between them. Her nipples seemed to be exceptionally large and red, and around them, admittedly only small and sparse, were black hairs. I managed to convince myself that I didn't fancy her – maybe solely because I knew Ruta was somewhere nearby. So I had behaved improperly with Lilli but not to her. But when I now tried it on with Lilli on a subsequent occasion Ruta's presence was not there to stop me, nor did Lilli seem to remember my previous hurtful rejection."

Ullo continued: "Well, if you do something with my stories, it'll be here that you'll get things wrong, strapping me almost masochistically to the Borms' orbit. You'll make me land on Lilli's red nipples because Lia was in the centre of gravity. And will say: OK, let it be, I will not refute your interpretation. But what I'm trying to say is this: I myself regarded my relationship to Lilli as a descent, and I freed myself from it, I don't know – over a month or six weeks. And not by reverting to the Borms . . ."

I wanted to taunt him. I wanted to shout: oh really? And I was about to bet him that he didn't free himself from the Borms' orbit for some years, if ever. So he could only fall towards this centripetally. Meaning that his next aerodrome proved to be none other than Lia's mother. With her 120 kilos . . . But I suddenly noticed his brow sharpen and there was, God knows, dark lightning in his slightly astigmatic look, so I kept my mouth shut. Yes, I suddenly refrained from putting my ironic thoughts into words, since I sensed his seriousness:

"Then, one day in early May 1940, towards evening, Uluots rang me on the intercom: 'Listen, Mr Paerand, I apologise for disturbing you, but the couriers are all out – could you please take this envelope to the Ministry of War? More specifically, to General Lille in person.' And he came in and handed me the envelope, and I went off."

I asked: "Have you any idea what was in the envelope?"

Ullo said: "It was the most important envelope I have ever had to deliver."

"Ohoh!"

"It determined my life for the following twenty years!"

"So what did it contain?"

"Haven't a clue."

"But how can you then say . . .?"

Ullo explained: "As I stepped out of the Ministry of War on to Pikk Street, a girl was walking some twenty paces ahead of me in the direction of the Russian Embassy and Stude's store. She was wearing a brown outfit. And had remarkable legs. And brunette curls – like some angel from a Memling painting – down to her shoulders. And all this was somehow familiar. But I didn't recognise her until I had got up close behind her and she turned her heart-shaped face over her left shoulder and looked straight at me . . .

"'Ah – Mr Paerand –'

"'Oh, Miss Maret – Miss Velgre, I mean to say . . . Weren't you teaching teachers to teach somewhere or other? Do tell me how life has been treating you? And how's your father?'

"And so forth. On the corner of Harju Street, near Niguliste Church, I invited her to go with me to the Colombia café for half an hour to have a chat. She agreed, and I was surprised at my own joy and elation. And so we began meeting, at least twice a week, in Tallinn cafés, while around us the drama of summer 1940 was unfolding. In the late summer, Maret sent her father off to the country. Because the old gent had tried to get in to see Vares to ask for financial support: Vares had after all been a good blue, black and white army doctor at the front in the War of Independence. One who had been awarded the Cross of Liberation. He had not accepted, out of modesty. The story that that refusal was a political protest against the Estonian Republic was slander at all events. Lord, it could surely be nothing but slander . . .

"Old Velgre was the only person I knew who had interpreted Vares's gesture in so naive a way. Then, and especially later, this interpretation could have brought down problems on his head, irrespective of whether his ailing memory was taken into account or not. Maret had seen the danger approaching early on, and fixed up a place for her father in the country. Not in Loobre where he had once worked as a headmaster and was remembered and known, but with his late wife's relations in the heart of Pärnumaa province, hidden behind large marshes and forests, where not a soul knew anything about either the old codger himself nor his War of Independence stories, which had now grown dangerous. And where it was hoped there would be no one around to dispute against when he slandered the Prime Minister for being a Red.

"At the end of August 1940 I went to visit Maret at her flat on Erbe Street. She had done up the back room nicely and had made some coffee. We sat on the sofa at the low table. Of course, I had come prepared with a bottle of liqueur and sinful thoughts. But what do I mean by sin? At any rate she let it happen. In, by the way, a rather odd manner – enjoying and suffering it at one and the same time. This was always the case later on, too. At first forgivingly, at any rate coolly, then suddenly kindling – hotly, passionately, ecstatically. Till suddenly she was broken, pudent, sad to her inner core. And then, bit by bit, not only sad, but sad-sad-joyful, then sad-joyful. As if she had, in the meantime, conversed with God, and He had forgiven her for her moment of joy. And I really didn't understand this behaviour. But what I soon did begin to notice was that she allowed me into the first room of the flat, her own room, allowed me to sit down in the armchair in there, look through her bookshelves. Although she didn't yet invite me to her divan with its cushions and its orange bedspread. Our romance always took place on the divan in the back room. She only allowed me into her bed once we had been to the registry office to get married. And I can say: in the second week of the war, during the first days of June, that's what we did . . . When . . ."

At this point I have to interrupt Ullo's flow: I remember that it was the summer of '86 when he told me about it. It was 19 June. What triggered off the memory is when he said "when" . . . and then fell completely silent, got up, went to the open the French windows and went out on to the small yellow-brick balcony (somewhere I have called such a balcony on the gable of Old Town houses a flying brick boat) – Ullo went out on to the balcony and stood there, and I followed him out there and asked: "When . . .?"

And he replied, his back towards me as if throwing his reply to the winds, to the faded red-roof ridges, flecked with seagull droppings: "When, three days previously, with five roses in my hand, I had again gone to ask for Lia's hand. And was again rejected . . ."

So I replied – unable to act any more gravely than to utter a cheap pun: "I mean, your being unfaithful – or the fact that you were prepared to be so – still stemmed from faith? But isn't that how it tends to go?"

Ullo did not take the trouble to say anything to that. He continued to remain silent for a further ten seconds, then went on.

"And then I was married. As simple as that. I no longer know when you first got to meet Maret. Very early on at any rate. But I don't remember you visiting us on Erbe Street."

I said: "Maybe I didn't. Who would invite people over during their honeymoon? But I did come for a visit a little later. During the

German occupation. When you'd already been arrested. And then, later on, when you'd been released, and I visited you, and you told me of your prison adventures. But, Ullo – tell me again now, how *did* you get arrested that first time? I remember that the second time you were imprisoned during the German period had something to do with stamps, hadn't it? But the first one? Was it to do with the fact that you had worked for Barbarus? Well? And what was it like out at Patarei in those days . . . ?"

26

U LLO CONTINUED HIS STORY during that June 1986 session with some pleasure, after being rather tongue-tied at first. The notes are lying before me now in the open exercise book. But they could have been ten, or even a hundred times more detailed. It goes roughly like this:

In early August 1941, when he had already become convinced that Barbarus would not be returning to Tallinn, Ullo decided to become ill. By that time his certificate of employment at the Praesidium of the Supreme Soviet would no longer necessarily shield him from being forced into joining the Red Army. But the *insufficientia valvulae mitralis*, which had got him out of the Estonian army military service some six years before, was still with him. This diagnosis, against which a question mark had been put at the time, could now serve to at least win time as regards a call-up to serve in the Red Army. All the more, since the Russian naval hospital, located in Kadriorg Park itself, only a few hundred metres from where Barbarus worked, had a number of Estonian doctors working there during that summer of 1941. Among these was one Dr G.P. That was indeed how I had designated him: Dr G.P. Nowadays, the combination of letters makes me squirm a little as I have forgotten his real name and initials. But I can't find that out without a relatively hopeless amount of archive work. The letters are the result of some mathematical trick I did with the actual initials. Over the decades, I have managed to forget how the trick works. At any rate, he could not have been Gustav Püümann, a name immediately recognisable to anyone with even the slightest knowledge of the Estonian doctors' register, one that reached the annals of history, Püümann being one of our signatories of the Treaty of Tartu in 1920. And who was most likely a lifelong colleague of Dr Joonas Berends, Ullo's uncle, working as he did in Tallinn as a doctor.

No, it was not him. But I can no longer establish who it in fact was.

In this cryptogrammatical game, my own inconsistency does make me laugh rather. Why did I bother to encrypt the doctor's name in the first place? For childish reasons of security. When I was making notes in 1986, the walls of the empire were already foundering, but strong powers were still at work within the shadows of these walls. Although the likes of, say, Comrades Kumm and Jakobson of the KGB were no longer present in Tallinn, Comrades Pork and Kortelainen and their factions were still around. So the fewer people who could be identified in the notes, the better. But the notes I took still allowed dozens and dozens of people to be identified, including Ullo, of course. He was exposed for all to see, only concealed, perhaps, by the odd abbreviation, gap or break in the dry pages, added for jocular purpose. And dozens of others shared a similar fate. The concealment of the identity of a doctor (whose deeds in 1941 could still cause him trouble in 1986) was in effect a game.

At the beginning of August 1941, Ullo had gone to the naval hospital in Kadriorg on account of heart problems. Because of his job at the Praesidium, he got an appointment without any difficulty. He had gone to the said Dr G.P. for tests for a week, for two, for three. He was in the company of sailors and their officers, initially only those who had been wounded during operations carried out in the Gulf of Finland, two Estonian professors from the Technical University, presumably draft dodgers like Ullo himself, but I no longer remember who, and a number of other people. The building was fairly deserted and quiet, and it remained like this for several weeks in a row. Maret had come to visit him daily and brought him extra food and newspapers. During their walks in the adjoining park, she told him who had been arrested during the last week, after the large-scale deportation in June. And in Hundikuristiku, there where Resev, then Minister of the Interior, was to build a villa, but which at the time was merely scrub and bushes where hares, tramps and Forest Brethren liberation guerrillas had ruled, they had fallen into one another's arms and afterwards, still panting from their exertions, had pressed their ears against the ground under the rustling grasses of late summer and listened to hear whether the sound of German artillery was coming closer.

Soon they could actually hear it when an artillery duel took place in the city, between those approaching from the south and those standing on the sea roads to the north. Suddenly, with a throb of engines and dust, accompanied by the stench of petrol and the shouting, a throng of black-uniformed sailors and their officers arrived over Lasnamäe ridge, some with bandaged heads, seeking first aid and yelling, as they moved towards the harbour: "To the ships! Every last man to the ships!" The sick at the hospital immediately split into those, mostly Russian sailors, who rushed off to the port and those, mostly Estonian pseudo-sick, who dispersed, with a hint from Dr G.P., to places such as the central boiler house of the hospital. Ullo was, of course, among the latter group.

One hour later, the first Germans were driving over that same ridge at Lasnamäe, firing a few rounds into what had by now become total silence.

And now they were here. Had been for almost half a year. Along with everything their arrival brought. Everything that their arrival had done to people's psyches. Initially, the ease of liberation, a huge relief among the majority of the population, and a great fear among the minority. Ullo's feelings were mixed. For experience proved, after the first few weeks, that Ullo's proximity to such a traitor as Barbarus put him on a knife's edge. ("Ah, Mr Paerand has also stayed behind?! Wouldn't have thought you'd have dared . . . Accidents could happen . . .") God knows who had said that as he strolled with Maret in the snow of Kadriorg Park, with in the background the castle into which the German Governor-General, Litzmann, had moved a week before.

Ullo was on a knife's edge. Till the knife snapped shut. And Ullo was trapped by the fingers. By the neck. I can't now recall, nor have I anyone left to ask, who denounced him, and how and when he was arrested. I can only imagine from what I've heard that the arrest occurred in the usual manner, in the middle of the night, at Erbe Street. He would have been taken to the Kaarli Church hall, the SD building, under the watchful eye of Mikson or Viks or some such person.

"Aha, you're one of those fucking Red bastards, eh . . . ?"

And so forth. I have no idea how he reacted. Based on what I saw of his behaviour at testing moments, I'm pretty sure that his bearing would have been supercilious – yet not to the extent that it would have seemed provocative.

He was notified that some commission or other had sentenced him to six months in prison for Communist activities – and so he'd ended up in Patarei, with rows of striped prisoners, gluing together boxes (as was no doubt also practised at the time at the lunatic asylum by the more mentally able patients) and in his free moments lying on his straw mattress and writing poetry, in as much as the crowded nature of his confinement would allow. For now, exactly as in Soviet times, there were some four thousand prisoners in a prison designed in Estonian days for about one thousand. Among them, a few cultured people such as the poets Sirge, Rummo, Sütiste and Kangro, plus, of course, the cartoonists Gori, Tiitus and anyone else who had, during the Soviet year of occupation, made ex officio and complicit cartoons of Adolf Hitler and were now in pretty deep trouble. There was also the more or less nameless mass of what had till recently been Communist apparatchiks, who would be summoned in threes and fours in the night, and who never came back.

During the second or third week Ullo found a way of sending Maret a message. Maret, the sprightly angel that she was, had immediately rushed off to somewhere or other, if not the old Omakaitse barracks on Vaksali Avenue, then to an old military library building, or older part of the present one – at any rate, to Colonel Tilgre.

I remember how Ullo once described this man as Irish-looking. This description would suggest that he was red-haired and had a sportsman's persistence of character. After checking up on the facts with Uncle Joonas, the colonel indeed proved to have the latter quality. During this conversation, Ullo had produced the explanation about how he and Barbarus had got to know one another, and had managed to reach Sandberger himself. Then the commission decided to quash the punishment meted out to Ullo, and he was set free. As likely as not in March '42. He was even offered a job which, under prevailing circumstances, was a quite acceptable post: at the *Hindade Teataja* – the organ of the Prices Commission. The place: I don't know any more, somewhere on Brokusmägi Hill, in one of two buildings there with old mediaeval walls, in the fourth of the small back rooms belonging to the Prices Commission, as the editor of the little bulletin which had a staff of three. His superior was the Commissioner for Prices, Saar. God knows where he hailed from, but he was someone who, in his director's pride, had risen to be almost a minister, a toytown minister for all I know, he may even have been a member of the Vapsid. Critical voices would say in a whisper that he was actually a Rooskie, but those more observant, among them Ullo, were quite prepared to admit that old Saar was neither arrogant nor revolting (as bosses in those days often tended to be) nor was he by any means stupid. One could even say what one or two of his subordinates had said, i.e. that he was a clever enough ne'er-do-well. "Heil Hitler" salutes and greetings were not practised at the Prices Commission, something which by 1942 had become the order of the day up on Tõnismägi Hill where that Estonian quisling, Dr Mäe, held out and elsewhere. At the Prices Commission, almost the opposite atmosphere reigned. For instance, above the writing desk of the Commissioner hung, of course, a portrait of Hitler. But believe it or not, on the back of that portrait there was still, with his back to the room, Stalin. For which the Commissioner would no doubt have been removed had this become known. Or he must have had solid backing.

Putting together these *Käseblättchen* didn't involve much effort and Messrs Ibrus and Kleinod managed it with some speed. They would fetch from the Commissioner's desk the current price tables and the police statistics on the fines given to businessmen who sold for unacceptable prices. These bulletins also contained information on changes in the prices boards of the counties and towns. But when Ullo wanted to publish his own poem – or God knows whose – in praise of the prices policy of the Estonian autonomous administration, the Herr Factor phoned him personally from the printers'.

"Mr Paerand – how are you? Am I reading this right:

> *Eesti rahvas on ju nõus,*
> *et kui püsib hoos ja jõus*
> *meie rinde ründe rangus,*
> *pole mingi hinnatõus*
> *üldse tõus, vaid hoopis langus . . .*

That is to say:

> *The Estonian people are agreed*
> *that if the attack of our front remains*
> *dashing and forceful*
> *then no price rise is a rise*
> *but a fall instead . . .*

209

". . . like that?"

"Yes, that's right."

"Mr Paerand, if you'll forgive me – have you gone completely stark raving mad?"

"Ha-ha-haa. Don't you think it'll pass the censor? Well then, censor it yourself. Goodness me, what's the problem?"

But at the same time, Ullo felt, after being released in the spring of '42, a new itch to put pen to paper. And luckily – or maybe unfortunately for the composition of what is written here – among my papers there is a text written by Ullo at around that time. Almost a short story. And I see no good reason to leave it out. When I consider how this tale continues, well, quite the contrary.

27

U LLO'S TEXT READ:
       During the lunch break, I had the habit of dropping in at
       Feischner's upper lounge. The oppressive wine red and
black of the room was somehow out of place, however eminently
suitable a colour combination, given the times. The café had
acquired these colours in what had been a completely different
world in the late thirties. In the prevailing atmosphere of light-
headedness and frivolity, the colours formed a strangely
harmonious contrast: outside, on Vabaduse väljak – i.e. Freedom
Square – the dusty faded lilac sunshine of those summers – and
then suddenly here indoors – not Stendhal's chivalry and nobility of
Le rouge et le noir, but the kitsch red and black of empty mimicry,
colours which became suddenly most appropriate: the dark red of
Soviet blood, the black of Soviet coal, a combination of colours
which remained steadfastly symbolic with the arrival of the
Germans: blood and violence.

On such late mornings in the heart of summer, there was much
else which blossomed against the background of the dark red
panelling and black upholstery. Dresses from yesteryear, blouses
and skirts sewn by hand in the indigence of war. High-combed,
blonde curls of perms, the blonder, the more Aryan-attractive.
Translucently gleaming silk stockings, which the women had
managed to rustle up from goodness knows where, since the
stocking factories had now begun to make parachutes and produce
the hemp used for making the hangmen's ropes. And finally those
strapped shoes with wooden heels and a fiery pattern which
enhanced the shape of calves, the delicacy of ankles and the naive
charms of toes.

I looked around the lounge. Just as on previous days. Of course there were Germans as well – blue, green and grey flecks among the general public. Like lead, not that cast molten into water for luck, but a baleful sprinkling of the metal, it occurred to me. Young officers, still wet behind the ears, who had placed their high caps next to their coffee cups, of course containing ersatz coffee, and who were muttering among themselves or chirping to Estonian girls.

There seemed to be no free places until I spotted someone beckoning. Of course I instantly recognised the beckoner. The instantaneity of such recognition always depends, at least in my case, on aesthetic qualities. And although in this instance it was perhaps not a question of platinum or gold, it was at least a happily clear silver: a young lady – yes, what was her name now – Õispuu or Lillenurm or Kullerkann, in other words, Bernhard Linde's latest flame. That same Bernhard Linde, a man who had always remained a trifle mysterious, was somebody whom I had known since childhood. I remember him from when we were living in our flat on Raua Street. We moved from there when I was eight, so this was a true childhood acquaintance. And now I had met him again, a few months ago, after the June coup d'état on my way to visit another childhood friend who had remained an amicable blockhead despite having grown up by now – Jochen von Brehm. Mr Linde had emerged on to Pikk Street, recognised me and took me back with him into his apartment – to look at the books he had recently bought and to have a chat. And so I began to go round to his place on a regular basis. Because the books he had were exceptionally interesting – and when the Baltic Germans were leaving the country he had been in the habit of buying them off them. His interest in the welfare of my parents and myself was genuine. And the coffee served up by his young wife was still, in the spring of 1942, the real thing.

Linde had remained more or less the same, these last twenty years, as when Nikolai Triik had painted his portrait back in 1914, though he had grown a shade fatter and his hair greyer and wispier. At any rate, the blonde beauty, his fourth or fifth wife, to whom he introduced me as the son of old friends of his, was at least thirty years younger than himself. He was, of course, burdened by the reputation of being somewhat unreliable, ever since the bankruptcy of his Varrak publishing house in 1924. At the same time he had close friends – and what friends they were! – Tammsaare, Suits, Eliaser, Tuglas and the like, who were always prepared to vouch for his integrity. Perhaps not entirely with regard to his affairs with women, but at least in his sterling honesty in public affairs.

So anyway, I went over to young Mrs Linde's table when beckoned. On the way over, I noticed that at the same table as the young lady in her orange-peel-coloured dress sat a gentleman in grey. He was a relatively tall and thin individual of about sixty years of age – about the same age as Bernhard himself – with a small grey moustache. I remember at the time feeling a wry mixture of condescension and jealousy, plus, in this instance, a flicker of sympathy for the young lady: her husband's friends were by definition older men and therefore hardly interesting to a young woman . . .

"Mr Paerand – a very old friend of Bernhard's," said the young lady to her companion as I took a seat. "But here, Mr Paerand, is a true literary surprise. Oh yes indeed. This is the writer Arthur Valdes."

I swallowed my surprise – for it was indeed rather a surprise – for a few seconds, but could not help saying: "Very pleased . . . I mean, what I thought to be imagination has turned out to be real. In other words, Friedebert Tuglas's information on the death of Mr Valdes has proved to be premature. Wait a minute. Where and when did he say you had perished?"

Valdes replied in mild tones: "Oh, you know, we shouldn't blame him. He received the information from Sergeant Kusta Tooming who served in my detachment. A very decent chap. Tooming was wounded five minutes after me. Saw me fall, and told them later back home what he'd seen. Oh, but you mean where? And when? Near Ypres in Belgium. On 20 January 1916."

He lit his straight-stemmed pipe and blew out into the lounge at Feischner's, full of ersatz tobacco smoke, a cloud of light blue smoke, this with its characteristic smell from some captain's or admiral's brand of real tobacco.

I said: "Mr Valdes, well . . . for some reason or other I have the feeling that your, er, presence here is, shall we say, fleeting, not to say downright ephemeral. I shan't be asking you any questions about works you've written in the meantime. Not even whether your famous *Steps* has, by some miracle, managed to get published without our hearing about the event. Or do you perhaps have the manuscript with you now? But please allow me to hope that you will tell us of your life meanwhile – for the sake of the history of Estonian literature."

Valdes said, puffing at his pipe: "My dear young man. When you appeared in this lounge, looked around, and then made your way to our table, Mrs Linde managed to convey to me the essentials about your life. But please let us not speak about the history of literature. For the past twenty-four years I have written as good as nothing. All I possess is in my small house on the Channel Island of Alderney, which is at present in German hands. But in line with what is termed the *Estonian Biographical Dictionary*, I can say the following." He stopped his pipe anew, then continued: "I returned to the ranks at the end of 1916, as you already know . . ."

"With which rank?"

"The rank of captain. I ended my army service in France in 1922."

"I asked: 'But what about the British army?'"

"The same, the same."

"And if I may ask: with what rank there?"

Valdes smiled, his teeth slightly yellowed from pipe smoking, but otherwise quite healthy. "With that of lieutenant colonel. Well, as you appreciate, Tuglas has saddled me with some sort of military career. But from 1922 until the present war I was busy in, shall we say, various types of business activity in France."

"And where have you just arrived from?"

"From Paris. For although my physical home is between England and France, my spiritual home is Paris. I have, of course, arrived here via Vichy. I'm here almost on official business, and that is only made possible by crossing Vichy territory. At the present point in time."

"And what are you doing here – after a quarter of a century?" I asked, my curiosity getting the better of my discretion. "Visiting old friends . . .?"

"I was at the Lindes' place overnight. I had a chat with Bernhard until dawn. His wife had already gone to bed. In the morning I got to hear that I should leave today – to avoid any misunderstandings . . ." he glanced at his large American wristwatch, ". . . in fact, before the hour was out. There is a Swede, a Major Motander, who will take me with him in his motor boat. In fact, he is something of a literary officer and has translated Tammsaare into Swedish. So what I came for remains undone. You no doubt have an inkling as to what. Of course: I came to visit my alter ego. To drop in, after all this time, on Friedebert Tuglas. Because, look, Tuglas is – how shall I put it? – quite a vain fellow. Yet I would still trust him as I trust myself. But now . . ." he glanced again at his wristwatch, "Mrs Linde, Mr Paerand – people, friends, this place here, this country – you can imagine that I am very reluctant to leave – but I believe that there has been and will be enough experience of privation in this country, both in the past and in the future – enough to be able to survive this privation . . ." And he shook hands with Mrs Linde and myself. "In a word, until we meet again. If fate wills it."

He walked very upright towards the door and disappeared down the stairs. Mrs Linde said: "Let's sit here a moment longer. If he's being observed, then hopefully only by one person who will now be obliged to follow him. So that now no one will be observing us." And noticeably more quietly: "Tell me – are you thinking of travelling to Tartu in the coming days?"

"As it happens, I am. Tomorrow. I'm being sent off to Tartu by the boss to have a look at our branch there."

"In that case I have a request. Look, I don't want Bernhard getting mixed up in this. He's already in difficulties with the Germans as it is. He's so careless. Only recently, he again said something in defence of the Czechs, in connection with the destruction of Lidice. He was questioned on the subject by the SD only last week. But now –"

I said: "But now Arthur Valdes has stayed the night with you. And you think it likely – and quite rightly – that they were keeping an eye on him."

"Not only that," said Mrs Linde in a whisper. "Valdes left us a letter. For Bernhard to take to Tuglas, as he couldn't go there himself."

I said: "And you would like me to take it to Tuglas instead of Bernhard . . ."

215

My God, that Mrs Linde was, after all, very nice, with her soft colours and her girlish figure (hair the colour of wheat, bright blue eyes and a straight neck) – and along with all that she was a very intense woman. So I said, surprising even myself a little: "But what's the problem, my dear lady? I'll be off tomorrow morning. In a vehicle belonging to our institution, a lorry with a wood-gas generator. But we'll certainly make it there by tomorrow lunchtime. And tomorrow evening, I can deliver your letter. Do you have it on you?"

The lady behaved in a manner she must have picked up from a spy film. She threw a glance at her yellow straw shopping bag lying on the black café chair and said under her breath: "It's in there, inside the newspaper . . ."

She took a newspaper from the bag. It was the latest issue of *Eesti Sõna* and she placed it on the table between us and warbled on about the theatre and concert programmes which were printed on the back page. I took eager part in the conversation – and, staring intently into the eyes and at the mouth of the lady, I folded up the paper and shoved it in my pocket. And I thought to myself: if nothing happens within a couple of minutes no one has been watching what I was doing. Three minutes later, we paid the bill and left.

I escorted Mrs Linde to her door on Pikk Street and then rushed off to the Prices Commission. Messrs Ibrus and Kleinod were still enjoying an extended lunch, so to speak, and I myself noticed how Klaas's ashes of courage were glowing in my heart as in Till Eulenspiegel's: Arthur Valdes's one and only letter to Friedebert Tuglas! I took the folded newspaper from my pocket and pulled out the envelope. The notepaper had small blue-and-white checks and was of a type which had not been available in the shops here for years. In greyish type was written:

> To the Writer
> Mr Friedebert Tuglas
> Tartu

Then the thought struck me: if I turned over the envelope, would Valdes's address be on the back, i.e. Valdes's own, whether on

Alderney, in Paris or in Vichy France? If it was, I certainly ought to copy it for the sake of Estonian literary history. I turned over the envelope and, of course, the back was blank. And then I noticed: goodness, the envelope isn't even sealed! Or if it was, then only at the tip of the glued point – and it was glued shut so temptingly lightly. And my curiosity had somehow smouldered, warmed or dried open the letter as it lay in my pocket, through my shirt and my breast pocket and through the newspaper. But what is far more likely – and I needed this excuse to justify myself – is simply that the letter had been open all along. Perhaps it had been left open on purpose. For whatever reason. Perhaps it was meant for many to read – since the writer wasn't sure what the addressee would do with it.

In a word, I rushed over to the window which was criss-crossed with sticky tape for protection against flying splinters in case of bombing, and opened the letter. It was written in Valdes's very linear, almost engineer-like hand (the many sides to this man were quite baffling!) and it went like this:

Dear Friedebert!

You are, in as far as I know you at all, someone who likes to keep his distance. But as I am almost your twin brother, please allow me to address you familiarly, allow us to be on first-name terms. And allow me also to hope that you will read this letter with great care and attention.

In your time, you gave me literary credibility in the eyes of the educated class of Estonians, which on account of my passivity of the observer, but also on account of the caprices of violence, I have never been able to make good. And for that reason I am writing to you about an entirely different matter and which is now, in present-day Europe, of a good deal more importance than a literary Weltanschauung.

I have remained here, in a France overrun by Teutons, on the heels of events, with reason whispering in my ear, close to that phenomenon which the genuine Frenchman already knows, in pet-name terms or in hope, as the Résistance.

Like certain trees in the Bible, this at first sent forth shoots, sowed mustard seed, but by now it covers the entire country. And

217

this first seed and germination has extended a direct connection all the way to Estonia in a most peculiar way. And what is most fantastic of all – a connection to you. Friedebert – you yourself were in your time familiar with that restless spirit from the edges of the Tartu bohemia, whose name was Boris Vilde. It has never been established whether he was indeed related to our great writer Eduard Vilde. But, as we are both aware, he moved from Tartu, in the year 1928, to the more stimulating intellectual climate of Paris. And seven years later, when Professor Ants Oras, an individual well known to us both, and Monsieur Louis Pierre-Quint, whom I did not know personally, began to edit an anthology of Estonian short stories for publication in France and when problems arose for the translators, then B.V. was always prepared to offer help. Under circumstances which remain unclear to me, he translated two stories for this anthology, Eduard Vilde's "Casanova Takes His Leave" *and August Mälk's* "Gifts From the Sea". *And the anthology appeared with the Sagittaire publishing house in 1937 (but you can of course take it down from your shelf to check). Most of the anthology was translated by some Madame Navi-Bovet. I know from B.V. himself that he refrained from translating your own* "Popi" *and* "Huhuu" *only because he doubted whether he had the ability to successfully translate its especially clear colour and plasticity to a sufficient degree. He was, at any rate, convinced – as am I – that that story is the highlight of the anthology. Not perhaps in translation – this is again the work of Madame Navi-Bovet – but in originality, certainly. But why do I write:* "B.V. was"? *I will come to the point with tragic swiftness. He was working as a minor restorer at the Musée de l'Homme in Paris. In the very cellar of that museum, with that very B.V. as one of its instigators, a band of idealist conspirators was formed, mercurial, but nonetheless of iron will, who started what is now termed the* Résistance.

With regard to B.V. personally, he and his closer fellow conspirators were discovered six months later by the Germans and B.V. was executed this year, on the eve, by the way, of the anniversary of the Estonian Republic. Although the Résistance *suffered countless victims, it has made things hot for the Germans*

218

in a quite literal and hopeful way. And, by the way, French writers, even very well-known ones, took a significant part in its activities. If I fail to mention those names here, this is only out of caution and since I feel no need to write a whole catalogue. But I can assure you: you would be surprised if you found out who had connection with the Résistance.

And now, looking from a European perspective, there is no doubt that at this point in world history a similar movement is needed in Estonia, one which will be vital for our future freedom, politically, tactically and morally. Estonia is in urgent need of an Estonian Resistance Movement, and all the potential attitudes necessary are present. When the Germans were received with open arms one year ago, this was only because a month previously some 10,000 Estonians had been deported to Russia and 20,000 had been forcibly conscripted by the Soviets. This was understandable from a psychological point of view: the Germans had come as liberators from occupation and terror. But they had, and have, learnt nothing from history and instead made their presence, by the will of God you could say, intolerable within a couple of weeks. You know how they behaved in more detail than I do. So that there was, luckily, no permanent shift in attitude towards the German camp. But why am I writing all this, to you of all people? Because you, Friedebert, are, as I have already said, my alter ego in my old home country about whose fate we are both concerned. Friedebert: someone has to take it upon themselves to coordinate the core of the Estonian Resistance Movement. Someone has to consolidate this core and give it an ethical impetus. Tell me, can you imagine anyone more destined for this task than you yourself?

I am far from entertaining the thought that you ought to act as some kind of major or colonel in the underground, someone who coordinates the distribution of rifles and explosives. You would need to find a real major or colonel for such a role. But the electric impulse to set the whole matter in motion should come from you. The spark igniting the fuse should be you.

Of those Estonians who stayed behind in our country, only you have the authority. Your extraordinary rise to becoming a literary master, your revolutionary activity (which was a little too short-

219

lived to suffice for the rest of your life), your experiences as an observer of Western Europe, your apolitical status in formal terms and closeness to the Social Democratic point of view, makes you the only suitable candidate (tell me if you know another) to consolidate matters and include acceptable forces from the left. By the way, this left-wing aspect is where there is a great difference between the Estonian and French resistance movements. In France the Communists have played a significant role. In Estonia this would be unimaginable. Firstly, because in France there are Communists by the hundred or at least fellow travellers among the leading intellectuals, perhaps the inheritance of Anatole France, while in Estonia such do not exist (the Soviet year proved that fact). And the band of the new faithful consists of only three people. I am thinking of your old friend Hans Kruus and our colleagues Semper and Barbarus. As for Communists of the lower ranks, there is only a minimal number among Estonians, whether they be careerists or idealists. But they have been infiltrated from Russia by thousands of souls. And together they may nevertheless form a significant force against Estonian independent nationhood. So, I think it impossible for the Estonian Résistance to have any dealings with most of them. But what I am trying to say is this: in principle, this matter ought to be left to you to decide. All the more, since during Mr Molotov's visit to London (while on his way back by plane from the USA), the British government signed a wide-ranging agreement covering matters of cooperation. Which means that Russia plays a major role, a worryingly major role I would say, in all the various variants of our national future, which in turn requires a balanced decision with regard to cooperation with the Communists. This will be a decision for you to make, given the fact that you have known all our prominent Red leaders personally, right from the start, or at least from last year.

Do I again have to spell out to you your suitability, undoubtedly a binding quality, your supreme suitability for this, element by element? Well, maybe I do, so here are the qualities making it your duty to volunteer for this position: your undeniable authority among both the older and younger generations. Your experience of conspiracy. Your revolutionary halo. Your knowledge of the world and of people. Your intermediary political position. And, last but not least, your unequivocal patriotism, which you have not cheapened by using hackneyed phrases. The fact that you seem to have shut yourself up in the ivory tower of neutrality will allow you to operate in public long before being forced to go underground. For sooner or later you will have to do so.

In truth, maybe I am writing this letter out of a sense of envy and for reasons of revenge, on account of your achievements in tranquillity while I, at least in literary terms, have not succeeded at all. Our old friend Tassa, whom I chanced upon in Switzerland, at very characteristic moments may have something to say about all this, if he doesn't start fantasising, as is his wont. But yes, maybe I want to drag you out of your peaceful, literarily fertile, world of writing out of sheer spite. Drag you out and goad you into taking the same risks as those with whom I've been mixing these last few years.

Be that as it may. My dear old friend: I appeal to you – for the sake of Europe, Estonia and yourself – sacrifice your peaceful life of writing for the sake of the common good. I am far from thinking that what I am saying to you is in any way a sanction, but I fear that the truth is this: my inescapable respect for you will be damaged should you refuse the imperatives of the moment, which you have been called to fulfil.

Dear friend who shares the same fate (we ought to share this, since we were born on the same day, only we do not know the hour of our birth, and any difference could affect our respective natures) – my dear friend, do not think I will give this up lightly now that I have made such an arduous journey to Estonia. You will understand, in your capacity not only as a weaver of decors but also as a psychologist, that I am only desisting from meeting you personally for a weighty reason: the higher command to avoid taking unnecessary risks. I obey, and cannot explain what risks the author runs by refusing.

At any rate, I hope that you, Friedebert, will do what I expect of you, as if my expectation were for you a higher command.

Kind regards,

A.V.

Tallinn, 28 June 1942

The following evening I went along with the letter to Tallinn Street, number 16, the Tuglases' place in Tartu. Unfortunately, I did not meet Tuglas there. His wife, Elo, accepted the letter in the hall. I had stuck down the flap of the letter again, just in case. It would not have been right to say who the letter was from – that was something I should maybe not have known.

"Regrettably, Tuglas has gone to rest. He's been having his headaches again," said Elo Tuglas apologising in her routine manner. "But I'll give it to him as soon as he wakes up."

So I wasn't able to explain to her who the letter was from. I may even have done so had not her irreproachable, if somewhat aloof, affability put me off doing so.

For the next couple of months, I overcame my embarrassment and the sensational letter took on ever more dramatic proportions in my mind. Eight weeks later, when I was again in Tartu to check up on our office there . . . No, I didn't look up the Tuglases at home but Mrs Tuglas happened to step out of the door of Café Werner and bump into me. I said: "Excuse me, madam . . ." and I walked with her round the corner towards the River Emajõgi.

"On the evening of 29 June I brought your husband a letter from Tallinn. He had gone to bed. I'm not going to ask anything about the contents of the letter or about Mr Tuglas's reaction to it. But please allow me to ask: did he receive it?"

She looked at me from under the brim of her broad white summer hat with her grey eyes framed by dark lashes. She was a bright lady with a triangular face, whose premature fading was perhaps not apparent, so self-assured was that face gazing out atop her straight and regal neck, and she said: "You – was it you who brought the letter? What was the name again?"

"Oh, madam – I did introduce myself when I brought the letter – but of course – I apologise . . ." And I told her my name.

Elo Tuglas shook her head. "No. I don't remember."

I said: "I was given the letter in Tallinn in Feischner's café by Mrs Linde."

"You mean Bernhard Linde's wife? Oh dear, that means nothing to me. Bernhard has had so many . . ."

I explained: "Mrs Linde had received it from her husband . . ."

222

"You mean from Bernhard?"

"Yes, exactly . . ."

"But Bernhard is a fantast! Was it a letter from Bernhard to Tuglas? If so, it need never have been written!"

"No, madam, it wasn't from Bernhard Linde . . ."

"Well, well. And who had written the letter, then?"

"It was from Arthur Valdes. Via Bernhard Linde. To be handed on to Mr Tuglas . . ."

Mrs Tuglas burst into a clear ringing laugh: "Arthur Valdes's letter, you say?! Ha-ha-ha-haa! Young man – you give the impression of being an educated person – don't you know that Arthur Valdes simply doesn't exist?!" We stopped at the ruins of the Stone Bridge across the river. Mrs Tuglas said: "Yes. I'm taking a little boat here to get me over to the other side. But please remember: I have no recollection of you bringing me any letter. Especially one from Arthur Valdes. Valdes is no more than a literary joke of Tuglas's from many years ago, a hoax in other words, upon which one or two others such as Tassa and Gailit embroidered. So that if you did bring us such a letter, it must have been written by some such epigone. Some psycho-terrorist or other . . ." Mrs Tuglas uttered these last words with a good deal of inner resentment as she stepped into the boat, but she did wave, now standing in the boat, with her long white glove which looked like a small, slender seagull.

I shouted: "But I saw the man with my own eyes. I spoke to him for some while. I even shook his hand!"

Mrs Tuglas shouted back: "Some kind of tomfoolery, don't you understand?!"

I turned around and walked back towards the City Hall, thinking: even if I myself began to doubt whether I had ever delivered such a letter, her words "psycho-terrororist" confirmed that the letter had existed. Not only had I read it, but she had too. The question remains as to whether she showed it to her husband. For reasons of love and caution she may very well have simply burnt it.

28

I WILL HAVE TO BREAK from following in Ullo's footsteps for a moment, in order to return soon, this time not alone, but in the company of another classmate from those years, Elmar Loo – or at least his shadow.

Elmar Loo was the son of a notary and a schoolmistress and was a schoolmate of both Ullo's and mine back at Wikman's. He had been one form below me, five below Ullo. Ullo would at least have known him by sight from early on, but they were not initially acquainted. Nor was I until we got to know one another at university in Tartu or, more specifically, at the Amicus. And after that student society had been closed down by the Russian authorities, just after the Soviet coup of 1940, we had kept in touch, until we had observed one another enough for a certain conversation to take place.

This occurred in a flat in Tallinn belonging to the parents of my then wife Hella. The flat was in a building which was bombed out of existence one year later. Hella and I had arrived there from Tartu and intended staying for a few days – I'm not sure precisely what we came for. Elmar came to visit us there with his Kaarin. The historical nature of the flat's address can be seen merely by looking at its name. Up to 1938 it had been called Kentmann Street, then, owing to the overzealous efforts of the city fathers it was renamed Konstantin Päts Street after the President incumbent. Then the new city fathers insisted on its being called Jaan Kreuks Street, after the murdered Communist revolutionary, then again Päts or Kentmann Street, then, a couple of days before the time I am going to tell about, it became Hermann Goering Street. Till the traces of snowballs and horse droppings were so densely packed around the street name board of the National Bank building that one night this was replaced, and the street once again became either Päts or Kentmann Street. It was there, on that street which had become a mirror of history, that Elmar came to visit us. With Kaarin, a student like himself.

My bookish father-in-law, old Oolep, and his dentist wife had gone off to the country to visit relatives. Looking back on it, I feel Elmar had known about this all along.

The four of us were sitting by the sawdust stove, a large cylindrical piece of tin which had been turned into a stove now that fuel was scarce, on which we burnt what sawdust we could lay our hands on. The stove stood blazing in the middle of old Oolep's chilly parlour. The flickering glow that escaped through the cracks in the casing lit up minimally the pictures of the master and mistress of the house, half-length portraits of the stern literary critic and his mild wife, in dynamic poses as painted by Peet Aren in the twenties. We'd just eaten beetroot tops, something quite usual considering the times we were living in, and were sipping at Dr Mäe's Tears. Not to such an extent that the voluptuous brunette Kaarin's cooing "r"s had sharpened, or that the volleys of laughter of Hella, with her long legs like a fawn and her Grecian profile, had grown any louder. But sufficiently nonetheless for our chat to begin to stray on to criticism of the world at large. Field Marshal Paulus's army had capitulated at Stalingrad. Five thousand Estonian lads had been sent off by the Germans to join the Estonian Legion of the SS. Voluntarily, of course. And so forth. Then Kaarin beckoned to Hella and took her off into our bedroom, for what I presumed was girly talk. With hindsight, I would say that Elmar may have signalled for her to do so. When just the two of us remained, Elmar said in a rapid, quiet voice, looking me straight in the eye, his three-quarter-moon face half hidden behind his thick spectacles: "Listen – have you heard that they're starting – or rather, have already started up – a group aiming at Estonian resistance?"

I had in fact heard something of the sort. Ex-student Taheva had mentioned something about it the previous week in his flat on Vilmsi Street. But had said too little for me to now say: yes, of course I know. At the same time my pride didn't allow me to simply say: no, I haven't heard. So I replied: "Well, let's assume I haven't . . ."

Elmar continued: "I'm speaking to you on behalf of that group. But I must first ask you not to ask me who belongs to it. Because, as you will understand, I would not be able to answer. Half of them will be known to you, anyway. I have been asked by the group whether you, in

225

principle at least, could take on assignments. That's Point A. Point B is: would you be able to find, under the same conditions, two entirely trustworthy men? The group is working on the three-man model – two men for whom you are responsible, for the benefit of the Third Way which represents the future independence of Estonia from both the Russians and the Germans."

I replied, as I remember, without thinking for very long: "A: in agreement. B: I can think of one such person at least."

Of course, the one person who sprang to mind was Ullo. His exceptional powers of observation balanced out his fondness of risk-taking, and his very large, I will not say absolute, independence of judgement made him indispensable for work of a conspiratorial nature.

When, a week later, I had discussed the matter with him, at his place on Erbe Street, in a rather rapid and hushed voice, even though Maret wasn't at home, Ullo only took a dozen or so seconds to reply. And said with a hairline smile on his face: "I actually needed a push like this one. Something has to be done, though I'm afraid that in the end Linton will sell us out to Stalin."

He continued smiling. Prophetically, I would say now. I asked: "Who's Linton?"

"Oh, a portmanteau name. For private use. It's made up from the name Lieutenant Pinkerton, who was a bastard and abandoned Cio-Cio-San, and the ends of the names Franklin and Winston. But what is my first assignment to be?"

This was to arrange Dr Taheva's trip to Finland or, more accurately, Sweden. What do I mean by "arrange"? Ullo had merely to coordinate matters that had been arranged beforehand. Because the grey uniform of an *yliluutnantti* – a Finnish first lieutenant – which the doctor had to wear hadn't actually been sewn up by Ullo, but was the work of Finnish military tailors. It was a genuine uniform in as much as its shape and some ribbons pertaining to some middling order on the front of the jacket were real, though there was no Mannerheim Cross. Some *vänrikki* – a Finnish second lieutenant – looked him over before departure.

The doctor was travelling on a Finnish naval communications vessel and was to arrive at the quayside with a number of suitcases. It had been arranged that Ullo would receive the keys to the doctor's flat on

Vilmsi Street from me and take the suitcases from there to the harbour, only a short distance away. The doctor himself would come separately to the port. They would meet with split-second timing and Ullo was to help the "*yliluutnantti*" get his suitcases on board. The papers in the pocket of the *yliluutnantti* were, of course, false. The correct details had been filled out on the correct form, even the stamps were real, and yet the whole was completely false. So Ullo dropped in on me at the Commercial Bank at ten o'clock one April morning to collect the keys. Ah yes, the Commercial Bank. I have written somewhere how I visited my classmate Endel Haag who was a secretary at the bank. During normal times there were three bank directors, but now, during these crumpled days of war, the number had been reduced to one. Endel had installed himself in the office of the second or third director. The director in question having no doubt died in Siberia by then. And in March '43, I happened to bump into Endel on the street and he said that he wanted to go down to Tartu to sit some exams, but that the director, who had admittedly been in the same student society as he himself – the Vironus – but who was an eternal pedant, had asked Endel to find a replacement for the month or month and a half this process would take. So would I stand in for him? The post – almost a sinecure – was paid at the rate of two hundred Ostmarks per month. I agreed, and worked for six weeks at the Commercial Bank during spring 1943. So it was here that Ullo came to collect the keys.

I gave him them. And his pass for the harbour; the keys real, the pass forged. He wasn't in any great hurry, but there was no real time for conversation either. I looked up into the sky from the highest windows, perfectly suited to a director's office, and said: "You're going to be caught in a heavy shower. Make sure that doesn't cause you any problems."

The next day he told me, with a grin:

He had managed to get to Vilmsi Street while it was still more or less dry. The keys had worked OK, and he had had no problem getting into the doctor's flat. But there, near the door, stood a neat row of five suitcases, each a metre or so in length, the other dimensions as appropriate. Not to speak of the weight involved. So he had stood there, quite at a loss what to do. Because he would have had to go to and fro between the flat and the harbour three times, leaving the first two suitcases under the watchful eye of the doctor while he fetched the other two, then the last one . . . At that point it had started to rain. And no mere shower which would be over in five minutes. With the vehemence of a shower, but continuous, the sky covered with clayey blue clouds from edge to edge. The downpour could very well last a whole hour. But Ullo only had fifteen minutes to spare.

So he had snatched up two of the suitcases – he hadn't managed to squeeze a third under his right arm – locked the door to the flat, and emerged on to the street under the clatter of rain on the tin roof of the porch. He put the suitcases down on the dry steps, spat into his palms, inhaled deeply for the forthcoming marathon and was about to seize hold of the suitcases again when he spotted a horse-drawn cab going in the direction of the harbour, the roof up to protect the driver from the rain. Nothing more convenient could be imagined. A true deus ex machina if ever there was one. Or actually, only the machina.

I said: "Anyone with such enormous good luck must be born for tasks of that sort . . ."

Ullo went on: "I shoved twenty marks into the cabbie's palm. Well, when we heard yesterday that the price of gold is two marks and seventy-eight penni per ounce of gold, that was a king's ransom, but against the background of actual prices not too shocking an amount. To take me and my five suitcases to the harbour."

Ullo had put the suitcases on, and under, the seat of the cab and heaved himself up on top. He could no longer watch to see if he had attracted any attention. Seven or eight minutes later they were there: at the harbour gate with its barbed wire and barrier and sentry box dating back to Russian times.

A German in black sailor's uniform, presumably an NCO, poked his head out of the sentry box and Ullo shoved the false pass under his nose to check with suitable matter-of-factness. Whereby Ullo said in a moderately jovial tone of voice: *"Ich bringe die Siebensachen von meinen Chef. Der Oberleutenant ist entweder schon da oder kommt gleich."*

The *yliluutnantti* had arrived at the right moment and showed the sentry his forged documents which were more than in order. The matter was arranged in a moment. And then they, Ullo and the doctor, each lifted two suitcases from in front of the sentry box, leaving the sentry to keep an eye on the fifth, and walked the hundred metres in the abating rain to the ship, the *Aunus* which was moored at the quayside. They put the suitcases on the gangway, the doctor left them there and started rummaging for his boarding papers, and Ullo went back for the fifth suitcase, presumably wondering why the hell anyone performing such a complex mission would start messing about with such a lot of luggage. When he had nearly reached the gangway again, he saw the impatient doctor had picked up two of the suitcases and was proceeding on board carrying them. At the top of the gangway, a lieutenant was standing to check the papers of those boarding and he saluted the *yliluutnantti*. Although the doctor had practised his role as a military man in front of the mirror on Vilmsi Street, and walking about in Kadriorg Park, he now got into an unexpected flap. He would have to return the salute but was prevented from doing so by the blasted suitcases. And now, with both hands full, he did not know how to react to the salute according to the book.

He put both suitcases down on the gangway and gave – such an accursed mix-up would make the wisest man do the stupidest thing – this dyed-in-the-wool left-handed man, gave the lieutenant a salute with his left hand. And got into such a panic from this muddle, chiefly from the fear of being found out, that he picked up the suitcases, turned on his heels, and descended the gangway once again. Ullo lifted the fifth suitcase almost against his chest and said in Finnish, smiling to the lieutenant at the top: "*Kaikki kunnossa, herra yliluutnantti. Ei mitään unohdettu . . .*" – "Everything in order, sir. Nothing left behind . . ." Whereupon he hissed at the doctor: "Stop larking around. Turn round and go back up," and once again, glancing furtively at the lieutenant standing at the top: "*Hyvää matkaa, herra yliluutnantti. Keskiviikkona palaatte, eik näin?*" – "Have a good journey, sir. Back on Wednesday, what?"

Ullo left the harbour and three days later came the news that the doctor had managed to travel on from Helsinki to Stockholm that same evening.

29

L ET US ASSUME THAT Ullo received assignments from the Third Way over the space of one year. From early spring '43 until early spring '44. A number of his assignments also involved me slightly, I heard the odd word said about others, about the rest nothing. But if I were to include all their reminiscences, my tale would become badly proportioned.

However, I cannot keep entirely silent about Ullo's achievements. For fifty years all those who could have said anything on the subject have kept their mouths hermetically shut, for obvious reasons. So his efforts, I won't call them heroic deeds, perhaps instead meddlesome pranks, can at least be briefly listed.

These can be split up into brief, one-off assignments and ones which continued over a period of time and, of course, into those which were innocuous enough, if a little risky, and those which were very risky indeed. Among the more or less innocuous ones were a few which tempted him to demonstrate his gallantry. For instance, when he had to accompany a young lady from her parents' large manor farm somewhere on the Latvian border over a shaky bridge across the flooding River Mustjõgi to a railway station and from there to Tallinn where the young wife Taheva could join her husband Dr Taheva, so that the latter could better concentrate on some liaison mission to visit our diplomatic representatives in London and Stockholm and wherever else.

For this mission, Ullo asked the Director of Prices for three extra days off following the usual free Sunday and helped the young lady, who luckily had only three rather than five suitcases, to the station at Karula. The trip to Tallinn involved eight hours sitting in a dark unheated carriage. Ullo read poetry by Under, Visnapuu, Alver, et cetera, to the young lady who grew ever jollier and more frolicsome.

They ate tasty home-made sausage sandwiches and jam tarts which she offered him in between the poetry, since in wartime there were no restaurant cars on trains. By the end of the journey, Ullo was almost disappointed that others would be escorting the lady on from Tallinn to somewhere along the coast in the Virumaa province (the lady would then be conveyed abroad from the Vainupea Naze in some spirit smugglers' vessel or other).

On another occasion, Ullo was requested – a serious task, although his job made it quite easy – to write a survey of the pricing policy of the German authorities in Estonia. With special reference to the ravages being caused by the same.

Some weeks after writing this survey, Ullo was asked to assist his old acquaintance Colonel Tilgre and apply for a post at Omakaitse headquarters which was located at the Ministry of War on Pikk Street. As far as I remember, Ullo had previously worked there at the end of '42, as a translator, translating German rulings and other material into Estonian from German, and vice versa. But under cover of this main, or rather, ancillary, official assignment came his real job which was to keep the fledgling Estonian National Committee and all representatives abroad informed as to what the Omakaitse was up to, who was a member, how it was structured, its attitudes to the Germans, and the mood there. From time to time, I happened to hear that his information was extremely thorough and exact.

In summer 1943, he was given leave from his post at Omakaitse headquarters for a month or two. How he got it I do not know. We met as little as possible during that period, as had been agreed. And I perhaps heard later how he had spent his summer. No, in fact I'd already heard from his Maret during this break.

They had rented a summer flat, two tiny rooms near Raasiku station, in the road master's house. This road master, named Berends, was probably a relative of Ullo's. I don't know whether Ullo involved this road master with the face of a hooded crow in his affairs, but he certainly told Maret what was going on. One day, when he was off in Raasiku, Maret bumped into me on the street, invited me over to their flat and told me, her voice still a whisper, that Ullo had to write down the number of convict trains passing through the station, their time of arrival, number of wagons and prisoners and, if possible, the station they had set out from. He had put a blue chicory flower from the station yard between his teeth and gone over to chat to the SS-ers who were escorting the column of lorries which were to convey the prisoners from the station. Once there were 220, another time 400 Jews, old men, women and children. Sometimes they were in summer clothing, sometimes dressed for winter, afraid, hungry, smelling of ashes, silent.

"*Und wohin mit ihnen?*"

"*Wohin befohlen.*"

"*Klar. Die Leute hier in der Umgebung sagen: auf Waldarbeiten . . .?*"

"*Na also.*"

"*Die Baumstämme da auf den Dünen sind ja auch entsprechend dünn. Ich meine, entsprechend der Gebrechlichkeit der Leute . . .*"

"*Na und?*"

"*Nichts. Normal.*"

"*Na also.*"

He had walked with a full bucket, filled at the station well, towards the road master's house. At other times he took a bicycle, and his empty buckets, to the bilberry patch and told Maret she must stay home at all costs. On one occasion he came back at dusk. And kept silent till darkness fell. Kept silent the whole night. And the next morning. And then, when Maret asked him where he had been and what he had seen, he had tossed on to the table a child's overcoat made of red cloth, two foot or so long, with three machine-gun bullet holes in it, and dark encrustations round the holes in the red material.

Maret told me this in a whisper, shaking with emotion. And I convinced her that she and Ullo should for God's sake keep the information to themselves for their own safety. And try to believe that Ullo knew how much he could risk. I have written about this elsewhere, omitting any mention of Ullo. Any reader who recognises this theme may now know that it was based on Ullo's experiences.

But Ullo's (and, to a certain extent, also Maret's) railway reports were at least sent off, and found their rightful hearer. I don't know how much effect they had, or what became of them.

In the space of approximately one year, Ullo went three or four times to Tartu. He had just matriculated. In order to have good reason to travel to Tartu, he took several exams. But each time he arrived there, sometimes with the odd German in the compartment, when he would quote Rilke one time, Rosenberg another or – as his instinct dictated, remain completely silent – each time he had had with him in his imitation crocodile-skin suitcase a couple of well-chosen issues of British or American periodicals (such as the bright red issue of *Time* about the Red Army, complete with picture of Voroshilov on the cover), plus, of course, a handful of circulars from the Estonian National Committee. And on each occasion he had gone by the university chapel and, with the permission of the deacon there, had slipped a Browning or two into a drawer at the back of the empty church. Sometimes even a dismantled machine gun.

If Maret had not already been dead these fifteen years, it would not have been proper to discuss what I am about to relate. And that is Ullo's stamp-buying affair, which nearly proved fateful.

All I know is what Ullo himself told me, but he only mentioned it in passing, vaguely, and we had agreed that I would write everything down in a more or less systematic fashion. When I did write things down in 1986, we never broached the subject. And yet this episode was of crucial significance for Ullo's subsequent fate.

In December '43, during his fifteen-minute lunch break at Feischner's, as I would imagine (Omakaitse translators' lunch breaks were more strictly defined than those taken at the "Price Bulletin"), Ullo read there in a fresh copy of *Eesti Sõna* an announcement. Somewhere in the region of Jõe Street or Petrooleum Street a more or less complete collection of postage stamps was being sold. Austrian stamps maybe. I don't remember. These had been collected originally by one Mr Brehm, the father of Ullo's friend Jochen.

Ullo was a philatelist in the same way as he was a chess player. He could discipline himself to the extent that he could force a stalemate on Keres himself. But under normal circumstances, he would get into a terrible muddle right from the first move and then, about a dozen or more moves into the game, he would begin to interest himself in working out a plan to extricate himself from it. I will have to leave the projection of this kind of character on to the world of philately to the reader, since my knowledge of philatelists and their world is too slight. At any rate, Ullo went to the address mentioned in the paper one December evening.

He found a low wooden house, and the flat consisted of four badly heated rooms, but it was respectably tidy, propped full of objects which contrasted oddly with the poor district and the little box of a house. There was a dining table with carved legs under an embroidered (though rather dusty) tablecloth, twelve carved chairs around the table, mirrors with crystal candelabra, heavy armchairs and sofas, unexpected *fin de siècle* paintings in the style of Stuck and Co., in matt gilded frames.

At the door to the flat, the lady of the house came to greet him and she turned out to be the owner of the stamp collection. She was a woman in her forties, no, a lady rather, wearing a woven maroon housecoat, with curly dark hair and eyes as if from a Byzantine icon, certainly a lady, who spoke with intangible softness, both German and Estonian with what was probably a Russian accent. Her knowledge of the stamp collection she was selling was surprisingly vague. Yet she wanted to know everything about Ullo right away. Who he was. What he collected. Or was he buying for a third party. And who that third party might be. And that they would have to "deescoss dzee whole matter calmly".

"Outside, dzere are eighteen degrees of frwost, and khere inside it is preetty chilly . . ." So would Ullo not wish to have a little glass of raspberry *nastoika*, before having a look through the albums?

I can imagine their drinks, and the next. Maybe even a third. Ullo was – despite a measure of skittishness – a realist and presumably asked right away, in order to conduct matters in a businesslike manner, what the collection was going to cost, but initially he was not to find out. So he returned to Mrs Nadja Fischer's place three or four times. In the dark dining room in the blackout, with the embroidered tablecloth removed, in the pinkish glow of some table lamp, they began, between glasses, to leaf through the albums. It became clear to Ullo, in as much as he could determine, that the collection was unique, at least against the background of local stamp collections. Its provenance was partially explained to him. It had clearly belonged to some Baltic German who had emigrated. "Herr Baron" had left it behind. Ullo could not understand if he had left it to Mrs Fischer, in order to use it as she saw fit. And now the good lady wanted to sell it, either on her own initiative, or to follow instructions sent by the Baron from Germany. Nor did Ullo really find out whether it was she or the Baron who actually owned the collection. But what he did obtain clarity about was something which was irrevocably and solely Nadja's own private property and with which she was, at least in Ullo's case, generous to a fault.

So I asked him straight out: "Ullo – so you mean you slept with her?"

And Ullo grunted a "Mmwell ..." and smiled the inanely triumphant smile which a man, when speaking to an old friend wouldn't, simply couldn't, completely conceal. Ullo added: once when Nadja had forgotten to lock the flat door after he had arrived, the stamp dealer Weidenberg had almost caught them in flagrante.

But with regard to the price of the stamp collection – Ullo had brought the matter up, discreetly of course, with Mr Brehm (Mr Brehm had left Estonia as part of the *Umsiedlung*, but had returned and now held a middle-ranking post with the *Zivilverwaltung*) and he, plus a few other people Ullo consulted, had given Ullo good grounds to believe that the spot value of the collection was around 50,000 Ostmarks.

When Ullo finally went over to Nadja's place to negotiate a price in concrete terms, she said she had decided to give the collection to him for 20,000.

Of course, Ullo hadn't got 5,000, let alone 20,000. But his father had been enough of a businessman for his son to have inherited some of the genes of a dealer. Or perhaps we all have a little of the dealer in us. Anyway, Ullo did. After Mr Brehm and others had mentioned the sum of around 50,000 to him, he had coolly gone back to Nadja. And now that Nadja herself had mentioned 20,000, only the slight raise of his left eyebrow would have been visible, if the room hadn't been so dark. But if Ullo was one, or 1.5, per cent a swindler, he was also, you could say, 15 per cent a realist.

After Nadja had mentioned the 20,000, Ullo dropped in on his Uncle Joonas who had recently told him, *sub fide doctorali* so to speak, that he had put his name, and that of his wife, on Pastor Pöhl's list, i.e. the list of potential refugees to Sweden. This list started to expand some three months later, in February 1944, but Uncle Joonas was a far-sighted man. And Joonas Berends was a name which would fit in perfectly with the list of Swedish or pseudo-Swedish names. All the more, since some great-grandfather, Sacharias or whatever, a Swede and an itinerant miller for the manor houses of the province of Harjumaa, really did occur in his family tree. But against this background of potentially moving to Sweden, and this was clear to Ullo too, Uncle Joonas's large stash of Ostmarks would soon end up as mere waste paper. If, that is, he didn't manage to discreetly exchange them for the equivalent amount in a stronger currency. Stamps with permanent value were, for such a practical man as Uncle Joonas, something much better than most things for such a boat trip, even including golden bars.

Uncle Joonas listened thoughtfully to Ullo's story. He had clearly pitched the story just right, not too indifferently, nor too enthusiastically, for Uncle Joonas had said: "If you're sure they're not fleecing you, and you can get it straightaway for 15,000 Ostmarks, I will have the money ready for you tomorrow. Such offers are very thin on the ground."

And Ullo, usually so Napoleonically decisive, now fell into a crisis of indecision, which was just as Ullo-like as his Napoleonic decisions. As he told me, he could hardly go to Nadja the next day with Uncle Joonas's 15,000 (plus the 5,000 he had scraped together himself) and plonk them down on her table. He muttered: "You understand . . . Once I knew I'd be doing her out of around thirty grand . . ."

But in order to present the themes in this text in the same order as the Great Stage Producer in the Sky served them up to us, I will have to make a swerve backwards in time and mention something else: the last assignment given to Ullo by the Estonian National Committee, a reasonably civilian and thus not a dangerous one which was left unfinished, and which I happen to know a little more about than the others he performed in this line of activity. A little more, since he turned to me for assistance – in the naive assumption that my skills in international law, the subject I was studying at the time, would make me better informed in these matters than he was.

In the summer of 1937, among the important political guests to arrive from time to time in Estonia, was the Secretary-General of the League of Nations, the Frenchman Joseph Avenol. The press, in this period under Päts, dealt with him as was usual during the so-called "Period of Silence" – the visit was much publicised since, after all, it was proof that Estonia was being taken seriously in terms of diplomacy, but the press kept completely silent about its content. A few experts did, of course, know everything, but among the public at large a vague rumour arose that the government was supposed to have asked Monsieur Avenol to intercede on its behalf in arranging a largish loan from a couple of Swiss banks. Later, quite a few years later, it was said that we were to get the loan and, later still, that the banks had

236

begun negotiations, and, finally, that agreement had been reached. But the loan itself did not materialise before the Soviet Union occupied the country in 1940.

Now, in late '43, early '44, people in the Estonian National Committee and diplomats serving abroad raised the question: if we in fact were in such a poor financial state now, shouldn't we try to find how it stood with the past loan application, or indeed with the loan itself? Would it not be possible to obtain some of the sums involved in cash – in order to promote the struggle abroad and resistance back home?

Solutions to this problem lay largely abroad. Primarily, of course, in Switzerland itself. There, in Geneva to be specific, was the penultimate Foreign Minister of the Estonian Republic, still in good health, who could prove to be a key figure in the interests of Estonia. I imagine that all the sources and people involved were consulted. I remember going along to Rajajõgi, the then director of the Hansapank bank, and with his intercession brought Ullo in contact with old Mr Kivisild. This man seemed rather absent-minded on first acquaintance, but turned out to be a shrewd old fellow and had no doubt been one of the directors of the Estonian National Bank during the loan talks. So he would know about all the paperwork involved.

Ullo had started to write a little text on the matter. Maybe he had, even the same day when coming back from his office, sat at his table, instead of going off to Nadja's to weigh down the silky smooth skin of the lady's ears with ruby earrings, and fleece her at the same time. Or perhaps it was that same night in January that his Maret, someone more worried than he, was woken by knocking on the door.

The SD men read out their arrest warrant and took Ullo with them. The search they made of the flat was quite cursory. So cursory, in fact, that they did not find the notes Ullo had begun writing, notes about the loan to the government, which would immediately have aroused the suspicions of the German Security Police. The papers were left where they were by those searching the flat – under the green cartridge paper covering Ullo's writing desk. Maret removed them after they had left.

Both of them, Ullo and Maret, assumed that Ullo's arrest had something to do with a leak among his Estonian National Committee contacts, which was really worrying, more so for Ullo than for Maret.

Because only Ullo would know of all the risks he had run. Including those assignments which could be termed downright frivolous or even amounting to hooliganism. Such as when, instead of distributing statistics according to some code or other, he had the rather grumpy typist write out four copies of the tables instead of the required three, so that the first was on file, the second sent to the General Commissariat, the third to the SD, and the fourth either to our man in Helsinki, Mr Warma, or to Ambassador Laretei in Stockholm. Or when there had been a leak and the car taking the post from Tallinn to the Vainupea Naze, or the motor boat which took it on to Helsinki, was stopped by the Germans and searched, quite to be expected under the circumstances.

Maret's partial ignorance of all these events meant that things were maybe not so hard for her. But she would get to know the real state of affairs regarding Ullo a week or two later, after experiencing that leaden palm pressing on her heart or mind, day and night, while she was trying to get to talk to someone at SD headquarters and at the public prosecutor's office looking at all those stuffed turkeys, *Sturms* and *Platzers* and what have you, with a gaze as innocent and profound as she could muster, in her shiny rubber galoshes, not too rustically or foolishly, but with a certain naive allure, with the drops of melted snow from the street still clinging to her angelic curls.

For Ullo, everything was clear right from the morning of his arrest, from the time of his first interrogation: once again they brought up his service in Barbarus's anteroom. On the second or third day, he was given a hint why. A smallish dark-haired boy in civvies exchanged a few words with him while they were waiting for the chief interrogator to arrive. Someone whose behaviour towards Ullo gave him the feeling (and quite rightly too) that the Third Way may have had a hand in getting this boy a job right there at the fourth B-Section of the SD. While the two of them were alone together waiting for the previous day's interrogator, a sullen militia lieutenant, the boy asked: "Do you happen to know Mr Weidenberg?"

Ullo said: "You mean the stamp dealer?"

"Exactly."

"Don't really know him as such . . ."

"Mmm . . ." mumbled the boy, adding: "You should know who your *friends* are . . ." accentuating the word "friends" so that it immediately

238

became obvious to Ullo: he had been arrested after Weidenberg had complained about him. Weidenberg had naturally been eager to lodge a complaint in order to rid himself of a rival – maybe with regard to the ownership of Nadja Fischer, God only knows, but doubtless with regard to the ownership of Nadja's stamp collection.

30

A S A RESULT OF HIS second arrest, Ullo survived the
notorious March bombings of '44 by being resident in Patarei,
otherwise known as Tallinn Central Jail or the Arbeits- und
Erziehungslager Revalis. He was unscathed by the bombs, but this was
hardly surprising considering the prison was affected as little as the
port, some half-kilometre away, which was the only target in the whole
city actually worth bombing. The Soviets, however, did manage to
destroy some thousand houses and kill seven hundred people in
residential areas.

Ullo's second arrest meant that when the April wave of arrests was
in full swing – i.e. when, on the Führer's birthday, throughout the
country some four hundred Third Way activists, according to some
sources, were rounded up – he happened to be in prison and remained
entirely unaffected.

Later, it was whispered that it was hard to establish whether the
wave of arrests by the SD was occasioned by incompetence or sheer
bad luck. The man whose task it had been to pack the next batch of
post in an oilskin bag for it to be conveyed overseas walked with the
appropriate suitcase to the appropriate block on the Pärnu Road in
Tallinn. There, in a certain flat, the letters would be given their final
sort.

When the man with the suitcase had stepped into the doorway
leading to the stairs, he suddenly realised that on the pavement, some
twenty paces from the door, he had seen, well, if not precisely
someone he knew, then the face of an SD lad. And this instantly
triggered his instincts. He had gone up to the door of the flat in
question, but passed it and stopped on the stairs, observing it from the
shadow of the lift shaft. Five minutes later, two men stepped out of
the flat door, two men who simply looked suspicious. They descended

the stairs and left the building. The man with the suitcase was now certain: the SD had a watch on the flat. So he would have to leave the building as surreptitiously as possible. If he took the suitcase with him he was bound to attract attention. It would be exceedingly unfortunate were it to fall into SD hands. So he considered for a moment what to do. Then descended the stairs, entered the unlocked cellar leading to the boiler house and looked around him. Near the central-heating boiler was a kind of boxed-in enclosure, separated from the boiler room by a low partition and half full of coal. The coal shovel was lying there too. The man with the suitcase took the shovel, shovelled some coal away from the partition, put the suitcase on the space he had freed on the concrete floor and put a couple of dozen shovelfuls of coal on top. A few hours later, as evening began to fall, he intended to come back to retrieve the suitcase unobserved. He went back to the main door and peeped out on to the street, waiting for a suitable moment to leave. The SD lad had crossed the street and was strolling on the opposite pavement. And when he looked the other way, there were five or six people walking along his side of the pavement, but in the opposite direction past the door. So the man, now relieved of his suitcase, slipped in among them and was gone.

But when the man, or rather someone sent by him, came to retrieve the suitcase, it was gone.

Much later, it transpired that the old red-nosed alcoholic of a caretaker had poked his beak into the affair. He was a servile little man without any sense of responsibility who would gladly have cringed to the Third Way, but in this situation cringed to the powers that be. This weather-beaten-faced blockhead had found the suitcase and taken it with him, no doubt in the hope of finding money. To his great chagrin, he found only papers. He did, however, get the impression that, if God were on his side, they might just be of interest to the SD. So he took his booty and placed it on the desk of the people at the Security Services office.

"*Halt! Auf den Fussboden setzen! Nicht doch auf den Tisch! Das Stück ist zu dreckig . . .*"

So the caretaker put the suitcase covered in coal dust on the linoleum floor, three paces from the table, and remained standing there rolling his eyes and snuffling – hoping that at least a couple of bottles of Dr Mäe's Tears might come his way . . .

I don't know, I don't think anyone does, whether the caretaker ever got his Dr Mäe's Tears – the tears of Judas. But his act brought plenty of distress and affliction down on the Estonian nation.

The fact that the Germans got hold of the information led to technical assistants helping the Third Way to be rounded up. But a number of members of the Estonian National Committee itself were also arrested. Others went underground or fled abroad. And some remained public figures and their links with the Third Way were never discovered by the German occupiers.

Some of the arrestees were obliged to admit to a limited amount of guilt, on the strength of the contents of the suitcase. Yes, so-and-so had collected the odd scrap of information at work. These were yelled at and accused of being enemy spies. They, in turn, claimed that they had operated on the orders of foreign representatives of the Estonian Republic and that these were, for the time being, the only legitimate organs of the Estonian government. They were then bawled at, though without being beaten up, initially at least: all those Warmas, and Tormas, and Lareteis would simply scuttle over to the British with all the information they received! Now that there was no actual Estonian government as such, these men had become the paid running dogs of the British. And the British would immediately send the information received on a silver salver to their friends in Moscow! Do you not understand?! Objectively speaking, you're all, down to the last man, spies for the Reds, spies for Moscow, Stalin's spies!

And it must be said that it was pretty hard to argue against the accusations. Because objectively what was said was (thanks, for instance, to the achievements of Mr Philby) true to a large extent, more than they themselves realised.

Of course, those caught in this initial sweep of the net were mostly fish of lower or peripheral value. They were filtered back out to liberty over the summer period. On 18 September, Ullo's former boss Professor Uluots, who had gone underground, wrote a decree (according to the Constitution of the Republic of Estonia, the Prime Minister would fulfil the tasks of the President in the case of the latter's absence) forming a government for Estonia whose Prime Minister was Otto Tief, a barrister, known for holding down posts in various previous Cabinets.

On 18 September, during the daytime, prisoners of little

importance were released from Tallinn Central Jail according to a list of names received from the SD. The following was decreed: thieves – free; small-time Reds – released; full-time Reds – taken by lorry to the woods at Kose, and shot in the back of the head. At the same time, a large number of evacuees arrived at Tallinn Central Jail from provincial prisons, on account of the advancing Soviets. No one knew what was to be done with them.

On that selfsame day, Maret was told at Public Prosecutor Platzer's office that Ullo – presumably regarded as a small-time Red – would be freed within a day or two. At the same time as my Hella was told that I would be sent off to Germany within the next few days. So Maret rushed off home in great hopes to await Ullo's arrival – and waited with some impatience. That evening, Ullo, with some chit declaring his release in his pocket, having negotiated the strange chaos of the blacked-out city, found his way through the drone of the lorries driving towards the harbour and through the dark choking rain of ash caused by the burning of documents, and arrived home in a yet darker Erbe Street.

Maret of course knew, but Ullo was likely not to have done, that I too had been rounded up during the wave of arrests in April. On the afternoon of the 18th, Hella brought me a package containing warm clothes, food and vitamins for my journey to Germany. The guard, who brought it to me in my cell, and who had been a pretty hardened soul until recently, had distinguished himself over the past week by bringing the paper to my cell in the evening (this was safe to do in the case of single cells) and mumbling: "What it doesn't say in the paper is that Finland pulled out of the war yesterday." Or: "The BBC announced this morning that the Americans crossed the German border in the West yesterday."

Now, when he pushed Hella's package through the hatch in the cell door, he muttered: "They've told your woman that they'll be sending you to Germany. Don't believe a word of it. You'll be freed. I know . . ."

At eleven o'clock that evening, movements and muffled voices could be heard in the corridor. Then the door crashed open and my newspaper guard beckoned – pssst – out into the corridor. A few men were already standing out there in the virtual darkness. In the end, there were about nine of us. As far as I could make out, they were all

Third Way lads. The guard took us – strangely silent and without the usual bawling – through several corridors and an iron grating door. He disappeared somewhere and our escort was now a man in a cloth cap with a face which looked reddened by drink. We followed him for quite a while. I remember telling my neighbour Armin Kask, a hydrologist, some political crack or other under my breath while at the same time trying to observe: phew, we've passed the corridor to where they carry out executions, also the store where we would be collecting our belongings on release, and also . . . And then we were in the goods yard of the Central Jail. We stumbled in the dark over the legs of prisoners who had just arrived and been told to sit down on the pavement. Then, still almost in darkness, the back gate of the goods yard creaked open and we were outside. We looked around – where were the military police, the dogs, the lorries? The worst scenario would be a trip to the woods at Kose, a less grim alternative would be the port at Paldiski and then off to Germany. Darkness. Silence. Above our heads the bright September stars. Then our guide who was standing in our midst screwed up his eyes and whispered, through the cloud of spirits on his breath: "Lads – the shit's over for now. Now, every man jack of you – skedaddle!"

Not until a few days later did it emerge how so crazy, blind, murky and shamefully lucky the escape of nine of us had actually been.

Ten minutes after our liberation, the head of the jail, the odious Viks, along with a lorry, dogs and military policemen, had begun calling out prisoners from a list. Seventeen prisoners, half of whom had just been liberated ten minutes before. But the other half still remained! And were taken away to the barking of Mr Viks – to Stutthof and other such places in the circles of hell.

How Ullo's release on the 18th had been effected is something I never heard any more about. And for the next forty years, I only heard the odd sentence about what he did immediately after his release. Until that time in spring 1986 when he let go of a bit more, in order to lead up to a session where he would spell out the details. It was a session which never took place.

31

U LLO ARRIVED HOME AT seven on the evening of 18
September 1944. He was hungry, as if he had never even seen
the packages Maret sent him. He had only been able to
consume about one-eighth of each package, having to share the other
seven-eighths with some of his fifty or so cellmates. He was hungry,
but not yet weak at the knees. He kissed Maret before shaving off his
beard. He then put on clean clothes and rushed out.

Although he had been in the Patarei prison during and ever since
the 9 March bombing of Tallinn, he had heard about it from accounts
that had leaked into the prison and could imagine the destruction.

On his way home, but not before he had crossed the square at
Raekoja plats, he saw the destruction with his own eyes. And saw it
even more clearly as he tried unsuccessfully to make his way through
the rubble on Harju Street in order to reach Vabaduse väljak. Harju
Street no longer existed. There wasn't even a decent path through the
ruins. So, because it was dark he had made a detour along Great Karja
and Little Karja streets. And now, on his way back into the centre, the
damage to the city struck him more forcefully than before. The
Estonia Theatre had been reduced to unreal sooty-flecked rubble
against the lilac sky to his left, with the blackened stumps of trees
along the avenue, and the sooty eyeless façades of buildings – and
between these, in the silence without even a breeze, wafted the
sudden nauseating stench of the burnt city. The men who came to
Patarei after the bombing had already noticed that peculiar smell, but
it had never reached the prison itself. Surprisingly fresh sea air
had poured into the largely broken windows of the prison cells. But
now, on the avenue, perhaps because the ruins themselves were
invisible in the darkness but you could feel the smog on the skin of
your face, the stench became suffocating: burnt walls, ash, pitch and

– God knows – the charred and rotting human remains from beneath the rubble.

I do not know where Ullo spent the next four nights and days. I do not know whether he first rushed off to Jõe Street, or whatever street it was – after Mrs Nadja Fischer. For some reason I imagine he did go there, but I'm not sure if he went there straight from home. To somewhere off to the left of the Narva Road. But there, half the quarter had vanished and Ullo stumbled over the heaps of rubble, the stones and the twisted metal. Near the foot of a chimney stack he found a tiled stove and for a moment he thought that this was the one that had stood beside the sofa with its raspberry-coloured cushions. He then realised that this one was twice as big as Nadja's had been. Nadja's stove must in its time have been wonderfully warm for the soles of Ullo's feet (his legs stuck out over the edge of the sofa). On touching this one he found it cold, cold to the core . . .

Across the street stood a more or less intact stone house with a chink of light emerging from its blacked-out windows. Ullo knocked for a long time, till finally someone opened the door.

"Oh, no. We know nothing about this place, nor about anybody, for that matter. We're refugees. From Narva. Been here a couple of months. When they put us here, things were no different to what they're like now. They say people have been killed here in the neighbourhood. And some have gone off to Germany on refugee ships. But we don't know anything for certain. Mrs Fischer? Never heard of her . . ."

From there – presumably – Ullo had gone to Palli Street and had rung the Klesments' doorbell. Why just there? Maybe simply because the Klesments' flat was nearby. But also perhaps because the one-time government counsellor was the only person from the higher echelons of the Estonian National Committee who Ullo was on first-name terms with.

Klesment was supposed to have opened the door in person and yelled through a light haze of cognac: "Ah – Paerand – jolly good!"

Ullo had thought to himself (right there in Klesment's entrance hall, I think he said): Why the hell do we in Estonia think of Churchill's weakness for whisky as a sign of British heroism, while we regard the sharpest minds' fondness for cognac over here as a manifestation of chronic alcoholism . . . ? Ullo himself never – well, hardly ever – drank more than just over a glass of anything.

Klesment had sat Ullo down in an armchair in his study and handed him a glass of cognac.

"Where've you just turned up from at this hour? Prison? Because of your Barbarus sins? Ho, ho, ho, ho-o-o! But jolly fine that you've come. Today, of all days . . ." He had adjusted his fingers around his glass to release his index finger and raise it to emphasise his point. "By the way, I just arrived back yesterday from Helsinki, and today Uluots has announced the Estonian Cabinet."

When Ullo kept silent at this pronouncement – simply in the hope of hearing something exciting – Klesment did not disappoint him. He took a swig from his glass and said: "I don't know why it's taken him so long. Wisdom, cowardice . . . God only knows. Anyway, it's done now. Tief is Prime Minister, formally only as proxy. Because Uluots himself is not the President, but only the Prime Minister pledged to the President, isn't he? I've become Minister of Justice. Well, that doesn't mean a thing. For we haven't got time to get law courts running. Only courts martial, at most. But that's Holberg's problem, as he's become Minister of War. Or maybe it's Maide's as he's Commander-in-Chief. But anyway, Tief and his team will have their hands full this evening. You can imagine all the hustle and bustle. So if you have no objections, I'll phone Tief – it's half past eight right now – and say that a chap'll be turning up to be at his disposal . . ."

Ullo had replied: "Objections? Of course not. I feel it's my duty. Only one thing – shouldn't you tell Professor Uluots? He knows me, and Mr Tief doesn't."

To which Klesment had uttered: "No, no, no. But then again . . . You've just come out of prison, so you presumably don't know. No one is being allowed to see Uluots. Tief is acting in his place. Uluots is a sick man. In actual fact, a very sick man. But if anyone asks, I haven't told you."

Over the six months that had passed since the March bombings, half the telephones in Tallinn had been put back in order. Klesment's phone call to Tief had sounded roughly as follows:

"Good evening, sir. Recognise my voice? Course you do. Listen, you need an assistant or two right now, don't you? Well, to help with the packing. And so forth. If you see what I mean. What I'm trying to tell you is, there's this young man. From the State Chancery. I know him. A clever and discreet young chap. He'll tell you his name himself. I'll give him a chit to take along with him. Yes. I'm staying home. You don't need me right now. Phone me tomorrow as soon as you do. Oh, and how's things with Jüri? No change. I don't know. Nobody knows. He doesn't know himself either. Tomorrow or the day after. Good night."

Ullo of course immediately realised that the Jüri mentioned must have been Uluots. But he had just been called a discreet young man and therefore refrained from asking what it was that nobody knew . . .

Then Ullo went to the half-destroyed building of the Lending Bank, to an apartment which had more or less remained in one piece up on the second or third floor. The door was opened by some long-limbed officer with a head like a bird's egg. Later, he got to know that this was a colonel – or as of the following morning, Major General, and head of the armed forces, Maide. Ullo no doubt said: "I've just been sent by the Minister of Justice Klesment – on the orders of Prime Minister Tief."

He was asked to show Klesment's chit and was led to the third or fourth room of the apartment where Tief was with the Head of Chancery, the lawyer Maandi. Both were unassuming-looking figures, of medium height and of eastern Baltic stock, Tief around fifty years of age, pink-faced Maandi around forty and sporting glasses. Tief's innate authority and concreteness of purpose soon, however, became apparent.

"Mr Paerand," he said, "write down these eight addresses. On a small piece of paper in case you have to swallow it. The Germans can stop you in the street and search you. Mr Maandi, tell the soldiers in the kitchen to give Mr Paerand one of the bicycles from the cellar." Then to Ullo: "Ride round to all eight addresses and give each man, or some other trustworthy family member – you can be the judge of who is trustworthy – the message: tomorrow morning, ten o'clock, at the Red Tower Café."

Ullo of course understood that the Red Tower Café was a coded way of referring to the place where they had arranged to meet.

"Any questions?" asked the newly-appointed Prime Minister exigently.

I can imagine that Ullo felt provoked by the rather risibly military way he was being treated. He may have thought that the manner of a War of Independence captain was a little too visible in this Prime Minister.

248

"There are," he answered, "two in number. Number one. If I am asked who I am, what am I to answer? Number two. If no one opens up, can I leave a message under the door, or in the letter box?"

I can see Tief answering him in all seriousness: "Who you are? Depends on who's asking. If it's a German policeman, then you're a drunk who's got the wrong address. If it's the person you're looking for, then you are the courier of the Government of the Estonian Republic. If you're not sure who it is, decide for yourself. According to circumstances. Second question. Yes. Write a note if needs be. Tomorrow, ten o'clock. Red Tower Café. Like that. And now write down the addresses."

Ullo cast his eye over the eight addresses. "No need," he said. "I've memorised them."

"Memorised . . . ?" asked the Prime Minister with some astonishment. "Where does Minister of War Holberg live, then?" He had picked up the sheet of paper and now covered the addresses like an examining schoolmaster.

Ullo replied: "Pikk Street, number 40."

"OK then. On your way," said the Prime Minister with a smile.

The courier of the Government of the Estonian Republic went into the kitchen with the Head of Chancery. There were four or five men in Finnish army uniform, their sub-machine guns on the table, their pistols in their belts. Government security. First day on the job, like the government. Maandi ordered one of the soldiers to go down to the cellar and get Ullo a bicycle. As they were about to leave the kitchen, the Head of Chancery called them back and asked Ullo: "Got a weapon?"

"No."

"Then we'll give you one. Just in case . . ."

Ullo shook his head: "No. It could cause problems."

Maandi shrugged his shoulders: "It's up to you."

So the courier of the Government of the Estonian Republic set off on his bike through the dark and anxious city to inform those members of the Estonian National Committee and the government who lacked a telephone of the meeting next day. Having no phone connection could be because lines were still severed, or as a result of the SD cutting through them, or because the person in question was in hiding, away from home.

Ullo started with Kuristiku Street near the park at Kadriorg, visiting the house of a former director of the Estonian Bank and now a member of the Estonian National Committee. Pärtelpoeg opened the door himself and from their meetings in Eenpalu's waiting room, Ullo recognised the sour-looking but in actual fact quite jovial and stately old man immediately.

"Minister of Finances, sir, I have a message from Prime Minister Tief. Could you be at the Red Tower Café at ten o'clock tomorrow morning."

"Nnnnng . . ." mumbled the minister standing in his half-dark hallway. "What's going to happen there?"

Ullo said: "As far as I can gather – the Estonian National Committee and the government will be holding a joint meeting, during which the Estonian National Committee will be handing over power."

"Well, in that case, my presence isn't, at least initially, of paramount importance," opined Pärtelpoeg.

I imagine that Ullo replied, a little taken aback: "I would have thought the opposite."

I will repeat: I don't really know precisely who Ullo went round to that evening in order to invite them to the meeting. He probably found about half of the eight people, unable to reach the other four. Rather against his expectations, he had found Ernst Kull and Oskar Mänd, the former a publisher from Tartu, the latter an editor from the daily *Päevaleht*. Against his expectations, because they had been the last of the Estonian National Committee to be in prison that morning, the morning of the 18th, and their wives had been told that it had not yet been decided whether they were to be set free or sent to Germany. Now, at any rate, they had been released.

Ullo met Kull in an apartment on the Pärnu Road (God knows who its actual owner was) – the man was fearful, as if electrified, but in an odd way, he had an electrifying presence. The trembling nostrils of his long fox's snout and questions in a half-whisper, while grasping and calculating everything.

"So it's going to be the Red Tower?"

"That's what I've been told."

"Were you told where that is?"

"No."

"Well then. All the better, all the better. Then see to it that representatives from all the four parties get invited. And from the largest opposition movements. Not only invited, but are actually present. So that there'll be no wrangles later on about the legitimacy of the government. And Uluots will of course be brought . . ."

He gave a very nervous, very brittle handshake to Ullo as he left.

And then – somewhere on Liivilaia he visited Oskar Mänd's with his head of tousled red hair and his small ironic eyes. He had the bony face of a satyr as a result of his hunger cure of the past six months.

"Do they think they'll actually be able to achieve anything?"

To which Ullo no doubt replied: "Presumably . . ."

And then he visited Mr Holberg, the Minister of War, on Pikk Street, whose telephone must have broken down the previous day because in principle he had a phone as he had already been working in a high post at the General Inspectorate. And the post merited one.

"*Ja. Wer da?*" asked the Minister of War through the letter box, in the official language of the nation. But he did open the door on the mention of Prime Minister Tief's name. Ullo also knew Holberg by sight, as he had rushed through the anteroom, both in Eenpalu's and Uluots's time and from Gori's famous caricatures. A small, brisk stubby little man who resembled his former boss Colonel Soodla more than Soodla did himself. All the more so, since he had one of those east Baltic apple noses under which sprouted a black Hitler shoebrush moustache, something which Soodla would not have permitted himself.

"What was the name again? Paerand? Mmm. Met you at some time or other, have I . . . ?"

"Yes, sir. Twice in Prime Minister Eenpalu's anteroom. Once in Prime Minister Uluots's."

"Mmm. Mr Paerand – tell him – Prime Minister Tief, that is . . ." He paused a moment to think how he should formulate his reply, and in so doing clearly changed his mind. "Tell him that I shall be coming."

And then, if I'm not mistaken it was somewhere out along the Paldiski Road, Ullo visited Susi the lawyer, and stood at the writing desk at the home of Education Minister Susi, in his half-dark flat with blacked-out windows.

"Ah, ten o'clock at the Red Tower? What I would like to ask is: why at that hour – why ten o'clock? Why not at eight? Why not at six? I don't think we'll pull it off. I suppose they are all right as hours – but it's *time* we so badly need."

He was a very friendly fifty-year-old, greying at the temples and whose bearing was less of a minister and more of a schoolmaster, and an exacting one at that. Exacting while nevertheless appearing rather apologetic:

"Of course you're not to blame for our tardiness . . ."

Then the door opened and the lady of the house looked into the study. The master said to Ullo: "This is my wife, Ella . . ."

Ullo said: "I know the good lady. Ten years ago she stood in for two weeks for our history teacher at Wikman's. Your good wife taught us about the Committee for National Salvation and the Provisional Government, when Mr Tiimus had pneumonia."

The master of the house replied: "And now Mr Paerand is bringing me an invitation to attend tomorrow's meeting of the government."

"Then you have to go . . ." said the lady quite clearly, though there was a trace of fear in her voice.

"Perhaps I ought to . . ." said Susi, a little defiantly, yet almost happily. Ullo took a good look at the legal gentleman. And would have looked longer, had he known that the Great Stage Producer in the Sky let this little minister be overtaken by the wheels of Stalin's torture machine, to enable him to teach his bunkmate, national traitor and artillery captain Alexander Solzhenitsyn, the basics of bourgeois democracy. With some success, though the studies in question were never fully completed.

32

I REPEAT AGAIN: I DO not know what Ullo got up to during those days. But he hinted that he played a part in the meeting the next morning, or at least some role against its backdrop.

The meeting took place in the Estonian Land Bank building, code name: the Red Tower Café. It wasn't red as such, but did have a red-and-grey striped tower, and a Red episode in its history: in 1918, this building housed the headquarters of the Estonian Communists' military units for a number of months. But the 1944 meeting did not presume to follow previous occurrences. It was only held here owing to the fact that Tief had been a legal consultant for the Maapank bank since the 1930s, maybe one of its directors afterwards, and used the attractive office in the bank building. And, when necessary, used the boardroom too. As now, for the meeting on the morning of 19 September.

I do not know whether Ullo was actually present in the room itself during the meeting. If he was, then more likely for the first part consisting of the joint meeting of Estonian National Committee representatives and the government. He would hardly have been present once the members of the National Committee handed over their powers to the government which then continued in session alone.

Ullo said: "I looked out of the south window of the hall. Straight across stood the old part of the Estonian Bank edifice, a building you'll remember. And I thought: how closely, how curiously, our various versions coincide – physically, spatially, historically and ethically. Fifty paces from here, the Estonian Republic was proclaimed in 1918. By the next day, the Germans had arrived. And here we are proclaiming the continuation of that republic. And what I fear is that the Russians will arrive within the next few days. The Germans came for nine months. How long are the Russians going to stay . . .? Not for longer, God forbid. Or are they . . . ?"

As the first worried-looking men entered the room, Ullo, still at the window, will inevitably have thought: "I can't really believe they're going to succeed. But I feel that although the fate of thousands of individuals does depend on it, one thing is more important than victory or defeat, and that is to make an attempt." Looking from one building becoming historical over at another, which had its history behind it, Ullo thought: "In life, the road itself is more important than the goal."

An observer once told me (either Helmut Maandi, former Head of Chancery when I met him in Stockholm in 1990, or Ullo himself some forty years after these September days) about how depressing the Minister of War, Holberg, looked at that first meeting on 19 September 1944, or the following day.

At the meeting, the military top brass (Maide, Sink and so on) were quizzed as to what chances there were for successful resistance against the Russians who had broken through the positions in the Blue Hills on the previous day, and were moving westwards along the Narva Road. All those asked had a few ideas, maybe ones which offered little hope, but were at least presented with hope. Until the Minister of War himself took the floor.

"Gentlemen, I have listened to you and am rather surprised at your wishful thinking. Or rather, at the fact that you have been ill informed. I cannot tell which it is. I've just come from the Inspectorate up on Toompea. I have the data from this morning. Resistance is regarded as useless. The Inspectorate is busy burning papers. Soodla has sent his officers home to pack and is doing so himself. And I'll be doing the same – so that I can make the ship sailing for Danzig tomorrow. And I would suggest you all do likewise." Holberg stood there for a moment longer – a small thickset man, his eyes almost shut in his pale and angular face, his little moustache sticking out obstinately. He stood for a moment facing the set expressions of the ten men, then marched out of the room.

I can imagine that after that – this *is* according to Helmut Maandi's recollections – Tief took the role of Minister of War upon himself. Someone wondered whether the Cabinet shouldn't consult Uluots, to which Tief said: of course that would be normal procedure, but it was, unfortunately, impossible. And why? Because Uluots had left the country this very morning. Some of the ministers cried out: "How can that be?! He does, after all, embody our continuity!"

And Tief had replied: "For that very reason. If anything should happen to any of us, then continuity will not be broken. If anything were to happen to Professor Uluots, then continuity would be broken for ever." And then, in a lower voice: "Besides, there is something which some of us will already know – Uluots is gravely ill. He's got stomach cancer. All the more reason . . ."

I only have the vaguest idea what happened next. Ullo mentioned that they had decided to print issue Number One of *Riigi Teataja* – the Estonian *Hansard* – giving the make-up of the government and a number of its decrees. Maandi was given the task of printing it and wanted to take Klesment with him to have someone on hand, should there be any editing to be done there at the print shop. But Klesment (who was known to be rather lazy) had muttered: "Now listen here, what possible editing could be needed at the printer's? The typesetter will ask whether he ought to write the 'republic', of 'Estonian Republic', in capitals or lower case. Capitals, I think. Though I'm not sure. Such things are known by – wait, where's he got to – that chap Paerand from the Chancery."

So Paerand walked or, rather, strode (since the much shorter Maandi was running on ahead) across Viru Square. More or less parallel to them, a dozen or so lorries with canvas roofing formed a column and moved off towards the harbour, their drivers wearing bluish-grey German forces greatcoats. A gaggle of younger towns-people carrying shoeboxes came from the direction of the Old Fire Station, some with four, some with six: a shoe shop had clearly been open somewhere or, God knows – had been jemmied or even smashed open and the looters had clearly arrived en masse. Somewhere near the harbour someone fired a short volley of machine-gun bullets.

There was no guard standing at the main entrance to the ETK cooperative's tobacco factory. Maandi in front with Ullo following up behind, they rushed into the yard. The three- or four-storey office block had been hit and was burning at one end so that the directors had moved to a nearby industrial building which turned out to be the factory itself. Behind it stood a small stone building, maybe in fact an annexe. They negotiated their way through the tobacco factory. On account of the scarcity of raw material, the workforce had been

255

reduced to half strength some while back, and had ceased production altogether the previous week in the light of current events. Maandi managed to find a stooping man with red whiskers and a pair of old-fashioned spectacles with oval wire frames. He had hustled them into the building behind. From the pocket of his blue overalls he also produced the keys to this back building.

And then they were standing in the tiny tobacco factory print shop, before them, on a smallish writing desk, an electric press, next to it a table for loading, and shelves for the metal slugs. And all around them were plywood boxes containing labels for cigars and cigarettes, which were printed as needed here at the factory. In the open boxes on the wall in front were small stacks of lilac labels for Karavan cigarettes, beige ones for Marets and blue, black and white ones for the Ahto brand.

Red Whiskers stepped behind the table and typeset the sheet of paper from Maandi's briefcase within ten minutes: *Riigi Teataja, Number 1, 19 September 1944.* He set Uluots's decree about the formation of the government and nine government decrees appointing officials – Colonel Maide as Chief of Staff, Oskar Gustavson as Head of Audit, and so forth, plus the announcement that at the afore-mentioned, Cabinet members swore oaths of allegiance on 18 September to the Prime Minister acting on behalf of the President of the Republic.

Ullo asked: "Where were the oaths taken?

Maandi looked over his shoulder at the red-whiskered typesetter and said in a low voice: "Yesterday evening, in a ward at the Central Infirmary."

What did this mean? Was it a sign that Chance, Fate or God still wanted to rescue the newly reborn republic by a hair's breadth, or was this a sign that Death was severing links with the past? Red Whiskers asked Ullo to help him lug the necessary quantity of paper, very fine French paper, by the way, from a wall cupboard to the large table by the press.

Some while later, Ullo told me what Maandi had said about this paper. It had been stocked up here at the label-printing shop, during the Soviet year, by a far-sighted individual who had bought up the stock from some warehouse or other, even though labels were printed here on cheaper, poorer quality paper. But the purchase had been effected at a time when there were still remainders of stocks to be bought up, and when it had already become clear that such material as French paper would never again be replenished. So the paper was bought up, although the printing house had not yet found a use for it. Until the Estonian National Committee in the early spring of 1944 had got so far as to enquire as to the chances of getting their texts into print. And two or three members of the committee who at the same time belonged to the board of the Estonian Tobacco Company had found this tobacco-label printing house eminently suitable. Which it certainly was. But not in the way Reigo and others had thought, it wouldn't raise suspicions, being so small and out-of-the-way and used for purely commercial ends. Reigo had ordered the printing of such important documents, as he considered those of the National Committee to be, on French paper. The first circulars had been prepared and distributed and of course had ended up in the hands of the SD and had caused just enough of a stir there.

Young gentlemen in black leather coats had appeared at a couple of the printing houses to conduct searches. These were no doubt at the places where the dailies and periodicals *Eesti Sõna*, or *Vaba Maa* and *Uhistöö* were printed, and they found nothing there. Then the searches ceased. Not on account of the torpor or any pro-Estonian feelings on the part of the SD, but on account of the competence of their specialists. SD experts had realised that paper of such quality as that which the so-called National Committee of the Estonian Republic had just been printing, was simply no longer available in Estonia. Consequently, the circulars had been printed abroad. And such a conclusion made printing the next batch of material by the committee a good deal easier.

When the telephone rang, the printing press had been clattering for well over an hour and had clunked out at least several hundred copies of the *Riigi Teataja* which were now lying in a large tin box. Ullo picked up the receiver. Klesment was on the other end:

"Ulrich, tell the secretary that he should get the appropriate number of *packets of cigarettes and arrange for their distribution*. You come back to the *Café* quickly. Right?"

"Right!" replied Ullo with some childish jauntiness. "I'll bring a packet or two in my pocket. Nice to have a puff with one's afternoon coffee."

Red Whiskers found Ullo an old fibre suitcase (which had, incidentally, also been made in this selfsame workers' cooperative venture, the ETK, something which should be borne in mind as things come full circle) and Ullo crammed in a couple of hundred copies of the latest issue of the *Riigi Teataja* for the Prime Minister's desk at the National Bank.

I do not know what Ullo did with himself the next few hours. Another Cabinet meeting was to be held that afternoon and although he, of course, would not be taking part, he must have been somewhere nearby throughout the course of the meeting. Because who else but he could have told me that now and again Maandi would leave the meeting room and send someone, maybe one of the sentries, on some errand or other. Sometimes he had summoned people waiting in the corridor into the meeting: some JR 200 officers, one with his arm in a sling, who had just yesterday been retreating before the Russian advance from near Puurmanni or the direction of Porkuni, plus some telegraphists in Finnish, German, and Estonian Omakaitse uniforms. And some of Ullo's old schoolmates flitted past – so that he saw them but they didn't see him – Hellat and Jõgi who were liaison officers between Finnish Intelligence and the Germans, and were in fact working for the Estonian National Committee. And Captain Talpak, who was supposed to have arrived from Finland on the heels of the JR 200 and whom the Germans had threatened with arrest, rushed past. He came back out into the corridor ten minutes later, a paper in his hand, showing he had been promoted to the rank of major and made Commander for Tallinn. And went up to the ensign who was the head guard of the government: why not come and be his adjutant. Because he, now in command of Tallinn, had to form a unit made up of just about anybody, JR men, *Leegion* men, *Wehrmacht* men, those from the Omakaitse, anybody at all – to keep order in the city if there were clashes with the Germans that afternoon. On a couple of occasions, Ullo had eavesdropped on the conversations in the corridor and maybe heard, as the door to the meeting room opened: "But where the hell is Pitka?"

At nine that evening, the Cabinet meeting took a break. Some of those present phoned home and about ten minutes later, wives had turned up with sandwiches and thermos flasks filled with ersatz coffee. Tief had asked the wife of the caretaker of the Maapank Bank to bring three jugs of hot tea and rusks. Klesment had clearly also rung his wife and she brought along some relatively hard black bread cut into thin slices, and made into sandwiches with some cod fillets that had been fried in a drop of oil. Klesment offered Ullo one.

"Go on, take one. It was me who got you to come here in the first place. Have to see you don't starve to death. The rest can look after themselves."

Ullo took a glass of tea with saccharin and a mouthful of cod sandwich.

Then Susi, a sheet of paper in his hand, stepped up to Ullo and pulled him aside, into the bay of the window.

"Mr Paerand. I've been given the job of putting together a government declaration, about the present state of Estonia and the duties of citizens. A pretty short text. To be distributed in the form of placards. Here it is. As much as I could get done during the meeting. I read it out to the Cabinet and nothing important was added. Run your eyes over it. Perhaps you've got some comments. Then take it straight to the printer's. See how big a format they can manage. A couple of hundred copies. To be stuck on to walls and fences right away tonight . . ."

Incidentally, Ullo mentioned something about this declaration to me at the time. But when telling me, he didn't start to divulge its contents. That was going to be the subject of a future session, i.e. the next time we met, or the one after that, during summer 1986. Which, as you know, never took place.

The text of the Declaration below comes from a later copy made by Helmut Maandi, how much later I am not sure, but it is more or less what Arnold Susi, Minister of Education, put down on paper on his return from the camps, as found among his papers by his daughter after his death in 1984.

DECLARATION OF THE GOVERNMENT OF THE REPUBLIC OF ESTONIA TO THE ESTONIAN PEOPLE

Today, in a decisive moment for Estonia, the Government of the Republic of Estonia has been created, which comprises representatives from all the democratic parties of Estonia.

Estonia has never voluntarily renounced its independence or recognised either the Soviet or German occupation of our country.

259

In the present war, Estonia remains an entirely neutral state. Estonia wishes to live as a sovereign nation in peace and fellowship with all its neighbours and does not wish to support hostilities against either of the warring powers.

Hitler's forces are retreating from Estonia. The Government of the Republic has decided to restore Estonian independence. Soviet forces are pushing forward into Estonian territory. The Government protests in the strongest possible terms against this action.

Estonia is a small nation, its army is too weak to resist an invasion of our country for any length of time. But the Government of the Republic of Estonia will continue in its struggle for Estonian independence with all means available to it and invites all citizens of Estonia to remain true to their people and the concept of sovereignty.

The sovereignty of the Republic of Estonia will continue!

With this text (or one extremely similar) Ullo hurried at around ten on the evening of 20 September 1944 through a city pregnant with danger and worry, in the darkness, and to the rattle of machine guns.

No doubt he was still on the street when the air raid began. It was not immediately evident as the first bombs fell, but it soon became clear that this was going to be an air raid second only in vehemence to that of 9 March. Or with regard to purpose, this was indeed the more devastating. This time we were not being bombed by squadrons of women pilots with their heads full of the Women's Day of the day before, those who had principally destroyed dwellings, and hit a cinema or two, plus two theatres: the Workers' Theatre and the Estonia. On 9 March not one bomb hit the primary target, the harbour. Now, on 20 September, mainly the port was being bombed. Although, given that the Germans were busy abandoning it, it would – from a Soviet perspective – be a Soviet port within a couple of days and might have been spared the Soviet bombs, since those swarming on to the ships at this point in time were actually civilian refugees.

The harbour zone began about a hundred metres from the printer's. The light from the "Christmas tree" flares above the harbour did not penetrate the blackout material of the printer's which was lit inside by quite decent electric lighting. But the thundering roar of bombs was

260

quite deafening, drowning out the clatter of the composing machine. On the paper table, double folio-size sheets, folded double. On the composing table, letters one centimetre high: *In the present war, Estonia remains an entirely neutral state. Estonia wishes to live as a sovereign nation in peace . . .*

I can imagine the sound of the bombs exploding outside the windows, the walls shaking, Red Whiskers's narrow shoulders and stooping neck – him starting, freezing, as he pointed his sharp chin towards the ceiling at each explosion – will this one get us or not? – then stooping over his machine once more.

Unfortunately, I do not know Red Whiskers's name. I forgot to ask Ullo. And God knows if Ullo himself would have known, anyway.

I can imagine Red Whiskers having switched on his beautiful little printing press and just got it going, when the next bombs fell. The first explosion pretty close, the limestone walls shaking, and a little plaster falling from the ceiling. Red Whiskers throwing back his head and gazing at the ceiling. Ullo standing behind him and holding his breath. Hell – however much you think you're a free and independent agent, your breathing muscles act by themselves: they simply stop working, keeping your breath inside. And between the detonations – a hum-hum-humming sound from the sky, even more irritating than it would be without the clatter from the printing press. The next bomb slightly closer than its predecessor. Ullo screwing his eyes shut and perhaps counting the seconds – as we did in childish innocence between lightning flash and crash of thunder. Then comes the next crash – no nearer, even a tiny bit further away than the last, thank God . . .

Red Whiskers yells: "Oh damn and blast!" and Ullo opens his eyes. He sees the yellowish light from "Christmas trees" round the contour of the rectangle where a piece of blackout material had been dislodged, and doesn't understand why he hasn't noticed before. And now, all of a sudden, he does understand, a fraction of a second before Red Whiskers mumbles, because his voice is too suffocated to yell: "The power's gone . . ."

I don't know whether they tried to mend it or to go out into the yard to see whether the overhead or underground power lines were down. And, of course, the power station itself may also have been hit. Even if they could make out what had happened, this wouldn't help the printing of a government declaration.

I do not know if Ullo managed to get hold of a copy of the ready-printed Declaration or not. If he did, it was no longer of any use to foster the rebirth of the republic. If he did, then it was only the one copy in order maybe immediately, or maybe when the air raid was over, to take it to Susi or Tief at the Red Tower Café. Where it remained, as the government fled two mornings later. The placard with the Declaration was too large to fold into the lining of a hat, as the only member of government to escape to the West, Maandi, had done with a copy of the *Riigi Teataja* which ended up, lightly moistened by sea spray, in friendly Sweden. As did Maandi himself, partly by making his way on foot across the quaggy straits between the holms off the island of Hiiumaa, partly by rowing, partly by motor boat.

I do not know.

33

W HAT I DO KNOW, OR at least I think I do, is this.
Ullo came back home to Maret at about two in the
morning. There was a power cut on Erbe street, so Maret
lit a candle and they looked at one another in the candlelight. Maret
thought: if I knew he was really mine, I could be happy, even with the
collapse of the world around us. She freed herself from Ullo's silent
embrace and whispered: "Come with me . . ."

Ullo did not react right away. He looked at his wife and thought: She
really has a lovely face. Between its brown locks and with her soft little
chin her face reminds me – of what? Of a long, oval shield, raising the
question: *was führt sie im Schilde* – ? A stupid question – when she has
such eyes: greenish grey, by candlelight, deeply black, but in reality
greenish grey, greyish green. Quite special. Loving. Terribly sincere.
And those troubled lips . . . God – the lips of the historical moment. To
think with Under's image . . .

Maret again whispered: "Come . . ."

She went in front, Ullo followed. Maret stepped out into the darkened
yard through the back door and across to the door of the shed. She took
a key out of her apron pocket, opened the padlock, stepped inside,
locked the door behind Ullo and indicated with the light of her torch.

Leaning against the pile of firewood were two bicycles, the one next
to the other. Each had a bundle tied to its carrier.

"What are these . . .?" asked Ullo.

"One's yours, the other is my father's," said Maret.

"I can see that," said Ullo. "But what are they for?"

"I think," said Maret, "that we'll be needing them."

Ullo said – and realised that he hadn't really thought about what was
going to happen next: "But why? The government has three lorries to
get to the coast in."

263

Maret said: "You're not a minister. Though you never know. Anyway, I can well imagine that there are three times as many people wanting to go as could squeeze into those three vehicles. So I put a few belongings in a bundle and pumped up the tyres . . ."

"And how are we going to get a place on board ship?" asked Ullo.

"That'll be a matter of luck," whispered Maret. "But you can't stay here . . ."

Ullo pulled her towards him. He pressed his nose into his wife's hair, smelling camomile, and listened. From somewhere in a northerly direction, maybe out on Paljassaare Island, explosions could be heard. In the darkness, the Germans were blowing up abandoned buildings and equipment. Ullo thought: If Maret has decided the way she has, then it was very likely to turn out in that way . . . But in order for it to happen and for us to get safely across the water . . . And he drew away from Maret and said hoarsely, and louder than necessary: "Just so that you know: three days before we got married, I went to Lia and asked to marry her. And was given the brush-off."

Maret was silent for a moment. Ullo thought: If I hadn't drawn away from her just now, to make my confession, I would have felt her stiffen. But now I didn't . . .

Maret said in a whisper: "Lia's been in Germany for ages. Why have you brought this up now?"

Ullo said: "So that it got said. To turn over a new leaf. To put things right."

When Ullo was in bed with Maret at his side, he heard through the ebbing roar of his blood more explosions coming from Paljassaare or the Sõjasadama naval base and suddenly thought: God, he'd never told Maret about Nadja Fischer! And now, at this time, after all that had just happened and was meant as a token of apology, a good omen for everything to come, he found himself quite unable to broach the subject of Nadja. He thought that his incapability of turning over a new leaf would guarantee the failure of their escape plan. Even if they reached the shore at Puise or wherever, there would no longer be room for them on the boat. Or if they did find a boat, their boat would sink, with them aboard.

At six o'clock in the morning, Ullo kissed Maret's eyebrows and intended to leave without waking her. But she put her arms around his neck and looked at him with her green-shot eyes.

264

Ullo said, with the conviction of spontaneity: "I think the government's going to be leaving Tallinn today. I'd better go and hear what they intend to do after that. Then I'll come home again. And then we will decide about where and how . . ."

At half past six, Ullo was at the Maapank Bank. Maandi led him through the bustle of civilians and military people to the Prime Minister's office. Tief cried out, one cheek still covered in shaving foam, razor in hand: "Jolly good, you've come! Susi has assured me that you're a polyglot. Men of my age have learnt mostly Russian, those a bit older a little German also. But English – that's our blind spot. It's said that you know the English language pretty well. Well, do you?"

"Not particularly well, of course. But I have some knowledge of it . . ." said Ullo, shrugging his shoulders. "All I know's what I learnt at school. But what's this all about . . . ?"

"You have to translate yesterday's Declaration into English and read it out over the radio."

Tief had wiped his cheek clean and poured himself, from what could be judged by the smell, a little *Rasierwasser* – aftershave – from a German officer's flask into his palm and rubbed it on to his face.

Ullo asked: "Does the government have a radio station which can be widely heard?"

The Prime Minister replied: "We have to make the attempt. Here's the text."

Reaching across the desk, he handed Ullo the text whose printing had been interrupted the night before during the bombing.

"I'll give it a try."

I can imagine Ullo taking the Declaration, glancing at it, the text now more or less in his head – and thinking: How the hell am I going to cope with this on the strength of the English I learnt from old Viruskundra at Wikman's and picked up from browsing though a couple of hundred books at random – and entirely without practice?

"Do we have any dictionaries?"

The Prime Minister hands him the latest edition of Silvet's English–Estonian dictionary, the one from 1940, then says: "Only this one."

Ullo knows full well that this is the only one they have. The one he really needs, the one from Estonian into English, simply does not exist, at least not in an edition for beyond school use. But this is the only place Ullo has a chance of finding the words he does not know.

"Sit down over there and make a start," says the Prime Minister. Ullo goes to sit down in one corner of the sofa and tries to make a start. He did, after all, say he would give it a try. Here goes . . .

Declaration of the Government of the Republic of Estonia.

Today – (but for foreign listeners one ought perhaps to add the date of the Declaration, i.e.) *the 18th of September 1944, in a decisive moment for Estonia* (hopefully, *decisive* is more precise than *conclusive* or *determinating*, or what have you . . .) so: *in a decisive moment for Estonia* . . .

At that point there is a knock at the door of the Prime Minister's suite, and the door swings open unexpectedly. In steps Chief of Staff Maide, a major general since the evening before. He wipes his egg-shaped head with a handkerchief and cries out: "Prime Minister! Do you know where Pitka's got to? We have to get in contact with him!"

Tief replies: "Where precisely he is I can't really say. He's somewhere in the south-eastern sector, setting up the front. He's supposed to be arriving at the manor in Kohila by three o'clock this afternoon."

Head of Chancery Maandi gestures to Ullo and leads him out of the Prime Minister's office. Into the small room behind. This is the bank director's secretary's office, a dozen square metres in size and filled with files. There is a desk and a typewriter.

"Carry on in here . . ."

Ullo carries on.

He is translating a cry of desperation from the Estonian nation, based on the English that Viruskundra, Miss Jakovlev, taught him. During whose lessons, Miss Jakovlev, an acerbic spinster complete with lorgnette who had trained at the Smolny Institute, had spoken Estonian, in as much as she did so at all, with a horrific Russian accent. Well, she was not, of course, openly hostile to things Estonian. Such an attitude would have been unthinkable at any grammar school where Wikman was headmaster. But in her supercilious and silent irony, Viruskundra's attitude towards Estonia was indisputable. A slight Russian accent had also crept into her diction when she spoke English.

So, anyway – *Today, the 18th of September 1944, in a decisive moment for Estonia, the Government of the Estonian Republic* (don't really know whether that should be written in capitals or not . . . But when reading it out over the radio you can't see that anyway, thank goodness) *entered his* – or *its* – *functions* – *duties*? The fact that the four democratic parties are all represented in government . . . You can't really say *to the Government belong* – Better to write *The Government includes representatives of all four democratic parties* – And then, the core of the whole Declaration: *Estonia never voluntarily* – but here it comes – *relinquished, yielded, surrendered, abandoned, assigned, gave up* – presumably there's also a seventh way of saying it – but which one is the right one? [And I don't know either. Nor do I know which word he chose in the end] – *her independence, nor has ever recognised or recognises the occupation of her territory either by Germany or by the Soviet Union. In the current war Estonia remains an absolutely neutral country. Estonia wishes to live in independence and friendship with all her neighbours, supporting neither the one, nor the other, of the belligerent sides* . . . And so forth. Picking his way, as if sleepwalking, among dozens of alternatives . . .

Twenty minutes later, he had knocked together a typewritten text. He went through the half-open door and peeped into the Prime Minister's office. There, five or six men, mostly in uniform, were standing at Tief's desk with one of them explaining that in the night the Russians had dropped parachutists just beyond Lake Ülemiste. Some of them had been captured. What should be done with them?

Ullo did not hear Tief's exact words, but I imagine he would have said: Take their weapons off them – he caught Maandi's eye and beckoned to him.

He led the Head of Chancery to his little cell and said: "Shouldn't there be a short explanatory text before the Declaration is read out over the air waves? Please ask the Prime Minister."

Maandi came back a moment later.

"Write the text yourself and translate it. Make it as short as possible."

Ullo wrote: *Attention! Attention! Attention! You are listening to a broadcast from the Government of the Republic of Estonia. We are reading you a Declaration of the Estonian Government.*" The text of the Declaration followed.

Maandi took Ullo with his text to a vaulted room in the tower of the Maapank. The window looked out on to the grey autumn sky and the smouldering ruins of the Estonia Theatre. On an old writing desk covered in green baize stood a large greenish open suitcase containing a military radio transmitter in camouflage colours, complete with microphone. Maandi showed him how to switch it on and off.

From half past seven till ten that morning, i.e. for two and a half hours, Ullo sat at the table and spoke into the black wire-clad tuber of the microphone: *"Attention! Attention! Attention! You are listening to a broadcast from the Government of the Republic of Estonia"* – Ten. Twenty. Thirty. Thirty-nine times. He tried to articulate as clearly and correctly as possible. Part of his voice seemed to evaporate into the microphone, some part of it rebounded, and Ullo felt it on his lips and face. As he uttered those seemingly meaningless words, which felt like no more than vibrations, all manner of quite irrelevant, or frighteningly specific and relevant, thoughts flickered through his head. He thought of himself as a five-year-old and his pet dog, born to be stroked, who had quite incomprehensibly committed suicide; the sagittate body of the dog like gold in the sunshine, having wriggled through the bars of the balcony, in the void. And then his own flash of thought years later, like a gulp of ice-cold sparkling mineral water: ah, it would be perfectly possible to step, at will, out of all this . . . At the same time as his mouth read: *Hitler's troops are leaving Estonia, but the troops of the Soviet Union are invading it. The Government of the Republic expresses its most resolute protest against the invasion* – at the same time another lobe of his brain was debating the question as to whether these radio announcements would have any effect. Most likely, of course, the effect would be nil, because no one would be listening to them. Because the signal from the equipment was so weak . . . But if someone should hear what was being said? Then it would depend on who was listening. Most likely, closest by, some German communications vehicle, if there still were any left in Tallinn. But if there were – then a group of men with helmets on their heads and with machine-guns at the ready could storm in through the doors of the bank, dividing into two groups as they approached the stairs: tramp-tramp-tramp-tramp with their iron-studded jackboots – into the cellar, the other half tramp-tramp-tramp-tramp up the staircase to the tower. But if my message were to be heard somewhere out in the Finnish archipelago, what would the radio people there actually do? They would spit: "We will be fighting against the Germans in Lapland tomorrow – yet the Estonians are getting rid of the Germans from their country without so much as lifting a finger! We're covered in

268

blood from our long fight against the Russians – while they want to be rescued, just like that. *Perkele.*"

But what if some British ear were to hear what I'm reading out? Let's say on Gotland. Are they really there on the island? Of course they are. And what if one of them hears what I'm saying? Things would start moving to further our cause – this would perhaps be the ideal variant. Could it happen? Not very likely, but still always possible. My words would be reported back to London. How long would that take? Under ideal circumstances, a matter of minutes. And, let's imagine they reached the ideal authority there. Within half an hour, Churchill would have got to hear of it. Why not? If we're dealing here with the ideal scenario. Churchill lights a cigar and mutters: "Ladies and gentlemen, this is just what I've been waiting for . . ." He presses a knob and says: "Give me Mr Cripps. Yes, that's right, our Ambassador in Moscow!" (This is the best possible scenario, don't you agree?) And a minute later he, Churchill, says: "Go to the Kremlin, *old boy*. No, no, not to Molotov. To Stalin. He promised me he'd give the Balts the right to self-determination, although he never envisaged actually doing so. Tell him: a new Government of the Republic has taken up office in Estonia. And we have never regarded such a government as anything other than legitimate. Despite everything. Let Stalin halt his forces at the line they have reached by ten today. I want to discuss the whole matter with him. That's all." And then the Red Army stops in its tracks. Why not? At precisely the same spot where it stopped back in 1918. At least in the north-east . . .

But no such thing happened, although Ullo, from about the thirtieth time he read out the Declaration, had added: *the Government of the Estonian Republic with Professor Jüri Uluots as Prime Minister* – in the hope that anyone listening would regard Uluots's name as a sign of continuity of government . . .

Nothing at all happened. Did no one hear his broadcast? If they did the information was not sent on. If sent on, to somewhere of no use. Even if it was of use, then the recipient wasn't quite the right one. Even if it was sent to the right people, then any ensuing action for the benefit of the Estonian Republic was – how shall I put it? – as expected.

At ten o'clock, Ullo stopped broadcasting. Not only because apart from the crackle and whine of background noise, the world in his

269

earphones remained completely silent, but also because Inglist or some such person came to him and said: "You can stop now. Go and see the Prime Minister."

An Estonian in captain's uniform and dusty boots was pacing around Tief's office nervously. A small, weathered man with demanding button eyes, a tiny wisp of a moustache in the middle of his prematurely wrinkled face. Tief introduced him.

"This is Captain Laaman, Admiral Pitka's Head of Operations. Mr Paerand, go along with Captain Laaman. The Admiral needs a liaison officer between his staff and the government. Neither he, nor I, have got a spare officer, so take the job on yourself. Captain Laaman will escort you. Take this with you. Get a review of the situation as it stands with him. If at all possible, have a word with the Admiral himself. Find yourself transport, so you can be back to report to me this evening."

I don't remember the Germans having anything similar to a jeep, or a Willis-type vehicle, but Laaman and Ullo went off in something of the sort, a BMW. By what route? I do not know, but they went in a generally easterly direction. All I remember are a couple of incidents which Ullo touched upon later in times when such things just weren't yet discussed on principle, but in days when, instead of his usual one and a half glasses of brandy, he would have three.

Ullo said: "When we'd got through scrub and bushes somewhere or other, I looked at the captain at my side. He was gripping the steering wheel, half crouched over it with a frighteningly concentrated expression on his face. He spoke in a loud voice, so that he could make himself heard over the roar of the engine.

"'We're two weeks behind. Well, at least a week. So I don't think we're going to succeed. But we're going to give it a try . . .'"

Ullo thought: In other words, this old War of Independence veteran – a man the Estonian government kept in prison for five years, and who had fled to Germany with papers making him out to be a Baltic German – has now become the keenest of the keen, someone who is prepared to give it a try.

And then – which manor house was it now: Kabala, Nabala, Anija or Hagudi? – they had approached it following the long wall behind the park. Ullo grabbed the captain's wrist as he had seen something moving in the bushes at the wall. Just then, some men in grey Finnish uniforms had bawled at the car from the bushes. The captain pulled a blue, black and white flag the size of a handkerchief from inside his tunic and waved it under the nose of the men as with a squealing of tyres he came to a standstill at the gates to the park.

"Report what's going on!"

A young lad with blue, black and white flashes on his sleeve and wearing the uniform of an *Oberfähnrich* had jumped out from the bushes on to the edge of the road.

"Captain Laaman, sir, the third company of the 'Pitka' combat unit, thirty-seven men in all, under the command of Ensign Treier, has moved in to take the manor house, sir!"

"Take it from whom?"

"From the Germans retreating from around Porkuni . . ."

"Take it? But whatever for?"

"The aim is to supplement our weapons reserves, sir!"

"And how many of them are there?"

"Intelligence reports suggest there aren't any more of them than we are, sir!"

"Hm. Take into account the fact that the manor house provides them with a defensive advantage. But – do it. What are you waiting for?"

The ensign said with uncertainty: "I would have liked to suggest to them that they leave the building but . . ."

"In order to do – what?" asked the captain in a demanding tone of voice.

"Give up their arms, then let them make for Tallinn on foot."

"Give it a try."

The ensign mumbled: "But I don't know enough German . . ."

The captain said: "Nor do I."

And Ullo thought: Yet Laaman was quite prepared to get papers proving him to be a German . . .

The captain said in a low voice: "Well, get on with it, then!"

Thud! Thud! Thud! The soldiers nearest the low wall jumped over it. Those in the middle ran, thump, thump, thump, in a scrum through the back gates of the park and tried to find cover in the bushes and behind fences. Ullo told me: "The reason I remember all that thudding and thumping so clearly was because my ears were cocked wondering whether the rumble of Russian tanks could perhaps already be heard from the Narva road . . ." Not yet. Behind the mostly broken windows

271

of the two-storey whitewashed building nothing stirred. The captain, Ullo and the ensign darted in through the park gates and crouched behind an acacia hedge. The captain thrust the weapon which he had picked up off the floor of the jeep, into Ullo's hand. The nearest windows of the manor were some fifteen paces away.

Ullo said: "I'm going to try to say something to them." And he yelled in the direction of the house: "*Hallo! Kameraden! Hört zu!*"

He found it awkward to speak, crouched as he was, and began to straighten up, but caution forced him back into the cover of the bushes. He said in the direction of the house: "*Wir sind keine Bolschewisten! Keine Banditen! Wir sind . . .*" With his left hand he pulled out a white handkerchief from his pocket and with his right he took the blue, black and white flag from Captain Laaman's grasp, popping his pistol into his pocket . . . "*Wir sind . . .*" He raised both hands, gripping the two emblems in the air to their full extent . . . "*Wir sind die gesetzliche Armee der Regierung der neutralen Estnischen Republik. Wir fordern euch auf: legt eure Waffen im Hause nieder. Wer unbewaffnet durch die Hintertür auf den Hof kommt, kann ungehindert nach Reval weitergehen. Sonst müssen wir das Haus angreifen. Wir möchten ein Blutvergiessen gerne vermeiden. Es kommt auf euch an. Ich werde bis zehn zählen – Eins – zwei – drei – vier . . .*"

He counted slowly, his voice high-pitched and strained. There was no movement from the house. When he said *acht*, someone behind the hedge lost his nerve. A grenade flew in through a smashed window and an explosion was heard from the room. Ensign Treier ordered an attack. Ullo rushed up to the wall of the house, along it, and in through the back door. A scrum of five or six men crowded in with him. This was clearly a manor house which had been used as a school. It was a little the worse for wear, somewhat looted, the floors all mud from soldiers' boots. Ullo had time to think: so now I really am in the thick of it . . .

The house was empty. The Germans must have only just left. But they had not done so quite as innocently as first appeared. From somewhere under the stairs, curses could be heard in a mixture of Finnish and Estonian. A soldier stormed up to the window of some small room and threw something out into the yard. Ullo heard the dull explosion of a detonator. Luckily, no one was hurt. It transpired that the Germans had lugged eight crates of bullets and three of tank mines from under the stone staircase to the floor above. They found it all too heavy to take with them as they retreated.

"They had left the building some twenty minutes before our arrival," Ullo said. "They were hardly aware of our existence, of the existence of the Estonian Republican Army. Had they known, they wouldn't of course have consented to leave their supplies for us to use. What the JR 200 boys had stumbled upon was a battery with detonator and alarm clock attached. If they had discovered it one minute later, the whole lot would have gone up including the ammunition, taking at least the central part of the manor with it."

When Ullo brought the subject up twenty years ago, upstairs on my tiny brick balcony under the night sky, maybe after an exceptional fourth glass of brandy, he said: "That lad in his Finnish uniform who found the detonator and threw it out of the window – that was Raimond Kaugver, that's right, the author of *Forty Candles* and other works. He was eighteen years old at the time . . ."

34

ULLO AND CAPTAIN LAAMAN journeyed on, driving south in a wide arc, to somewhere near Ambla. There they had encountered groups of men left over from the border guard regiment, some marching, others in green lorries. Captain Laaman had conveyed to the major there the order from the Admiral to rally as quickly as they could in Kohila – not really an order as such, more of a request. The central thrust of the new defence front would be concentrated there. Ullo saw from the major's weary, angry and mud-splashed face that he maybe took the request as an order after all – but whether he would actually carry it out was something he himself would decide.

They had driven through the village of Kose – the buildings shut to the world, the streets deserted, the frightened church locked up and silent – and sped in a westerly direction through vague hamlets. The captain had handed the map over to Ullo. Ullo had folded the appropriate part of the map, which dated back to Czarist times, open on his knee. Given his job as navigator, he hardly had time to look at the passing countryside. They rushed through the drizzle past the fields and scrubland of central Harju province, through what seemed to be a completely deserted stretch of landscape. Though they did pass straggling squads of soldiers moving west. The captain waved his blue, black and white flag above his head and stopped the car. He ordered Ullo to take a pistol and be ready to shoot – but this had not proved necessary. The captain ascertained which section the soldiers, who were partly in German uniform and partly in those of the Omakaitse, belonged to, and gave them the order and direction in which to proceed: "To Kohila! On the Admiral's orders! Quick, march!"

"Take up positions on the west bank of the river and in the factory buildings. The Admiral is in the school. Contact him. I can see you have some anti-tank bazookas. Keep them at the ready, they'll be needed for sure. By the time you get there, there'll hopefully be soup tureens in the school, and the soup in them still warm."

When the captain and Ullo arrived, the soup was already cold. Some hundred or so soldiers had trooped into the school, yet again a former manor house, for their soup. They sat in the doorways to classrooms, at the school desks, on the stairs in groups, holding their mess tins and half-loaves, some still in Finnish, German or Estonian uniform, but mostly in civvies, some with military appurtenances such as belts or map cases. Mostly youngish sunburnt lads, some were very young with pinkish complexions, hardly sixteen years old.

The captain said to Ullo: "Come on, the Admiral is in the headmaster's study."

He wasn't. They were taken to the school kitchens. And there he was standing against the backdrop of two empty soup tureens, arms akimbo, right in the middle of the room, explaining something to a sergeant in uniform trousers and jackboots, who was wearing a white chef's hat. The captain bawled out: "Admiral Pitka, sir! The Prime Minister has sent you a liaison chappie. This is him."

Pitka was an almost small man and was seventy-three years of age. After three months' toil in the name of this glorious undertaking he looked unexpectedly worn out. He was in civvies, wearing a grey hat with a ribbon soaked in perspiration on his head, and a light grey summer suit, bagged at the knees, its jacket too large for him.

He raised his left hand with spread fingers to hold back the captain and Ullo:

"One moment, please."

He turned his ruddy old man's face towards the captain and Ullo, and looked at Ullo, as Ullo later told me, with his indeflectable blue-eyed stare, but then looked back at the cook.

"You mean to say that this chap has been stealing? How many loaves?"

"Twenty whole loaves, Admiral Pitka, sir!"

Ullo followed where the Admiral's thumb was pointing and saw a man standing next to the soup tureens, in the brown shirt of the Omakaitse, no longer all that young, perhaps around forty, stubby. His whole bearing radiated the wish to become much, much smaller still, to become a speck of dust, to be somewhere else entirely.

275

The Admiral asked the presumed thief: "And why did you steal? Were you that hungry?"

The man uttered, barely audibly: "I live a kilometre away from here. Our farm is full of refugees. They wanted to eat . . ."

The Admiral gestured for him to be quiet and turned again to the cook. "What do you propose?"

The cook, a man with bulging cheeks and fair eyelashes, raised his head. "In such an instance, Admiral Pitka, sir, he should be shot!"

"You think so . . .?" asked the Admiral, almost coaxingly.

"Yes, sir, Admiral Pitka, sir!" said the cook, quite sure of himself.

"Mmm, yes, well . . ." muttered Pitka. "They stole during the War of Independence as well. At first. But we understood: execution is a luxury. We couldn't allow ourselves such a luxury. Captain . . ." he turned to Laaman – " . . . summon the head of the guard."

The captain went out and came back a minute later with a lieutenant. The Admiral said, indicating the thief with his thumb: "Give this fellow a good thrashing. A thorough one, but not so much that he can't rejoin the ranks. Quick, march!" And then he said to the captain and Ullo: "Let's go . . ."

He swayed slightly as he walked, moving forward in surprisingly large strides. Ullo thought that it was as if movement of his hips was painful to him. He tried, in the twenty seconds the walk took them, to summon up what he knew about the Admiral.

He was from the inland province of Järvamaa, but was clearly someone with broad horizons. He had attended three nautical schools and was a ship's master on voyages abroad from the age of twenty-three. He had spent twenty years at sea, then he was in the shipping business in Britain and Estonia. And suddenly, in 1918, he became a central figure in the birth pangs of the Estonian state, commanding schoolboy volunteers, the Kaitseliit home guard, armoured trains, the navy. Pitka was someone who had started from nothing but built himself up into a force to be reckoned with. He considered operations which even the most sober of encyclopaedias describe as *foolhardy*. Inevitably, there were dozens of stories about him. Like this one: he is standing on the bridge of the minesweeper the *Lennuk* and fights a duel with the fortress at Krasnaya Gorka. The *Lennuk* has four-inch guns, the fortress, eighteen-inch ones. The *Lennuk* has sailed provocatively near to the fortress – otherwise it wouldn't stand a chance of hitting it. Then the pillars of water from the shells from the fortress's eighteen-inchers begin to move worryingly closer. And he yells: "*Suitsu! Suitsu!*" and since Admiral Cowan, a Briton, is standing at his side observing the breakneck operation, he also shouts, for the sake of clarity "Smoke! Smoke!" whereupon the Briton opens his gold cigarette case and offers him a Camel or Lucky Strike. He is terribly hurt: only the day before he had explained to the Briton that he had never in his life held a cigarette between his lips. And now this "sir", Sir Walter, imagines Johan, who happens to have the same surname as that pseudonymous scribbler Ansomardi, to have spat upon his principles from one day to the next! Or is it that this backwoods Nelson is so shit-scared of the Russian guns that he needs a smoke? And why should he have to say *smokescreen* or *curtain of smoke* anyway, when every Estonian understands that although he's shouting "Smoke!" what he really means is a layer of it between them and the enemy . . . Pitka was soon to become a rear admiral in Estonia; in Britain, he would even become a "sir" himself. *His Majesty the King of England – in full appreciation, Sir John, of your extraordinary merits –* or whatever the set phrase is when you are knighted . . . Then in his native land, sudden strife erupted. Overnight he became an exaggerator, slanderer, unpatriotic dog! And why? Because he had started his own periodical entitled *Valve – Watchman –* in order to expose corruption in Estonia. The result: he left Estonia for Canada a deeply disillusioned man, and ran a farm and a sawmill somewhere near Vancouver for seven years. He returned in 1930, on account of homesickness, as he has said, and was appointed director of the Estonian Cooperative Society, the ETK. He wrote his war memoirs, tried to build up a merchant fleet for Estonia, and its light industry. He financed some kindly English eccentric who wanted to produce a large Maori–English dictionary. I do not know what the eccentric did it for, but Pitka paid out in the hope of proving global linguistic links between the Maoris and the Estonians . . . At first, he was a leading figure among the Independence War Veterans – the Vapsid – but when this movement began to show totalitarian traits, trouble arose and they had to do without him. And one evening, at his farm in Kiltsi, the same evening that the formation of the Vares government had been announced on the radio, he put on his hat (maybe even the same one he was wearing now walking towards the headmaster's office in the whitewashed corridor in Kohila, but in

277

much newer condition) – anyhow, he put on his hat and said in passing to his wife: "Helene, I'm going to take a short walk . . ." No less and no more. So that she could say with a clear conscience: "I haven't a clue where he's gone." But perhaps also so that his wife could not know, since either side, the Germans or the Russians, could start squeezing the information out of her, since both time and space were ripe for such things to occur. He found a motor boat which had been hidden in the reeds and chugged through the German naval blockade all the way to Finland. He stayed there for four whole years, and still no one knows how he survived or with whose help he stimulated and encouraged our national struggle. Two months ago he returned with a group of Estonians who had fought in Finland (whom the Germans took from him) and tried to knock together an army for the Tief government to defend Tallinn from the Russians. For a day, two days, three, a week, a month, till, God willing, the world would take notice and give the Estonian people under threat of suffocation a sign. In a word, the old man was trying to promote a cause in which His Majesty the King of England had already decided to betray him to Yosif Vissarionovich . . .

I have no idea what was discussed there in the school at Kohila, housed in the study of the former Tohisoo manor house, a kilometre or so from Kohila village itself. Or what the Admiral said there. Ullo was in any case mostly there in the role of listener.

I can imagine the Admiral sketching out to Ullo the next moves of his plan in order that Ullo might, in turn, inform the government. He made no requests to the government, at least no significant ones. Because he must have known that it had no way of granting them.

Ullo asked the Admiral whether the Cabinet had discussed which part of Estonian territory could hold out longest against the Russians and could be best defended against them. (And Ullo thought to himself that it was a daft question given that this was the issue most preoccupying the government at the time.) Ullo wondered whether the Admiral had considered Hiiumaa? Sitting in the government corridor he had thought about it, then dismissed this idea.

The Admiral said: "But of course. But Hiiumaa? No. Because we haven't got the tonnage to transport a couple of thousand men, even one thousand, plus equipment, over there. What is more, we just don't have the time."

I don't know whether the Great Stage Producer in the Sky had actually wished to emphasise the drama of the situation in so cheap a manner, but at that very moment the old crank-up telephone on the wall rang. The Admiral picked up the receiver.

"Pitka." A pause. "Yes. By some miracle . . ."

Ullo expected to hear what miracle it was. But it transpired that all it consisted of was that the call had actually got through from Tallinn. Pitka continued.

"Yes, I'm listening." Pause. "Yes, I understand." Pause. And then, in a very flat voice: "Yes, OK."

He replaced the receiver and looked for a moment at the white-washed wall, his back to Laaman and Ullo. Then turned, with what for such an elderly, weary man was unexpected rapidity, to face them.

"That was the Chief of Staff . . ." (And Ullo, as he told forty years later, had started and for one fleeting moment thought: Laidoner.) ". . . Major General Maide. He notified that the government is abandoning Tallinn tomorrow and travelling to the coast at Puise where it will try to get to Sweden."

"And what does that mean . . .?" asked one of the two.

"It is a command from the Chief of Staff. For me to dismiss the combat units. The government has ceased to resist and is leaving the country. Don't you understand?"

Maybe the Admiral still clung blindly to his belief that he would succeed, as we had succeeded back in 1918, in working something out, triggering off a new War of Independence. He stood there for a good while weighing up whether or not to take orders from the, well, not exactly self-styled and certainly fully legitimate, but nonetheless completely new Chief of Staff. Perhaps he wouldn't have done. But the greater the stage producer, the more he will cling to the established order by exercising a certain lack of imagination. No, no, I'm not here thinking of that old man as the Grand Producer, standing there with his trimmed grey beard thrust forward, his grey tattered old hat and his penetrating eyes staring into infinity . . . Incidentally, when I once asked Ullo about Pitka's appearance during those times, I remember his reply: "Listen, I've lived in Jartu less than you have, but I do remember the odd face. There was that professor of children's diseases, Lüüsi, Ado Lüüsi. Whose chief claim to fame was his beautiful daughter – Mrs Oras, wasn't she? When I now compare my memories of what Lüüsi and Pitka looked like, they seem so similar that they merge." So when I mention the Grand Producer, it is not the twin of the professor of pediatrics I was thinking of, but History itself, at any rate History as it played itself out in time and space, over here and out there. So I am not exaggerating, not much at any rate, when I say that at that very moment there was a knock at the door and some pale ensign bawled out: "There are nine Russian tanks entering the village from the Angerja road!"

The Admiral stood there in the middle of the room for a moment. If he hadn't had a beard, you would have clearly been able to see his clenched jaw. His bright enamel-blue eyes, the eyes of a child, in fact had narrowed and become silver, since he, Lord, surely . . . But why shouldn't the eyes of an old man like him grow moist? Anyhow, he almost shouted at Laaman and Ullo: "Come on!"

They went out through the tiny vestibule and through the crowd murmuring and shouting their disaffection. Someone cried out: "Admiral Pitka, sir! There are Russian tanks in the village! Command us over to the main road, sir. We've got bazookas."

Pitka grunted: "I know. One bazooka and nine tanks."

They went through the door of the schoolhouse. The hubbub receded. The rumble of tank tracks could be heard, about a kilometre from the school. Pitka said: "Men. I've just got orders from the Chief of Staff in Tallinn. This unit is to cease all hostile activities. Dismissed! Spread out in the woods! Vanish – into thin air! Till things improve. Quick march!"

Some of the lads ran to get their weapons, packs or mess tins. Some shouted: "Admiral Pitka, sir! We don't agree! Fuck it, we'll hold out!" One of them yelled, almost in tears: "Admiral Pitka, sir, this is betrayal! Betrayal . . ."

No one knows whether Pitka heard these words or not. He beckoned to Laaman and Ullo and sauntered, sway-sway, over to Laaman's car. The tall ensign followed.

"Admiral Pitka, has the order to thrash the criminal been revoked?"

"What criminal . . .?"

"The bread thief, sir!"

Pitka stopped in his tracks. "No! The order stands! Give him a good thrashing!"

The ensign tried to set matters right: "But, Admiral Pitka, the bread is Russian bread now, isn't it . . .?"

Pitka bawled: "An Estonian shouldn't steal bread, even from his executioners!" Then he said impatiently to Laaman and Ullo: "Come on!"

Off they went. In that same open BMW in which Laaman and Ullo had arrived. Somewhere on the country road between Hageri and Haiba a young lad in Omakaitse uniform came riding on a motorbike in the opposite direction. Pitka stopped him. Who was he, and where was he off to? He'd come from Omakaitse headquarters and was on his way to Vasalemma, to report that the Commies had dropped parachutists near the woods at Lümandu.

"Take this man to Tallinn instead," said Pitka, indicating Ullo with his thumb.

The lad asked: "And why should I obey your order . . .?"

"Because I am Admiral Pitka."

The lad jerked to attention and replied: "Then OK, sir."

Ullo got out of the car on to the muddy road and Pitka said: "One moment," and came up to him. He indicated to Ullo to follow him and they walked away along the edge of a ditch. Thirty paces from the motorcyclist he came to a halt, turned to Ullo and said: "Tell Tief: I've stopped as ordered. Not least because the government has left the country, so I'm no longer taking any responsibility for those men who could still get killed. And tell him not to wait for me at Puise. I'm not coming. Clear?"

"Clear . . ." said Ullo, in what would have been a pretty muffled voice. The old man shook him by the hand, in a quite unsoldierlike way.

When Ullo got on the motorcycle, he did not know that of those returning to everyday life he was, well, if not one of the very last, then at least among the last ones who had seen the old man alive (or dead). Nor did he know how anxious Soviet intelligence were that the old man had vanished into thin air. It is now generally known how all those picked up or arrested were asked the question routinely, but in angry tones: "*A gdye vash Pitka?*" I myself ended up under interrogation fifteen months later and I had had nothing whatsoever to do with the Admiral, but the question was put to me nonetheless.

To return to Ullo, the Omakaitse lad from Haiba took Ullo to Tallinn by motorcycle. What Ullo did there in the early evening of 21 September is anyone's guess. Around half past seven he was off yet again, now no longer in the company of the Admiral and his entourage in their BMW, but on an ancient Husqvarna bicycle and another slightly newer one, complete with bundles attached to the baggage racks – he and Maret.

The dark, grey, windy sky with the occasional shower augured an early dusk. They cycled over the old stone bridge at Pääsküla, with Ullo thinking that it really ought to be blown up. So that the Russians, when they took over Tallinn the next day, couldn't move their tanks directly in a south-westerly direction. But it wouldn't be much of an obstacle, they would drive over its ruins and through the shallow river.

Ullo and Maret had decided to cross the bridge and continue south-west along the road to Pärnu through the autumn evening, arriving at the coast by lunch the next day. Their exact destination was something they would have to figure out overnight. Puise would be most obvious. Ullo knew that many politicians and civil servants fleeing from Tallinn would be heading there. But maybe for that very reason, it didn't seem very clever to go there. On the other hand – maybe the members of the Cabinet would still be there at lunchtime the next day. So that Ullo and Maret sitting there among the thousands of people, gradually blown into wet, grey and cold despair, would immediately be spotted by Tief or Klesment or Maandi in the nervous crowd of those hoping for a boat to freedom. And they would take them to one side, happy to have met them. "Jolly, jolly, jolly good that we spotted you – the government motor boat is over there in the bulrushes. And for you there is, of course, room." Something like this could hardly be hoped for. And experiencing anything else would be vastly disagreeable. They would still have the night to discuss the matter. Because the darkness would force them to spend the night somewhere en route.

In the gathering gloom the road to Pärnu was hardly swarming with travellers, but there was a surprising number nonetheless: cars, with only blackout slits as headlights, and one or two driving entirely without lights. Most cars still used for civilian purposes had already sped past. Nor were there many horse-drawn carts full of belongings. But as for handcarts stacked up with bundles or suitcases, with four or five people pushing and pulling or walking alongside, these could be encountered every hundred metres or so. Plus refugees with rucksacks or suitcases, singly, or in groups. Cyclists were very much of a rarity.

282

Ullo and Maret managed at first to cycle past and through the straggling mass of refugees with ease. One expected, and one unexpected, observation: what was to be expected was that movement was occurring principally away from the city, away to the south-west. Unexpected was that all movement occurred almost entirely without sound. All those clustered around carts and handcarts or in groups carrying rucksacks walked in silence. Ullo and Maret did not encounter any snatches of conversation, cries, shouts, voices. It was as if the whole escape were occurring in a dream.

Somewhere, maybe in Rahula or some such village, Ullo rode up alongside Maret and said: "It's so dark now that we really ought to start thinking about spending the night somewhere. But any of the large farmhouses along the main road would be dangerous. You never know how quickly the tanks could catch up with us. So we should take the first lane we come across on the left."

Which they did. They cycled in almost complete darkness for a kilometre or two, through fields and scrubland and ended up in the yard of an unknown farm. They leant their bicycles against the wall by the door, knocked, and stepped inside.

A paraffin lamp was burning in the living room. In the flickering light they saw that the large, low-ceilinged room was not full to the brim with people, but there were three or four clumps of refugees who had already made themselves at home there. Four or five people and a couple of children, a family no doubt, had grouped themselves with their bundles in the corner behind the stove, and a second group had taken over the wooden sofa, a product from the Luther Plywood Manufactory, as could be found in any railway station waiting room or farmhouse. And somewhere against the wall in the gloom were yet more strangers, in pairs or alone. Ullo greeted them and said: "Who do you have to ask if you want to spend the night here?"

Someone pointed with his chin to the door to the adjoining room. "The farmer's wife's gone in there." And when Ullo made a move towards the door, someone added: "She'll be out soon . . . There's some sick person in there . . ."

So they stood waiting in the middle of the room, and Ullo whispered to Maret: "There are already too many people here. Let's ask if we can sleep in the hay, or on bales of straw."

A moment later the farmer's wife appeared. She was a brisk, thickset woman of about sixty years old, a kindly enough person but showing no particular enthusiasm at the arrival of yet more refugees. So Ullo decided to pre-empt her.

"My dear lady, I can see that there are already too many people here. So we would like to ask – could you spare some hay or straw in the attic or similar?"

"I suppose we can manage that . . ." said the farmer's wife. "Come this way and I'll show you."

They went through the porch and out into the yard and Maret, walking at the heels of the farmer's wife, apologised for the trouble they were causing. "Such crazy times . . ."

The farmer's wife muttered over her shoulder: "Whatever you do – some go, others stay, and some even manage to arrive . . ."

Maret thought that there was something a little vague about her words and said: "And you've got someone who's ill back in the house . . .?"

"Not been regarded as an illness up to now," said the farmer's wife, "but it probably soon will be."

"So what's wrong . . .?" asked Maret.

"It's just that Tiina would have to choose today – or tonight – to bring a baby into this world."

They found a ladder propped up against the barn. The farmer's wife lit their way with a torch. She said: "Don't you go leaving them bicycles there by the front door. It wouldn't make any difference, but what with all those refugees . . ."

They brought their bicycles into the barn and clambered up on to the straw. In the safe haven of the darkness exhaustion overcame them, erasing their own escape and the apocalyptic flight of thousands from their consciousness.

When Ullo awoke in the complete darkness, he thought for a moment that he could hear the distant rumble of tanks coming from the main road. He tried to listen, then realised: the rain was pattering against the shingle roof and nothing more could be heard clearly through that noise. He switched on his torch for a moment, found the ladder and went down into the yard. He walked away from the building so that the patter of rain on the roof no longer muffled other noises. But the rain on the grass and bushes, more of a rustle than a patter, still prevented him from hearing anything from the road. Then

284

he heard Maret calling quietly: "Ullo – is that you down there?"

When he confirmed that it was, Maret came down the ladder. "What is it? Have you heard something?"

Ullo said: "No. But I'm listening . . ."

Then they both heard: "What's that?" asked Maret. They listened to noises coming from the blacked-out back room. Ullo said: "The mewling of a new human being."

After dozing off for another couple of hours they had continued on their bicycles, taking a southerly route. It was still raining. Under a dark lowering sky, they pedalled through grey, seemingly deserted villages towards Risti Church, hoping to reach the northern part of the western coast by lunchtime. They still had more than a hundred kilometres to go.

Somewhere near Nahkjala, the road became visible in the morning light but was still hard to see in the tunnel of quivering wet alders. Then Ullo rode level with Maret and braked, as did Maret. They stood beside one another in the mud, and looked into each other's eyes. Ullo said: "Listen – I'm not sure whether . . ."

Maret whispered: "Neither am I."

Ullo asked: "What?"

Maret said: "I was wondering – are we doing the right thing, fleeing?"

Ullo asked: "You mean, when thousands leave, a million ought to stay behind . . .?"

Maret whispered: "And when all those who are born here have to stay . . ."

Ullo took Maret's hand. He said (I imagine with as much feeling as he had ever done in his life): "Let's stay too!"

Maret asked: "But do you think you'll manage . . .?"

"With a bit of luck," said Ullo, his face glowing despite the wetness and chill around them. They turned their bicycles around in the direction of Tallinn.

35

I SAW NEITHER ULLO NOR Maret for ten years.

In October 1944, a week or so after the new occupation, which was of course officially announced as being a liberation, I travelled down to Tartu, and stayed there for fifteen months.

I think that everyone connected to the Third Way avoided contact with other supporters of the cause over those months. But not only on account of the dangers involved. The merciless attempts of the Soviet occupation forces to process all those connected with the Third Way through the courts became clear to better informed people within a few weeks. One after the other, people were arrested, mostly from the government, towards the end of that year. And the fact that they were treated in a way befitting Ivan the Terrible is evident from the fact that one of their number, Oskar Gustavson, the Head of State Audit, jumped out of the fourth-floor window of Security Services headquarters on Pikk Street, dashing himself on the cobblestones below. Before the people from the Security Services building managed to pick him up, a passing car took him off to hospital where he died a few hours later.

Danger was certainly one factor. But more pertinent in the circumstances was a realisation which even the most blind had arrived at: that our Third Way had become No Way. It felt like being clubbed over the head. The West had ceased to support the rebirth of the free Baltic states. By the summer of 1945, the West had sold us out to Stalin on three separate occasions: in Teheran in 1943, in Yalta in 1945, and for a third time in Potsdam that same year. In 1946, we were sold out for the fourth and final time. As these events unfolded, our betrayal became all the more clear and it felt, as I have said, like a blow to the head with a club. A blow which made us realise that all resistance was futile.

In 1944–5 Ullo, myself and our peers were still too young to meet over cups of coffee and glasses of cognac to reminisce about things that had occurred a couple of months, or a couple of years, before. These events were all too painfully present in our memories. If we did meet, then it was to discuss how to continue. But world politics had given us our answer: our cause had been deemed to be absurd, since all those who could have saved us and could have shown their support had abandoned us.

We knew no details, other than the odd fragment of unchecked news that came our way. There was no one in the world whose job it was to inform us. Nor was there anyone who could act as an information courier, as the members of the government were, with the silent consent of the West, now in a Moscow jail, awaiting judgement by General Ulrich, notorious already from the 1937 show trials. The ministers were sentenced to hard labour, the Chief of Staff was shot.

All we heard were whispers of the negotiations taking part in the West. About Yalta, for instance, people would whisper that on one occasion, presumably in the second week of February 1945, Stalin, while walking towards the wing where Roosevelt was staying, strode alongside his wheelchair and asked him, through an interpreter of course: "Mr President, you've spoken in passing about holding free elections to determine the future of the Baltic states. Very well. I will take the responsibility myself to see that they are organised. Only – do they need to be conducted with international observers present? Or is that not necessary? Because, you see, in the current logistical situation it could be difficult to get them to their appointed destinations. So that the elections could be postponed for an inconvenient amount of time . . ."

Roosevelt had swallowed four tablets, just before setting off in his wheelchair. Because sharp, blinding headaches had been troubling him since taking off for the Crimea and had still not abated. Especially not here. And he was hovering between the fear that he had taken his tablets too late to stop the headache, and the hope that the tremors would soon subside. Against the background of the rustle of the wheelchair rolling over the asphalt, Stalin's comically soft and slightly sing-song sentences were so Georgian of intonation, so un-Russian, that even the monolingual and by now sclerotic ear of Roosevelt could recognise them. Then he heard what the interpreter said, and suddenly realised what the words meant.

"This is a problem of peripheral importance," he thought. "Why should he be afraid of international observers – as he seems to be? What I really ought to do is brace myself and stand up on these poor legs of mine which have not obeyed me for a quarter of a century now – I ought to brace myself (although after all the concessions we made at Teheran with regard to Eastern Europe, it would no longer mean anything), straighten up from my slack and stooped position, and, now wedged firmly in place, say: 'Dear friend' (but in fact – why dear friend when we've got such deep suspicions about the guy?). But why not say dear friend, since Winston expressed to me in private yesterday – in as much as we can have a private conversation around here – his eager desire (he did not explain why) that the fellow, i.e. Stalin, should *like* him. Quite risible in itself, quite the confessions of an old woman. Anyhow, I ought to say to him: 'Dear friend – it should definitely be in the presence of international observers, for your own sake. So that the half of the world which sympathises with fascism – you yourself stress at every turn it still exists and is more powerful than we suspect – will not call into question the legitimacy of those elections at some future date!' Yes, I ought to demand those elections take place under international observation. That's the least that could be done . . . But if I now start becoming inflexible and begin to gainsay him, my headaches will inevitably turn on me! And Dr Donovan will notice in an instant. He never loses sight of me as he walks there among my bodyguards. He would no doubt order the bodyguards to pick up the wheelchair and run off with it to our residence, causing unnecessary panic in so doing. And I, swaying and bouncing up and down in between the heads of my bodyguards, would probably pass out – as has happened once before, though only for a moment, luckily, and only with Americans present . . . So what I'll say to Stalin (and in my revolt against doctors' orders, a little louder and more rapidly than I would have liked), feeling how the pressure of fear emerges with the words, how I crumple like a rag and feel liberated, is: '*Dear Mr Stalin* – of course we are not going to demand the presence of international observers!' And then, as if this were not humiliating enough to rid myself of my fear of headaches, I will add – in a bout of self-abasement and self-defence – and lying through my teeth: 'Because we trust you!'"

"Mr President, I thank you for your trust!" replies Stalin without the soft sing-song of his half-whisper changing one jot, the pencils of the secretaries noting down this exchange flashing above their notepads. Stalin stops and allows the extraordinarily pale President and his entourage to move away. And he walks off to the residence occupied by the Soviet delegation, softly humming "Suliko" to himself.

What we hear spoken about in whispers is something like that. The good Lord only knows where the rumours have come from. Less is known of the analogous conversation which took place between Uncle Joe and Churchill. But this must also have taken place with a measure of apathy or weariness caused by whisky and kidney pains, as history has shown.

So much for the futility. Now the dangers involved. I will provide one personal example of such dangers hovering over us at that time.

I was working for those fifteen months I mentioned above as a junior lecturer in the Department of Law at the University of Tartu. In the absence of the professor responsible, I gave lectures in juris-prudence. One evening in February 1945 – and why could it not be the same as when the conversation between Roosevelt and Stalin took place – I had just finished giving my lecture. The majority of my students, not quite starving but certainly underfed, not quite dressed in rags but poorly clothed, had already dispersed, making their way through the rubble of the winter city, the ashy smoke from which could still be smelt in the darkness. Three or four students were still hanging around in the cold lecture theatre which nonetheless still had electric lighting. I knew their names but nothing else about them. Except for one who was closest to the rostrum and was rummaging in his briefcase. Vinnal, a former lecturer in civil law and a one-time Amicus buddy of mine, had once muttered: "Peerna – watch out for him."

Peerna was the son of a professor of medical science. He was born with serious physical deformities. He could only move about in a sidelong gait. His small head sat awry on his shoulders so that he would always be looking to the left, and he couldn't use his right hand very well. Nor could he speak either fluently or freely. But the skewed position of his head did not prevent him from being observant within the field of vision he was afforded, and his slow answers were strikingly precise. And as for Vinnal's warning – why should it not be heeded?

I was not the only one to realise in those days that Soviet Intelligence exhibited a disproportionate interest in using people with physical defects. God only knows whether this tendency was based on experience of their usefulness, or whether the KGB entertained the pathological theory that crippled people would suffer from complexes and would therefore be easier to manipulate than average people, the root cause sometimes being a fear of saying "no", on account of their problems, and at other times being an ethically unrefined urge to avenge. As I say, I cannot tell whether behind this business lay experience on the part of the "watchers", or whether it was part of their overall philosophy (I would like to think the latter). In this instance, things went like this:

As I began to leave the lecture theatre, Peerna was suddenly standing there, blocking my path in his oblique way. I tried to negotiate my way round him, but he was too quick for me and made an attempt at a half-whisper. Although he didn't have his voice particularly well under control, he tried to make what he said clearly audible to the three or four left in the room, so they could, if necessary, be used as witnesses.

"Comrade Sirkel – I fear that Estonia has now been sold down the river in the Crimea. Comrade Sirkel, we ought to do something about it! We really must! Tell us what we should do. You should know! You've got the experience and the contacts that we don't have! We'll come to your place – me and some friends – real Estonians. Do you understand what I mean: supply us with arguments, guidelines, tell us what we have to do . . ."

We looked one another in the face for an instant from very close range. His darting bright grey eyes avoided mine. He had small drops of sweat on his forehead. It wasn't easy for him.

I thought to myself that if the sons of old professors – whether on account of physical defects or not – allow themselves to get mixed up in this game, where will it all end? I weighed up my courses of action for a split second, searching for what I should say, and replied: "You, Comrade Peerna, should keep well away from such matters, because your life is in danger all the more. I'm thinking of how years in a labour camp could affect your health. In your case, it wouldn't take years, but months, even weeks, before . . ."

He took a step backwards and I managed to pass him. The following months he came loyally, twice a week, to my lectures. He wrote down everything I said with care. He greeted me diligently, but never again entered into conversation with me.

There were still eleven months to go before I was kicked out of the department. And a further nine years before I managed to escape back to Estonia. Or "returned" as official documents would have it. And then it was some time more before I went to visit Ullo and Maret. For despite the liberalisation which the Khrushchev era meant for us, such a singed crow as myself did not hurry to restore old contacts during my first few weeks of freedom.

36

SOMETIME DURING AUTUMN 1955, I had heard from some former schoolmate or other that Ullo and his wife were living on Erbe Street in the same place as ten years previously. I went over late one Sunday morning, since I was a writer and thus free to choose my own working hours.

Nothing had been built on that street for the past ten years. A few of the buildings that had been damaged or half burnt in the March bombings had been knocked down. Acacia bushes the colour of yellow rust had grown up to the windows in front of Ullo and Maret's little low house. Despite its relatively sheltered nature, it seemed to stick out more than ever before, given its sparse surroundings. There was the thick dusk of acacia and the dark rusty colour of darkness in the porch. I started; good Lord, this is of course Maret! She recognised me immediately. But this was an *old* woman . . . Of course: Ullo would now be forty, Maret a few years older. Forty-four at the most. I had no idea what the last ten years had done to Ullo, and I suddenly thought that I didn't really know what had happened to me these last ten years either. But at any rate, Maret was unexpectedly old for her age. Her face had a brownish hue with liver spots at her temples and wrinkles at the corner of her mouth – which were most visible when she forgot to smile.

But mostly she didn't forget. She smiled with a kind friendliness, with an understanding gentleness. There they were, still living in the same house. But now they had a third room too – in the third year of Soviet rule, they had brought Maret's father to live with them. Because he had become too ailing to be looked after by distant relatives. Ullo had managed to get one room in the neighbouring flat to use as their own. The door was bricked up and access was constructed via their own back room, and her father had lived there until his death, two years before. Now Ullo had, well, a workroom or a study or whatever, thanks to the fact that the building was luckily so run-down that no serious bidders for the flat ever came along.

Maret and I entered that third room and sat down. There were a number of old petit bourgeois armchairs, a settee, a tiny writing desk whose mahogany top had long ago split down its length, the crack filled in with putty. In front of the bookshelves and under the two windows were two tables standing in the full light. On one table was a small, but quite unexpected display: seven or eight models of cannon, ranging from twenty centimetres to half a metre in length, made of top-quality iron and brass and lacquered to prevent verdigris or rust from forming. The older ones were carved out of wood and painted, the newer ones on gun carriages, with cranking handles and levers, and on wheels. It was the history of artillery in miniature, ranging, as Ullo later explained, from a falconet used by Charles VIII of France (around 1480), up to a British field gun from the last century with a 76.2 millimetre calibre . . .

Maret smiled apologetically, but maybe with some pride too. "Well, that's what he's been occupying his time with recently. They're all scale models down to the last detail."

I sat down in an armchair between the writing desk and the models. "You mean to say he made them himself?"

"Who else? We wouldn't have the money to . . ."

"And he reads such books while he's making them?" I had picked up a book lying on the writing desk. It was Camus's essay collection *The Rebel*, but in Swedish: *Revolterande människan*. I don't know whether I'd actually heard of Camus at the time.

"Where would he be able to get such books from?!" I asked.

"He has an aunt who's an expert on music in Moscow. His late mother's half-sister . . ."

I cried out: "Hang on a minute – has Ullo's mother died?"

"Yes," said Maret quietly. "It was her heart. Seven years ago now. Anyway, this aunt – she's been allowed to make the odd trip now and again, so now and again Ullo gets books from her . . ."

"But Camus – why in Swedish?"

"Oh, by sheer chance," said Maret mildly (which made me think: she must have forgiven Ullo for his snobbish traits ages ago) – "Ullo says that he's reading good literature, researching into the existential way of thinking and learning Swedish at one and the same time . . ."

I said: "That's typical of him. Where is he, by the way?"

"At work," said Maret approvingly.

I cried: "On Sunday morning? That *too* is typical of him. But where's he working? I don't even know . . ."

"At the suitcase factory. On Ahtri Street."

"And what does he do there?"

"Makes suitcases."

"Since when?"

"Right from the start. Or right from the end, if you like. Ten years now."

So that's how it was. That day was a rest day at the factory and Ullo had to work that day so he could have the next Saturday off. To be able to attend some postcard collectors' day in Rakvere or Viljandi.

I told Maret I would go along to the factory to see Ullo. But Maret said that it wasn't that easy, because outsiders weren't allowed on the premises.

"I'll phone the guard on the gate. They'll let you through."

They still had a phone. Actually, not still, but again, as Maret explained. Because the secretary of the trade union had allotted him one because he, like Ullo, was a postcard collector. Maret smiled wryly and said: "Hobby buddies. Ullo is an expert when it comes to small deals . . ."

Maret phoned, and they said I could come, and I was there within half an hour.

By some fluke, the factory was located just to the north of the cooperative venture compound, the ETK, where Ullo had, eleven or twelve years before, in the annexe of the tobacco factory, tried to print the Estonian Government Declaration. But the suitcase factory was itself a typical two-storey limestone industrial building, access to which from Ahtri Street was effected by passing a typically Soviet security guard, a quite suspicious but rather dozy old codger who let me in once I had mentioned Comrade Paerand and his wife's recent phone call.

The factory was deserted, as is usual for a Sunday. In the more or less bare workshops, the spiked and riveted white-ribbed skeletons necessary for assembling the end product were stacked up to the

294

ceiling. Near the large curved blades of the guillotine, sheets of fibreboard lay in piles, plus a stapling machine for affixing the locks, and there were shelves round the walls of a further workshop with grey cardboard boxes from a factory in Leningrad on them, some of which had been ripped open, the nickel locks showing through greasy oiled paper.

I followed the instructions given by the guard on the gate, but found my way more by smell, following the increasing odour of acetylene as I went upstairs and into a corridor to the right – up to a grey door, marked PAINT SHOP in black letters. From inside, the whirr and chug of the vacuum compressor could be heard, which ceased when I knocked.

"Who is it?" A curiously muffled voice, which I would not have recognised as Ullo's, had I not known that he was there.

"A visitor."

I can imagine him hearing something familiar in those four syllables and racking his brains to think back ten years (a dog's ability to distinguish 30,000 different scents springs to mind), but he did not of course manage to remember. Though I'm pretty damned sure he gave it a try. Four seconds later he said: "Just a moment."

The door opened swiftly and closed again behind the back of the man stepping out into the corridor. The cloud of acetylene which wafted out was cut in two by the door but managed nevertheless to thrust its lung-tickling fingers down my throat and breathe my eyes full of sting.

The man who had just come out of the paint shop was wearing an overall flecked with brown and grey stains and had something of Don Quixote about him (the tall stature, the thinness, the smallish head thrust back, size 45 shoes with the right-hand shoe turned slightly inwards at this moment of doubt). It could have been Ullo, but I could not see his face because he was wearing a gas mask. There were paint splashes on the glass eyepieces and a veiny hose dangling down. Some piece of ALMAVÜ equipment left in stock and for civilian use. He, at any rate, recognised me immediately. With his left-hand rubber glove he pulled off the right-hand one and shook my hand. Only then did he take off his mask and hang it on a peg on the wall. I said, indicating the mask: "Perfect mimicry on your part . . ."

Ullo had to laugh. We went some ten paces further where there was a Red Corner, and took a seat under the metre-square coloured poster of Stalin.

I asked: "Well, how long has it been, now . . .?"

Ullo said: "Don't remember exactly. Must be – ten years, ten months and one week."

I said: "But to return to mimicry . . ." I started in a slightly louder voice to compensate, as the picture behind us had awoken in me the automatic tendency to speak in hushed tones.

Ullo said, rather interrupting me, but at normal volume: "That's it. Diving into the depths of the proletariat as protective colouring. You know that when Maret and I decided to turn back at the coast, she asked me: 'Do you think you'll manage?' And I answered her: 'With a bit of luck.' And it's held . . ."

Looking back on it, I now understand that what I should have asked Ullo is this: How come they've put you under constant pressure, but you always manage to come out on top? And why have they never touched you? Unfortunately, I left the question unasked at the time. Nor did I ever ask him at any time afterwards.

37

B
UT AS FOR MIMICRY AS protective colouring, and the
insuppressible provocation connected with it, I will here
present Ullo's poem which raises quite a few questions.

I do not know whether the name Manolis Glezos means much to people nowadays, but in the summer of 1941, it was for a short time one of the hottest names in the news. Not, of course, on the *Nachrichtendienst* but on the BBC.

By April 1939, Mussolini had invaded Albania. When Greece subsequently refused to accept Italy's further push into the Balkans and refused to afford Italy the assistance she demanded, the Italians pushed on and invaded Greece too. But after three weeks of occupation they were finally pushed out by the Greeks in November 1940 with unexpected ease. So powerful was the counter-attack that the south of Albania fell into Greek hands, which was something the Germans couldn't allow. Especially since British forces had landed in Piraeus and elsewhere to support the Greeks in March '41. In April, the Germans themselves launched "Operation Marita" which ended with the fall of Athens to the Germans on 27 April, followed by the famous invasion of Crete by German parachutists on 1 June.

Against this background, the name of Manolis Glezos flickered briefly into prominence in that part of the world opposed to the Germans. He was an unforgettable event, at least among thinking young people, despite the fact that we ourselves were living under the bloodstained steamroller of history, what with the first large-scale deportations and then, a week later, the war coming to our door. Despite all that, or maybe because of it, Manolis Glezos and his activities remained in our memory for all time.

After conquering Athens, the Germans had erected an iron pole on the slanting marble roof of the Parthenon and there they raised their

297

own red flag with its black swastika on a white field. And on the night of 31 August, the eighteen-year-old student Glezos had climbed up and torn the flag down. Tore down the conquerors' flag from the symbolic altar to European tradition and spirit.

This was a prank which to a certain extent compensated for the merciless thrashing the British had received on Crete. But not only that. Glezos's gesture was an incomparable injection of hope, strength and decisiveness into the body of those fighting against Hitler throughout the world. What later occurred with Glezos himself, what he believed in, or how he was maybe even exploited (member of the Communist Party, editor-in-chief of the Communist periodical *Avghi*, arrested three times and condemned to death by the Greeks themselves, to be liberated by the Reds or fellow-travellers – ending up being awarded the Lenin Peace Prize) was not known in the late summer of 1941, not even by Glezos himself, not to speak of those people (especially those back here) who had turned their hand to writing poetry about him.

Ullo's typewritten poem, on two now yellowed DIN format sheets of paper, has at any rate survived. To which I will add: I don't know when he wrote it, don't remember when he gave it to me.

> *Gory wound*
> *in my breast, a*
> *flag*
> *flag*
> *flag*
> *flag*
> *a dagger*
> *stabbed a million times*
> *into the giant heart*
> *of the people's Hellas*
> *the red of shame*
> *on the marble cheeks of the caryatids*
> *not conceded even by chimerical night*
>
> *Resounding in the ears in secret silence from*
> *unprecedented shifts of the souls*
> *to the right, more to the right, to the extreme right*

to the hope inert, bog pool
to the hydra swamp of compromise
to the complacency of maggot-pink betrayal
not feeling even in Attica's light-eager day
the blush
in which withers the ensouled Greek marble's
eternal youth

Will not from the vast ruins of human nature
from the secret fissures of ruin
maybe stretch
into the distant day of the sons
no one rushes
like a sword to the left
have the cruel Moiras corrupt to the last enticed
the deed-greedy ace of Heraclidae

And he went –
desperationlovefuryfearjoy labyrinthine
in the sinuous passages of intertwining-clashing brain cells
time flows
from the left chamber of the heart of Ariadne's thread –
eyes wide open
with the stony stone of eternity
the caryatids grew amazed
at the birth of a legend
washing away the desecration with enflamed pride

When I saw
the alien flag
as a lash of a horsewhip
on the highest tower of the stronghold
it lashed me in the face

And I went
past
adopting the trick of indifference
past

on a thousand days
although my duty . . .

But no court condemned me
for this . . .

Must you
Manolis
now pay my ancient debt

What – do I not have a debt?
because you paid it for me
paid it for us all
and on account of everything
on account of the laws of Solon
of the wild rosemary chalice of Socrates
of the twelve columns rising like a fugue
against the silvery-blue sky
from Poseidon's temple at Cape Sunion
on account of breasts
Sappho's wondrous breasts
smelling of myrtle olives sun
turning the Mytilene nights into song

Manolis Manolis
it is so like you
smiling understandingly
from the Acropolis heights
of the deed
to forgive deedlessness

Yet I could not
forgive myself
we could not forgive ourselves
were we to pass by you
today whom the slow-witted executioners
still not realising
that you live in millions

300

condemn to death
to death
since
with gentle and bold hand
you swept away the blush of shame
from the caryatids' cheeks
from the anxious face
of the entire continent in chains
waiting for the call to arms

As I have already mentioned, I do not know when the poem was written. But everything depends on that fact. Almost everything. Locating it in the space between genius and mediocrity is not dependent on the date of its birth. Technically, it remains a draft by someone quite gifted. But as for the content of the poem, the position of the poet in relation to world events of the day, these do indeed depend on how and when it came into being. As, I suppose, is always the case. It is rare, however, for such dependence to be so patently obvious.

Let us imagine that Ullo wrote the poem immediately after hearing, shall we say, a BBC broadcast, thus becoming acquainted with Glezos's feat of daring. The poem would then be a spontaneous reaction – the earlier the reaction, the more ebullient – against the arbitrary power of the Germans over Greece and the whole of Europe. Written in the first week of September 1941, it would represent a general manifesto against the Germans, and as such would have to remain in the desk drawer in the Estonia of the day.

But what would it mean if Ullo finished the poem on, say, 31 May 1945? Or in 1946? Or in 1956? The fourth, fifth or fifteenth anniversary of Glezos's deed? When Hitler's Germany had been recently crushed, or on the other hand had collapsed long before, and an "Ariadne's thread" emerging from the left-hand chamber of the heart no longer showed the way into the underground of the swastika-clad labyrinth, but led to Glezos's ceremony of honour at the Kremlin in Moscow? The later the poem was written, the more one-sided its context, for instance 1963, when Glezos was awarded the Lenin Prize.

At whatever period in history Ullo wrote the stanzas, there are

301

inevitably lines among them where the erudite and literary surge of praise changes tack suddenly, becoming something simpler, more personal, more painful:

> *When I saw*
> *the alien flag*
> *as a lash of a horsewhip*
> *on the highest tower of the stronghold*
> *it lashed me in the face*
>
> *And I went*
> *past*
> *adopting the trick of indifference*
> *past*
> *on a thousand days*
> *although my duty . . .*

Do we need to ask, is it possible in Estonia ever to ask, what kind of flag is alien, and what is our own? When it was Ullo himself who had once told me (he'd seen it with his own eyes – presumably on 18 or 19 September 1944, and the agitation in his voice was still there when telling the story some fifteen or so years later): he had cycled up the incline on Kaarli Avenue in central Tallinn to about where the tennis courts stand opposite Kaarli Church. In full daylight, I would suppose, perhaps on his way home to Erbe Street. He glanced to his right and saw Tall Hermann Tower and saw the swastika'd flag sliding down the mast. And had stopped his bicycle in surprise. And had noticed a huddle of people around the foot of the tower and saw, with a lump in his throat, the blue, black and white flag being hoisted. And he also saw, some twenty paces nearer the church, a man wearing the sand-coloured uniform of an Estonian captain with four golden chevrons on his sleeve stop right in the middle of the carriageway, stand to attention and salute the flag, raising his hand up to his cap. And then he saw a *Sturmbannführer* in his greenish uniform approach the captain from behind, pull out his revolver, and fire. A shot rang out amid the Indian-ink silhouettes of the lime trees. And the *Sturmbannführer* put his revolver back in its holster as he strode crunch-crunch-crunch-crunch on the gravel in the direction of the church. The captain remained lying on the ground in the avenue.

Ullo set down his bicycle and ran over to the man. As he ran he thought he recognised his workmate Lieutenant Veski from Omakaitse headquarters, who had unexpectedly been promoted to captain. But no: this man was much younger and quite unknown to him, his mouth, with its narrow ginger boyish moustache, set in a crooked smile. His face was still warm, Ullo felt this as he turned the man's head. The captain's cap had fallen on to the sand. The sand was bloody under the captain's head, in the ribbon of the cap was a bullet hole, and there was a bullet hole in the man's neck.

Ullo told me what he was thinking: The *Sturmbannführer* is some fifteen paces away. If he were to look back he would see me bent over his victim and could shoot at me too, so I won't look, won't look, won't look to see if he's looking. I think God understood the situation – "You see what I mean: the blind revenge of the *Übermensch* at his flag being lowered, and another raised . . ."

I recounted: "And because someone saluted and someone was watching, his heart in his mouth – that was what you said about yourself, wasn't it – with your heart in your mouth?"

Ullo said: "At that moment – definitely."

Nor do I have my doubts: even though Ullo might have written the poem in profoundly Soviet times and stuck in a few "necessary" Red curlicues, these were only attached to give him, in theory at least, a chance of publishing the poem.

> *When I saw*
> *the alien flag*
> *as a lash of a horsewhip*
> *on the highest tower of the stronghold*
> *it lashed me in the face*

which should, in fact, have read:

> *When I saw*
> *alien flags*
> *as lashes of horsewhips*
> *on the highest tower of the stronghold*
> *they lashed me in the face*

I mentioned his theoretical chance of publication. Because in practice he was hardly likely to have even made any attempt to do so. And this was the case with every other line he ever wrote in his life, especially during the last forty years of it.

38

WHAT DID HE OCCUPY himself with all those forty years?

For at least the first thirty of them, with suitcases. Sometimes brown ones, sometimes grey ones, probably even black ones now and again, but in the main brown ones. They were made out of grey cardboard that had a striped pattern in relief, and which was delivered from the paper mill on Lasnamäe by lorry, then stacked up in slipshod piles in the factory storeroom. Till the sheets of cardboard were cut into suitably sized pieces and Ullo in his gas mask sprayed them a little brighter grey than they would have been by nature, or the odd one black, but chiefly brown, brown, brown. So Ullo even ended up writing a poem about them, a few lines from which I reproduce here:

> *Our suitcase grey-black-brownishness*
> *is a sure sign*
> *in which line*
> *red society is leading us . . .*

Ullo said: "Yes, yes. Now don't snigger, but even the paper suitcase linings which were stuck into them were on principle always patterned in pink. So could it be assumed that their colour on the outside was pure chance and quite lacking in ideological significance?"

The suitcases had nickel staples, nickel locks, and nickelled reinforcements made out of cheap brass. The fibreboard was chocolate coloured – the colour of faeces if you like.

Even if Ullo had only managed to make one suitcase a day, this would still have come to some 10,000 over those thirty years. But at the factory, they worked on the basis of some plan involving a division of labour, and they had a workforce of thirty: ten men and twenty women. Work started at eight thirty and lunch was from eleven thirty till twelve. The working day ended at four thirty. During the average working day, thirty people assembled some one hundred suitcases.

I asked Ullo once what sort of people worked there.

Ullo said: "All kinds of people passed through over the thirty years, but mostly incredibly ordinary. Not one of them with a whiff of mystery. Or the mystery was so well concealed, that . . ."

I asked: "As well concealed as in your case?"

He continued: "Just the odd one would get the gift of the gab when he'd had a few . . ."

I asked, rather astonished: "Did you take part in their drinking bouts?"

Ullo countered: "What do you mean by their drinking bouts? They didn't arrange any kind of regular drinking sessions. But I did go along, once in a while. Especially in the forties and in the early fifties, when I was still trying not to stick out too much . . ."

Any fears that their products might flood the market were entirely ludicrous. Because the market from Vilsandi to Vladivostok could easily have swallowed up the production of a hundred such suitcase factories. Even though few travelled to foreign destinations. Such travel only occurred in high and rarefied circles of society, and there was no real information on what kind of suitcases they used. But as for domestic travel, if people didn't exactly travel from Vilsandi to Vladivostok, they did go to Leningrad, to Moscow, and trips grew in number to, for instance, the Black Sea coast. So the suitcases made by Ullo and his colleagues were ever more in demand. Until – because Ullo and Maret did have a certain carefree spirit – they packed their own belongings into one of the factory's suitcases, an entirely new one and, *nota bene*, a light grey one, bought a train ticket and took themselves off, they too, to Adler or Sochi or some such place. They were not exactly short of money. As well as Ullo's wages as a suitcase maker, there was Maret's salary for teaching Estonian language at some secondary school. Maret didn't really spend money on anything much, and while Ullo did spend regular sums on his philatelic or philocartic or philomenic activities, this never amounted to one kopeck above a quarter of his salary. By putting aside a bit for a big summer holiday, they had managed to save enough within four or five years until, to their own surprise, the trip was actually granted in early April 1949, as far as I remember. And I'm not wrong about this dating, as I seem to remember Ullo was telling me about the trip (ten years afterwards) in the same breath as about the March deportations of that year.

"Because after the deportations all around us during the nights of 25 and 26 March, Maret couldn't get to sleep, even after taking a double dose of sleeping tablets. We decided a change of air might do her good. And it did, to a quite amazing extent . . ."

As far as I know, their 1949 holiday remained the only bout of mischief and luxury they ever indulged in, if it could be called that. It was like all trips to the Black Sea by ordinary people. Ullo and Maret did not even try to stay at an elite sanatorium, nestling among the breathtaking, if dusty, splendour of some princely, or at least aristocratic, stately home, where the guests received, thrice a day, pork or lamb cutlet with gravy made from lard and pepper, plus a mountain of macaroni (let me repeat: thrice a day, and on each occasion a glassful of smetana to go with it). Because to be accepted for those, they would have had to be put through the appropriate trade union sieve, and to remain in the sieve they would have had to exhibit an appropriate level of political correctness, something that Ullo would deride and Maret felt ashamed of.

So their spring was spent, as was common for lesser mortals, in some small private house on the edge of town and near the sea, in a poky little room which the host family had made available to them by moving themselves out, during the high season, into some little Wendy house or shed. As for board, they took care of that themselves. Ullo would light the fire in the stove with beech twigs and would bring in water from the well on the street corner. Maret would boil up chicken stock in an ancient saucepan dating back to Czarist times (*lend-lease* stock cubes were still on sale, at least in the Black Sea resorts). With the soup they would munch some pretty decent local *lavash* – which wasn't some type of French cow, as Ullo commented with a chuckle, but simply white bread or, rather, a kind of pancake. Or wallcake, to be more exact. As the things were baked in such a way that the lumps of dough were thrown up on to the walls of the oven and the bread was ready when it fell on to the oven floor. As Maret had seen done in the back room of the bread shop. To the chicken stock and *lavash* they would add cool and mild wine which the neighbour would bring in an earthenware jug. Then they would stroll the half a kilometre down to the beach. The sea was a dull blue in colour and cold, so that there was no question of anyone bathing, except for somewhere far off, where rowdy and vodka-soaked lads from the Kola Peninsula rushed in and out, in and out of the water, all the while criticising the Black Sea as being too tepid compared to what they were used to up north, and told tall stories about swimming in holes in the ice on the shores of the White Sea.

The beach itself was more or less deserted. Instead of sand, there was grey shingle and tamarisk bushes, among which it was warm enough in the spring sunshine. There were grey egg-shaped stones for the benefit of those lying on the shingle – to look at in their post-coital melancholy – and around them an endless variety of ovals and spirals drawn by the Lord on the pebbles with His white fingernail, hieroglyphics, from which an interpreter of such things could read the fate of the whole world. Ullo and Maret took some ten kilos of these pebbles with them when they left, and some of them even ended up in my desk drawer. What else was there for them to take back, at that time and from that place?

On the trip back they stopped in Yalta for a short while.

"Why Yalta?" I asked. "I would have understood if it had been Hersonesos . . ."

"Yalta is a very important spot."

"In what way?"

"From an Estonian point of view, you could say."

"How?"

"There, side by side, within the space of a few kilometres, are the best and the most revolting things Estonia has ever been given by Russia."

"Being?"

"Chekhov's house and the Livadia palace."

"Oh?"

"Well, Chekhov's house as well as Chekhovian tradition are an embodiment of Russian humanism. Sentimental I'll grant you, but at least it is the focal point of profoundly humanist values. And the Livadia palace – as a symbol for the conference in the Crimea. Where Stalin ultimately outwitted both Roosevelt and Churchill and turned them into his henchmen. It was one of the blackest deeds committed, in Eastern Europe at least. Also with regard to Estonia. So that . . ."

I very much wanted to return to that topic later, but it was not to be. As regards returning to topics, sometime during the 1980s he mentioned in passing that between his childhood trips and this one to the Black Sea, he had made one more, about which he had been silent for decades for good reason. In August 1939, three weeks before the Second World War broke out, he had been to Holland and probably England too. The administrative assistant to Prime Minister Eenpalu had gone to The Hague at the last possible moment, but not for reasons of state. After a gap of ten years (and, as he did not yet know, for the last time) he wanted to meet his father.

I also wanted to return to that topic with Ullo, especially after he had given me the freedom to use these conversations in a literary way, as I saw fit. But we never had the opportunity.

Ullo and Maret returned to Tallinn in the late spring of '49. Maret's health had improved so much that she could rely on the dose of sleeping tablets she had taken before the deportations. But she never got down below two tablets a night. She did make the attempt, but would only manage to sleep till half past three or four, and then thrash about until seven, her mind full of dreams until the time she had to get up. One such *idée fixe* was the following:

She has to go to a congress of Estonian-language teachers. She already knows what is to be decided there: to change the alphabet in which Estonian is written from Latin to Cyrillic. To turn the repugnant Cyrillic alphabet of the conquerors into something cosy, close to home and belonging to the Estonian people. To adopt the same alphabet as all brother nations. This much she already knows. But suddenly she can no longer remember where the congress is to take place. She can't remember whether it is to be held in the ruins of the Niguliste Church, of the Grand Marina cinema, or of the Estonia Theatre. So she wanders the streets of the shattered capital. Good Lord, by now they should have managed to clear away all those collapsed walls and masses of tangled iron standing outlined against the cold ashen sky, but there's more of it than ever. They should have managed to clear up all the ashes and cinders from the conflagration the city has undergone, but there's more now than in the days immediately after the fire. They could at least have swept away the snow so that the paths between the drifts weren't so hopelessly blocked. But the snow has been trodden into the streets and is now so mixed up with ash that the drifts, growing ever higher, are heavily streaked with grey as if semi-liquid concrete had been added. Maret just doesn't get through. In one-quarter nightmare mixed with three-quarters waking anxiety, she snuggles up as close to Ullo as she can. Through her angel curls streaked with grey she can feel the sharp chin of her husband and the stubble on his unshaven cheeks. She shudders lightly. Then the alarm clock wakes her with its jolting ring as happens every morning. It is a jolt that is both liberating and oppressive. The start to the day is a weft of pleasant and tolerable threads, by turns.

From day to day, the problems vary a little. Maret's life. And Ullo's: 30,000 suitcases, and his collections, among which are the model cannons. Slowly their third room has been taken over by them. Which can be interpreted – though it would be childish to put too much stock in the interpretation – as a threat to blow up the world. God only knows . . .

Thirty years and 30,000 suitcases. And then, some signs of poisoning, as I heard, I don't know what kind. Presumably it was from the acetylene which he inhaled in small doses, so it was imperative to change jobs. And at about the same time – or perhaps already before – one even more important change in their lives, which I only heard about later and didn't get to know much about even then: divorce.

After twenty years of marriage, Ullo and Maret got divorced. Why? Those observing never know the intimate details. Nor did I rush to ask. At least not from Maret. I heard about their divorce from mutual friends. It was the beginning of the sixties. During those times, I only bumped into them, Ullo and Maret, that is, on the odd occasion. Perhaps we had unconsciously been avoiding one another for eleven years, on account of various dangerous matters from our common past.

Perhaps half a year after I'd heard of their divorce, I met Maret on the street. I don't remember where exactly. Could it have been crossing that grassy space near the Baltic station where the statue to Kalinin stood for some twenty years? What I do remember very clearly is what Maret looked like and how she behaved.

She was wearing a bluish-grey outfit in a discreet check, with a hint of shoulder pads, which had been in fashion ten or more years before. And the flat heels of her blue chamois leather shoes were a trifle worn round the edges. Maret's head was uncovered on that sunny day in early spring – uncovered, and I noticed: I could no longer see the grey spirals in her long hair which used to curl down over her shoulders. And then I understood why. Not that she'd cut them off or dyed them. It was just that Maret's prematurely grey locks had blent into a larger mass of uniform grey.

There weren't many people on the footpath past Kalinin. Had there been, we would perhaps not have spotted one another in the crowd. Now we had seen one another from several dozen paces away and had recognised one another. I'm not sure what I looked like to her. She seemed to have grown older and even thinner. Her bright blue eyes looked out from even more darkly pigmented sockets than before, and her whole appearance was more pronounced – an alert sadness, a mild feeling of hurt, a proud apology.

We approached one another. We slackened our pace. I greeted her. She responded. Then some passer-by walked between us. We had, Maret and myself, turned some twenty degrees towards each other, foolishly, searchingly, expectantly. And I had time to think: like some figures in a *Glockenspiel* who stop only when the clock strikes, but even then never meet. I remember exactly how I hoped and feared that she knew very well what would force me to stop and speak to her – I hoped, because it was the natural thing to do. And feared? I feared she would no doubt try to convince me (that too being quite natural) that it was Ullo's fault that they had parted. I feared nodding to Maret's words and, yes, feared saying: Dear Maret, that I just cannot believe! Even though I knew Ullo well enough to suspect that Maret's accusation could ring true . . .

But by then we had passed one another and were moving off, she too, as I believe, in a mixture of embarrassment and relief.

Soon afterwards, Ullo gave up his job spraying sheets of cardboard on account of symptoms of poisoning, and moved to another: stapling the already painted cardboard to the frames. He still managed another 10,000 suitcases. Or even 20,000.

39

IT STILL TOOK HIM over a dozen, maybe fifteen, years to produce his 20,000 suitcases. In the early part of this new epoch, former schoolmates of mine said that Ullo had got himself a new woman. Oh yes? Which one? Or rather, what kind of woman?

"*O la laa!*" said former classmate Penn in the best nasal French drawl he could muster. I had known Penn at Wikman's. He was the son of a piano-maker and had finally ended up as a drama student. In June 1941 he was one of the first batch of 10,000 to be deported to Russia along with his parents who had died in the process. Penn himself had arrived back in Estonia about fifteen years later, at any rate after Stalin's death. He had worked as some sort of bast-shoe plaiter for an agricultural brigade in the Kirov oblast, a kolkhoz blacksmith in the same oblast, a copper miner in the labour camp in Karaganda, and a bassoon player in the Lutfi orchestra at the cultural centre in the town of Kokui. "Oh, there were all manner of *Luftmenschen* there apart from myself . . ." Once back in Estonia he had with him a certificate which proved that he had become ping-pong champion of the Kazakhstan SSR in 1954. I saw him for several years, over at his little workshop on the Tartu road, where he mended smoothing irons and electric razors and passed on the odd bit of information about the old boys from Wikman's. There was never anything indiscreet about what he said about them. The problems Wikman old boys had with their mistresses and wives always played a very modest part in anything Penn would tell, one could even say a minuscule part.

"Who's Ullo's new woman? Some young artist. That much I know. Done a few years at the institute. Now working for the window-dressing brigade for the Kaubamaja department store. What sort? Mmmmm . . ."

"And where d'you hear all that from?"

"Ah well, *quelle question*. From *Monsieur Oullo*, your one-time friend, when he came to me to have his iron fixed. It was a Siemens one, made of iron dating back to Hindenburg's time. Kept bringing it in every couple of weeks. Then comes the lady – clip-clop-clip-clop – smiles, pays and takes the thing home with her. You did ask me how I know . . ."

"But what's she like?"

"As I already said: mmmmm. Clear, or not?"

"Not really."

Penn clicked his tongue and raised his thumb. But I still didn't get any explanation as to what Ullo's new wife was like. I did meet them a few times over the next couple of years, on the street or at the theatre. I don't remember the occasion on which Ullo introduced us, but he certainly did do so. Ullo's wife, by local standards, was particularly dark-haired, with a pageboy-style haircut and large eyes. She was at least half Ullo's age who, by then, was approaching sixty, and she was stouter than Liza Minnelli, but with the strange intensity of that film star.

As I said, Ullo was almost sixty. When he had approached that age closely enough, he handed in his papers and, as he himself later told me, retired the week after his birthday, to devote his time completely to his collections. He went from one stamp or postcard collectors' gathering to the next and drove hard bargains with the predominantly old Russian or Jewish men, retired bookkeepers or pensioned-off majors, who were prominent at the time in the world of collecting. Or he would drop in at workshops, such as Penn's on the Tartu Road, to have the mahogany barrel for some mediaeval cannon bored out, or have the wheels for a gun carriage turned, to his exact specifications.

He lived in more than straitened financial circumstances during those times. His wife's salary as stage designer, plus his own pension, came to a total of maybe two hundred of the roubles of the day per month which, as people say, is a lot to die for but little to live on. Now and again he managed to do small deals on stamps or postcards, mostly good ones, since the dealer gene he had inherited from his father was still present in him. And these helped them along, although only in the short-term, small scale as they were.

Then one day he was made an unexpected proposal: to go out to work again. No, no, not as government adviser to Comrade Klauson, or as assistant to Bruno Saul. But not back to the suitcase factory either. I don't actually know whose idea it was and who approached him, nor is it really important. But an offer was made for him to become the head of the warehouse run by the Publishers' Committee. And this would still leave him on a full pension, something unusual for those times. Behind the offer was no doubt someone with an observant eye. This person, Ullo's proposer, must have looked beyond the seemingly total unsuitability of Ullo for the post. He must have seen Ullo's ability to be able to feel such solidarity with his four or five subordinates that they would desist from indulging in the usual habit among Soviet warehousemen of being light-fingered. They would follow the example of their rather daft boss, and his penchant for being hellishly pedantic. And one more of Ullo's qualities of which, as it turned out, I had up to then only had an inkling of. This was his extraordinary memory with regard to space and objects.

Why he wished to give up the relative independence of the pension he was now used to, and swallow the bait of the Publishers' Committee, is not hard to explain. As I said earlier, he actually kept his pension and what with the supplements he now received, he would be earning three times the standard pension, now taking home some four hundred roubles a month, to which his wife's salary was added. His responsibilities were, in his own eyes, minimal. And the other conditions of the job suited him fine. I did go and see him once at the warehouse, when he'd been working there for around a year. This must have been in the spring of '86. It was somewhere south of the Leningrad road, just before Lagedi.

It was an enclosure, about a hectare square, with a high fence round it, one part filled with some kind of building materials in piles and stacks, and in the other part stood three medium-sized hangar-like buildings with arched roofs. The building material – the breeze blocks, the bricks and the timber – was all stored here in neat stacks. Ullo explained that the committee intended to build a printing works plus two or three storehouses for books, that building material could, of course, be obtained under special permit issued in Moscow and in the meantime, all the material had to pass through Ullo's warehouse before being taken to the building site.

"Well," I said, "I see your stacks are quite a bit neater than those of other warehouses, but –"

"Not neat enough . . ." said Ullo. "I know that myself. But this is the only possible proportion of order and disorder that can be maintained around here. The only proportion, under prevailing circumstances."

"What do you mean by that?"

"I can't tolerate greater chaos. Our system can't tolerate greater order. Our system in the broadest sense of the word."

His three warehouses with their tin roofs and foam-rubber insulation were the pinnacle of warehouse organisation in Estonia at the time, not a peak standing out sharply against its surroundings, but at least a small area, almost a plateau, a summit compared to the rest. The warehouses had been bought from Finland and erected by Finns, and they stored a more refined type of construction material: glass, tiles, seventeen lavatory pans which were even made in Czechoslovakia, and so on. Plus rolls of printing paper, decorative paper, cardboard for book covers, paper for flyleaves, leather for book spines, printer's ink – even gold leaf. Of the various types of material which were supposed to be stored here, only half the types of stock were present, but still . . .

"How much is it all worth?" I asked.

"Mmm – about one and a half million roubles."

But at the southern end of the third warehouse Ullo's predecessor, clearly someone who liked his creature comforts, had had an office for the warehouse keeper erected. And I remember Ullo telling me that when he had come to have a look round before deciding whether to take the job, he had been taken first into this office. The only time I came here to visit him we went into that selfsame office.

"It's rather a small room," Ullo said. "Same then as it is now. Still a good writing desk. Good chairs. Even that copy of Wiiralt's *The Preacher* was on the wall then. A copy, of course, otherwise it would have disappeared by now. When I came for my interview, the snow had melted on the strip of lawn outside the window and three yellow crocuses were peeping up their heads towards the sun, though I saw them through the bars on the windows. But I didn't feel I was being imprisoned, as people like you would perhaps have done. I felt the bars protected you from the outside world. So I decided to take the post as warehouse keeper."

If I remember rightly, it was just after that little trip to beyond the suburb of Lasnamäe that I phoned Ullo and he came to our place and we made the arrangement for me to start noting down the story of his life ("I will, of course, give you my notes to look through, but to what purpose I'm not sure. You're not going to be making a scientific treatise out of them but I still ought to look over the factual details. If you do write anything, you'll be distilling the lot, turning it all into literature . . .").

During the summer months, Ullo would cycle to work and he used a kick-sled in winter. He would sit there for long evenings after work, getting no end of satisfaction out of what he was doing.

"Ullo, people have said that you wrote things in the evenings."

"Well, what if I did?"

"What kind of things?"

"Nothing at all. At least nothing to do with my life. That's your prerogative."

Later on, I heard that he would sometimes take along his Liza Minnelli and a bottle of rare Crimean or Greek wine to the little warehouse keeper's office. His bosses at the committee were said to be satisfied with him nonetheless. But eighteen months later, in the summer of 1987, Ullo suddenly resigned.

I heard about it some months later. Our conversations followed no regular pattern. After each three- to four-hour session we would arrange the next one. After the fifth session we decided that as I was now going away for the summer with my family, I would ring him when I got back to Tallinn that September.

That year, my wife and I stayed at our summer house near the Kassari Naze on Hiiumaa until early October. I had a deadline hanging over me, but the manuscript was only half finished. When we arrived back in Tallinn at the end of the first week in October, my work was still not quite rounded off. I of course had Ullo's next session at the back of my mind. I felt we still needed a further four or five sessions to finish the interviews – but there was no real hurry. What was pressing on my mind at the time was an article about the philosophy of heritage protection. There would be plenty of time later on for historical-cum-literary conversations with Ullo. As we always tend to think in such circumstances.

Someone in Tallinn then told me that Ullo had left his job at the warehouse one or two months before. I thought: At least now we'll have more time to get on with our interviews with no interruptions.

316

One sunny morning in early November, I stepped out on to the six-metre square balcony of my workroom in an attic in the Old Town, nestling among the steep tiled roofs. The maples in the yard were half bare by now and the wind had blown some of the rust-coloured leaves up on to the concrete floor of my balcony. I stood there a moment – and suddenly Ullo came sharply to mind, and the fact that I had not yet rung him. I thought: Perhaps he has come to mind just now because our last "interview" happened in June, precisely here, in two striped deckchairs . . . Then I heard through the open door: the phone was ringing. As I entered the room, I dislodged some maple leaves with the tip of my shoe and heard their dry rustle between two rings of the phone . . .

It was Ullo.

"I want to see you."

"Same here. Come over to my place."

"No."

"I'll come over to Erbe Street. What time would be convenient?"

"No."

"Ullo – what's wrong with you? I can hardly hear you. Where are you anyway?"

"In Seewald."

He answered instantly, without the slightest embarrassment, in a strangely emotionless voice. Entirely without the humour I would have expected of him. Because if he was where he said he was, this was likely to be no more than some game of self-protection.

"They say you've left your job. Are the two things connected, by any chance?"

"No. Ward Two. Room 76."

He put down the receiver. Or had it taken out of his hand. And I asked myself something which was quite feasible at the time: was the KGB behind this in some way? Quite likely it was. I don't know whether Ullo had ever supported the Estonian National Heritage movement – but a couple of weeks before, a meeting of the Heritage Club at Tarvastu had been banned. Banned to such an extent, in fact, that the empty and stubbly fields of wheat and rye with the tracks of combine harvesters, not to mention the fields of potatoes, had been suddenly swarming with "potato pickers" for two days wearing suspiciously new overalls and jackets. And the groves in the forest were full of "entomologists" who wandered with butterfly nets over their shoulders and automatic pistols in their pockets. So Ullo's unexpected sojourn at the Seewald Mental Hospital could very well have had something to do with the KGB.

I was there within half an hour. The grounds of the mental hospital were still almost idyllic, as when, more than forty years before, I had wandered through them for the first and last time – up to then – in the summer of 1943, to go and see the shrink Dr Viidiku who I had consulted about how to get out of being recruited for the SS *Leegion*. And after my visit he had conducted me on a brief guided tour of the wards. I wasn't shown the ones for the severe cases, so what I remembered of the place was not the boredom, greyness and torpor of the faces there, but the marked contrast between the freshness of the park and stuffy air of the wards and, most of all, the way the door handles were constructed so that you could use them but would be unable to cling to them . . .

Room 76 of Ward Two was, in the autumn of 1987, quite a civilised place for patients who had their own rooms. I thought to myself: his Minnelli must have arranged this for him. The staff were obviously quite kind to him there, which wasn't always the case in such hospitals during those times. Even the sister who took me to his room was pleasantly attentive and closed the door discreetly behind her.

Ullo was lounging on an iron bed, painted white. He was wearing a grey hospital shirt. He had pushed aside his flannelette blanket. He eyed me from an unrecognisably grey face, covered in slight beads of sweat. The window, barred of course, was wide open and the ward was the temperature of a November morning.

I said: "Listen, I'll just close the window . . ."

Ullo said: "Do. So we can have a talk."

I thought to myself: Another case of persecution mania. Another chap who thinks he's being observed. But the fact that it had happened to him of all people was quite unbelievable . . .

I shut the window. Ullo said: "You must open it again when you go. I don't want to incubate in here."

"OK." I sat down on the stool. "First things first. Why did you leave your job at the warehouse?"

"Boredom."

"And how did you end up in here?"

"I came here."

For some strange reason, Ullo had never been inside during Soviet times. So I could not tell whether he was parodying the phrase that had been used in Soviet prison documentation for decades. When a prisoner had to sign the statement that he had been brought by so-and-so to such-and-such a place he was persuaded to write *I came* instead of *I was brought*. But perhaps there was no hint of parody in Ullo's reply after all.

"And what's wrong with you?"

"Poisoning."

"What's your being here got to do with poisoning?"

"Poisoning causes psychic disturbances."

"What's been poisoning you?"

"The basic substance is acetylene."

"But that was twenty years ago! You used a mask while you worked, didn't you?"

"Without a mask I'd have been dead for twenty years."

"But twenty years have passed since you had any contact with acetylene."

"It's a cumulative poison. Which, under certain chemical conditions, explodes, so to speak."

"What do you mean by 'certain chemical conditions'?"

At that moment there was a knock at the door and the sister, the same brisk nurse who had escorted me, stepped inside. She was carrying a dish of some kind of porridge on a tray.

"No! No! No!" Ullo cried, almost in a rage. "Leave us in peace for a minute!" It was only after this cry and outburst of helpless rage that the scales fell from my eyes and I realised just how sick and weak he'd grown physically. The sister – they were used to it – smiled pleasantly and turned to me and said: "Try and persuade him. It can't go on like this. He's not eaten a thing for two weeks now. If he continues his hunger strike, we'll have to force-feed him. And that'll be unpleasant. Try and talk him round . . ."

Ullo motioned for the sister to leave and commanded: "Check that the door's properly shut."

When I had done so, and Ullo was reassured that the door was in fact shut, he suddenly made a rapid movement – pulled open the drawer in his bedside cupboard, whisked something out, it looked like an old blue school exercise book. He thrust it into my hand.

"Put it in your pocket!"

"What is it?" I folded the exercise book in two and pushed it into my inside pocket.

"My supplement – to your notes. To be read at home. And do what you want with."

I asked: "But listen, what did you mean when you said that the acetylene would explode under certain circumstances?"

He said in a whisper, evasive, yet trying to arouse interest: "Why the curiosity? Just a certain mixture of gases."

"Which gas do you have in mind?"

He said, still in a whisper, but with the ghost of a smile on his face for the first time during our conversation: "Futurium. Go now, if you will."

I rose from my stool and said: "OK then. Thank your doctor for making an exception for me. Next visitors' day is Friday. I'll come and see you then."

He motioned with his hand, or indicated the door, rather sluggishly I have to say. I did not understand the gesture, and thought that he was putting out his hand for me to shake – though we had never practised such niceties in all the fifty years of our acquaintance. I took his hand. It was alarmingly limp and strangely cold. And because of this – somehow wrong. And I understood: he had not meant this as a farewell handshake, simply a gesture . . .

Before I got the bus outside the hospital gates, I went into the main building and dropped into Dr Rohtla's office and asked him, with the privilege of an old friend of the family, what he could tell me about Ullo.

This freckled young man with his shock of tousled ginger hair and the nose of a weasel was, despite his innocent appearance, one of the greatest experts in his harsh field of medicine.

"Ullo Paerand . . . ? A most interesting case. His story about acetylene poisoning, which he will have told you too, is, of course, 95 per cent fantasy."

I asked: "Only 95 per cent . . . ?"

"Well," said the doctor, pouting his lips, "let's say 99 per cent then."

I asked: "But not quite one hundred?"

He hesitated. "You see, in medicine the boundaries between phenomena are rarely absolute."

I said: "And those between life and death?"

He parried: "Even those are rarely as clear as we would like to think. They aren't where we tend to locate them . . . Anyway, as I was saying, the acetylene tale is no doubt fantasy. But he has others too."

"For instance?"

"For instance? The white wall of his ward, there at the foot of the bed – at times he thinks it's a screen. Behind his head there is a projector which shines pictures on to the wall."

"What sort of pictures?"

"Radio waves, for instance. Some kind of signals. Sometimes people too. Once he had a conversation with Churchill."

I had to smile. "Churchill has been dead for twenty years . . ."

The doctor raised his pink hand: "So you see – that's how relative death can be . . ." and changed his tone of voice. "So the diagnosis in the case of your friend Ullo is some sort of schizophrenia. We're still working on it. But one thing's for sure: he's got a very weak heart."

That Friday I couldn't go to see Ullo. I can't recall what stopped me going. Was it something important, some appointment, some job I had to do, some other more important engagement – or was it simply the fear that I would have to pretend? Such pretence would arise the moment he started talking about the radio waves on his screen . . . Perhaps I felt this need to dissemble could grow exponentially and I would feel my inability to behave appropriately should I meet Ullo's wife at the hospital. The following Wednesday she phoned me. I didn't recognise the voice for all the sobbing until she said her name. Ullo had died the morning before. After his second heart attack.

I was shocked, as can easily be imagined, but there was more than that. I muttered my words of condolence, then asked hurriedly: When did he have his first heart attack? I had never heard anything about that one. His wife, God, now his widow, said in sobs that I wouldn't have heard about it because it had only come to light now, recently, when a cardiogram was made at the mental hospital.

Ullo's funeral took place in the usual invisible manner, at the old chapel in the Rahumäe cemetery. It was a secular burial where no one had anything personal or sensible to say, with an out-of-tune violin duo and a couple of dozen mourners in cheap grey clothes assembled around the coffin. And the mourners, more than I had expected, stood in the late-autumn sunshine at the Berends family grave surrounded by a moss-flecked wall, and Ullo was laid to rest – with a heap of blindingly yellow sand piled up between his mother's grave and his own.

Among those standing there were a number of Ullo's classmates from Wikman's whom I recognised despite their old men's faces, plus others, no doubt from the same school, whom I no longer recognised. In all likelihood, there were also people from the suitcase factory and the philately club, plus other collectors.

Ullo's wife was sad of course, but very brave with it. When candles had been lit and I again shook her hand at the graveside, she repaid my handshake with zeal and said, almost expressing her condolences to me: "Oh, I understand – you were such old friends . . ." which made me think shamefully enough: What do you understand – when I'm not even sure myself. But when she understood I was moving away from the grave in order to go back into town, she cried: "No, don't go now – come to the wake! It's just round the corner . . ."

And indeed it was, in a small restaurant, a hundred paces from the south gates of the cemetery. Everyone had, the men as well as the women, thought that late-autumn morning was going to be warmer than autumn days can prove to be. We were now all feeling the cold after standing by the grave, and all those who drank spirits shivered during their first glass, but gradually shook off their numbness. Including me and another mourner who ended up sitting next to me at the same table.

He was quite a bit younger than both Ullo and myself, and belonged to that group of mourners I had not known before. But when the first glass had been raised, we soon overcame our diffidence.

This was a smallish man in his forties, rather nondescript at first glance. I have forgotten his name but I remember my first impression of him: both his head and his face were somehow round and smooth, as if turned on a lathe. But made out of particularly gnarled wood. His small tediously grey eyes suddenly livened up. And his enunciation was unexpectedly coherent. He had been a colleague of Ullo's at his last place of work, not in the building materials warehouse itself, but on the board of the committee. I did not quite grasp what his own post there was. But he gave a summary of Ullo's activities with regard to the committee.

322

Tensions arise between the older and younger generation in any society. Those who cannot find anything better to talk about tend to trumpet abroad these tensions, calling them conflicts. Conflicts do arise, but in nine cases out of ten the conflict is normal organic tension. Which may be stronger in a certain time and place than at other times elsewhere. For us here on the eastern shores of the Baltic Sea such tensions are very much in evidence right now. Because the boundary of biological age tends to coincide at present with the borders of our ways of thinking and upbringing: on the one hand, those who have personal experience of a lost world and, on the other, those whose corresponding lobe of the brain rings empty. But to talk or write about a specifically local conflict between generations is no more than a silly-season tale to fill column inches.

For the older generation, the way youth treats us – with an inferiority complex – is expressed either as superiority or, depending on the type of person – as servility. One of these attitudes always dominates. The more intelligent the balance, the more unassumingly and veiled the attitudes.

My neighbour at Ullo's wake was undoubtedly a very intelligent man. So his slight servility to Ullo and his generation should thus be borne in mind. All the more so, given the location where our conversation took place – as with funeral talk anywhere. After my third glass I ventured to ask whether he knew anything about why Ullo had left his job. And he explained in an instant. It stands to reason. A scandal led to his dismissal. A smallish one, but such as came to the ears of the committee. At least at a particular level of seniority there.

My neighbour said: "Look, even I don't know what shape the books were in when Ullo took on the job . . ." And I thought with growing unease: *Et tu, Brute?* Were you, Ullo, also involved in some shady business dealings?

He continued: "At any rate, he'd taken over the warehouse according to the rules. And his bosses grew more pleased with him as the months went by. Until, about a year later I think, there was some dispute with some trade delegate about materials. The committee phoned him up at the warehouse and asked how many cans of, let's say, white lead paint there were in stock according to the warehouse books. And he replied: 1,411 kilograms. When the committee came to check, it turned out that there were indeed 1,411 kilos of white lead paint in stock, but the entry had gone missing from the card index. Actually, it wasn't missing from the card index. Because there was no card index for it to be to be missing from. It emerged that Comrade Paerand had not made an inventory at all."

At that point, someone from diagonally across the table interrupted our conversation. It turned out to be another person who had worked for the committee and who wanted to correct what my neighbour had just told me. "Listen, there was, of course, a kind of inventory in Paerand's diary." But my neighbour was adamant: "No, there wasn't! There simply wasn't! I was especially interested in that whole business. I mean, he had an inventory in some filing cabinet or other – but this was only the old inventory, with entries up to when he'd been taken on. But from that time onwards, he never added a thing. So all the movements of goods were noted only in Paerand's head. There was a hell of a to-do. The chairman said that they should have Paerand arrested. Then they started checking how much had been stolen. At length, it turned out that every nail, so to speak, was where it should have been, every last item. Every gram of material was there. Everything. Even down to the last sheet of gold leaf. So the chairman had Paerand summoned. I was present during the conversation. The chairman said severely – and we all know what a pain he could be – 'Listen here, Paerand, what the hell have you been getting up to?' He had the inspector bring up the old inventory cards and place them on his desk under Paerand's nose. 'I could not believe my eyes – for the past eighteen months you've made no entries at all! What is the meaning of this?' But he, the late Paerand . . ." said my neighbour at the table enthusiastically, his eyes shining, ". . . came back with an explanation instantly. There simply aren't people like that left in our generation. He asked: 'But what do you need an inventory for?' Who, of our generation, would put a question like that? Paerand answered his own question: 'To keep some kind of check on the correspondence between the numbers on paper and reality. But what do they guarantee?' He stretched out his hand and pulled a greyish card from one box, glanced at it, tore it in four and placed the pieces in his pocket: 'Well, what do these figures correspond to? One hundred and seventy-seven kilos of maroon synthetic leather, left over after binding copies of Comrade Gorbachev's speeches – swish, gone! It's in the warehouse all right – but not here! And how can you effect that sleight

324

of hand? With one rapid flick of the palm! One act of petty hooliganism. But if the information is stored not in a filing cabinet, but in the warehouse keeper's head, you would have to commit murder to erase the record. So in this way your materials would in effect be better safeguarded.' He smiled, showing his long teeth. 'But – to avoid tempting you . . .' And he placed his letter of resignation on the chairman's desk. And I say again: our steam-rollered generation no longer has anybody of his ilk!"

40

Now all there is left to say is a word or two about that blue exercise book with its cross-ruled paper, which he pushed into my hand during my last visit. Several pages of small neat handwriting in ink. Now the paper is slightly yellowed, the ink slightly faded.

I did, of course, read it through immediately, and again after Ullo's funeral. Then it got mixed up with my papers and, I have to admit, fell into oblivion. When I got the idea of writing this story of Ullo Paerand's life some seven or eight years later, I gathered together all the things I had in various drawers about him, and it was then that the blue exercise book came to light again. I felt its contents should be published with the rest of his story. At first, I thought that Ullo's own text would require my commentary over and above the explanation as to how it fell into my hands; I owed the reader a guide as to how to interpret Ullo's text – in as much as I myself understood it. But at length I dropped the idea. For what could I have added apart from an interpretation which would remain just that – and which would by its very nature be nothing more than an attempt to pump into my readers' heads the interpretation I myself preferred? Do I have the right to do so? No, in the case of Ullo's own text which follows here, I will refrain from such commentary. Here goes:

At first, I thought it might be some painting by Maurice de Vlaminck. I must have seen a number during my childhood, but only very vague memories remain. About the man himself, Vlaminck that is, I really know nothing at all. Because we simply don't have his book of memoirs, *Tournant dangereux*. So I don't know whether this is a dangerous bend in the river, a dangerous manoeuvre or a dangerous veer.

The picture before me does not depict the bend in a river, more the mouth of a river, if it's a river at all, but perhaps it's a sea bay. Water flowing from left to right maybe, spreading out to the right into the sea which is out of the picture, or a bay, from right to left, penetrating the land and narrowing into a bay, where the neck of the river is off picture to the left. The water, whether sea water or river water, is mainly a yellowish grey with light blue patches and completely smooth, as if painted so that viewed from the left it seems that its surface is lightly coated veneer (which is indeed perhaps what it is), but viewed from the right, the deception is complete: the water is not only wet, but moving, alive. So you can clearly imagine the figure walking down through the grassy bank and over the fathom-wide sand, and over the foot-wide strip of shingle into the water, ever deeper, gradually taking on the shape of a human being.

But I do not leave the slope of the bank. Instead, I stay on the path and look around me diffidently.

Across the river or bay, maybe some 150 metres in width, there is a greyish-white bank, similar to the one here, with white, grey, yellow houses on the decline. These are mainly low, with attic roofs. This is clearly a settlement, or the outskirts of some town, whose habitation becomes more dense to the left. I walk along the ridge of the bank towards the neck of the bay – or upriver – then the trees begin to meet me. All deciduous, as far as I can make out. Tall, without branches lower down, gnarled, with trunks which look as if they come from southern landscapes, not from here, and with crowns that have spread rather than grown upwards. And which have something Japanese about them. There, in the shade of these odd trees, is something very much in keeping with home: a white park bench.

Exactly the same park bench that used to stand under the trees on Kaarli Avenue. I hasten my step, almost run towards the familiar park bench, across the puddles in the sand of the way – it has rained in the night – across a glittering pool of blood in among the puddles, into an earlier epoch – and sit down on the bench.

The morning river – or sea – sparkles between the trees. I sit there and feel – or think that I feel, of course I only imagine that I feel – the park bench is still wet from the night rain. My bottom and back can feel the moist chill through my trousers and shirt. My feet in their thin slippers have become wet from the puddles on the avenue but not from the pool of blood which glitters there. That I have managed to avoid. I know whose blood it is. But I can't quite remember. I sit there and wait.

For what? For whom? Ah yes, for Grandmother, who will come out of church and take a seat next to me. We used to sit there on the odd occasion. In 1922. When I was six. The stout Mrs Trimbek with her eyes as blue as the heavens who was supposed to have spoken to Koidula in her young years. And who told me earlier than other people of the Dog Snouts. Now she no longer speaks about them. Because now we know more than enough about them. Grandmother Trimbek and me.

I sit under the strange trees, feeling at home in this strange place on my familiar park bench. And, of course, Grandmother doesn't arrive. But good Lord – here she comes!

There in front, between the river bank or sea shore and the park, below the deciduous trees with their silhouettes like pines, stand houses. At first, I didn't really pay any attention to them. But there they are against the glittering background of the river or sea, among the trees with their broad crowns. At the edge of the avenue there are three sets of gates, three wicket gates with white stone gateposts. Through those furthest from the avenue, though they are not that far away, Grandmother is coming. But not walking, she is being brought, in a wheelchair with nickelled spoked wheels. But it's her all right. In her black hat and coat, a little hunched, but still sitting somehow straight. And stout and stumpy as I remember her. The wheelchair turns towards me and draws nearer. I cannot see who is pushing the wheelchair. This tall, bony man could almost be my brother. My twin brother. If I'd had one.

The wheelchair approaches. I watch it with no surprise. Not even at the fact that I don't rush over to Grandmother. Nor at the fact that she clearly doesn't recognise me. But how could she, having been dead for nearly forty years? Nor do I show surprise at the fact that the nearer she comes, the less familiar she grows. The more her face disappears into shadow, from above into her black hat and from below into her white shawl.

And then – but this is no surprise to me either – the wheelchair has come up to the bench where I am sitting, and my twin brother lifts that person I still to an extent regard as being my grandmother out of her wheelchair and seats her on the park bench. I think to myself: What does it matter? No escaping now. But I move slightly away from my bench neighbour nonetheless. Not much room for me to do so at my end of the bench. Nor do I want to make my neighbour notice my retreat – and I think instantly: I'm not sure this is because I still think of her as my grandmother or because to a certain extent she no longer is . . .

And suddenly I understand: this figure there on the bench, a couple of paces away, this indolent yet rather stiffish old woman – is in fact a humpbacked old man! His headgear which I first thought to be a soft velvet cap is – and how could I not have seen it right from the start – a shiny round, starched hat, and under his double chins at the neck of a raglan coat a strip of white collar can be seen and the wings of a black bow tie winking at me. The old man has screwed up his eyes, now squeezed between his thin eyebrows and the bags under his eyes. So I cannot see his eyes (or, rather, the eye on my side of him) but I seem to see a curious glitter there. The old man's nose is, at any rate, too ridiculously snub to be considered dignified and his wide mouth under it seems all the more tense, his lower lip curled. And this gives his round, immobile and obtuse face something you have to take seriously.

The weather is chilly, but it is clearly early spring and the clothes the old man is wearing, especially in this sunny park, are somewhat odd. He is totally unknown to me. But I hardly have time to accommodate this strangeness when I am already asking myself: isn't there, despite his strange appearance, something familiar about him? And more than just a little?

After this revelation I am of course struck dumb (as one is in dreams) but only because I am stifling a cry: this is none other than my long-lost father!

The smallish, almost slim and certainly very spry man as he was has, over the forty years, become unrecognisably fat. And the air of a master of bankruptcies and deals, which was his eternal aura for many, has forced him to come to terms with his especially authoritative behaviour . . . I know that I cannot know this, but I am sure of it. I am sure of it, and decide: if I'm now here and he's sat

329

down on the same bench as myself, I ought at least to give him a sign . . .

I open my mouth, but he beats me to it. He is well over eighty, but still beats me to it. The corner of his mouth forms an ironic smile as he turns towards me and says: "I see that you have come, young man, from there – from far up north? Or the north-east, to be more precise? From behind the Iron Curtain? And you harbour strong prejudices towards us?"

He doesn't recognise me. And how could he, since he has never seen me since I was a boy? For the last time – forty years ago, and only those few hours – in The Hague, in Ipswich, I no longer remember where it was.

I say: "It wasn't me who drew the curtain between us. It isn't a curtain anyway, but a wall. A wall of indifference, sir. I did not build that wall." (After forty years, I didn't feel we could be on first-name terms.) "You yourself built that wall, sir, when you abandoned us on the other side in cold blood! Me, my mother, all of us . . ."

He raises his puffy pinkish paws as if to ward off something. "My dear young man – not us. But the history of Europe! The history of the world!"

I say: "Don't use history as an excuse! It wasn't history, it was *you*! Your ruthless business affairs! Your treacherous connections!"

I notice that I am actually shouting at him: "You – you – Father – you betrayed us . . ." I shout at him: "Father! You never used to drink! Never used to smoke! At least throw away that slobbery cigar! Throw away that whisky! You think I don't know that you're hiding it in the chamber pot under your wheelchair! Throw the whole lot away into the sea or the river, whichever it may be! Then we can go on together. And if you've had children over here too – my half-brothers, my half-sisters – maybe I've seen them – call them over – and admit your guilt to them, your guilt, your guilt, Dad – then we can make peace . . ."

He remains silent. He looks at me scornfully. I wake up with a start. Out of one dream into another. He's not there. Yesterday's gone too. The white park bench is empty. But the dream's oppression remains.

*

You finish it, if you can. I can't. I always leave everything ridiculously half finished.

I know that you will immediately start talking about the swerves of conflict between fathers and sons. And about the human injustice that inevitably rises from it. About the corrosive poison of disappointment which eats away at the clarity of the picture – God knows. Maybe old father Berends really is more or less innocent of our degradation. And Roosevelt was guilty of everything. Yes. You know, I heard that somewhere recently, just before I ended up in the madhouse. They were supposed to know already in the USA that Roosevelt must have suggested that America could support the spread of socialism in India to Stalin, even before Teheran. Even despotic, enlightened socialism was more acceptable than the feudal imperialism of the British which was so widespread out there . . .

Well, if it was like that, there's nothing more to be said about Estonia and Eastern Europe!

But may God be praised, I do know one thing: I need no longer weigh up these matters on a pharmacist's scales. Now it's up to you!

And yet – which court has ever freed any of us from this responsibility . . . ?

LIST OF POLITICIANS AND CULTURAL FIGURES

There follows a list of (mostly Estonian) politicians and cultural figures referred to in the novel. The chapters in which they appear are noted at the end of each entry.

Johannes Aavik (1880–1973) was the most influential renewer of the Estonian language. He introduced a whole range of neologisms, many based on Finnish, and reduced the number of Germanised grammatical features. Originally from the western island of Saaremaa, he was educated in the Ukraine, Finland and at Tartu University. He fled to Sweden in 1944, and continued his linguistic research there, while many of his exiled compatriots ended up working in factories and forestry. [Chapters 9, 12 and 15]

Aleksander Aberg (1881–1920), Estonian wrestler. Won the world championship in London in 1904. [Chapter 14]

Adamson-Eric (1902–1968), painter, sculptor and applied artist. There is a museum devoted to his work in Tallinn. [Chapter 20]

Alexander Alekhine (1892–1946), Russian world-champion chess player 1927–35 and 1937–46. A memorial championship was named after him. [Chapter 19]

Betti Alver (1906–1989), poet whose neoclassicism has been compared to that of T. S. Eliot. She published the collection of poems *Tolm ja tuli* (*Dust and Fire*) in 1936, but became a persona non grata after her husband Heiti Talvik was sent to Siberia, and she was banned from publication for the rest of the 1940s, and the 1950s. She returned to literature in the 1960s when her translation of Pushkin's *Yevgeni Onegin* appeared and she enjoyed a revival as a poet, now in a more personal style, during the 1970s and 1980s. [Chapters 15, 20 and 29]

Ado Anderkopp (1894–1941), journalist, sports organiser and minister under Päts. [Chapter 17]

Peet Aren (1889–1970), a painter who studied in St Petersburg and initially adopted Russian Impressionism, moving on to painting stylised Expressionist landscapes and city views. Fled to Germany in 1944, and from there to New York in 1949, where he remained. [Chapter 28]

Barbarus, real name **Johannes Vares** (1890–1946), is better known under his pen name. He is perhaps the most colourful real-life figure in the novel and was, at various times in his life, a poet, dandy, doctor and prime minister. Barbarus studied medicine, qualifying in 1917 and practising as a general practitioner in Pärnu from 1921 to 1939. He was drawn to socialism and the international Clarté movement of committed left-wing writers, whose ideas he tried to introduce in Estonia. He became a member of Estonian PEN in 1927. When Estonia was occupied for the first time by the Soviet Union in 1940, the leading member of Stalin's politburo, Andrei Zhdanov (see below), proposed that Barbarus be made (puppet) prime minister of an Estonia now totally under the control of the Soviet authorities. When the Germans invaded in 1941, Barbarus was evacuated to Russia, returning to what was once again Soviet Estonia in 1945. Disillusioned by now with the Soviet system, he committed suicide the following year. Barbarus's poetry is full of grand gestures and was influenced by French Modernism, which is hard to square with his activities as a propagandistic Soviet poet during World War II. Barbarus's collection *Kalad kuival* (*Drying Fish*) is regarded as one of his best achievements, containing a blend of allegory and empathy. [Chapters 16, 20 and 25]

José-Raúl Capablanca (1888–1942), Cuban-born chess master. World champion from 1921 to 1927. [Chapter 19]

Kaarel Eenpalu (1888–1942) was born Karl Einbund, but changed his name when it became chic to Estify it (cf. Ullo Paerand himself, the former Ulrich Berends). He was Estonian prime minister in 1938–9 and died in Soviet captivity in 1942. [Chapters 14, 21–4, 31 and 38]

Rutt Eliaser (1914–1996), writer of Siberia memoirs entitled *Eight Careers*. Originally trained as a lawyer, she was arrested and sent to Tomsk, Russia, in 1941, returned to Estonia and worked as a teacher, only to be rearrested in the March deportations in 1949 and sent to Krasnoyarsk. She worked in a brickworks, sovkhoz, factory, hospital, as a factory inspector and as a publisher's proofreader, finally emigrating to Sweden in 1977. [Chapter 27]

Salo Flohr (1908–1983), Czech chess grandmaster. Orphaned in World War I, he became a Soviet citizen in 1942 following the annexation of Czechoslovakia by Germany some years previously. [Chapter 19]

August Gailit (1891–1960) wrote novels tinged with grotesque fantasy and eroticism. He was initially a sarcastic cynic and wrote a Spenglerian vision of decline in the 1920s. However, after his escape to Sweden in 1944 he wrote with nostalgia about the tragedy of losing one's homeland. [Chapter 27]

Gori (1894-1944), real name Georg Tõnisson, was the leading Estonian cartoonist and caricaturist of the 1930s. A prisoner of war of the Germans during World War I, he spent some time in a German concentration camp during World War II. [Chapters 26 and 31]

Alexander Jaakson (1892–1942), a veteran of the Estonian War of Independence, became Minister of Education under Päts and tried to instil a militaristic spirit in schools. Jaakson was arrested during the Soviet occupation in 1940 and died in Russia in 1942. [Chapter 24]

Johannes Jakobson (b. 1921), a leading Estonian Communist Party propagandist. [Chapter 26]

August Jansen (1881–1957), Estonian painter. [Chapter 24]

Mikhail Kalinin (1875-1946), Soviet Communist Party leader. The statue referred to when the narrator passes Maret used to stand in the grassy space between the city wall and the Baltic station in Tallinn. Kalinin's wife was born in Estonia. [Chapter 38]

Aino Kallas (1878–1956) née Krohn, was a Finnish short-story writer, born in Viborg. She married the Estonian diplomat Oskar Kallas and they lived in London together from 1922 to 1934, spending their summers on the Estonian island of Hiiumaa where Kallas wrote most of her stories, many of which are set in Estonia. [Chapter 15]

Bernard Kangro (1910–1994), poet, novelist and publisher, was at Tartu University the decade before Kross. Fleeing Estonia in 1944, he lived the rest of his life in Lund, southern Sweden, where he set up the exile Estonian Writers' Cooperative which published a great many Estonian books between 1951 and 1991. Jaan Kross edited a selected edition of his poems in 1966. [Chapter 26]

Sten Karling (1906–1987), Swedish art historian who produced a book about Narva several years before the city was destroyed by bombing in 1944. [Chapter 24]

Raimond Kaugver (1926-1992) was one of the most popular writers in Estonia during Soviet times. Fleeing to Finland in 1943, Kaugver returned to Estonia the following year and spent a further five years as a political prisoner in a Soviet labour camp in Vorkuta. He then worked as a tram driver until he became a professional writer in 1961. He tackled the controversial and complex subject of Estonians fighting for the wrong side and ending up in labour camps in his book *Forty Candles* (1966). *Letters from the Camps* was published in 1989. [Chapter 33]

Paul Keres (1916–1975) was an Estonian chess champion of international stature, first representing Estonia, later the Soviet Union. Keres tried, but failed, to flee to Sweden with his family in 1944. [Chapter 19]

August Kirhenšteins (1872–1963), Latvian microbiologist and leading Communist Party official in the Latvian Soviet Socialist Republic between 1940 and 1952. [Chapter 20]

Valter Klauson (1914–1988) was a motor transport expert, and a "Yestonian" (see Introduction). He was chairman of the Council of Ministers of the Estonian Soviet Socialist Republic from 1961 to 1984. [Chapters 21 and 39]

Lydia Koidula (1843-1886) was one of the first major poets to write in the Estonian language. She was brought up in Pärnu and attended the German girls' school there. She later moved to Tartu and became known as the "Nightingale of the River Emajõgi", the river flowing through that university town. Daughter of one of the first newspaper editors in Estonia, Johan Voldemar Jannsen, she married a Germanised Latvian doctor who took her to the Kronstadt garrison on the island off St Petersburg where he had obtained a post, a move which proved disastrous for her health and creativity. Several of her more patriotic poems have been set to music. In 1972, Kross published a novella, *An Hour in a Swivel Chair*, which mentions Koidula and her father, while mostly dealing with the exploits of her brother. [Chapter 2]

Johan Kõpp (1874–1970), theologist, historian, educationalist and Vice-Chancellor of Tartu University from 1928 to 1937. Fled to Sweden in 1944.

Karl Kortelainen (b. 1930), Communist official and head of the Estonian KGB in the 1980s. [Chapter 26]

Hans Kruus (1891–1976), historian and political activist. Kruus joined the Communist Party in 1940 during the first Soviet occupation but was accused of "bourgeois nationalism" and spent the early 1950s in prison. [Chapter 27]

Boris Kumm (1897–1958) was head of the Estonian KGB during the 1940s. [Chapter 26]

Johan Laidoner (1884-1953), Estonian Chief of Staff from 1934 to 1940 and chairman of the Estonian Olympic Committee during those same years. Educated at military academies in Wilno and St Petersburg, he chaired a League of Nations commission in 1925, appointed to establish the borders of Iraq. Laidoner died in Soviet captivity. [Chapters 2, 4, 17 and 24]

Ants Laikmaa (1866–1942) was born Hans Laipman and educated in Germany during the 1890s. He had better reason than many to Estify his German name, since "laip" means "corpse" in Estonian. He travelled all over Western Europe and for a while lived on Capri and in Tunisia. [Chapter 10]

Heinrich Laretei (1892–1973), artillery officer in the War of Independence. Estonian Ambassador in Sweden 1936–1940. Refused to return to Estonia after the Soviet takeover. His daughter Käbi Laretei is a well-known Swedish pianist and was once married to film director Ingmar Bergman. [Chapter 30]

Andres Larka (1879–?), Minister of War in the Provisional Government in 1918, he was imprisoned by Päts twice in the 1930s on account of his Vapsid connections (see Introduction). He was arrested in 1940 and died in captivity. [Chapter 24]

Johannes Lauristin (1899-1941) was an erstwhile revolutionary who died aboard ship as the Communists were being evacuated from Tallinn. His widow Olga (b. 1903), also a revolutionary, was head of the Estonian branch of the Glavlit Soviet censorship apparatus for a short while. [Chapter 21]

Kalju Lepik (1920–1999), whose short poem 'The Painter' appears in

337

Chapter 9, was one of the most important Estonian exile poets. After studying business, archaeology and Mediterranean history, he was drafted into the German army. He fled to Sweden in 1944, where he worked in a hospital kitchen, a radio factory and as bookkeeper in the Swedish Central Bureau for Statistics. His daughter now heads the chancellery of the Estonian government. [Chapter 9]

Bernard Linde (1886-1954) was a scholar, essayist, theatre critic, translator, journalist and a prodigious traveller. In 1916–17 he served in the Czarist army in Minsk and Wilno, moving to Siberia in 1918, then travelling the following year via Japan, China, India, Egypt and Great Britain back to Estonia. He was variously editor and head of a publishing house. During the twenties and thirties he visited many countries in central Europe while working as a freelance journalist. He also wrote biographies of Balzac and of the Czech statesmen Masaryk and Beneš. Linde was arrested in 1951 and after his return from the labour camps three years later, his health broken, he died that same year. [Chapter 27]

Karl-Sigismund Litzmann (1893–1945) German Commissar-General for Estonia during the German occupation of 1941–1944. His surname, if not his actions, caused much hilarity among Estonians, since "lits" is the Estonian for "whore". [Chapter 26]

Georg Lurich (1876–1920), champion Estonian wrestler and weightlifter, competed in Western Europe and the USA. [Chapter 14]

Oskar Luts (1887–1953) was the popular author of a series of novels, *Spring* and its sequels, in which the same main character Joosep Toots appears. [Chapter 21]

Helmut Maandi (1906–1990) was the only member of the Estonian National Committee (Eesti Vabariigi Rahvuskomitee) to succeed in fleeing to Sweden in 1944, where he published his memoirs.

Uku Masing (1909–1985), a theologist, was Estonia's major religious poet. His poetry is rich in references to Eastern religions. He was a prodigious linguist and during the 1930s learnt Arabic and produced a grammar of ancient Hebrew. During Soviet times he had difficulty making a living on account of his avowedly Lutheran views. [Chapter 15]

Hjalmar Mäe (1901–1978) was the Estonian Quisling during World

338

War II. His official title was Erster Landesdirector of Estonia during the German occupation, and he also held the post of Minister of Education. Dr Mäe had studied in Austria, became a schoolmaster, and took part in an attempt by the Vapsid (see Introduction) to stage a *coup d'état* in 1935. He was sentenced to twenty years hard labour, but was then freed in an amnesty in 1938. Mäe lived in Austria after World War II. "Mäe's Tears" refers to a type of spirits and Jaan Kross puns on this coincidence of names. [Chapter 28]

August Mälk (1900–1987), novelist and playwright. His story "Gifts from the Sea" describes life in a fishing village. Mälk fled to Sweden in 1944. [Chapter 27]

Kirill Meretskov (1897–1968), Soviet Chief of Staff. Member of the Communist Party from 1917. Fought in the Spanish Civil War and wrote about the annexation of Estonia in his memoirs. [Chapter 24]

Kersti Merilaas (1913–1986), poet and translator of poetry and drama from German, French, English and Russian. She was married to the poet August Sang. Her collection *Maantee tuuled* (*Winds on the Highway*) touches upon contemporary social themes. [Chapter 20]

Mait Metsanurk (1879–1957) was the pseudonym of Eduard Hubel, novelist and playwright. Metsanurk wrote most of his novels and plays between 1910 and 1930, including *The Unmarked Grave* (1926) which is written in the form of diaries by a revolutionary who has gone underground, and deals with vacillation and the conflict of ideas. [Chapter 6]

Roman Nyman (1881–1951), Estonian painter and set designer. [Chapter 24]

Ants Oras (1900–1982) studied English literature at Tartu, Leipzig and Oxford universities and was a professor at Tartu University from 1934 to 1943. He escaped to Sweden and taught from 1945 to 1949 at Cambridge University. From 1949 to 1972 he was Professor of English Literature at Gainesville, Florida, where he died. His interests included the poetry of T. S. Eliot. He started translating at the age of fifteen and translated works by Poe, Pushkin, Heine, Bernard Shaw, Virgil, Shakespeare and Goethe into Estonian. He also translated various Estonian poets into English and German. [Chapters 15 and 27]

Justas Paleckis (1899–?), Lithuanian writer and leading Communist Party official in the Lithuanian Soviet Socialist Republic between 1940 and 1971. [Chapter 20]

Konstantin Päts (1874–1956) was the most powerful Estonian politician during the troubled 1930s. During those years, Päts's autocratic rule as Riigivanem, State Elder, the equivalent of premier or president, was similar to, though milder than, that of Ulmanis in Latvia, Smetona in Lithuania, and Piłsudski in Poland. Päts died in Soviet captivity in the Kalinin oblast of Russia, and his remains were reburied in Tallinn in 1990. [Chapters 21, 23 and 29]

Friedrich Paulus (1890–1957), Field Marshal and commander of the German army during the siege of Stalingrad in November 1942. [Chapter 28]

Kristjan Jaak Peterson (1801–1822) was the first ethnic Estonian to write contemporary poetry, mainly modelled on Klopstock and Herder. Although he was known for having written poems in German, his Estonian poems were not rediscovered until some eighty years after his death. He was educated in Riga and Tartu and also translated *Mythologica Fennica* from Swedish into German. In 1975, Kross published a short novel *The Meteor* which deals with the life and times of Peterson. [Chapter 16]

Johan Pitka (1874–1944) was a sailor and then a naval officer. During the Estonian War of Independence in 1918 he led naval operations as a rear admiral. He lived in Canada between 1924 and 1930, and founded the Estonian Cooperative Movement on his return home. He fled abroad once more in 1940, this time to Finland, where he hoped to coordinate the Estonian struggle for freedom. Returning to his native land in the fateful year 1944, he fell defending Tallinn and environs against the advancing Red Army. [Chapter 34]

August Pork (b. 1917), "Yestonian" (see Introduction) propagandist and head of the Estonian KGB during the 1960s. [Chapter 26]

Kristjan Raud (1865–1943), a painter of Estonian national themes in a neo-Romantic style inspired by Symbolism and Jugendstil. Many of his works allude to the Estonian national epic, the *Kalevipoeg*. [Chapter 10]

Baron Otto Fabian von Rosen (1683–1764) was the author of the notorious Rosen Declaration of 1739 in which he, as district magistrate, claimed that Estonian and Livonian peasants had been serfs since the thirteenth century and therefore all their property belonged to the lords of the manor. In Rosen's opinion, all matters of buying and selling serfs, plus their corvée, were the responsibility of the nobility only, and not of the state. [Chapter 9]

Alfred Rosenberg (1893–1946), a Baltic German, was born in Tallinn and educated in Tallinn, Riga and Moscow. He joined the German National Socialist Party in 1919 and became editor of the Nazi newspaper the *Völkischer Beobachter*. He was Hitler's chief ideologist, acted as German Foreign Minister from 1941 to 1945, and was executed after the Nuremberg Trials for war crimes. [Chapter 29]

Paul Rummo (1909–1981) was a poet and a Communist sympathiser. He edited an edition of poetry by the exiled Marie Under. His son Paul-Eerik Rummo is a major poet. [Chapter 26]

August Sang (1914–1969), poet and translator of poetry and drama from German, French, English and Russian. The husband of the poet Kersti Merilaas. [Chapter 20]

Bruno Saul (b. 1932) was the first Estonian-speaking Communist premier of the ESSR, after a string of "Yestonians" (see Introduction). [Chapter 39]

Johannes Semper (1892–1970) was educated in Pärnu and later became well acquainted with the St Petersburg literary scene and Russian Symbolism. A major early influence was Émile Verhaeren, over a hundred of whose poems he translated. Semper also translated novels by Hugo, Zola, Stendhal, Daudet, Gide, and poetry by Rimbaud and Verlaine, plus Boccaccio's *Decameron*. He was also a literary critic. His own poetry underwent changes from Symbolism to political commitment, via Expressionism, and his left-wing sympathies led him to attend many PEN congresses in the 1930s as Estonian delegate. In 1940, Semper became the Minister of Education in the puppet Communist government, only to be sacked as head of the Writers' Union and thrown out of the Communist Party in the early 1950s for "cosmopolitanism and bourgeois nationalism". [Chapters 14, 20 and 27]

Rudolf Sirge (1904–1970), a prose writer and sports reporter who took part in an abortive round-the-world voyage in 1932. During the German occupation, he spent a year in prison. After World War II, his writings tended towards Communism. [Chapter 26]

Gustav Suits (1883–1956), one of the most accomplished poets of the Young Estonia movement (see Introduction). Like Tuglas, Semper and Barbarus, Suits held radical left-wing views, and was of romantic revolutionary inclination in his younger years, spending 1905–17 in exile in Helsinki where he taught Finnish and Swedish at the Russian grammar school. On returning to an independent Estonia, he became Professor of Literature at Tartu University. In 1944, he fled to Sweden where he continued to work as a stipendiary of the Nobel Institute, researching nineteenth-century Estonian literature. [Chapter 27]

Gustav Sule (1910–1942), athletics champion, lecturer in economics and bank official. Sportsman of the Year in 1934. Died in Russia in a labour battalion. [Chapter 17]

Juhan Sütiste (1899–1945), poet, playwright and theatre critic. Sütiste (born Johannes Schütz) started out in life as a watchmaker's apprentice, then fought in the Estonian War of Independence as a schoolboy reservist. He later studied philosophy and law and was a keen sportsman, winning the javelin in the Student Olympics in Rome in 1927. Later in life, Sütiste tended towards Communism. [Chapter 26]

Rein Taagepera (b. 1933), an exiled Estonian sociologist, political scientist and essayist who predicted the downfall of the Soviet Union. He stood unsuccessfully for President of Estonia in the 1990s and has now started a political party of his own. [Chapter 23]

Anton Hansen Tammsaare (1878–1940) is regarded as Estonia's greatest novelist. Only once travelling outside of Estonia in his lifetime, he chiefly described life in Estonia in his novels. He was deeply influenced by German philosophy, especially Kant. He is best known for the five novels forming the *Truth and Justice* quintet, written between 1926 and 1933, which examine both rural and urban life. This quintet has appeared in French and is being translated into Finnish. [Chapters 8, 22 and 27]

Aleksander Tassa (1882–1955), artist and short-story writer. Like Tuglas and Vilde, he led a nomadic life during the first two decades of the twentieth century, living and working in the Netherlands and Scandinavia. Was close to the Noor Eesti movement. [Chapter 27]

Karl Terras (1890–1942), long-serving Head of the Estonian State Chancery from 1921 to 1940. Member of the Kaitseliit (see

Introduction). Arrested in 1941 by the Soviet occupier and died the following year in Russia. [Chapters 21–23 and 25]

Otto Tief (1889–1976), a lawyer who became Minister of the Interior under Uluots. He tried to revive the Estonian Republic on 18 September 1944, as the Germans were retreating. Sentenced by the Soviets to ten years in a labour camp, which he spent in Siberia and Kazakhstan, later in the Ukraine. Died in the Latvian SSR. [Chapters 30 and 31]

Romulus Tiitus (1906–1982), cartoonist and newspaper caricaturist. [Chapter 26]

Jaan Tõnisson (1868–?), was one of the first Estonian politicians in Czarist times to formulate a clear national policy for an independent Estonia, resisting both the Russification and Germanisation of the country. When independence was achieved, he continued as editor of the daily *Postimees* (*Postilion*) and represented the more left-of-centre opposition to the right-wing tendencies of the then premier, later President, Konstantin Päts. Tõnisson was arrested by the Soviet occupiers in 1940 and was never seen again. [Chapter 1]

Indrek Toome (b. 1943) was the last Soviet premier of the Estonian Soviet Socialist Republic and now works in real estate and property development. [Chapter 21]

August Torma (1895-1971), Estonian diplomat. He was a liaison officer between the Estonian and British forces in Archangelsk during the War of Independence, and subsequently a diplomat in various countries including Lithuania, France and Belgium. In 1934, Torma became Estonian ambassador in London and also the Estonian League of Nations representative. After the Soviet occupation he remained in Britain as *de jure* ambassador. [Chapter 30]

Nikolai Triik (1884–1940), portrait painter and illustrator for the Noor Eesti series of albums, his work drew from Symbolism, National Romanticism and Expressionism. [Chapter 27]

Friedebert Tuglas (1886–1971) was one of Estonia's leading twentieth-century writers. Educated at a Russian-language school, he was an autodidact from then onwards, never attending university. As a young man, Tuglas spent many years in exile on the Åland Isles, in Finland, Belgium, Switzerland and Paris on account of his left-wing views, thus avoiding arrest by the Czarist secret police. Starting out as a Realist, then Symbolist short-story writer, he went on to found the Estonian literary monthly *Looming* (*Creative Endeavour*) in 1923. In 1916, Tuglas published a spoof obituary for the non-existent writer, Arthur Valdes (Chapter 27). In the 1930s, Tuglas published *Little Illimar*, an autobiographical novel describing the idyllic childhood of a boy growing up in the countryside. He also published travel diaries from his trips to Morocco, Spain and Italy, and was made an honorary member of the London PEN Club in 1937. In 1944, Tuglas tried, but failed, to flee Estonia with his wife. Tuglas fell into disfavour in the late 1940s for criticising Stalin's cultural policies. He was reinstated during the post-Stalinist thaw in 1955, when he was again allowed to publish under his own name. [Chapters 20 and 27]

Elo Tuglas (1896–1970), who also features in the Arthur Valdes story, was the wife of Friedebert Tuglas. She published a couple of volumes of interesting diaries. [Chapter 27]

Jüri Uluots (1890–1945) was Estonian Prime Minister just before the Soviet invasion of 1940. He previously taught law at Tartu University when Jaan Kross was a student there, and made a futile attempt to form an independent Estonian government in the confused days of 1944 as the Germans were leaving, the Russians returning. Officially, the President would have to make all appointments, but Uluots, already gravely ill with cancer, appointed Tief (see entry, and Chapter 31) as his deputy since Päts, still regarded as the legitimate President, had been arrested years before. Uluots made it to neutral Sweden, but died shortly afterwards. [Chapters 16, 23, 25, 26 and 30–33]

Marie Under (1883–1980), poet. Her key collections were written in the late 1920s. She also translated plays by Maeterlinck, Rimbaud, Schiller and Hasenclever during that decade. Like Tuglas, Marie Under was made an honorary member of the London PEN Club in 1937. Her poetry collection, *With Troubled Lips*, appeared during the German occupation in 1943. The following year she fled to Sweden, and Tuglas and his wife moved into her former home in Nõmme, which is now a museum dedicated to both writers. During her period of exile, Marie Under worked for a decade at the Drottningholm Palace Museum as an archivist, and died in Stockholm. [Chapter 33]

Mati Unt (b. 1941) is a major Estonian novelist and theatre director.

He has staged plays by Strindberg, Weiss, Gombrowicz, Havel and many others. He started producing stories and novels in the 1960s and brought modernism to Estonian prose. His short novel *Murder in the Hotel* is reminiscent of Kafka, and in 1990 he published two of his best novels, *There are Things in the Night* which deals with man's relationship to electricity, and *Diary of a Donor* which deals, in his usual eclectic and intertextual way, with vampirism. [Chapter 5]

Jaan Vahtra (1882–1947), post-Impressionist painter. [Chapter 20]

Aleksander Vardi (1901–1983), born A. Bergman, impressionist portraitist. [Chapter 20]

Boris Vilde (1908-1942), Russian poet of Estonian origin and a founder member of the French Résistance during the Second World War. His name appears on a French monument to those Résistance fighters who fell in battle or otherwise died for France. [Chapter 27]

Eduard Vilde (1865–1933), a prolific Estonian author of left-wing sympathies. *The Mahtra War* tells of the farmers' unrest in the late 1850s when Estonian farmers were punished by the Czarist authorities. Many were also deported to Siberia, whence the title of another Vilde novel, *To the Cold Land*. Vilde also wrote *Maltsvet the Prophet*, which deals with a religious fanatic who swept people along with his crazed form of Christianity. Like Tuglas, Vilde led a nomadic life between 1905 and 1917, living in many places including Berlin, Vienna, Brussels, New York and Copenhagen. The story "Casanova Takes His Leave" was published in 1932 and is largely autobiographical. [Chapters 4 and 27]

Henrik Visnapuu (1890–1951), poet and playwright. Studied in Germany after which he worked for the Estonian national information service and in publishing. His most productive years as a writer were the 1920s. Fled in 1944 to Germany and from there to Long Island, New York. [Chapter 29]

Alexander Warma (1890–1970), naval officer in the War of Independence, he studied international law and worked in the Soviet Union as an Estonian diplomat. Escaped to Sweden in 1944. [Chapter 30]

August Ludwig Weizenberg (1837–1921) was the founder of a national Estonian style of sculpture using white Carrara marble from Italy. He lived in Rome between 1873 and 1890, and the following quarter of a century in St Petersburg. [Chapter 10]

Andrei Zhdanov (1896–1948), one of Stalin's closest colleagues who supervised Stalinist ideology and culture. When Estonia was occupied in 1942, Zhdanov was sent to Tallinn to govern there. [Chapter 24]